MW00916025

THE FIST

CONVERGENCE WAR
BOOK 5

M.R FORBES

Published by Quirky Algorithms
Seattle, Washington

This novel is a work of fiction and a product of the author's imagination.
Any resemblance to actual persons or events is purely coincidental.

Copyright © 2024 by Quirky Algorithms
All rights reserved.

Cover illustration by Tom Edwards
Edited by Merrylee Lanehart

CHAPTER 1

Grand Admiral Strickland's boots echoed on the hangar deck as he approached, each step measured and deliberate. Alex's heart rate quickened, a swirl of anticipation and dread coiling in his gut. Both familiar and alien, the man before him possessed his father's face, but unlike his father, this man's features were etched with lines of cruelty and ambition.

The Grand Admiral came to a stop mere feet away from Alex, his piercing gaze sweeping over the three Scorpions. For a long moment, he said nothing, simply studying them with an intensity that made Alex want to squirm. He held his ground, meeting the man's stare with as much defiance as he could muster.

Finally, Grand Admiral Strickland broke the silence, his voice carrying the same authoritative timbre as Alex's father, but with an undercurrent of cold amusement. "Well, well," he said, a small smile playing at the corners of his mouth. "This is certainly...interesting."

He turned to Alexander, who stood at rigid attention. "You've done well, son. They're remarkably similar to you and your squad, aren't they?"

"Thank you, sir," Alexander replied, his voice carefully neutral. "As I reported, the resemblance is uncanny."

The Grand Admiral nodded, returning his attention to Alex and his team. "Indeed it is. I must say, I'm quite fascinated by this turn of events. It's not every day one encounters such perfect doppelgängers." He paused, his smile widening slightly. "I don't suppose there's a version of me running around out there as well?"

Alex felt Jackson and Zoe tense beside him, their silent question clear through their neural link. *What do we tell him? How much do we reveal?*

Before Alex could decide on a response, Grand Admiral Strickland's expression hardened, a flash of impatience crossing his features. "Come now," he said, his tone sharpening. "Surely between the three of you and those neural augments of yours, you can come up with a lie faster than that."

Alex felt as if he'd been punched in the gut. How did he know about the augments? They'd been so careful to keep that information secret. He glanced at Jackson and Zoe, seeing his own shock mirrored in their eyes.

The Grand Admiral's smile returned, but it didn't reach his eyes. "Oh yes, we know all about your little enhancements. We have them, too. But if you're at least as smart as my son, I'm sure you already figured that much out." He took a step closer. "Let me give you some free advice. The more forthcoming you are with information, the easier things will be for you. I'm not an unreasonable man, but I do have my limits."

Alex remained silent, his mind racing. How much did they already know? How much should he reveal? He couldn't shake the feeling that every word—or lack thereof —might be a potential misstep in a game with rules he didn't fully understand.

After a moment of tense silence, Grand Admiral Strickland's expression soured. He turned to Alexander, his voice sharp. "Why exactly did you bring them to the hangar bay? This is hardly the place for a proper interrogation."

Alexander straightened, a flicker of nervousness crossing his face. "I...I wanted to see if they would attempt to escape, sir. To test their capabilities and verify if they truly were copies of myself and my team."

The Grand Admiral's eyes narrowed, his voice dripping with disdain. "Of course they are. Didn't you read the reports from the anomaly? Didn't you listen to Gray's report? Didn't you see the damage they did on FOB Alpha with your own eyes and put it in your own report!" His voice raised to a shout.

"It...it's just so hard to believe," Alexander said, sounding more like a scared child than the second most powerful man in the Strickland Federation.

"Yes, it is hard to believe. I'll give you that, son. But use your head. What's harder to believe is that your mother's faction might have the resources to pull off something like this. To find people who look identical to you and your team, considering the resources she had left? And how many of my Marines died for this test of yours?"

Alexander opened his mouth.

"Well? Answer me!" Strickland snapped.

"F...four units, sir."

Strickland rounded on his son. "Four units? Twenty-four Marines? Do you think that just because we conscript them, they have no value?"

You know, Jackson said through his neural implant. *I almost feel bad for your evil twin, Gunny. This is painful to watch.*

Poor guy is totally beaten down, Zoe agreed.

Good, Alex replied. *I don't have any sympathy for him. He could have stayed with Admiral Yarborough. He chose this.*

"N..no, sir. I just needed to—"

"Enough," Strickland cut him off with a wave of his hand. "What I want to know is where they came from, how they got here, and why." He turned back to Alex, his gaze boring into him. "And I intend to get those answers, one way or another."

Without taking his eyes off Alex, he addressed Alexander once more. "Take them to the interrogation compartment. Then meet me in my ready room. I want a word with you in private."

"Yes, sir," Alexander replied, his voice tight with suppressed emotion.

If this is how he treats him in front of us and his team, I can only imagine how he'll come down on him in private, Zoe said.

As Alexander and his team began to herd the Scorpions out of the hangar bay, Alex caught a glimpse of the Grand Admiral's face. There was no warmth or hint of the man he knew as his father. Only cold calculation and the promise of unpleasant things to come.

The journey to the interrogation compartment was tense and silent. Alex worked to formulate a plan to turn this situation to their advantage. But with every step, the reality of their predicament became more apparent. They were deep in enemy territory, with no clear path to escape or rescue.

When they arrived at their destination, Alexander's team efficiently secured them to thick chains attached to the bulkhead. The restraints were heavy-duty, clearly designed to hold individuals of enhanced strength. Alex tested them subtly, feeling no give whatsoever.

"Watch them," Alexander ordered his squad. "I'll return shortly."

Alex decided to take a risk as the door closed behind Alexander, leaving them alone with the rest of his squad. He'd been silent until now, but if they were going to have any chance of survival, let alone escape, they needed information. Maybe he could talk some of it out of their guards.

"Do you mind if I ask you a question?" he said, eyeing all four members of Alexander's unit. He already knew the answer, but he needed an in.

"Yes," their Sarah replied. "Why don't you just stand there and stay silent."

"It's not a delicate question," Alex said. "I was just wondering what your unit name is. We're the Scorpions."

"We don't care," Sarah snapped.

Alex shrugged as best he could in his restraints. "Come on. I'm just making conversation. I figured since we're probably going to be spending some quality time together, we might as well get acquainted."

SF Zoe scoffed. "You think this is a social call? You're prisoners, not guests."

"Fair enough," Alex conceded. He paused, then added, "I couldn't help but do a headcount. You have five members."

The Marines exchanged glances, clearly unsure how to respond. Finally, Sarah growled at him again. "I said, shut up."

"It wouldn't happen to be PFC Theo Makris, would it?"

The sudden tension in the room was palpable. When one of the Marines spoke, Alex immediately recognized Theo's voice. "How do you know that name?"

"Lucky guess," Alex replied, trying to keep his tone light. "In our universe, Theo was part of our unit, too. He had to retire for medical reasons. Cancer."

Theo visibly paled. "Cancer?"

Alex nodded. "Yeah. Caught it early, thankfully. But it was enough to take him out of active duty. Maybe you should get checked out, just in case."

Theo opened his mouth to respond, but Sarah cut him

off. "Don't engage with them. They're trying to get in your head."

"Hey, I'm just trying to help," Alex protested. "Look, I know we're on opposite sides here, but—"

"Even if I did have cancer," Theo interrupted, his voice low, "it wouldn't matter. The Scarabs...it's a lifetime commitment. No way out."

Alex wanted to pat himself on the back for getting the unit name from them when they hadn't freely offered it.

Jackson sighed. "You could be dying as we speak, man. You catch it early enough, you can get that treated."

Theo didn't answer. Sarah stepped between them. "That's enough," she snapped. "Makris, don't say anything else." She turned to Alex, her eyes hard. "Let me make something very clear. I know what you're trying to do. We probably have similar training. You won't make any friends here. Not with us, not with anyone on this ship. So save your breath."

Alex held her gaze, seeing the conviction in her eyes. But beneath that, he caught a flicker of something else. Uncertainty? Curiosity? He couldn't be sure, but it was enough to give him hope. Maybe, just maybe, not everyone in this universe was as devoted to the cause as they appeared.

Before he could further pursue that line of thought, the door slid open, and Alexander strode in, followed closely by Grand Admiral Strickland. The atmosphere in the room instantly shifted, tension crackling like electricity.

"Well," the Grand Admiral said, his eyes sweeping over the assembled group. "Shall we begin?"

CHAPTER 2

Alex steeled himself, knowing that what happened now would likely be unpleasant. But as he met the Grand Admiral's gaze, he made a silent vow. No matter what happened, he would find a way to protect his team, complete his mission, and make it home.

Grand Admiral Strickland's eyes locked onto Alex, a predatory gleam in their depths. "Now then," he said, his voice deceptively calm, "let's dispense with the pleasantries, shall we? I have questions, and you have answers. The only variables are how long it takes to get those answers from you and how unpleasant the process becomes."

He began to pace slowly in front of the restrained Scorpions, his hands clasped behind his back. The posture was so familiar, so reminiscent of Alex's father, that for a moment he felt a pang of longing. But the cold calculation in the Grand Admiral's eyes quickly dispelled any notion of familiarity.

"Let's start with something simple," Strickland continued. "Where did you come from? And don't bother with lies or evasions. I assure you, we have ways of verifying your claims."

Alex glanced at Jackson and Zoe, a silent conversation passing between them through their neural link. They had prepared for this, had spent countless hours crafting a cover story during their confinement. But now, faced with the reality of interrogation, Alex wondered if their carefully constructed lies would hold up.

Taking a deep breath, he decided to start with a version of the truth. "We're from another dimension," he said, his voice steady. "A parallel universe, if you will."

The Grand Admiral's eyebrow arched slightly. "Interesting. And how did you manage to cross between dimensions?"

"It wasn't intentional," Alex replied, sticking to their agreed-upon story. "We were investigating an anomaly in space—a rift, we called it. Something went wrong, and we found ourselves here."

Strickland nodded slowly, his expression unreadable. "I see. And what was the nature of this...investigation?"

Alex hesitated, knowing they were treading on dangerous ground. Too much truth could be as damaging as an outright lie. "We were part of a research team," he said carefully, "studying the effects of the rift on local spacetime."

"A research team?" The Grand Admiral's tone was skeptical. "With your combat skills and augmentations? You'll forgive me if I find that hard to believe."

"Where we come from, the military often assists with scientific endeavors," Zoe chimed in, following Alex's improvisation. "Especially when they involve potential security risks."

Strickland's gaze shifted to her, his eyes narrowing. "Is that so? And what exactly did you hope to gain from this research?"

"Knowledge," Jackson said, his voice firm. "Understanding of the universe and its mysteries. Isn't that what all scientific pursuit is about?"

The Grand Admiral's laugh was short and harsh. "How very noble. But let's cut to the chase, shall we? You expect me to believe that your presence here was all some cosmic accident?" He stopped pacing, turning to fully face them. "No, I think there's more to this story. Much more. And I intend to uncover every last detail."

With a sharp gesture, he summoned Alexander to him. "Prepare the neural link," he ordered. "It's time we got a more...direct look at what's going on in their heads."

Alex felt a chill run down his spine. Neural link? That didn't sound good. He exchanged a worried glance with his teammates, seeing his own concern mirrored in their eyes.

As Alexander moved to comply with the order, Strickland turned back to the Scorpions, a small smile playing at his lips. "I'll give you one last chance to tell me the full truth voluntarily. It will be much less unpleasant for you."

Alex met the Grand Admiral's gaze unflinchingly. "We've told you the truth," he said, his voice steady despite the fear churning in his gut. "Do your worst."

Strickland's smile widened, but it never reached his eyes. "Very well. You've made your choice. Remove his restraints."

Sarah moved beside him, taking his arm to release it from the chain.

"You can't seriously think this is the galaxy you want to leave to your children," he whispered. Their Sarah had planned to spend fifteen years in the Corps and earn a full retirement package before seeking a husband and having a few kids. Maybe this one had once thought the same way.

"Scarabs are forever, asshole," she snarled back, unclasping the chain from his wrist but keeping her grip on him.

"They don't have to be," he replied.

"Bring him over to the link," Strickland ordered.

She pulled him across the compartment to a simple-looking chair with extensions on either side of the headrest. "Sit," she snapped.

Alex had no choice. He sat.

Alexander helped Sarah restrain him once more.

"I wouldn't try to wriggle free of this if I were you," Sarah said. "If you break the link mid-probe, you'll die instantly."

"Mid-probe?" Alex asked. "What are you going to do to me?"

"The tricky thing about the neural augments," Strickland said, approaching the device. "They're implanted directly into your brain. That makes them incredibly useful for their designed purpose, making you and your squad a unit of super-soldiers. Efficient killers with unparalleled teamwork. But it makes them useful for other purposes, as well. We originally developed the neural link to recover information from spies after a mission, and to corroborate the reports of our augmented Marines when they returned from the field. But they've been quite useful as an interrogation tool against the enemy, especially because the more you resist its efforts to look into your mind, the more it hurts."

Sarah adjusted the extensions on the headrest until they were in line with the position of his augments and locked them in place. Alexander activated the device, which hummed softly. A projection appeared off to the side, currently not displaying anything.

"Let's begin," Strickland said. "I'm curious to see what secrets lurk behind those familiar eyes of yours."

The first jolt of electricity coursed through Alex, and he gritted his teeth against the pain. He knew this was only the beginning. The real test was yet to come.

Grand Admiral Strickland leaned in close, his voice a menacing whisper. "Now, let's see what you're really hiding, shall we?"

With that, the neural link hummed to life, and the world around Alex dissolved into a haze of pain and fractured memories. Waves of discomfort flowed through Alex's skull, probing and searching, like fingers rifling through the pages of his mind. Images flashed before his eyes—snippets of memory, both real and fabricated, blurring together in a dizzying kaleidoscope.

Grand Admiral Strickland stood nearby, his eyes fixed on a holographic display that flickered and pulsed with Alex's brainwaves. "Fascinating," he murmured, more to himself than anyone else in the room. "The neural architecture is remarkably similar to Alexander's, and yet...there are subtle differences."

Alex fought to maintain control, to keep the carefully constructed false memories at the forefront of his mind. They had prepared for this, and had spent countless hours during their confinement crafting multiple believable alternate histories. Now, it was being put to the ultimate test.

A particularly strong pulse sent a jolt of pain through Alex's head, causing him to gasp involuntarily. In that moment of weakness, a true memory slipped through—a flash of the Wraith, his father's face, filled with determination as they prepared to enter the Eye.

"What was that?" Strickland demanded, leaning closer to the display. "Show me more."

The machine seemed to respond to his command, digging deeper. Alex gritted his teeth, focusing all his willpower on suppressing the truth, on projecting the false narrative they had created.

"I'm seeing...a research vessel?" Strickland narrated. "They call it the...Wraith? Interesting name for a scientific endeavor."

Alex's heart raced. They knew about the Wraith. How much more would they uncover?

"There's something else," the Grand Admiral continued. "A mission. Something about...stopping a Convergence?" He turned to Alex, his eyes narrowing. "What is this Convergence? Why are you trying to stop it?"

Fighting through the haze of pain and disorientation, Alex managed to choke out a response. "It's...it's a theory. About dimensional collapse. We were...studying it."

"Studying it?" Strickland's voice dripped with skepticism. "Tell me more."

Before Alex could respond, another surge of energy tore through him. This time, as sweat beaded his brow, he couldn't hold back his cry of pain.

"Gunny!" Jackson shouted, straining against his restraints. "Leave him alone, you bastards!"

Zoe's voice joined in, her usual calm replaced by fury. "If you hurt him, I swear I'll—"

"You'll what?" Alexander cut in, his tone mocking. "You're in no position to make threats."

Grand Admiral Strickland held up a hand, silencing the room. "Enough. This...Convergence. It's clearly more than just a theory to you. Tell me, what exactly were you hoping to achieve by coming here?"

Alex's mind raced, trying to find a plausible explanation that wouldn't reveal too much. It was hard to think at all through the pain. It went across his entire body, every joint throbbing, every nerve-ending burning. "We...we were trying to understand it. To find a way to stop it, if possible. Our dimension...it's in danger."

"And you thought the solution lay here?" Strickland pressed. "In our dimension?"

"We didn't choose to come here," Alex insisted, clinging to their prepared story. "It was an accident. A malfunction during our research."

The Grand Admiral studied him for a long moment, his expression unreadable. "I don't believe you," he said at last. Then, with a slight nod to Alexander, he said, "Increase the intensity. I want to see everything."

As the machine's hum grew louder, Alex braced himself for another onslaught. But this time, something was different. The pain was ten times worse. Worse than he had ever felt. He could feel his mental defenses beginning to crumble, and there was nothing he could do to stop it.

Images flashed through his mind in rapid succession and in random order—the battle at FOB Alpha, his father's face twisted with anguish as they were forced to leave him behind, the Wraith emerging from fold space near Wolf 1061c—but it was more than that. Other memories were mixed in. His childhood. His training. His family. Each memory felt like it was being torn from his grasp, laid bare for Strickland to see.

"Interesting," the Grand Admiral murmured, his eyes fixed on the holographic display. "It seems our guests have been quite busy since their arrival. Tell me, Alex—may I call you Alex?—what exactly were you doing at our forward operating base?"

Alex struggled to form a coherent thought through the pain. "We...we were looking for answers...about the Convergence."

"Answers?" Strickland's voice was skeptical. "It looks more like you were conducting a military operation. With the assistance of our enemies, no less."

Another surge of energy coursed through Alex, and he couldn't suppress another sharp groan of pain. Through the haze, he heard Jackson's voice, strained with concern. "Gunny, hang in there!"

"Silence!" Alexander barked, but Alex could hear the undercurrent of unease in his voice. Was he disturbed by what they were seeing? Or just annoyed by the interruption?

Grand Admiral Strickland's eyes narrowed as he studied the holographic display, his expression a mixture of fascination and growing anger. "This ship of yours, the Wraith...it's quite remarkable. Cloaking technology, advanced weaponry...hardly standard equipment for a research vessel, wouldn't you agree?"

Alex struggled against the neural interface, desperately trying to control his thoughts. But the machine was relentless, probing deeper into his mind with each passing second.

"Increase the intensity," Strickland ordered, his voice sharp. "I want everything."

As Alexander complied, adjusting the settings on the neural interface, the pain in Alex's head spiked to unbearable levels. He couldn't suppress a cry of agony as unbidden tears leaked from his eyes and streamed down his face. Images flashed across the holographic display faster than Alex could process them—the battle at the SF station, the Wraith's narrow escape, the desperate search for a way to stop the Convergence. Once more, they mingled with some of his most intimate memories.

Sweat poured down his face, mixing with his tears, as Alex fought with every ounce of his willpower to keep certain thoughts hidden, to protect the most crucial aspects of their mission. But the neural interface was too powerful, too invasive. It tore through his mental defenses, laying bare the secrets he had tried so hard to protect.

Strickland watched intently as the truth unfolded before him on the display. He saw the three dimensions, the impending Convergence, the Wraith's journey through the Eye. The connection between the vortex cannons and the growing instability between dimensions became clear, as did their alliance with Admiral Yarborough's FUP forces.

As the full scope of the situation became clear, Strickland's expression shifted from disbelief to fascination and finally to a cold calculation that sent chills down Alex's spine.

When the deluge of information finally slowed, Strickland straightened, his expression unreadable. "Well," he said, oddly calm, "that was certainly...illuminating." He turned to Alexander. "Deactivate his neural augment. We can't risk him using its capabilities again."

Alexander nodded, moving to comply. Alex felt a strange sensation wash over him, like a part of his mind going quiet. The constant background hum of the neural link with his team disappeared, leaving him feeling oddly hollow. And tired. He was so exhausted he could barely hold his head up.

"What now, sir?" Alexander asked, looking to his father for direction.

Strickland pointed to Zoe. "I want you to corroborate the memories. Use the link on her next, then the other one."

"Yes, sir," Alexander replied.

Grand Admiral Strickland was quiet for a moment, his eyes distant. Finally, he spoke, his voice cold and decisive. "If they want to join forces with our enemies so badly, then they can share in their fate. Once you're finished here, prepare them for transfer to the next ship headed for Teegarden."

"But sir," Alexander began, a note of confusion in his voice, "with what they know, shouldn't we—"

"Are you questioning my decision?" Soren snapped, cutting him off.

"N...no, sir."

"I want them to see firsthand what life is like for those who oppose the Strickland Federation." He turned back to Alex, his eyes hard. "You came here looking for answers, for a way to save your dimension. Well, congratulations.

I've been wondering what I'm going to do with the war machine I've built once the FUP and CIP are eliminated. Now I know." He whirled back on Alexander. "I'll have new orders for you soon."

"Yes, sir," Alexander replied.

With that, he strode out of the room, leaving Alex and his team alone with Alexander and the Scarabs. As they began to prep the Scorpions for transfer, Alex's mind reeled with the magnitude of what had just happened. He hadn't broken, hadn't given up the information willingly, but in the end, it didn't matter. The neural interface had stripped away his defenses, leaving his mind bare and vulnerable. Leaving him pulsating with pain from head to toe, his eyelids growing increasingly heavy.

As unconsciousness began to claim him, his last thoughts were of his father, of the Wraith, and of the billions of lives across three dimensions that now hung in the balance. He had failed them all, and the price of that failure was only beginning to become clear.

As the darkness took him, Alex knew that when he woke up, it would be to a whole new kind of nightmare.

CHAPTER 3

Soren sat in his ready room aboard the Wraith, his fingers drumming a restless rhythm on the desk as he waited for the latest status reports. The past few weeks had been a whirlwind of preparation and planning, but the capture of Alex and the Scorpions remained a constant thread in his subconscious, surfacing every time he had a break in activity and making it harder for him to sleep. Every moment not spent working toward their rescue felt like a moment wasted.

A soft chime from the door broke through his brooding thoughts. "Enter," he called out, straightening in his chair.

Keira and Ethan came into the room, both carrying data-pads. Soren could see the fatigue in their eyes, but there was also a tenacious edge that had become characteristic of his crew in recent days.

"Captain," Keira began. "I have the latest ordnance report. With the FUP's aid, we've managed to restore our stocks to eighty percent capacity. Obviously, it's not perfect, but it's a significant improvement from where we were after the station assault."

Soren nodded, allowing himself a small measure of

satisfaction. "Considering the FUP's limited resources, to recover that much ammunition is more than I'd hoped for. It will give us more options when the time comes."

"Aye, sir," she replied.

"We've also completed repairs on the minor shield damage we sustained," Ethan added. "The system is back to peak efficiency."

"Excellent," Soren said. "And how are the other engineering tasks progressing?"

Ethan's face lit up with barely contained excitement. "We've made some significant breakthroughs, Captain. My team has been working around the clock, and we've managed to squeeze more optimizations out of our systems."

"I'm listening," Soren said, leaning forward with interest.

"Well, sir, the big one is the vortex cannon. With Tashi and Lina's engineering help, we've automated the frequency adjustments. Now we can change its firing pattern with the flip of a switch, in the time it takes to reload. Which, by the way, we've cut down to just over a minute."

Both Soren's and Keira's eyebrows shot up in surprise. "That's incredibly impressive, Ethan," Soren said. "How did you manage that?"

Ethan grinned, clearly proud of his team's accomplishment. "Honestly, sir, you can thank Tashi for that. The kid's a whiz with wiring and circuit tolerances. He came up with routing paths and failovers I never would have considered possible." He chuckled. "He's so modest, he attributes his success to doing more with less when he was fixing shuttles back in the Dregs. They often didn't have replacement parts, so they had to find different ways to make things work up to spec, or over spec. His story's pretty inspiring, if you ever have time to hear it."

"I've heard some of it," Soren said. "Listening to Jane and picking up crew in the Dregs was the best decision I've ever made, outside of marrying and having children with her."

"Aye, Captain," Ethan agreed.

"Remind me to commend him personally," Soren said, making a mental note. "These improvements could make a significant difference going forward."

"That's what we're hoping for, sir," Ethan replied.

Soren nodded, a small smile tugging at the corners of his mouth. Despite the dire circumstances, he couldn't help but feel a surge of pride in his crew's dedication and ingenuity. "Outstanding work, both of you. Make sure your teams know how much I appreciate their efforts."

"Aye, Captain," they replied in unison.

As Keira and Ethan left the ready room, Soren's mind was already shifting to the next item on his agenda. He activated his comm unit. "Samira, get me Admiral Yarborough on video."

"Right away, Captain," came the prompt reply.

Moments later, Admiral Yarborough's face appeared on Soren's display. The lines around her eyes seemed deeper than the last time they'd spoken, no doubt a result of her stress.

"Captain Strickland," she greeted him, her voice weary but alert. "What can I do for you?"

"I was hoping you might have news about Alex."

Yarborough's strained expression tightened a little more. "I'm sorry, Captain. I can understand why you're eager for news. I haven't heard anything concrete yet. Our intelligence networks are stretched thin, and information from Earth is sporadic at best. Plus, it's not the most efficient process. We have to pass encrypted intel to sympathetic freighter captains, then wait for them to tranSat the messages through three or four hops to ensure security, before intercepting them and passing them through to the fleet. By the time we receive anything, the data's usually two to four weeks old."

Soren felt a familiar knot of anxiety tightening in the center of his chest, but he pushed the discomfort aside. "Understood. It's impressive you've managed to maintain a spy network at all, under the circumstances. What about Major Gray? Any sign of him?"

The Admiral shook her head. "Nothing definitive. But I'm more confident now that he stayed behind on Wolf and managed to escape to Earth. It fits with the pattern of information leaks we've dealt with in the past."

Soren's jaw clenched slightly. The thought of Gray, a man they had trusted, betraying them to the enemy still stung. But there was no time to dwell on past mistakes. "And the preparations for the Teegarden mission?" he asked, steering the conversation back to more immediate concerns.

"As we discussed, we're proceeding with the plan whether Alex is confirmed to be there or not. Our primary objective is to rescue as many FUP POWs as we can. Our current goal is to launch the operation three weeks from now. That will give the Fist of Justice enough time to reach Earth, for my ex-husband to interrogate the Scorpions, and then for a transport to take them to the penal colony. It's a delicate balance between allowing them to move the prisoners and not waiting so long that another leak can develop or we lose our window of opportunity."

"What does our force composition look like?"

"With ship rotations and needed repairs, we can commit twenty ships to the rescue operation," Yarborough replied. "It's not as many as I'd like, but it's the best we can do after what happened at FOB Alpha."

Soren frowned, a sense of unease settling in his stomach. "Admiral, I don't think that's going to be enough. As we've discussed, there's a high probability of increased security around the colony, and even the possibility that we'll be walking right into a setup. We need overwhelming force if we're going to have any chance of success. Neither one of us wants a repeat of FOB Alpha."

"We can't survive another repeat," Yarborough agreed. "I would commit more ships if I could, Captain, but this is all we have. There's no sense sending damaged, unreliable, or unarmed ships into the fight. They'll do more harm than good. We're stretched to the breaking point as it is."

Soren nodded, understanding her position even as he chafed against the limitations. "I know. In all honesty, I brought it up so I could segue into something I've been thinking a lot about lately."

"That sounds awfully familiar," Yarborough said.

Soren grinned despite himself. "I suppose it does. What can you tell me about the current state of the Coalition of Independent Planets in this dimension?"

Yarborough's eyebrows rose slightly. "The CIP? As I've mentioned before, they're holding fast to a neutral position in this fight, so as not to draw the ire of the Strickland Federation. That's above board, anyway. Below it, they have provided some support. Humanitarian supplies, mostly. Food, clothing, medicine. But every so often those crates of uniforms also contain less…savory equipment."

"But no direct military assistance?" Soren pressed.

"No," Yarborough replied, shaking her head. "They're walking a tightrope as it is."

Soren leaned forward, his eyes intense. "I've been wondering if we might be able to get them more directly involved. The Convergence affects everyone, not just our dimension. And the defeat of the FUP would have far-reaching consequences for the entire galaxy."

Yarborough's expression was skeptical. "I appreciate your thinking, Soren, but I don't see how we can convince them. They've been very clear about not wanting to escalate their involvement."

"Do they really think Strickland will leave them alone once the FUP is destroyed?" Soren asked, his voice rising slightly with passion. "They're a target whether they want to accept it or not. It's only a matter of time before the SF turns its full attention to them."

"I believe that as well," Yarborough said, her tone softening. "And deep down, I think they know it too. But fear is a powerful motivator. They're afraid of provoking Strickland into immediate action against them."

Soren nodded, understanding the dilemma. Then, his idea began to expand in his mind. "What if I spoke to them directly? As Strickland's doppelgänger, maybe I could help them understand the true scope of the threat we're facing, both from the Convergence and the Strickland Federation."

Yarborough was quiet for a moment, considering the proposal. "It's not without merit," she said. "Your unique perspective could be compelling. And if you can convince them of who you are, that might make them more willing to listen."

"Exactly," Soren pressed, sensing an opening. "We need allies, Admiral. Real allies, not just clandestine support. If we can bring the CIP into this fight, it could change everything."

Yarborough's eyes narrowed slightly, a calculating look crossing her face. "It's a risk," she said. "If Strickland found out we were trying to bring the CIP into the conflict more directly, it could provoke him into immediate action against them."

"It's a risk we have to take," Soren argued. "We're running out of options, and we're running out of time. Every day we wait, the Convergence draws closer. People in my dimension are dying, and the SF is tightening its grip on this galaxy. When they declare war on the CIP, and they will, you'll see the Fist's vortex cannon used multiple times in a short period. The Convergence will be all but assured."

There was a long moment of silence as Yarborough weighed the proposal. Finally, she nodded, a hint of her old fire returning to her eyes. "Okay, Captain. I'll see what I can arrange. No promises, but I'll reach out to my contacts in the CIP and see if we can set up a meeting."

Soren felt a surge of hope tempered by the challenges ahead. "Thank you, Admiral. I know it's a long shot, but we have to try."

"Agreed," Yarborough said. "I'll contact you as soon as I have any news. Hopefully within the next day or two. In the meantime, continue your preparations for the Teegarden Operation. We can't afford to lose focus on that, even as we pursue this new avenue."

"Understood," Soren replied. "We'll be ready. Strickland out."

CHAPTER 4

Soren grunted as he pushed through another set of pull-ups, his muscles burning with exertion. Around him, the sporadic sounds of heavy breathing and the occasional clang of weights cut through the somber undercurrent of what little activity was occurring in the gym. The place was emptier than Soren had ever seen it, not for lack of desire, but for lack of personnel. Following the losses at FOB Alpha, his Marines were down to two units of six, twelve members total, plus Lieutenant Moffit.

As he dropped from the bar, wiping sweat from his brow, Soren's gaze fell on Liam, who was spotting one of the Marines on the bench press. The lieutenant's resigned expression reflected both the general mood and his response to it. He pushed himself and his men harder than usual. Soren understood the impulse. Physical exertion was often an efficient way to process grief and anger.

"How are they holding up?" Soren asked, approaching Liam as the Marine finished his set.

Liam helped the man rack the weights before turning to face him. "As well as can be expected, sir. They're angry, frustrated. Itching for a chance to hit back."

Soren nodded, understanding all too well. "And you?"

A flicker of emotion crossed Liam's face before he schooled his features into a more neutral expression. "I'm managing, sir. Keeping busy helps."

"I know what you mean," Soren replied, his voice low. "The memorial service yesterday…" They had held a service similar to the one for the fallen Hooligans, but this time for the Marines and crew members lost on FOB Alpha. The hangar bay had been filled with a sea of solemn faces as they paid their respects to those they couldn't bring home. "It brought back a lot of memories. Too many good people lost."

"It's never easy," Liam agreed. "But it reminds us what we're fighting for."

Soren's jaw tightened. "Speaking of which, how are the preparations coming for the Teegarden Operation?"

Liam's posture straightened slightly, shifting into a more professional demeanor. "We've been running drills around the clock, sir. Working on breaching techniques, room clearing, and evac procedures. We'll give the SF hell when we get there."

"I don't doubt it, Liam."

As they continued discussing the finer points of the upcoming mission, Soren's comm unit chimed softly. "Captain," Samira's voice came through, "I have Admiral Yarborough for you on a priority channel."

"Thank you, Samira. I'll take it in my ready room." He turned to Liam. "Keep up the good work."

After a quick nod from Liam, Soren grabbed a towel and rushed out of the gym, wiping off sweat as he hurried through the passageways. Whatever news the Admiral had, he wanted to hear it five minutes ago.

Entering his ready room, Soren activated his terminal, connecting to the comms channel. Admiral Yarborough's face appeared on the screen, her eyebrows rising slightly at his appearance. "Captain," she greeted him, a hint of amusement in her voice. "I hope I didn't interrupt anything too strenuous."

Soren ran a hand through his sweat-dampened hair, suddenly self-conscious. "Just making sure I stay in fighting shape, Admiral. I'll be ready to join the Marines on the ground at Teegarden if that's what it takes to help bring our people back." He said it half-jokingly before realizing the truth of his words. He really would join the ground attack if he thought it would improve their odds. Then again, even in prime shape, he doubted he could keep up with the much younger Marines.

Yarborough's expression softened. "Your willingness to get your hands dirty is admirable, Soren. It's one of the many things that sets you apart from my ex-husband."

"Thank you, Admiral," Soren replied. "But I'm sure you didn't call to comment on my workout routine. What do you have for me?"

The Admiral's face grew serious. "Unfortunately, there's still no word on Alex or the other Scorpions, but I do have news regarding our other initiative."

Soren leaned forward, his full attention focused on the screen. "The CIP?"

Yarborough nodded. "I spoke with them as we discussed. Initially, they were...less than receptive. I tried arguing our case again, but they remained firm in their neutrality."

Soren felt a flicker of disappointment, but he recognized the look in Yarborough's eye. "But?" There was more to it than that.

"But," Yarborough continued, "I managed to convince them to agree to an in-person meeting. I told them we had new, compelling information that might change their minds about staying out of this fight."

"That's excellent news," Soren said, feeling a surge of

hope. Still reading her face, he didn't let himself get too excited. "What's the catch?"

She chuckled, shaking her head. "It's strange talking to you, Captain. You know all of my tells."

"My Jane has the same ones, and we've been together too long for me to ever miss one."

"The catch is that they want us to meet on Gliese 667 Cc, also known as Glaive. It's within the accepted boundaries of the CIP, but not by much. Easier for plausible deniability if the SF catches wind of our presence there. As a portal to the greater CIP, there's plenty of SF activity to and from the planet."

"So we have to be more careful about who sees me," Soren said.

"And me," Yarborough replied. "I haven't set foot on a CIP planet since the Grand Admiral branded us a terrorist organization. I would prefer not to start now, but I couldn't get them to agree to a meeting anywhere else. Going planet-side proves how serious I am about the intel I intend to share with them. Essentially, you."

"But it's risky," Soren said.

"Of course."

"The kind of risky I wish I had Alex here to help mitigate."

"We're on our own for this one, Captain. We'll have to take a small shuttle to Glaive to avoid attention. Just the two of us."

"That's…awkward," Soren admitted.

"At least you still love your wife," she replied. "That should make it easier for you."

"Maybe too easy. It's hard to look at you and not see her. I miss her more than I can say, and I'm worried about her. Earth will be a tough nut to crack in our dimension too, but if the enemy reaches it before I get back…"

"We won't let that happen," Yarborough replied. "There is one other wrinkle. Glaive is a ten day journey from here."

"And we're set to head for Teegarden in twenty-one days."

"That's right. We'll be cutting our return close."

"Can we delay the assault?"

"Not once we leave. And I don't think a delay is in anyone's best interests."

"Not if we can help it. If things go well, we might be able to bring some CIP ships to Teegarden with us."

"That would be a small miracle, Captain. One I'd gladly accept."

"I think if we're going to spend ten days on a shuttle, just the two of us, it's about time you started calling me Soren. Unless you can't stand saying the name."

"I'd rather think of you when I say that name than the Grand Admiral. You're welcome to call me Jane, but I understand if that's uncomfortable for you."

"I'd call it natural for me."

"You're sure it won't blur the lines between her and I?"

"I won't mistake you for my wife, if that's what you mean. There are a few differences between you two," Soren said. "But I can't help admiring you for the qualities you share."

"And I can't help admiring you for the qualities you don't share with the Grand Admiral," Jane said before she laughed. "Anyway, we need to leave as soon as possible if we want to make it back here in time for the Teegarden Operation. How soon can you be ready to depart?"

"Give me an hour," Soren replied. "I need to shower, change, pack, and get Jack up to speed."

"Of course," Yarborough said. "I'll send a shuttle over to collect you. See you soon, Soren."

As the screen went dark, Soren took a deep breath. Ten days alone on a shuttle with Jane's doppelgänger. He didn't know how well he was going to handle that. He just knew he needed to handle it.

He activated his comm unit. "Jack, can you come to my ready room immediately?"

"On my way," came the swift reply.

While he waited for Jack to arrive, Soren quickly informed Dana of the situation.

"Do you really think you can convince the Coalition to stand against the Strickland Federation?" she asked.

"If I can't convince them with the threat of the Convergence, I think I can make believers out of them with my tactical viewpoint. The SF will attack the CIP as soon as the FUP resistance is quashed. That's not an opinion. That's a guarantee."

"It makes so much sense, I don't know why they can't see it."

"Because they don't want to. The same way our FUP didn't want to see the threat of the Convergence. But burying your head in the sand only makes it easier for the enemy to cut it off without you ever noticing."

"Be careful out there, Dad," Dana said. "That's all I ask."

"I always am," Soren assured her just as the door chimed. "Enter."

Jack strode in, his expression curious. "How can I help you, Captain?"

Soren said a final goodbye to Dana before disconnecting and motioning for Jack to sit. Once he did, Soren quickly laid out the situation—the meeting with the CIP, the need for him to accompany Yarborough, and the tight timeline they were working with.

"Ten days there and back," Jack mused when Soren had finished. "Cutting it close for the Teegarden op, aren't we?"

"It's a risk we have to take," Soren replied. "If we can bring the CIP into this fight, it could change everything."

Jack nodded, understanding the gravity of the situation.

"Don't worry about things here. I'll keep the Wraith and crew ready for your return. To be honest, I don't expect much to happen besides waiting, anyway."

"That's what I'm hoping for," Soren said. He paused, meeting his friend's gaze. "Jack, if something goes wrong...if we don't make it back in time..."

"I'll do everything in my power to recover Alex and the others," Jack promised. "I know how important this is, Soren. I won't let you down."

Soren felt a wave of gratitude wash over him. "Thank you. I know I'm leaving the ship in good hands."

As Jack turned to leave, Soren called out, "And Jack? Keep an eye on Dana for me. You know how she can get when she's deep into her research."

Jack grinned. "Don't worry. I'll make sure she occasionally comes up for air."

With that, Jack left, and Soren found himself alone in his ready room. He gave himself a moment to close his eyes, the weight of responsibility settling heavily on his shoulders. So much was riding on this meeting with the CIP. If they failed to convince them, not only would the resistance end more quickly, the entire galaxy would fall to the SF. And, more worryingly, it was almost a given the Fist of Justice and its vortex cannon would be leading the vanguard, each ejection from its cannon pushing multiple dimensions closer to the brink.

Failure wasn't an option. Not when Alex was still out there somewhere, not when billions of lives across three dimensions hung in the balance.

With renewed resolve, Soren headed for his quarters to prepare for the journey ahead. Whatever challenges lay before them, he would face them head-on.

After a quick shower and change of clothes, he grabbed his pack and began stuffing it with necessities. He packed quickly, having carried out the same procedure hundreds of times before, and headed out of his quarters. Rather than go right to the hangar bay, he diverted to the lower decks, finding Liam and his Marines had moved from the gym to the training area.

"Going somewhere, Captain?" Liam said as he approached.

"I'll be away from the ship for the next three weeks," Soren said. "But I'll be back in time for the operation."

"And you came to say goodbye?"

"No, I came because I need a sidearm and a concealed carry holster. I was hoping we might have something suitable in the armory."

Liam grinned. "We're not really outfitted for concealment, but we can check and see if we have something in the Scorpions' supplies." Liam whistled to the sergeant leading the training exercise. "Testa, take over the class. I need to speak with the Captain."

"Yes, sir." The sergeant looked at Soren. "Captain." He moved back to his drills.

Liam led Soren through the passageways to a locked compartment that had previously been under guard. They didn't have the manpower to keep watch over the area now. He used his handprint to open the hatch and led Soren into a relatively sparse equipment room, containing everything Alex and his team had brought with them from Jungle. Not only did they find a waistband holster, but the pistol as well. Soren checked the magazine and put it in the holster, which he tucked into his pack. He wouldn't need it with Jane, of course, but once they were on Glaive…he wasn't taking any chances.

"Where are you headed, Captain?" Liam asked. "If you don't mind the question."

"I'd like to tell you, Liam. And it's not that I don't trust you, but after what happened with Gray…"

"I understand, sir. We can't be too careful. Rest assured, we'll continue to prepare while you're gone."

"Thank you, Liam. Jack has command while I'm away. If you need anything, bring it to him."

"Yes, sir."

Soren left the compartment and headed for the hangar bay, knowing an alliance with a CIP might be the only thing that prevented the SF from unwittingly causing a catastrophe. He was determined to do whatever it took to secure one.

CHAPTER 5

Alex's head throbbed as consciousness slowly returned, each pulse of pain a stark reminder of the neural link's invasive probing. He groaned softly, his eyes fluttering open to the dim lighting of the brig. The familiar sight of the cell's interior did little to comfort him, especially given the circumstances that had led to their return.

"Jackson? Zoe?" he whispered, his voice hoarse and barely audible. He tried to reach out through their neural link, only to be met with an eerie, empty silence. The augments were offline, leaving him feeling oddly hollow and disconnected after having them online for so long.

"Here, Gunny," Jackson's voice came from the adjacent cell, equally strained. "Feels like I went ten rounds with a Rhino-class warship."

"Make that twenty," Zoe added from her cell. "I don't think I've ever had a headache this bad."

Alex attempted to sit up, wincing as the movement sent fresh waves of pain through his skull. "Are you both okay? Apart from feeling like we've been put through a mental wringer."

"Define okay," Jackson muttered. "I feel like my brain's been turned inside out and scrubbed with steel wool."

"That's...not a bad description, actually," Zoe agreed. There was a pause before she spoke again, her voice barely above a whisper. "Gunny, I...I can still feel them in there. Rooting around in my memories. It's like they left muddy footprints all over my past."

Alex closed his eyes, understanding all too well what she meant. The neural link hadn't just accessed their surface thoughts or recent memories. It had dug deep, dragging up moments both treasured and painful, leaving him feeling exposed and violated in a way he'd never experienced before.

"I know," he said softly. "It's like they took everything that makes us who we are and laid it out for inspection. Everything we've ever thought, felt, or experienced."

"All our secrets," Jackson added, his voice uncharacteristically somber. "Our fears, our hopes. The things we've never told anyone."

"And now they know it all," Zoe finished, a tremor in her voice. "Forget about the personal stuff. They know everything about the Wraith, about the FUP resistance, about the Convergence. We tried so hard to keep it hidden, and in the end..."

"In the end, it didn't even matter," Alex said, finishing for her. "We gave them everything, even though we fought it with everything we had."

"I keep replaying it in my head," Jackson said. "Trying to figure out if there was something else we could have done, some way we could have resisted harder."

Alex shook his head, immediately regretting the movement as it sent fresh stabs of pain through his skull. "There wasn't," he said firmly. "We did everything we could. That machine wasn't designed for subtlety or gentle probing. It was made to rip information out of people's minds, regardless of the consequences."

"We've put everyone at risk," Zoe said.

"Not just our dimension, either," Jackson added. "If what the Grand Admiral said is true, he's planning to use this information to expand into the other dimensions once he's done here." His tone became mocking. "Why be the king of one realm when you can be the king of three?"

Alex clenched his fists, frustration and anger at odds with the guilt and pain. "We can't dwell on that now," he said, trying to inject some strength into his voice. "It wasn't our fault, and to sit here blaming ourselves is counterproductive. What's done is done. We need to focus on what comes next."

"And what exactly is that?" Zoe asked. "In case you hadn't noticed, we're still locked up, our augments are offline, and we're headed for a prison colony on some backwater planet."

"We're still alive," Alex countered. "As long as we're breathing, there's hope. We just need to stay alert, look for opportunities."

"Ever the optimist, eh Gunny?" Jackson said, a hint of his usual humor creeping back into his voice.

Before Alex could respond, the sound of approaching footsteps silenced their conversation. The brig door slid open, revealing Alexander flanked by the Scarabs. They had shed their power armor for a more standard fare but were still well-armed and armored enough to deal with the unaugmented Scorpions.

"Well, well," Alexander said, his voice dripping with mock cheerfulness. "I hope you all enjoyed your little nappie. It's time for a change of scenery."

Alex studied his doppelgänger's face, searching for any sign of the conflict he'd glimpsed earlier. But Alexander's expression was a mask of cold indifference, betraying nothing of his inner thoughts.

Alex decided to take a risk as the Scarabs moved to unlock their cells. "How are you feeling, Theo?" he asked, his eyes locked on the Marine.

Theo stiffened slightly, but Alexander responded. "That's none of your concern," he snapped.

"Actually, it is," Alex pressed. "You saw my memories. You know what happened to our Theo. Cancer's not something to mess around with."

"Shut up," Alexander growled, but Alex could see the flicker of uncertainty in his eyes.

"What's the matter, Alexander?" Alex continued, pushing himself to his feet despite the lingering pain. "Are you so desperate for your father's approval that you'll force one of your own squad to suffer? Is that what being a leader means to you?"

Alexander's face contorted with rage. Before Alex could react, his doppelgänger's fist slammed into his stomach, driving the air from his lungs. Alex doubled over, gasping, but he didn't miss the tremor in Alexander's hand as he pulled it back.

"You don't know anything about me," Alexander hissed.

Alex straightened, meeting his counterpart's gaze. "I know more than you think," he said quietly. "I am what you could have been, what you still could be if you'd just open your damn eyes and see what's really going on here."

Alexander's jaw clenched, but he didn't respond. Instead, he turned to the Scarabs. "Get them moving. We have a schedule to keep."

As they were roughly pulled from their cells, Alex turned his attention to the others. "Did you enjoy the show?" he asked, his voice carrying clearly in the confined space. "Digging through our memories, seeing what real Marines stand for? Honor, duty, loyalty and courage to do the right thing even when it's hard?"

He saw several Scarabs shift uncomfortably, their eyes darting away from his piercing gaze.

"You all know what the Grand Admiral is doing is wrong," Alex continued as they were marched out of the brig. "You've seen it firsthand. The way he treats people, the way he treats you. You're not people to him, you're slaves. More enslaved than you ever would have been in the FUP. And for what? To help a tyrant crush anyone who dares to stand up to him?"

"That's enough," Alexander snapped, but Alex could hear the strain in his voice.

"Is it?" Alex pressed. "Because from where I'm standing, it looks like you're all so afraid of him you'd rather kill millions of innocent people than stand up and do the right thing."

Alexander whirled on him, his hand going to his sidearm. In one swift motion, he drew the weapon and pressed it against Alex's forehead. "I said, that's enough," he growled, his finger tightening on the trigger.

Alex met his gaze steadily, unflinching in the face of the threat. "Go ahead," he said softly. "Pull the trigger. Go against daddy's orders. Show me you've got a spine of your own."

For a long, tense moment, no one moved. Alex could see the conflict raging in Alexander's eyes, the desire to silence him warring with...something else. Fear? Doubt? A flicker of the person he could have been if he'd made a single different decision?

Finally, with a frustrated growl, Alexander lowered the weapon. "Move," he snarled, shoving Alex forward.

The rest of the journey to the hangar bay passed in tense

silence. As they entered the hangar, Alex saw a shuttle waiting, its engines warming up for departure. A group of Marine Field MPs stood nearby.

"Your chariot awaits," Alexander mocked. "I'm sure you'll find Teegarden absolutely charming this time of year."

Alex turned to face Alexander one last time as they were handed over to the waiting MPs. "It's not too late, you know," he said quietly. "For any of you. And who knows? Maybe if you change your way of thinking, you'll find out what it feels like to breathe free air before it's too late for all of us."

Alexander's face twisted with mixed emotions—anger, uncertainty, and possibly regret. But before he could respond, one of the MPs grabbed Alex's arm, pulling him toward the shuttle.

Alex caught one last glimpse of Alexander and the Scarabs as they were herded up the ramp. Their gazes at him were hard, except for Theo's. He almost appeared to want to be with them instead of with his unit. He was most likely dying, and none of them seemed to care.

The shuttle door sealed behind the Scorpions with a hiss, cutting off Alex's view of the hangar. As they were roughly shoved into seats and secured with heavy restraints, he exchanged glances with Jackson and Zoe. No words were needed; they all understood the situation.

But as the shuttle's engines roared to life, carrying them away from the Fist of Justice and toward an uncertain future, Alex allowed himself a small, grim smile. They might be prisoners, battered and bruised, their secrets laid bare. But they weren't broken. Not yet. And as long as that remained true, there was still hope.

The shuttle accelerated, carrying them toward a long, smooth, rectangular vessel. A prison ship. The idea of it chilled Alex. Their dimension had no such thing. Had no need for it.

As the shuttle drifted into the vessel's hangar bay and Alex spotted additional MPs waiting to guide them to their next living arrangements, he was already planning, already looking for opportunities. They'd find a way out of this. They had to. The fate of three universes depended on it.

CHAPTER 6

Shoved in the back, Alex stumbled down the shuttle's ramp, his legs still unsteady from the neural link's invasive probing. The harsh lights of the hangar bay assaulted his eyes, forcing him to squint as he tried to take in his surroundings. The cavernous space was a stark contrast to the Fist of Justice's sleek, well-maintained interior. This ship was nowhere near as well-kept, with dirty, stained floors and dull, ugly bulkheads. No doubt, the crew running the ship sat securely near the bottom of the pecking order, the dregs of Strickland's navy, sent here to be useful and usefully forgotten.

As his vision adjusted, Alex's gaze fell on a mountain of a man standing at the foot of the ramp. His guard uniform stretched taut across his massive frame, his face permanently set in a scowl that would make even the toughest drill instructor think twice.

"Well, well, well," the man's voice boomed, echoing off the hangar walls. "What do we have here? Some fresh meat for the grinder?" He stepped up to the Scorpions, confusion crossing his hard face. "What the hell is this, some kind of joke? Commandant Strickland said he had special prisoners, but I didn't think he meant himself." He leaned in close to Alex. "Who the hell are you?"

"Nobody," Alex replied.

The guard smirked. "Damn right you're nobody. Keep playing it smart, and maybe I won't hate you quite as much as I hate everyone else. I'm Sergeant Major Briggs, but the only thing I want you to call me is Boss. You got that?"

"Yes, Boss," the three of them replied sharply.

"That's pretty good. Better than the rest of the sorry lot I've got on this shithole of a starship. But I can tell by the looks of you that you're all Marines. I don't know where the FUP found you or how they made you look like our honored Commandant and his squad, but I can guarantee the last thing you'll get on Teegarden is a warm welcome." He began to pace in front of them, his massive boots clanging against the deck plating. "And just to set the record straight, despite its name, there ain't no gardens on it, and there sure as hell ain't no tea."

Briggs stopped directly in front of Alex, leaning in close enough that Alex could smell the stale coffee and alcohol on his breath. "What we do have is hard work. Lots of it. And when you're done with that, you get to do some more. You'll sweat more than you ever thought possible, sleep less than you ever imagined, and then wake up to do it all over again. For the rest of your sorry lives. It's paradise, I assure you."

Jackson, never one to keep his mouth shut, piped up from behind Alex. "Sounds lovely. But not exactly in line with the Geneva Convention, is it?"

The words had barely left Jackson's mouth when Briggs spun on his heel, closing the distance between them in two massive strides. Without warning, he hawked and spat, a glob of phlegm landing squarely on Jackson's boot.

"Geneva?" Briggs snarled, his face inches from Jackson's. "Geneva belongs to Grand Admiral Strickland, boy.

And so do you. The sooner you get that through your thick skull, the easier your time here will be."

Alex tensed, ready to intervene if Briggs decided to escalate further. But the Sergeant Major simply stepped back, his eyes sweeping over the three Scorpions with undisguised contempt.

"Alright, ladies," he barked. "Time for the grand tour. Move out!"

A unit of guards fell in around them, their weapons at the ready as they began to herd the Scorpions out of the hangar bay. As they moved through the ship's corridors, Alex's trained eye took in every detail. The layout was efficient, designed to move large numbers of prisoners quickly and securely. But there were also signs of wear and tear, places where the veneer of spit and polish was starting to crack.

They passed through a security checkpoint, the guards eyeing them warily as they were scanned and processed. Alex noted the positions of the cameras and potential blind spots in their coverage. It wasn't much, but it was something to work with.

Finally, they reached a massive blast door. Briggs input a code, and with a groan of protesting metal, the door slid open to reveal the holding area beyond. The space was enormous, easily large enough to house a small frigate. Cells separated by steel bars, lined both sides of a wide central aisle, stacked ten levels high, with stairs and catwalks providing access. In the center of the ground floor, a raised security station allowed the guards to monitor the entire area.

"Home sweet home," Briggs announced, his voice dripping with sarcasm. "Get used to it. You'll be seeing a lot of it over the next few weeks. In fact, you won't be leaving it at all."

"Not exactly at full occupancy, are you?" Zoe asked as

they were led down the central aisle. Alex noticed she was right. Most of the cells appeared to be empty.

Briggs turned, his eyes narrowing. "What's that supposed to mean?"

"Nothing," Zoe replied, her tone carefully neutral. "Just an observation."

The Sergeant Major's face darkened. "If you must know, there aren't many FUP dissidents and sympathizers left these days. Most of 'em are already enjoying Teegarden's hospitality." His grin was all teeth and no humor. "But don't you worry. We've got plenty of room left for the likes of you three."

They reached a section of cells about halfway down the aisle. Briggs gestured to three adjacent units. "Your accommodations, ladies. I do hope you find them to your liking. If you don't, piss off."

One by one, the Scorpions were shoved into their cells, force fields shimmering to life behind them. Alex found himself on the left, with Jackson in the middle and Zoe to his right. As the MPs began to disperse, Briggs lingered, his eyes fixed on Alex.

"I've got my eye on you, maggot," he growled. "One toe out of line, and you'll wish you'd never been born. Understood?"

Alex met his gaze steadily. "Yes, Sergeant Major."

With a final sneer, Briggs turned and stomped away, leaving the Scorpions alone in their new home.

As soon as the guards were out of earshot, Alex turned his attention to his surroundings. The cell was small, barely large enough for a bunk, a tiny pedestal washbasin, and a toilet with no lid. But the occupant of the cell to his left caught his eye.

A woman sat on the bunk, her posture rigid and her eyes wary. She looked to be in her mid-forties, with graying hair pulled back in a tight bun. Despite the prison jumpsuit, something in her bearing spoke of military training.

"Hey," Alex said softly, careful not to draw the guards' attention. "I'm Alex."

The woman regarded him for a long moment before responding. "Cassandra," she said finally. "Cassandra Reeves."

Alex's eyebrows rose slightly. "Any relation to Marcus Reeves?"

Cassandra's eyes widened in surprise. "My brother. How do you know him?"

"We met briefly," Alex replied, choosing his words carefully. "On Forward Operating Base Alpha."

"Are you SF traitors, then?"

"Hardly. We were assaulting the station. He was on the bridge. In an SF uniform."

"Undercover," Cassandra said. "I assume since you're here the assault didn't go well."

"We were sold out by one of the FUP Marine officers. Marcus tried to warn us that we'd been made before it was too late but…well, it was too late for us at least."

"Do you know where Marcus is now?" she asked, eyes hopeful.

"I'm sorry," Alex replied. "He didn't make it."

Cassandra's lips pressed tight together and she nodded. "That sounds like Marcus. Always trying to do the right thing, even when it gets him killed." She paused, eyes tearing up.

Alex started to turn away and give her some privacy to grieve, but she spoke up before he could. "I was in FUP Intelligence, too. Marcus, he got me into it. A chance to do good. To do the right thing for the right people. He was up for anything to stop the Grand Admiral's tyranny." She motioned to the forcefield keeping her contained. "I guess I failed in doing that."

Alex shrugged. "You only fail if you give up."

She offered a sad smile. "I suppose you're right."

"How did they catch you?"

Cassandra's face darkened. "It's the dumbest thing, really. I didn't get caught because I messed up. I was just in the wrong place at the wrong time. The Strickland Secret Police raided the apartment complex I lived in. Swept up pretty much everyone in the place, FUP spies and SF civilians alike. Booked us all as traitors and sympathizers and brought us up to this ship."

Alex frowned. "Why would they arrest innocent, loyal citizens?"

"Because Strickland and his son don't care who they screw over," Cassandra spat, her voice bitter. "You look a lot like him, you know. Alexander."

"I've heard that a few times," Alex said.

"The Grand Admiral sold the people on security, on the idea that only he could keep them safe from both internal and external threats. And as long as they're not the ones being shipped off to Teegarden, most folks are happy to give up their freedom for that safety." She gestured to the cells across the aisle. "See those people over there? Half of them are probably more loyal to the SF than I ever was to the FUP. But it doesn't matter. Strickland needs his boogeymen, and we're it."

"That's disgusting," Alex said, realizing the situation was worse than he'd thought. Grand Admiral Strickland wasn't just a despot. He was a monster.

"You don't know the half of it," Cassandra replied.

"So how long have you been on this ship?" he asked.

Cassandra shrugged. "I lost track. A few months, maybe? Since there are no viewports, and they never dim the lights, time sort of loses meaning after a while."

"Intentional, I'm sure."

"Yes. They like to make us squirm. A few of the civilians

they rounded up have been taken away at night. When they come back, they're shivering and catatonic. I can only guess what the guards might be doing to them."

Alex could guess, too. A cold fury burned through him at the thought. It didn't matter what side they were on, nobody deserved that kind of treatment. "Do you know how long it'll take to reach Teegarden?"

"About two weeks," Cassandra replied. "Why? Got a hot date waiting for you?"

"Something like that. I'm curious how long I have to figure out how to escape."

Cassandra's eyes widened, a mix of surprise and admiration crossing her face. "Escape? I don't know if you've noticed, but we're on a prison ship that'll be in fold space soon enough. There's nowhere to go."

"I don't know about that," Alex replied, his voice low but firm. "I bet the bridge is pretty nice."

Jackson, listening in, finally spoke up. "Gunny, I don't know if you've been paying attention, but we're zero for our last two on that front."

"Because we were dealing with the damned Scarabs," Alex replied. "There aren't any Scarabs on this ship. Just the chaff that couldn't cut it. Augments or no, we should be able to run the gauntlet with ease, as long as we can get out of these cells and off the prison block. If you aren't plotting, then you've given up. And I'm not giving up."

Cassandra studied him for a long moment, her expression unreadable. Finally, she spoke, her voice barely above a whisper. "You're serious, aren't you? You really think you can pull this off?"

Alex met her gaze steadily. "I have to. There's too much at stake to give up."

A spark of something—hope, maybe?—flickered in Cassandra's eyes. "Well, if you're crazy enough to try, I might just be crazy enough to help. What do you need?"

Alex glanced around, making sure no guards were within earshot. "Information, for starters. Everything you can tell me about this ship, especially the routines of the guards."

Cassandra nodded, a hint of her old intelligence officer demeanor surfacing. "Of course, I've been keeping an eye on them, monitoring their movements and shift changes. I can do that. But I can't help you get out of this cage, or through those doors." She motioned to the blast doors at the end of the block.

"I know," Alex replied. "But we'll cross that bridge when we come to it. For now, let's take one step at a time."

As they discussed the guards' routines in hushed tones, Alex felt a familiar spark of resolve ignite in his chest. He knew escape was a long shot, and the odds were stacked against them, but he refused to just lay down and surrender.

The game was just beginning, and he intended to play it for all it was worth.

CHAPTER 7

Alex leaned against the cold metal bulkhead, his eyes closed as he focused on the rhythmic footsteps of the guards patrolling the prison block. It had been three days since their arrival on the prison ship, and like when they were trapped on the Fist of Justice, every moment had been spent observing, analyzing, and planning.

As Cassandra had warned, the harsh overhead lights never dimmed, making it difficult to gauge the passage of time. But Alex had quickly fallen into the routine of the ship, using the guards' shifts and meal deliveries as markers.

"Chow time," a gruff voice announced, breaking the monotonous silence.

Alex's eyes snapped open as a tray slid through the small break in the bottom of the cell's forcefield. The meal, if you could call it that, consisted of a gray, gelatinous substance that smelled vaguely of overcooked vegetables plus a paper cup of water. He grimaced but picked up the tray. Nutrients were nutrients, and he needed to keep his strength up.

"Bon appétit," Jackson muttered from the adjacent cell, his voice dripping with sarcasm.

"At least it's consistent," Zoe chimed in from her cell. "I'm starting to think the gray goop might be growing on me."

"Pretty sure that's mold," Jackson quipped, eliciting a snort from Zoe.

Alex allowed himself a small smile at their banter. Despite their dire circumstances, their spirits remained relatively high. It was proof of their training and their bond as a unit.

As he ate, Alex's mind wandered to their daily "exercise" period. Once a day, for precisely one hour, the prisoners were allowed out of their cells to stretch their legs in the central aisle of the block. It was during these times that the Scorpions had been meticulously observing the guards' routines and the layout of their fortified position.

The guards' station was a raised platform at the center of the block, offering them a clear view of the entire area. During exercise periods, they would arrange in a circle at the top of the station, rifles at the ready, their fingers never far from the triggers. It was an intimidating display, but Alex had noticed small details—the way certain guards favored one side, how they rotated positions, and the exact timing of breaks in coverage.

Most importantly, Jackson had observed one of the rifles being loaded and was positive they were armed with nonlethal rounds.

The Grand Admiral didn't want his prisoners dying before his guards on Teegarden could get as much hard labor out of them as possible.

"Cassandra," Alex said softly, turning toward the adjacent cell once he was sure the guards were out of earshot. "Have you noticed any changes in their routines?"

The former intelligence officer shook her head.

"Nothing significant. They're sticking to the patterns I described. Shift changes every eight hours, with a fifteen-minute overlap for briefing. The guard station is always manned by at least four, with two more patrolling the block. I'm sure you've noticed the guards don't spend much time actually guarding while we're in our cells."

"I've definitely noticed," Alex replied. "What about during exercise periods?"

"They double the number on the platform," Cassandra replied. "Eight up there, four on the floor. Always in pairs, never alone."

"Smart," Alex mused. "Harder to overpower or bribe in pairs."

"Exactly," Cassandra agreed. "But it also means they're spread thinner. More ground to cover, more angles to watch."

"Still, this would be easier if the block were full."

"Not necessarily. The SF prisoners are a wild card. Some of them might try to help the guards in hopes of being released."

Alex gritted his teeth. He hadn't considered that. "We'll have to—"

Their conversation was interrupted by the sound of approaching footsteps. Alex quickly turned away from Cassandra, pretending to be absorbed in scraping the last bits of food from his tray.

A pair of guards stopped in front of his cell, eyeing him suspiciously. "Enjoying your meal, pretty boy?" one of them sneered.

Alex looked up with a grin. "It's truly a masterwork of culinary delight. My compliments to the chef."

The guard's face twisted in anger, but his companion put a hand on his arm. "Leave it, Merv. Not worth the hassle."

As they moved on, Alex caught Jackson's attention.

Jackson gave him a subtle nod, indicating he'd been listening to his conversation with Cassandra. He would pass what they'd said on to Zoe when the opportunity arose.

Later, Zoe spoke up when the guards were well out of earshot. "I've been thinking," she said, her voice low. "If I could get through the bulkhead at the back of my cell to the wiring, I might be able to reverse the forcefield polarity."

Alex raised an eyebrow, impressed. "That's not a bad idea. But how do we get through the bulkhead?"

"The washbasin," Jackson chimed in. "It's bolted to the wall. If we could remove it..."

"We'd have access to the interior," Alex finished. "Good thinking, both of you."

Over the next few hours, all three Scorpions worked on loosening the bolts securing their washbasins to the walls. It was slow, tedious work. Without proper tools, they had to rely on improvised methods, using the edges of their food trays, bits of metal they'd managed to pry loose from their cots, and even their fingernails. Cassandra kept an eye on the guards, and they had to stop often to avoid detection.

From the tightness of the bolts, someone else had tried to get to the interior of the bulkhead this way before. But Alex had noticed the condition of the ship. It wasn't well maintained, which meant…

"I think I've got one," Jackson whispered excitedly. "It's loose."

Alex paused in his efforts, hope coursing through him. "Good work, Three. Keep at it."

But even with one bolt loosened, they were far from their goal. The opening would be small, barely enough to reach through, let alone manipulate wiring.

"We need more," Zoe said, voicing what they were all thinking. "Wire, tools, something to work with."

Alex considered their options. Then it hit him. "What about the guards' stun batons?" he asked.

"If we disassemble the electronics, we might have something to work with," Zoe answered, excitement creeping into her voice.

"But how do we get one?" Jackson asked. "It's not like they're just going to hand one over."

"We cause a distraction," Alex replied. "Something big enough to draw their attention and force them to use the batons."

"And then what?" Cassandra asked, her voice skeptical. "Even if you manage to get a baton, they'll know it's missing. They'll tear this place apart looking for it."

"Then we'll have to move fast," Alex replied. "Create the distraction, get the baton, open it up, pull the electronics, put it back together, drop the baton. If they try to use it, they'll likely think it's defective and toss it aside. They aren't engineers."

"How can we take it apart and put it back together that fast, and without being noticed?" Jackson asked.

"Easier than you think," Zoe replied. "The batons have a simple locking mechanism at the handle. All the electronics are inside the grip. I can do it in ten seconds."

"Jackson needs the asset," Alex said.

"I can probably teach you how to take it apart, Three. You don't need to be smarter than a fourth grader to learn."

"Very funny, Five," Jackson said. "This is a hell of a risk, Gunny."

"I know," Alex acknowledged. "But it might be our only shot. Leave the distraction to me. I'll figure something out."

As they continued to discuss the plan in hushed tones, the opening of the main doors echoed through the block. Alex fell silent, watching as a group of new prisoners was led in.

Most were directed to the SF side of the cell block, civilians by the look of them. But one figure caught Alex's attention. A man, walking with a slight limp, his face bearing fresh bruises. As he was led past them, Alex's blood ran cold.

It was Major Thomas Gray.

The traitor who had sold them out to the SF, leading to their capture and the disaster at FOB Alpha.

Jackson was the first to react. "Gray, you son of a bitch!" he raged. Zoe joined in, hurling insults and threats at the man who had betrayed them. The commotion drew the attention of the guards, who moved to intervene.

"Enough!" Alex barked, his voice cutting through the chaos. "Stand down, both of you."

Reluctantly, Jackson and Zoe fell silent, but their glares could have melted steel.

As the guards moved away, satisfied that the situation was under control, Alex turned his attention to Gray. The man looked broken. Fear, anger, and desperation were in his eyes.

"Major Gray," Alex said, his voice cold. "Isn't this an interesting turn of events? I thought you'd be living it up with your new SF buddies. What happened? Strickland didn't roll out the red carpet for his star informant?"

Gray's face twisted in a mixture of pain and bitterness. "I got what I deserved," he admitted. "It turns out the Grand Admiral isn't big on rewarding traitors. While his subordinates were beating the shit out of me, he told me that anyone willing to betray their own side can't be trusted." Gray's voice faltered. "He got everything he could, then dumped me here."

"Karma's a bitch, isn't it?" Jackson sneered.

Alex held up a hand, silencing his teammate. "So you betrayed the FUP, got twenty-five good Marines killed, plus two of my team—my family—and this is what you got for it? Excuse me while I die laughing, you asshole."

Gray's eyes darted between the Scorpions, a desperate gleam in them. "Look, I know you have no reason to trust me, but I want in on whatever you're planning."

"We're not planning anything," Zoe said. "What the hell could we plan?"

"I know what you're capable of. You aren't going to sit here and accept your fate. I don't want to, either."

"Like hell," Cassandra snarled from her cell. "After what you did? My brother died because of you. You deserve to rot here."

"Strickland had it right for once," Alex said. "You can't be trusted. You sold out your own people once. What's to stop you from doing it again the moment it benefits you?"

Gray's face hardened. "I can be an ally or an enemy," he said, his voice low and dangerous. "Trust me, you don't want me as an enemy. Not here."

Alex lowered his voice, speaking in a calm, cold tone. "If you know what we're capable of, then you're the one who needs to be careful. You know, just in case we do happen to get out of these cells. You'll be the first one we come after."

Gray's face contorted with rage. "You're making a mistake," he hissed.

"No," Alex replied. "I'm learning from yours."

With that, he turned away from Gray, effectively ending the conversation. He could feel the man's glare burning into his back, but he ignored it. They had bigger problems to deal with.

A low rumble vibrated through the ship. The engines were powering up.

"We're getting underway," Cassandra whispered.

Alex nodded. He knew they'd move out of orbit before coming to a stop to fold. "The clock is ticking for real now."

The vibrations intensified, and Alex could feel the subtle shift as the massive vessel maneuvered out of Earth's orbit.

Then, just as suddenly, it stopped, followed by the subtle change in the ship's vibrations as the fold drive engaged.

They were on their way to Teegarden. They had two weeks to turn their plans into action. If they could reach the bridge, they could cancel the fold and change course. He wasn't sure how they would find the FUP resistance at that point, but they would figure it out when the time came.

He glanced at Jackson, who nodded back with a smirk. "As soon as we get out of these cells, I'm going to kick your ass, Gunny."

"In your dreams, Three," he replied. "But let's make it count."

CHAPTER 8

The harsh buzz of the intercom echoed through the prison block, signaling the start of the daily exercise period. Alex stood at the threshold of his cell, muscles tense with anticipation. As the force field on his cell flickered and died, he took a deep breath, steadying himself for what was to come.

"Okay, maggots," Sergeant Major Briggs' voice boomed from the guard station. "You know the drill. You have one hour, starting now."

Alex stepped out onto the catwalk at his cell, eyes immediately turning to Gray. Jackson did the same, and for a moment Alex thought his squadmate might go after the traitor. He knew better himself than to ruin the plan by starting a fight with Gray, but Jackson was sometimes a bit of a hothead. Gray noticed them and quickly headed for the stairs in the opposite direction, settling the issue.

The prisoners made their way down the metal stairs to the main floor, the clanging of their footsteps on the catwalks echoing off the bulkheads. Alex kept his movements casual, but his senses were on high alert. He noted the positions of each guard, the angles of the security cameras, and the body language of his fellow inmates.

As the prisoners began to spread out, Alex spotted Gray at the far end. The traitor was making a beeline for the guard station, his posture rigid with purpose. Alex's jaw clenched, but he forced himself to remain calm. He'd expected as much when he declined Gray's bid to get in on their plot.

He maneuvered closer to the station, careful to stay out of the guards' direct line of sight. Gray's raised voice, tinged with desperation, carried just far enough for Alex to make out his words over the other hushed conversations across the deck.

"Listen to me," Gray hissed to the nearest guard. "Those prisoners, the ones that look like Commandant Strickland and his Scarabs? They're planning an escape. You need to—"

The guard cut him off with a harsh laugh. "Planning an escape? No shit, genius. Everyone here's planning an escape. Doesn't mean any of them are gonna pull it off."

Gray's face reddened. "You don't understand. These aren't ordinary prisoners. They're—"

"What I understand," the guard growled, "is that you're starting to piss me off. Now get out of my face before I decide to make an example of you."

With a rough shove, the guard sent Gray stumbling backward. Alex couldn't help the small smirk that tugged at the corners of his mouth as he watched the traitor's humiliation. It was a petty satisfaction, but given their circumstances, he'd take what he could get.

As Gray slunk away, Alex caught Jackson's eye and gave a subtle nod. They waited, biding their time as the other prisoners milled about. Finally, Alex squared his shoulders and strode toward Jackson, twisting his face into a mask of barely contained rage.

"You got something more to say to me, asshole?" he snarled, loud enough to draw attention.

Jackson, playing his part perfectly, rose to meet the challenge. "Yeah, I do. I'm sick of your bullshit, Gunny. You think you're so much better than the rest of us. But I know you're really just a piece of shit."

"Is that right?" Alex shot back. "I don't think I'm better. I know it. And if you've got a problem with that, why don't you do something about it?"

The tension in the air was palpable as the two men squared off. Then, with a sudden burst of motion, they were at each other's throats. They hit the deck, grappling and throwing punches. Though each blow was carefully pulled to look brutal without causing any bloody damage, they staged an altercation more than entertaining enough to pull in a crowd of spectators.

The prisoners' shouts and jeers egged the pair on until a trio of guards pushed their way through the crowd. "Alright! Break it up!" the lead guard bellowed, the electric sound of his crackling stun baton cutting through the commotion. Alex and Jackson paid it no heed. They continued their struggle, Alex pushing through the first jolt of pain that connected with his side, rolling them both toward one of the guards.

They collided with the man's legs, toppling him to the deck. His baton clattered to the deck after him, just the opportunity they needed for Jackson to roll on top of it. While Alex kept him locked there in a fake chokehold, Jackson's fingers worked frantically to open the baton's handle.

More shocks, as the other guards tried to subdue Alex, rained down on his back and sides. He gritted his teeth against the charges, only his early training and experience allowing him to absorb the electric impulses. One, two, three, four charges. His muscles spasmed with each hit, each one numbing him more and more, threatening to paralyze him temporarily. Just as his body began to turn rigid, his muscles numb and spasming, he felt Jackson give the slightest of nods against his arm. It was done.

Alex's grip on Jackson went slack with a final, powerful shock. He slid off him to the deck, rolling onto his back, his body twitching involuntarily as Jackson staggered to his feet. Coughing and bending down to clutch his knees, he coughed and pretended to gasp for air.

The pain for Alex was intense, but it was nothing like the neural probe had inflicted. He watched a guard roughly haul Jackson upright, the reassembled baton remaining on the deck.

"What in the name of Grand Admiral Strickland's perfectly pressed uniform is going on here?" Sergeant Major Briggs' voice boomed as he stalked across the prison block.

Two of the guards pulled Alex, still dazed from the stun batons, roughly to his feet. He swayed between them, unable to stand alone, grateful for their support even as he bristled at their rough handling.

Briggs stormed right up to Alex, his face tight with barely contained fury. "I give you maggots one hour, one measly hour to stretch your legs and this is what you do with it?" he roared, his breath smelling strongly of alcohol. "You think you're tough, boy? You think this is some kind of game?"

Alex remained silent, knowing anything he said would only worsen the situation.

Briggs turned his attention to Jackson. "And you. Thought you'd take on your superior, did you? Show everyone what a tough guy you are?" Briggs sneered. "Well, congratulations. You've just won yourself and every other sorry sack of shit in this block a one-way ticket to Boring City."

He stepped back, addressing the entire prison block.

"Listen up, maggots! Thanks to these two, recreation time is officially canceled for the remainder of this trip. Hope you enjoyed your little taste of freedom, because it's the last you'll be getting." A chorus of groans and angry mutters rose from the assembled prisoners. Briggs silenced them with a glare. "If you've got a problem with that, take it up with your new pals here," he growled, jerking a thumb toward Alex and Jackson. "Now, get back to your cells. All of you! Show's over."

Alex caught sight of Gray as the guards began herding the prisoners back to their cells. The traitor's face was a mixture of frustration and smug satisfaction. Alex couldn't resist the urge to twist the knife a little.

"Hey, Gray," he called out, his voice rough from the fight. "Thanks for the warning about us. Really saved the day there, didn't you?"

Gray's face reddened, his hands clenching into fists at his sides. "This isn't over," he hissed.

"You're right," Alex replied, his voice low and dangerous. "It's not. Remember that."

With a final shove from the guards, Alex stumbled into his cell, falling face-first onto his mattress, his legs still like Jell-O under him. The force field hummed to life, sealing him in once more. He turned over on his cot, his body aching from the stun batons.

"You okay over there, Gunny?" Zoe asked.

"I've had worse," Alex grunted, confident the loud chaos and distraction of the guards hustling the last few argumentative prisoners back into their cells was enough to mask their interaction. "Jackson?"

"Present and accounted for," Jackson replied, a hint of triumph in his voice, his voice dropping to a whisper. "And I've got a little souvenir in my pocket."

Alex allowed himself a small smile. "Nice work, Three," he muttered. Despite the pain, despite the cancellation of their exercise period, they had accomplished their goal. They were one step closer to freedom. "Zoe, what do you think we can do with this?"

"You'll need to describe the components to me, Jackson," Zoe replied.

Alex settled in as best he could while Jackson did his best to describe what he had stolen, pausing whenever the guards came too close or looked their way.

"Give me a few minutes to think it over," Zoe replied, her voice taking on the focused tone she got when tackling a technical challenge. "At first thought, I'd say we've got some promising components there. The power cell alone could be a game-changer."

As Zoe began quietly discussing with Jackson the potential uses for their new acquisition, Alex turned his attention to Cassandra in the next cell over.

"Quite a show you put on," she murmured, her voice barely above a whisper. "I hope it was worth it."

"It was," Alex assured her. "We're making progress. Slow and steady."

They had taken a significant risk today, but it had paid off. The components from the stun baton could be the key to their escape. But there were still so many obstacles to overcome. Even if they managed to escape their cells, they would have to navigate the heavily guarded prison block, make their way to the bridge, and somehow take control of the ship. All without their neural augments, without their usual equipment, and with who knew how many armed guards standing in their way.

And then there was Gray. Alex was confident he could handle him when the time came. In the meantime, the traitor was a wild card, unpredictable and dangerous. Alex had no doubt he would try to interfere with their plans out of spite or in a misguided attempt to curry favor with the guards.

Despite the challenges ahead, Alex felt a spark of hope ignite in his chest. They had taken the first step. As he drifted into an uneasy sleep, his body still aching from the fight, his last thoughts were of the Wraith, his father and sister. He wondered where they were now and if they'd come any closer to stopping the Convergence or at least figuring out the source.

He sure as hell hoped so.

CHAPTER 9

"Your turn," Jane said, a hint of amusement in her voice. "Unless you're planning to concede already?"

"Not a chance." Soren leaned forward in his chair, studying the holographic chess board floating above the small table between him and Jane. "I'm just weighing my options."

The soft blue glow of the pieces cast strange shadows across the cramped interior of the shuttle, adding an otherworldly quality to the already surreal situation. He reached out, his hand passing through the hologram as he considered his next move.

He finally moved his knight, capturing one of Jane's pawns. "There. Your move."

As Jane contemplated the board, Soren took a bite of his protein ration bar. The bland, slightly chalky texture was far from appetizing, but it was all they had for the long journey to Glaive. He washed it down with a swig of water, grimacing slightly.

"Not exactly gourmet cuisine, is it?" Jane commented, noticing his expression.

"It does its job," Soren replied diplomatically. "Though I'd kill for a real cup of coffee right about now."

Jane laughed, a sound that was achingly familiar yet subtly different from his own Jane's laughter. "You and I both. But I suppose we should be grateful we have supplies at all, given our situation."

She moved her bishop, putting Soren's king in check. "While you ponder your imminent defeat, why don't I fill you in a bit more on the CIP situation in our dimension? It might help you prepare for the meeting."

Soren nodded, studying the board intently. "Please do. The more information I have, the better our chances of convincing them to join the fight."

Jane leaned back, absently twirling a loose strand of hair around her finger. "Well, as I mentioned before, we never had an all-out war with the CIP like you did in your dimension. Instead, it's been more of a prolonged cold war, with tensions always simmering just below the surface."

Soren moved his king out of check, buying himself some time. "No major battles? No defining moments of conflict?"

"Oh, there have been skirmishes," Jane replied. "Disputed territories, the occasional firefight between ships. But both sides always managed to pull back from the brink of full-scale war. There was too much at stake, too much to lose."

Soren nodded, understanding. "A delicate balance of power."

"Exactly," Jane said, advancing a pawn. "When Soren...when the Grand Admiral came to power, he initially assured the CIP that he would maintain the status quo. He even provided humanitarian aid during some of their planetary disasters."

Soren's brow furrowed. "A gesture of goodwill? Or a strategic move?"

Jane's expression hardened. "Both, I suspect. It kept

them complacent, made them believe they weren't in his crosshairs. But we both know it's only a matter of time before he turns his attention their way."

"And that's why they've been helping the resistance," Soren concluded, moving his rook to threaten Jane's queen. "To stall the inevitable."

"Precisely," Jane said, deftly maneuvering her queen out of danger. "They've been increasing their military spending, but they're still no match for the Strickland Federation. It's a losing battle, and they know it."

Soren leaned forward, his interest piqued. "Do you have any sense of the size of the CIP Navy? Their capabilities?"

Jane paused, considering. "Last intelligence estimates put them at over two hundred ships. It's a respectable force, to be sure."

"But not big enough," Soren finished for her.

"Not even close," Jane agreed. "The SF has over a thousand ships, not to mention superior logistics and resources. The CIP simply can't compete on that scale."

Soren sat back, rubbing his chin thoughtfully. "No wonder they're hesitant to abandon their neutrality. They're trying to buy time, hoping for a miracle."

"Or waiting for the axe to fall," Jane added grimly. She moved her knight, putting Soren in check once again. "Check."

Soren leaned back, folded his arms across his chest and studied the board, his mind racing with possibilities both for the game and for their upcoming meeting. "I might have an idea," he said slowly. "Something that could change their minds about joining the fight."

Jane's eyebrows rose. "Oh? Care to share?"

Soren shook his head, moving his king to safety. "It's still the nucleus of a plan. There are too many moving pieces, too many variables. I'm not even sure I can make good on it yet."

"Come on, Soren," Jane pressed. "Give me something to work with here. Even a hint?"

For a moment, Soren was tempted to confide in her. The plan forming in his mind was audacious, potentially game-changing. But it was also incredibly risky, with consequences that could ripple across multiple dimensions. He needed more time to refine it, to consider all the angles.

"I'm sorry, Jane," he said finally. "But until I'm more certain of the details, I'd rather keep it to myself."

Jane studied him for a long moment, her expression a blend of curiosity and frustration. Finally, she nodded. "Fair enough. I just hope whatever you're cooking up in that brilliant mind of yours is enough to sway them. We're running out of options. And time."

"Believe me, I know," Soren replied. "If this doesn't work..."

He trailed off, unable to finish the thought. The consequences of failure were too dire to contemplate.

Jane reached across the table, briefly squeezing his hand. "Hey. One step at a time, remember? Let's focus on getting to Glaive first. We can worry about next steps once we're there."

Soren managed a small smile. "You're right, of course. Now, I believe it was your move?"

They continued their game. The quiet click of holographic pieces moving provided a soothing backdrop to their conversation. Jane shared more details about the CIP's political structure, their key leaders, and the delicate dance of diplomacy that had kept the peace for so long.

As they played, Soren marveled at the differences and similarities between this Jane and his own. They shared the same sharp intellect and dry wit. But there was a hardness to this Jane, a battle-worn edge that his wife had never needed to develop. It was a stark reminder of the divergent paths their lives had taken.

Finally, after a grueling match that stretched on for over an hour, Jane made her final move. "Checkmate," she announced, a triumphant grin spreading across her face.

Soren stared at the board in disbelief, then chuckled ruefully. "Well played. I thought I had you there for a moment."

"You very nearly did," Jane admitted. "But I've had a lot of practice over the years. Strategy games help keep the mind sharp when you're constantly on the run."

As they began clearing away the remnants of their meager meal, Jane stretched, her joints popping audibly in the confined space. "I don't know about you, but I'm ready to call it a night."

Soren nodded in agreement, feeling the fatigue settling into his bones. "Sleep sounds good. We've got a rematch ahead of us tomorrow, and I need all of my wits to beat you."

"You can't beat me with all of your wits, either," Jane laughed. She stepped toward her bunk, casually stripping down to her underwear. There was little room for modesty in the cramped confines of the shuttle. Soren found himself averting his eyes out of habit, though he couldn't help but notice the lean, athletic build that years of warfare had sculpted.

It was strange how different this Jane's body was from his own wife's. His Jane had softened over the years, her figure fuller and more rounded. This Jane was all hard angles and taut muscle, a physical manifestation of her harsh life.

As Jane pulled the privacy screen closed around her bunk, Soren felt a pang of guilt. Not for noticing the differences—that was only natural—but for how much he had come to enjoy this Jane's company over the past few days. The easy camaraderie they had fallen into, the shared jokes and quiet moments of understanding...it all felt dangerously close to a betrayal of his own Jane.

Soren settled into his bunk, staring up at the featureless ceiling. His thoughts drifted to his wife, on Earth, two dimensions away. He missed her with an ache that grew stronger with each passing day. The sound of her laughter, the warmth of her embrace, the way her eyes crinkled at the corners when she smiled—all of it felt like a distant memory right now.

And beneath the longing, a current of fear ran deep. What if the second dimension's FUP had already reached Earth? What if, even now, his Jane was in danger? The thought of her facing the horrors of interdimensional war without him there to protect her was almost unbearable.

Soren closed his eyes, trying to push away the dark thoughts. He needed to focus on the mission, on the thin thread of hope they were pursuing. If they could convince the CIP to join the fight and find a way to stop the convergence, maybe he could return home. Maybe then he could hold his Jane in his arms once more.

But as sleep finally claimed him, one thought lingered, refusing to be silenced.

What if it was already too late?

CHAPTER 10

Soren and Jane spent the remaining days of their journey to Glaive in a routine that blended monotony with moments of unexpected camaraderie. The cramped confines of the shuttle demanded a level of intimacy that, while initially uncomfortable, soon became almost companionable. And, contrary to his earlier beliefs, spending more time with this Jane didn't take away his love for his own Jane. In fact, it only added to it, as he found comfort in the two women's similarities, but also greater admiration for their differences. Admiral Yarborough became much more of an individual to him, and that was the best result for everyone.

Each morning began with a series of exercises designed to keep their bodies limber and their minds alert. Soren found himself impressed by Jane's discipline as she matched him rep for rep, her movements fluid and precise. It was during these sessions that he often caught glimpses of the woman she must have been before the war, before the weight of resistance leadership had settled on her shoulders.

"You know," Jane said one morning as they cooled down from a particularly grueling set of burpees, her breath coming in short pants, "I used to hate these things. Thought they were a waste of time."

Soren chuckled, wiping sweat from his brow with the back of his hand. "And now?"

Jane paused, taking a long drink of water before answering. A wry smile played at her lips as she considered her response. "Now? Now I think they're a necessary evil. Kind of like politics."

Soren raised an eyebrow, intrigued by the comparison. "Politics as exercise? That's an interesting analogy."

Jane shrugged, stretching her arms above her head. "Think about it. Both require discipline, stamina, and the ability to push through discomfort. And both leave you feeling exhausted and nauseated at the end."

He could only agree.

Their afternoons were often spent in fierce chess battles, the holographic board between them a battlefield of strategy and counter-strategy. Soren found that Jane played much like his own wife—aggressive, always looking for an opening, but with a patience that could stretch for dozens of moves before striking.

"Check," Soren announced, moving his bishop into position. He leaned back, a satisfied smile on his face as he studied the board.

Jane didn't react immediately. She leaned forward, her elbows on her knees, chin resting on her interlaced fingers as she studied the board intently. Her eyes darted from piece to piece, clearly calculating moves and countermoves. Finally, she spoke, her voice tinged with grudging admiration. "Hmm. Not bad, Soren. Not bad at all."

Her fingers hovered over her queen, then shifted to her knight. With a decisive move, she not only blocked his check but put his king in jeopardy. A triumphant grin spread across her face as she sat back. "But not quite good enough."

Soren's eyes widened as he realized the trap he'd fallen into. "Well, hell," he conceded, shaking his head in admiration. "I walked right into that one, didn't I?"

She only laughed with enjoyment.

As the days wore on, they found themselves sharing stories—carefully at first, then with increasing openness. Soren spoke of his children, of the pride he felt in their accomplishments and the worry that gnawed at him now that Alex was missing. Jane, in turn, shared tales of the resistance, of narrow escapes and hard-won victories.

"There was this one time," she said one evening, her eyes distant with memory, a half-eaten protein bar forgotten in her hand. "We were pinned down on Proxima. SF forces had us surrounded, no way out. The air was thick with dust. We could hear them closing in, shouting orders, the heavy tread of their boots getting closer with each passing second."

Soren leaned forward, intrigued, his own meal forgotten. "What did you do?"

Jane's eyes refocused on him, a hint of old pain mixing with the memory. "We were ready to make our last stand. And then this kid—he couldn't have been more than twenty—comes up with the idea to decrypt our comms and pay off a civilian to act as the commander of a strike force that had just entered the area. We made it sound like we had reinforcements incoming."

"Clever," Soren nodded appreciatively. "Did it work?"

Jane's laugh was tinged with both amusement and a hint of old pain. "Like a charm. You should have seen their faces when we finally made it out. The relief, the disbelief...it was something else." Her expression sobered. "Lost the kid a month later in another skirmish, but...well, his quick thinking saved a lot of lives that day."

Soren's face fell, recognizing the weight of command and the toll it took. "I'm sorry," he said softly. "It's never easy, losing people under your command, especially ones so young."

Jane nodded, her eyes meeting Soren's with a shared understanding. "No, it isn't. But we honor them by continuing the fight, by making sure their sacrifices weren't in vain."

On the tenth day of their journey, in a bid to stave off the creeping boredom, Jane surprised Soren by pulling up an old music file on the shuttle's computer. The strains of a slow jazz number filled the small space, the mellow tones of a saxophone weaving through the air. Before Soren could react, Jane had pulled him to his feet.

"Come on, Soren," she said, a mischievous glint in her eye as she tugged him toward the small space in front of the table. "Show me what you've got."

Soren hesitated for a moment, his body stiff with surprise. "I should warn you," he said, a self-deprecating smile on his face, "I'm a bit out of practice. It's been a while since I've had an occasion to dance."

"So am I," Jane replied, her lips quirking in a grin. "But I figure we can't be any worse than some of the diplomatic functions I used to attend. You should have seen some of those politicians try to waltz. It was like watching a herd of drunken elephants."

They moved together in the confined space, their steps more shuffle than dance, but there was a comfort in the simple human contact. As they swayed to the music, Soren found himself struck by the surreal nature of the moment— dancing with his wife's doppelgänger in a cramped shuttle in folded space.

"Penny for your thoughts?" Jane asked, noticing his distraction. Her hand was warm on his shoulder, her other clasped in his as they moved to the gentle rhythm.

Soren shook his head, offering a small smile. "Just...marveling at the strange turns life can take. If someone had told me a year ago that I'd be dancing in a shuttle with an alternate version of my wife in another dimension, I'd have thought they were crazy."

Jane's expression softened, understanding in her eyes. "I know what you mean. If someone had told me a year ago that I'd be dancing with a Soren Strickland who wasn't trying to kill me, I'd have thought they were crazy too." She paused, a wistful look crossing her face. "It's nice, though. Reminds me of simpler times."

"It does," Soren agreed. He took the occasion to dip her, and they shared a soft laugh before winding down the dance.

"We're just about there," she said, pointing to the countdown on the shuttle's dashboard. "Thank you for the dance."

"Thank you," Soren replied.

He followed her to the flight deck, dropping into the co-pilot seat while she sat and prepared to take the controls. They remained silent for the last two minutes of the journey before a flash of light deposited them into normal space. Through the viewscreen, a planet loomed before them, a massive ball of ice and rock, its surface a swirling canvas of white and pale blue.

"There she is…Glaive," Jane said, her voice tinged with relief and apprehension. "Last stop before we find out if this crazy plan of yours has any chance of convincing them to join the fun."

CHAPTER 11

Soren's eyes remained fixed on Glaive. As they drew closer, he could make out the sprawling domes—massive structures of transparent panels held in place by reinforced alloy —that dotted the surface, each one a self-contained ecosystem. He knew the planet also had a large city beneath the ice, for a total population of over one hundred million people. The orbit around Glaive was just as crowded, a mix of CIP and SF vessels moving in complex patterns to circumvent one another as they came and went.

"Quite a mix," Soren observed, noting the variety of ships. Freighters and transports made up the bulk of the traffic, their hulls marked with corporate logos and registration numbers. Among them, he spotted at least two CIP-flagged Komodos maintaining a watchful presence.

Jane opened a channel to orbital control, her voice steady and professional. "Glaive Control, this is shuttle Epsilon-937 requesting permission to land at Dome 12 spaceport."

There was a moment of static before a crisp voice responded, the slight distortion doing nothing to hide the bored professionalism in the controller's tone. "Shuttle

Epsilon-937, this is Glaive Control. Please transmit identification and state your business."

Jane glanced at Soren, a silent question in her eyes. He nodded, and she transmitted the prepared identification codes. "Transmitting now, Control. We're here on personal business. Just a quick stopover."

Another pause, this one stretching long enough to make Soren's palms sweat. He could feel his heartbeat quickening, the tension on the small flight deck palpable. Finally, the controller's voice returned. "Identification confirmed, Epsilon-937. You are cleared for landing at Dome 12, Bay 17. Transmitting approach vector now. Welcome to Glaive."

As Jane guided the shuttle through the planet's atmosphere, following the designated flight path, Soren rose to his feet. "I should go put on my uniform." He turned to head to the back of the shuttle. Jane's hand on his arm stopped him, her grip firm but not unkind.

"Not a good idea," she said, shaking her head. Her eyes met his, conveying the seriousness of the situation. "We need to blend in, not stand out. I brought some civilian clothes for you."

Soren frowned, his brow furrowing in concern. "Won't that make us look less official? I thought the whole point was to make an impression on the CIP leadership."

Jane's lips quirked into a wry smile. "Trust me, Soren. Once they see your face, they'll take us plenty seriously. But for now, we need to avoid drawing attention. There are eyes everywhere on Glaive, and not all of them are friendly."

Reluctantly, Soren nodded. Jane directed him to the compartment beside her bunk, where he found a pair of black slacks, a white shirt, and a black vest, along with a hooded coat, clearly designed to conceal his face. As he changed, Soren discreetly transferred his sidearm to the new outfit, carefully concealing it beneath the vest. Jane, focused on their descent, didn't notice.

The massive dome of the spaceport loomed before them, its apex splitting open like the petals of a flower to admit their shuttle. Soren marveled at the engineering required to create such structures in this harsh environment. As they passed through the opening, he caught a glimpse of a second aperture on the far side, allowing a larger shuttle to depart.

"Impressive," he murmured, eyes wide as he took in the scale of the operation."Do they ever get to close the apertures?"

"They have to eventually, or the mechanisms will begin to freeze. But it's all perfectly managed. The CIP may not have the military might of the SF, but they've got some of the best engineers in the galaxy."

She set the shuttle down with practiced ease in the designated bay. As the engines powered down, she turned to Soren, her expression serious. "Remember, we're just two more faces in the crowd. We get in, make contact, say our piece, and get out. Understood?"

Soren nodded, pulling the hood of his coat up to shadow his face. "Understood. Lead the way."

They exited the shuttle into the bustling spaceport. The cavernous interior was a hive of activity, with people moving purposefully in every direction.

As they made their way toward the exit, Soren spotted a group of SF Marines near one of the security checkpoints. His muscles tensed instinctively, hand twitching toward his concealed weapon, but Jane's hand on his arm kept him moving.

"Easy," she murmured, her lips barely moving as she spoke. "They're not looking for us. To them, we're just two more civilians passing through. Act natural."

Soren forced himself to relax, adopting a casual stride.

"Right," he whispered back. "Just two ordinary civilians on a perfectly normal trip."

Jane's soft chuckle was reassuring. "That's the spirit. Now, let's get to the maglev before our contact starts to wonder if we got cold feet." She shoved him lightly in the ribs. "Get it?"

Soren couldn't keep himself from laughing. "That was bad." And exactly the kind of jokes his Jane liked to make.

They boarded a maglev train bound for the underground city of Glaston. As the train descended, Soren was mesmerized by the view through the transparent tunnel, as formations of ice stalagmites gave way to solid rock and the geological history of Glaive.

"It's beautiful," Soren said softly, his breath fogging the glass as he leaned closer. "In a stark, alien sort of way."

Jane nodded, her gaze fixed on the passing layers of ice and stone. "It grows on you. The first time I came here, I thought it was the most desolate place I'd ever seen. But there's a certain majesty to it."

Suddenly, the tunnel opened into a vast cavern that left Soren gawking. The underground city spread out before them, a marvel of engineering and human determination. Towering structures reached toward the cavern's lofty ceiling, lit up by holographic projections of a clear blue sky. Parks and gardens dotted the landscape, and trees and flowers added splashes of color to the subterranean metropolis.

"Incredible," Soren murmured, unable to keep the awe from his voice. His eyes darted from one marvel to another, trying to take it all in. "It's like a whole underground world."

Jane nodded. "It is, isn't it? Proof of what we can achieve when we put our minds to it, and that not everything we build has to be built for war."

As they exited the maglev station, Soren expected Jane

to lead them toward some sort of government building. Instead, she guided him through bustling streets to a nondescript restaurant in what appeared to be a business district. The smell of cooking food wafted from the entrance, making Soren's stomach growl in anticipation of something more appetizing than military rations.

"Our contact is here," she explained as they approached the entrance, her voice low. "Less conspicuous than a government office. I can guarantee there are SF spies watching everyone going in and out of the government properties."

"That makes sense," Soren agreed.

Inside, Jane spoke quietly to the host, her posture relaxed but her eyes alert. "We have a reservation for three under Ryan."

The host nodded, his expression neutral. "Of course. Please, follow me."

They were led past the main dining area, through the bustling kitchen where chefs called out orders and the sizzle of cooking food filled the air, then down a flight of stairs. Soren's hand instinctively moved toward his concealed weapon. Jane seemed to sense his discomfort.

"Trust me," she whispered, her lips barely moving. "If they wanted to trap us, they would have surrounded the shuttle at the spaceport."

The stairs opened into what appeared to be a surveillance center filled with monitors and communication equipment. Technicians sat at various stations, focusing on screens displaying feeds from all over the city.

Their guide led them to a door at the far end of the room and knocked twice. A muffled voice from within called for them to enter. As Jane pushed the door open, Soren readied himself for whatever might be waiting on the other side.

Nothing could have prepared him for the sight that

greeted him. Seated behind a desk, dressed in a fine three-piece suit, was Wilf Delaney.

CHAPTER 12

Soren stood frozen, his eyes locked on the familiar yet utterly unexpected figure seated behind the desk. Wilf rose to his feet with a fluid grace that seemed at odds with the version that Soren knew. This doppelgänger of his crew member was impeccably dressed in a tailored charcoal suit that accentuated his lean frame, a far cry from the casual attire of the Wilf aboard the Wraith. A polite smile played across his lips as he extended his hand toward Jane.

"Admiral Yarborough," Wilf said warmly, his voice carrying a hint of an Irish accent. "It's good to see you again. I trust your journey was uneventful? No unexpected entanglements with our Federation friends?"

Jane stepped forward, clasping Wilf's hand firmly. Her posture was relaxed, but Soren could see the alertness in her eyes, the way she subtly scanned the room even as she greeted their contact. "As uneventful as one could hope for these days, Mr. Delaney. A few tense moments in the space-port, but nothing we couldn't handle. Thank you for agreeing to meet with us on such short notice."

Wilf's gaze shifted to Soren, curiosity evident in the slight tilt of his head and the way his eyes narrowed slightly. "And who might your hooded companion be? You spoke quite highly of him in your message, but I confess I'm intrigued by all the mystery. It's not often you bring a guest to our little chats."

Soren glanced at Jane, who gave him a subtle nod, her eyes conveying a silent message of support. Taking a deep breath, he reached up and slowly lowered his hood, revealing his face to Wilf.

The effect was instantaneous and dramatic. Wilf's eyes widened in shock, the polite smile vanishing as if it had never existed. His hand darted toward his side where Soren was certain a concealed weapon waited, the movement so swift it was almost imperceptible. The easy charm that had filled the room moments before evaporated, replaced by a palpable tension that crackled in the air like static electricity.

"What the hell is this?" Wilf hissed, his voice low and dangerous, all pretense of civility gone. His eyes darted between Soren and Jane, a mixture of fury and betrayal evident in his gaze. "Some kind of trick? A clone? Or have you lost your mind, Admiral?"

Jane stepped forward quickly, her hands raised in a placating gesture. Her voice was calm, but there was an edge of urgency to it. "Wilf, please. I know how this looks, I do. But I need you to trust me on this. What he has to say could change everything, not just for the resistance, but for all of us. For the entire galaxy."

"Trust you?" Wilf's voice was incredulous. "You bring the spitting image of the man who's been tearing the galaxy apart into my office, and you ask me to trust you? Give me one good reason why I shouldn't call for the authorities right now."

Soren remained perfectly still, acutely aware that any sudden movement could end in disaster. He kept his hands visible, his posture open and non-threatening. When he spoke, his voice was steady and calm. "Because if I were the man you think I am, Mr. Delaney, you'd already be dead. And because the Admiral is right. What I have to say could be the key to the end of the Strickland Federation."

For a long moment, the only sound in the room was their breathing. Wilf's hand remained near his concealed weapon, his eyes never leaving Soren's face. Finally, he spoke.

"Sit," he said, gesturing to the chairs in front of his desk. "Both of you. And start talking. But I warn you, one wrong move, one thing that doesn't add up, and this meeting is over. Understood?"

As they settled into their seats, Soren leaned forward, meeting Wilf's gaze. The intensity in the other man's eyes was unsettling; this Wilf was clearly a far cry from the easygoing engineer he knew.

"What I'm about to tell you is going to be hard to believe," he began, choosing his words carefully. "But I swear to you it's the truth. And if you trust Admiral Yarborough at all, you'll know that she wouldn't be here, wouldn't have risked bringing me here, if she didn't accept it as fact."

Jane nodded in agreement, her voice soft but firm. "It's true, Wilf. Everything he's about to tell you, as impossible as it might sound, is real. I've seen the evidence with my own eyes. And it's why we need your help. Why the entire galaxy needs your help."

Wilf's eyes narrowed, but he remained silent as he waited for Soren to continue.

Taking a deep breath, Soren launched into his explanation. He told Wilf about the Convergence, painting a vivid picture of the multiple dimensions teetering on the brink of collapse. He described his time on the Wraith in detail, recounting their harrowing journey through the Eye and the desperate battle against time to find a solution.

As he spoke, Wilf's expression shifted from skepticism to fascination. When Soren reached the part about their scientists identifying the Fist of Justice's vortex cannon as the cause of the instability, Wilf leaned forward, tense but amazed.

"So you're saying," Wilf said slowly, his voice tight, "that this weapon, this vortex cannon, is literally tearing open the fabric of reality? That every time it's fired, it's like...what? Ripping a hole in spacetime?"

Soren nodded grimly. "That's exactly what I'm saying. Every discharge pushes us closer to the brink. The energy released creates ripples in the dimensional barriers, weakening them. If we don't stop it, those barriers will eventually collapse entirely, and the consequences, well, we don't know the exact consequences. But it wouldn't be good for anyone. With the assistance of the CIP, we have a much better chance of destroying the Fist."

Wilf sat back in his chair, considering all they had said. For a long moment, he was silent, his eyes distant as he processed the information. Finally, he spoke, his voice flat and decisive. "No."

Soren felt a flicker of frustration, but he pushed it aside. Instead, he allowed a small smile to play at the corners of his mouth. "I expected you might say that, at first. It's a lot to take in, I know."

Wilf's eyebrows rose slightly, a hint of curiosity creeping into his expression. "Oh? You seem awfully calm for someone who just had their request for help summarily denied."

Soren leaned forward, his voice low and intense. "Tell me something, Mr. Delaney. What do you think the odds are that the Strickland Federation will attack the CIP the moment the FUP resistance is eliminated?"

Wilf shifted uncomfortably in his seat, his eyes darting

away from Soren's penetrating gaze. "We have defensive measures in place. We've been preparing for–"

"The odds, Mr. Delaney," Soren pressed, his voice firm but not unkind. "Give me a number. Be honest with yourself."

Wilf's jaw clenched, a muscle twitching in his cheek. He was silent for a long moment, clearly wrestling with the implications of Soren's question. Finally, he met Soren's eyes once more, his voice barely above a whisper. "One hundred percent," he admitted. "But every day we delay allows us to work on building another ship, further hardening our defenses. We're not just sitting idle, waiting for the axe to fall."

"I understand that," Soren said, nodding. "But those defenses, impressive as they might be, will crumble under the first major assault. Especially with ships like the Fist of Justice leading the charge. You've seen what that weapon can do. Imagine a strike force of them, all bearing down on your worlds, destroying entire fleets in seconds, while also further destabilizing spacetime. What do you think will happen to the CIP then? How long do you think it will take before all of your planets fly the Strickland Federation flag?"

Wilf's face paled slightly at the image, but his eyes narrowed, a hint of curiosity creeping into his expression. "You came prepared, didn't you? If you are a version of Grand Admiral Strickland from another dimension, then I imagine you have a similar aptitude for tactics and strategy. And you have something specific in mind. An offer we could refuse, but probably shouldn't. Am I right?"

Soren nodded. "You're perceptive, Mr. Delaney. I do have something in mind. It's not guaranteed, but I believe it offers better odds than certain defeat."

"I'm listening," Wilf said, his earlier hostility giving way to genuine interest.

"Reinforcements," Soren said simply.

Wilf's face twisted in confusion. "Reinforcements? From where? The CIP is already stretched thin, and the FUP resistance is barely holding on as it is. Unless you have a navy hiding in your pocket, I don't see how–"

"I don't have a navy in my pocket," Soren interrupted. "But I do have a navy, multiple navies, just on the other side of the rift we entered this dimension through."

He could see Wilf's expression slowly shift as his words sank in, a glimmer of hope replacing his understanding of the inevitable. "Go on," he said.

Soren explained the situation in the other realities, how the second dimension's FUP attacked the first, driven by fear of the Convergence. "If we remove the threat of dimensional collapse, they have no reason to continue fighting. The Strickland Federation becomes the real threat—not just to one dimension, but to all of them. If we can unite our forces across dimensions, we stand a chance of defeating them once and for all."

As Soren laid out his plan, he saw the wheels turning in Wilf's mind. The CIP representative leaned back in his chair, a thoughtful expression on his face. "It's a bold strategy," Wilf admitted after a long moment of silence. "Audacious, even. But how can you be certain that if we stop the Convergence, we'll have time to negotiate with these other forces and rally them to our cause? What if the dimensional rifts close immediately, leaving us right back where we started?"

Soren shook his head. "I don't believe they will. Based on what we've observed, it's more likely that the rifts will need time to heal. Think of it like a wound. Even after you've stopped the bleeding, it takes time for the tissue to knit back together. But I'll need to confirm that with our lead scientist, Dr. Mitchell."

Wilf drummed his fingers on the desk, his expression

conflicted. The silence stretched on, broken only by the soft hum of the building's environmental systems. Finally, he let out a long sigh. "I'll bring your proposal up the chain of command. It's intriguing, to say the least. Risky as all hell, but intriguing. Thank you for bringing this to our attention."

Soren felt a surge of frustration. "Mr. Delaney, I appreciate your willingness to consider this, but we don't have time to wait for bureaucracy, and neither does the CIP. Every moment we delay is another moment the Strickland Federation grows stronger, another chance for them to use that weapon and build another. We need a decision, and we need it quickly."

Wilf looked like a man caught between a rock and a hard place. "Captain Strickland, I understand the urgency of your situation, but you don't set the timeline here, and neither do I. The best I can do is relay all of this information and make a recommendation. To be clear, I'm on your side. But also to be clear, that doesn't mean a whole lot beyond the fact that I can get your proposal in front of the right people. The CIP leadership will need time to consider all the implications of what you've proposed."

Jane placed a calming hand on Soren's arm, her touch a silent reminder to tread carefully. "We understand, Mr. Delaney," she said placatingly. "Thank you for your time and for hearing us out. We appreciate your willingness to bring this to your superiors. Is there any way we can expedite the process? Perhaps arrange a meeting with the decision-makers directly?"

Wilf shook his head. "I'm sorry, but that's not possible. The security risks alone...look, I'll do what I can to push this through quickly, but I can't make any promises."

Soren took a deep breath, forcing himself to relax. Jane was right; pushing too hard now could jeopardize everything. He stood, extending his hand to Wilf. "Thank you,

Mr. Delaney. We understand the position you're in. I hope we'll hear from you soon."

Wilf hesitated momentarily before shaking Soren's hand, his grip firm. "You'll hear from us as soon as a decision is made. In the meantime, I suggest you keep a low profile. Glaive may be a Coalition planet, but it's undoubtedly crawling with SF spies. If they notice your presence here..." He trailed off, leaving the implication hanging in the air.

"We understand," Jane said. "Thank you again for your time."

"Thank you, Mister Delaney," Soren added, raising his hood to once more conceal his face.

The guard met them outside Wilf's door, guiding them back to the stairwell, where they passed through the restaurant and exited onto the street. Glaston still bustled with activity, the subterranean city's artificial day cycle in full swing. The holographic sky above them showed fluffy white clouds drifting across a perfect blue expanse, starkly contrasting the icy reality outside the cavern.

"Well," Jane said quietly as they walked, her eyes constantly scanning their surroundings. "That went about as well as we could have hoped. At least he's willing to consider the proposal. Wilf has more influence than he lets on. If he pushes for this, there's a good chance the leadership will listen."

"In my dimension, Wilf was a drug-addicted spacer with a revoked license before I picked him up and added him to my crew. How did he get to be such an important cog in the CIP machine?"

"I don't really know. But what you saw down there was a branch of CIP Intelligence. He's one of their top operatives. It also doesn't hurt that his mother is a member of parliament."

Soren nodded, though frustration still gnawed at him. "I

just hope they make their decision quickly. Every moment we waste is–"

A sudden, sharp crack that echoed through the street cut off his words. Jane stumbled, a look of shock crossing her face. "Soren," she gasped, her voice tight with pain as blood began staining her white blouse. "I'm hit."

CHAPTER 13

Soren's instincts kicked in the moment he heard the crack of gunfire, the sound echoing off the cavern's artificial sky with an unnatural resonance. Without hesitation, he grabbed Jane and pulled her down behind the nearest cover, a delivery van—one of very few vehicles in the city— parked at the curb. They hit the ground hard, the impact jarring his bones. The grass along the sidewalk provided little cushioning, the beauty of its perfectly manicured green blades a stark contrast to the chaos erupting around them.

"Jane!" he hissed, a second shot ringing out, the projectile thudding into the truck above their heads. Soren cursed under his breath, his eyes locking onto the crimson stain spreading across the left shoulder of her crisp white blouse and soaking into her vest, both front and back. The fabric was darkening rapidly as it absorbed her blood. "How bad is it?" he asked, concern etching his brow.

She grimaced, her face pale but determined, jaw clenched against the pain. A thin sheen of sweat had broken out on her forehead, glistening in the artificial sunlight. "It could be worse," she managed through gritted teeth, her breath coming in short, sharp gasps. "I don't think the bullet hit bone, but my arm is useless. I can't move or feel it."

"Stay down," he ordered, his voice low and urgent, his eyes scanning their surroundings as he drew his concealed weapon. Grateful now for his foresight in bringing it, the weight of the pistol felt reassuring in his grip as he scanned the street, trying to get a glimpse of their attacker.

The street had emptied within seconds, civilians scattering like startled birds at the first sound of gunfire. The eerie quiet that followed was broken only by the wail of approaching sirens, the noise bouncing off the cavern walls.

Slowly, carefully, Soren began to rise. The street stretched out before him, the perfect facades of the buildings now ominous in their emptiness.

He had barely shifted his head around the van when another bullet whizzed past, so close he felt the displacement of air ruffle his hair. The projectile embedded itself with a sharp crack in the wall behind him, sending chips of stone flying. Soren ducked back down, his heart racing, a bead of sweat trickling down his temple.

"Even though we're still under fire, we need to move," he said, turning back to Jane. Her face was growing paler by the moment, the blood loss clearly taking its toll. "The restaurant's only two blocks away. If we can make it back there—"

"No." Jane shook her head, her expression grim. "If they have one shooter, they have multiple," she said, her voice tight with pain and urgency. "This isn't some random attack, Soren. Coming here was always risky, but the SF has never moved on me like this before." She paused, wincing as she attempted to shift her head up higher against the van's paneled side. A fresh trickle of blood seeped through her fingers. "Strickland may be accelerating his timeline. He knows he can act with impunity on CIP planets. They won't do anything but rattle their sabers, and maybe summon his diplomats for a slap on the wrist."

Soren's jaw clenched at the implications. "We can't stay here," he said, his eyes continually scanning their surroundings for any sign of movement. Every shadow, every flicker of light seemed to hide a potential threat. "We're sitting ducks."

As if in response to his words, a series of sleek drones appeared overhead, their sensors sweeping the area with eerie blue lights. The devices moved with an unsettling precision, their soft hum adding to the surreal atmosphere. For a moment, Soren felt a surge of hope. Perhaps the local law enforcement would be enough to drive off their attackers.

Seconds later, a group of armed men in suits emerged from the alley beside the restaurant. No doubt members of CIP Intelligence. They'd barely made it to the street, heads turning to hunt for the attackers, when a hail of gunfire tore through them. The men dropped where they stood, their bodies jerking grotesquely as multiple rounds found their marks.

The drones fared no better, exploding in quick succession as precise shots shredded them. Shards of metal and plastic rained down, clattering against the pavement.

"Damn it," Jane breathed, her eyes wide with shock. "It's like there's an entire army out there. Where did they come from so quickly?"

Soren didn't panic, his tactical mind rapidly assessing their options. They couldn't stay where they were. It was only a matter of time before their attackers closed in. His eyes landed on a narrow alley about twenty meters off to his right.

"There," he said, nodding toward it, the narrow recess shadowed and cluttered with waste receptacles. It wasn't much, but they needed to make a run for it, and the alley was their best shot at putting some distance between them and their attackers. "Can you move?"

Jane nodded, her face set with determination despite the pain etched in the lines around her eyes. "I'll manage."

"Okay. On my mark." He slipped his left hand into her right armpit to help her up. "Stay low, and don't stop for anything. Ready?"

She nodded, clasping her left hand to her wound, and Soren took a deep breath, preparing himself for what was to come. The weight of the pistol in his other hand was reassuring, but he knew their odds were slim. "Three...two...one...now!"

They burst from behind the delivery van, keeping low as they sprinted toward the alley. The air around them erupted with gunfire. Bullets whizzed past with terrifying proximity, chipping the pavement at their feet and ricocheting off nearby surfaces with sharp pings. Soren felt the heat of a round as it passed inches from his ear, the close call sending a jolt of adrenaline surging through his system.

Soren raised his weapon, firing blindly behind them to prompt their attackers to cease fire and take cover. It didn't work. A bullet grazed his shoulder, tearing through his coat and stinging his flesh.

They were halfway to the alley when Jane stumbled, crying out in pain as it jarred her injured shoulder. He pulled her back up, wrapping his arm around her to half-drag, half-carry her as they continued their desperate dash. A bullet clipped the sleeve of his coat. Another round shattered a nearby window, sending a shower of glass cascading over them. Tiny shards bit into Soren's exposed skin, but he barely noticed, his entire focus on getting Jane to the relative safety of the alley.

Just as they neared their goal, a figure stepped out from the corner of a building, weapon raised. Time seemed to slow as Soren registered the immediate threat. Without breaking stride, he shifted his aim and squeezed the trigger twice in rapid succession. The first shot went wide, but the second found its mark before the man could fire. He crumpled, his gun clattering to the ground.

They reached the alley, the relative shelter of its narrow confines a welcome relief. The clutter of dumpsters forced them to weave an erratic path, but they couldn't afford to slow down. Soren urged Jane forward, his eyes constantly scanning for threats.

"We need help," he said between breaths, acutely aware of the blood still seeping from Jane's wound. The entire left side of her blouse and upper sleeve was stained crimson now, the fabric clinging wetly to her skin. "You must have agents of your own here. Someone we can trust."

Jane nodded. "Just one," she admitted, her voice strained, her face twisted in pain. "Not too far from here. If we can reach him..."

They emerged from the far end of the alley just as their pursuers entered it behind them. For a heart-stopping moment, Soren thought they were finished. The open street before them offered no cover, and they were exposed. Vulnerable.

A law enforcement drone zipped overhead, its sensors locking onto the SF attackers. It opened fire, the fast-buzzing fire of its weapon, the sound eerily similar to the rip of tearing fabric. One of the pursuers went down immediately, his body jerking as multiple rounds found their marks. The others dove for cover, momentarily halting their advance. It bought Soren and Jane precious seconds before the drone exploded in a shower of sparks and twisted metal.

Soren didn't waste the opportunity. He urged Jane forward, putting as much distance between them and their pursuers as possible. They sprinted across the open street, painfully aware of their vulnerability. Every step felt like it could be their last, every shadow a potential threat. Soren's eyes darted from side to side, expecting an ambush at any moment.

He caught sight of a public tram up ahead, stopped at a station, its doors open as passengers boarded. "There!" he shouted, pointing toward the tram. "If we can make it—"

His words were cut short as a man emerged from an alley ahead, weapon raised. Soren's training took over. In one fluid motion, he brought up his gun and fired three times. The shots were clean, dropping the man as his shot blew past them. He didn't take the time to look back to see where it went. The shooter's body crumpled to the ground, a look of surprise forever frozen on his face.

More drones converged on the area, their high-pitched whine mixing with the deeper rumble of approaching vehicles. Soren caught glimpses of military-style trucks filled with what he assumed were local law enforcement, speeding toward the scene from down the street. But he wasn't ready to trust that Glaston's defenders weren't compromised.

"Almost there," Soren urged as they neared the tram, the vehicle preparing to depart, its doors starting to close. It would be tight, but they could still make it. With a breathless burst of speed, he pulled Jane behind him, his feet pounding the ground. His muscles burned with the effort, his lungs heaving as he pushed them both to the limit.

He shoved his gun into the front of his belt an instant before they practically fell through the narrowing gap between the doors as they slid shut and the tram lurched forward. His free hand shot out, grabbing a nearby pole to steady them both before they could sprawl across the laps of the wide-eyed couple sitting in front of them. They stood there momentarily, breathing heavily, the adrenaline coursing through their systems.

As Soren helped Jane to a seat, the other passengers

eyed them warily, shrinking back from the sight of Jane's bloodstained clothing and Soren's now-exposed face. A child began to cry, quickly hushed by its frightened mother. Otherwise, fear kept them all silent, no one daring to raise an alarm.

Replacing his hood, Soren remained standing, positioning himself between Jane and the other passengers. They rode in tense silence for two stops, every second feeling like an hour. Finally, Jane nudged Soren's hip. "This is our stop," she whispered, her voice tight with pain.

Having to virtually hold Jane up now, Soren kept his head down, acutely aware of the eyes following them as they exited the tram. Jane pointed the way, her steps faltering slightly as the adrenaline began to wear off. Within minutes, they entered a nondescript apartment building, its facade blending seamlessly with the others on the street. The lobby was deserted, their footsteps echoing as they made their way to the elevator.

The enclosed space made for a tense ride up, the cab's interior seeming to close in on them. Soren positioned himself in front of Jane, ready to shield her if the doors opened to reveal an ambush, but when the doors opened on their chosen floor, the hallway was mercifully empty.

Jane pointed to a door at the end of the hall, her hand shaking slightly with fatigue and weakness from blood loss. Soren approached it ahead of Jane, rapping his knuckles against the metal with more force than was strictly necessary.

The door opened a crack, revealing a man's face. His eyes widened in shock at the sight of Soren, a mixture of fear and disbelief flashing across his features. Then his gaze fell on Jane, taking in her bloodstained clothing and pale complexion. Without a word, he threw the door wide, ushering them inside. Soren allowed himself a moment of relief.

They had made it.

"Admiral," the man said, quickly securing the door behind them, engaging multiple locks. "What in the stars is going on? And why are you with...him?" His hand moved toward a weapon at his hip, uncertainty written across his features.

"Stand down, Samuel," Jane said, her voice strained but carrying the unmistakable tone of command. "He's with me. And as you can see, I need your help."

CHAPTER 14

As the door clicked shut behind them, Soren quickly scanned the apartment, taking in every detail. It was a modest space, sparsely furnished but meticulously clean. The living area was dominated by a worn but comfortable-looking couch flanked by two high-backed chairs. A small dining table with four chairs occupied one corner, while the kitchenette along the far wall gleamed with well-maintained appliances.

The man who had let them in—Samuel as Jane had called him—was unremarkable in appearance. He had the kind of face that could blend into any crowd. His salt-and-pepper hair was neatly trimmed, and his plain clothing seemed thoughtfully selected to avoid attention.

Samuel's gaze darted between Soren and Jane, his hand still hovering near his weapon. "Admiral," he said, his voice low and tense, " we need to stop your bleeding. What happened out there?"

Jane grimaced, her good hand pressed against her bleeding shoulder. A thin trail of blood had begun again to seep between her fingers, staining the cuff of her sleeve. "Ambush," she managed through gritted teeth, her face pale with pain and blood loss. "SF agents, I think. They were waiting for us. Professional hit squad, not your average thugs."

Samuel's eyes widened, then narrowed as he looked at Soren again. His voice was laced with suspicion as he spoke. "And him? Why does he look like–"

"Later," Jane interrupted, her voice strained.

She swayed slightly on her feet, and Soren instinctively reached out to steady her. "I promise, we'll explain," he said. "Right now, we need to get this bleeding under control. Questions can wait."

Samuel nodded, his training clearly kicking in as, for the moment, he pushed aside his questions. "Right. Of course." He turned to Soren, his words clipped and efficient. "Help the Admiral out of her vest and blouse while I get the medical kit. Be careful not to jostle her arm too much."

As Samuel disappeared into what Soren assumed was the bathroom, he turned to Jane. Her face was ashen, a sheen of sweat glistening on her forehead. "Let's get you seated," he said softly, guiding her to a chair at the table.

With gentle hands, he helped Jane remove the blood-soaked vest and then her blouse, careful not to move her injured arm more than necessary as he unbuttoned her blouse before sliding it off her good arm. "This is going to hurt," he warned. "But we need to get a look at that wound. Are you ready?"

Jane nodded, her jaw set. "Just do it," she said, her voice tight with pain. "It's not like I haven't been shot before."

As Soren peeled the fabric, gooey with thickening blood, away from her wounds, Jane hissed in pain but didn't cry out. She fisted her good hand, her knuckles white with the effort of maintaining her composure.

The wound was uglier than Soren had feared, but not as bad as it could have been. The bullet had passed clean through her upper shoulder, missing the bone as she'd said but leaving a ragged hole on both her front and back. The flesh around the exit wound was larger and particularly swollen, but the bleeding had slowed to a steady trickle on both sides.

"At least we don't have to go digging for a bullet," Soren muttered.

Jane managed a weak chuckle. "Small mercies, I suppose. Though I can't say I'm looking forward to the recovery process."

Samuel returned, a sleek medical kit in his hands. The contents looked far more advanced than standard first aid equipment. He knelt beside Jane, his movements quick and efficient as he used clean towels to wipe up the blood around the wound.

"This might sting a bit," he warned, applying an anti-septic solution that fizzed and bubbled as it made contact with the torn flesh. "But it'll help prevent infection and then deaden the area a bit."

Jane blew her breath out in small gusts and nodded, but she remained silent as Samuel worked. He pulled out a small, pen-like device from the kit. Its surface covered in tiny, blinking lights, and a thin, needle-like probe extended from one end. "Tissue probe," he explained, noticing Soren's questioning look. "It'll give us a better idea of the internal damage."

"We don't have anything like that where I'm from," Soren said.

Samuel looked confused. "Where are you from?"

"I'll explain later."

The man nodded, the probe beeping softly as he inserted it into the wound, its lights flashing in complex patterns. Jane winced but held still, her breath coming in short, controlled pants.

After a moment, Samuel frowned, his eyes scanning the readout on the probe's handle. "Looks like there's damage to the tendons and nerves," he reported, his voice clinical but tinged with concern. "The good news is, you should regain full feeling and function. The bad news is, it'll take a few weeks, and you'll need some physical therapy to get your range of motion back."

Jane nodded, her face pale but determined. "A healing pod would speed things up. But that's out of the question for now."

Samuel continued to work, picking up a long, slender device with lights at the end and applying a familiar-looking gel to it, slathering it with the stuff before turning to Jane. "This is going to hurt."

"I know," she replied, bracing herself.

"What is that?" Soren asked.

"Like a healing pod, but localized, and not quite as efficient. It'll fix the worst of the internal damage," he said, using the distraction of his explanation to telescope the device into the bullet hole. Jane let out a quick, reserved bleat and then grabbed onto Soren's arm as it worked its way through her wound until the tip came out the other side. Jane's fingers had dug so hard into Soren's flesh he thought her nails might have drawn blood, but she didn't cry out.

With that done, Samuel reiterated his earlier questions. "Now, would one of you mind telling me what the hell is going on? And why you," he looked at Soren, his eyes narrowing with suspicion, "look exactly like Grand Admiral Strickland?"

Jane took a deep breath, wincing slightly as the movement jostled her arm. "It's a long story, Samuel. One that's going to sound completely insane, I warn you." She paused, gathering her thoughts. "The short version is, he's not our Soren Strickland. He's from another dimension, one where things turned out differently."

Samuel's eyebrows shot up, his hands pausing in their

work momentarily. "Another dimension? You can't be serious."

"I assure you, we're entirely serious," Soren said, his voice grave. He met Samuel's skeptical gaze steadily. "I know it sounds impossible, but it's the truth. We came here because we need the CIP's help. There's a threat looming that's bigger than just this dimension's war."

Samuel's eyes darted between Soren and Jane, clearly searching for any sign that this was some elaborate joke. Finding none, he shook his head slowly. "Alright," he said, his voice cautious. "I'm listening."

As Jane and Soren took turns explaining the situation, Samuel listened intently, keeping the device within Jane's wound. His expression shifted from skepticism to shock and finally to understanding and acceptance.

When they finished, he sat back on his heels, shaking his head in disbelief. "That's a lot to take in," he said finally, his voice quiet. "But if it's true, it explains why Strickland moved against you so boldly. He's not going to wait much longer to go after the CIP, is he?"

"No, I don't think he is. The attack today was brazen, even for him. Either he's growing impatient, or he has new information that's emboldened him."

"Alex," Soren breathed, the realization hitting him. "If he got him to talk…"

"He may have come to the same conclusion about the CIP that you did," Jane agreed. "Either way, if he knows what Alex knew, it makes him all the more dangerous."

"At least it's also more likely that Alex is alive."

"I'm sorry," Samuel said. "Who's Alex?"

"My son," Soren said. "In a twisted way, this might actually work in our favor. For once. If the CIP sees how imminent the threat is, they might be more inclined to listen to my proposal."

"A silver lining, I suppose," Jane mused.

"I need to get some supplies," Samuel said. "New clothes for both of you, some food, and a few other necessities." He indicated the healing device attached to Jane's arm. "Can you hold this in place for the next hour? It needs time to finish its work."

Soren nodded, moving to take Samuel's place. "Of course. I'll keep an eye on it."

As Samuel prepared to leave, he paused at the door, his hand on the knob. "I'll be back as soon as I can." With that, he slipped out, leaving Soren and Jane alone in the apartment. The silence stretched between them, filled only by the soft hum of the healing device and the distant sounds of the city outside.

"Tell me about Samuel," Soren said finally, his curiosity getting the better of him. "How did he end up here, working for you?"

Jane shifted slightly, trying to find a more comfortable position in the chair. "It's quite a story, actually," she began, a hint of fondness in her voice. "He was with FUP Intelligence when your counterpart took over. He was in IT, not a field agent. Brilliant with computers, but he'd never held a gun in his life."

She paused, her eyes growing distant with memory. "When the initial roundup happened, when Strickland started purging anyone he saw as a potential threat, Samuel managed to escape. He used his tech skills to fake his own death in the system, then hitched a ride on a cargo ship bound for Proxima."

"Resourceful," Soren commented, impressed.

Jane nodded. "Very. That's where I connected with him. He sought me out, once he knew I wasn't backing my ex-husband." She smiled slightly. "Well, let's just say he was eager to help. He's been living on Glaive ever since, acting as our eyes and ears between the SF here and the CIP."

Soren nodded, a new respect for the unassuming man

growing in his mind. "He seems capable. You're lucky to have him."

"We are," Jane agreed, her voice soft.

"I'm sorry you were shot," Soren said. "It's my fault you're here."

"Don't be ridiculous. This is war, Soren. It's not realistic to expect to escape unscathed."

"I know a little about that." He turned slightly, using his free hand to lift the back of his shirt.

Jane's eyes widened as she saw the scars on his back. Some were thin and faded, barely visible against his skin. Others were thick and ropey, a testament to deeper, more grievous wounds. He'd hidden them from her during their time together on the shuttle, not wanting to talk about his experience as a prisoner of war, but now he changed his mind.

"Souvenirs from my time as a CIP POW," he explained, his voice matter-of-fact as he told her all about his torture. "We all carry our battle scars. Some are just more visible than others."

After thirty minutes, Soren turned the healing device off and switched it to her exit wound. They fell into a comfortable silence until Jane restarted the conversation. "I've been thinking about how we're going to get off this planet. I'm not sure—"

The sound of the door opening cut her off. They both tensed, relaxing only when they saw it was Samuel returning. He carried a large bag Soren assumed contained new clothes, along with several smaller packages.

"How are you feeling, Admiral?" Samuel asked as he sat down the packages.

"I can feel my arm again," she replied. "It's a start. We were just talking about our exit strategy."

Samuel gestured to the healing device on Jane's arm.

"Let's get that out first and close up the wound properly. Then we can start planning your next move."

With practiced hands, Samuel removed the healing device and began to suture Jane's skin, using a tool that seemed to close the wound and dissolve the stitches simultaneously. The torn flesh knit together before their eyes, leaving only a thin, pink line where the bullet had torn through.

Jane flexed her fingers experimentally, her face a mix of relief and frustration. "I still can't move it much. It feels... heavy. Unresponsive."

"Therapy will take care of that," Samuel said, his voice sympathetic, but adamant. "Healing devices can accelerate healing, but they can't work miracles. You'll need to be patient." He turned to Soren, his expression serious. "You mentioned an exit strategy. I assume you want to get back to your shuttle."

"It's our only way off this rock," she explained.

Samuel smiled before moving to a seemingly blank section of wall. He pressed his hand against it, and a hidden compartment slid open. He pulled out a sleek briefcase. "This," he explained, "is how you get out of here alive." He set the case on the table and opened it to reveal a compact surveillance terminal. The device flared to life, its screen revealing a request for security authentication. Samuel let it scan his face and thumbprint.

"Let's see what we're dealing with," he muttered, before entering a long passcode to log in and then tapping expertly on the keyboard. "First, let's check the law enforcement chatter. See how much they know about what went down earlier."

As Samuel worked, Soren and Jane listened intently. The news was mixed–the local forces had taken casualties, but they'd managed to eliminate the SF attackers. Reports were still coming in, and the authorities seemed to be struggling to piece together exactly what had happened.

"That's something, at least," Soren said. "But it doesn't mean we're in the clear. They'll be on high alert now, watching for any suspicious activity."

Samuel nodded, his attention still on the screen. "Agreed. Now, let's take a look at the spaceport." He pulled up a series of security feeds, his eyes scanning the crowds. "I've got facial recognition software identifying known and suspected SF agents," he explained, pointing to a series of highlighted figures on the screen. "And...it's not good. There are a lot of them. More than I've ever seen here before."

Soren frowned, a thought nagging at him. It was a long shot, but... "Samuel, can you check the records for any comms from the CIP intelligence field base to Glaive's Planetary Council? Specifically in the last few hours?"

Samuel raised an eyebrow but complied. "I happen to have access to the CIP's internal systems. Of course, they don't know it." He laughed as he tapped into the CIP Intelligence network. After a moment, he shook his head. "Nothing. It's almost too quiet."

"What about Wilf Delaney?" Soren pressed, leaning in to get a better look at the screen. "Can you locate him?"

A few more keystrokes, and Samuel had pulled up a feed showing Wilf still in his office. The CIP representative sat at his desk, poring over what looked like reports. His personal comm device sat idle on the desk.

"He hasn't spoken to the council," Soren said, his voice thoughtful. "But he apparently made a private call. It could be nothing, but..."

"But it's suspicious," Jane finished for him, her expression grim. "What are you thinking, Soren?"

"I'm thinking that Wilf may have arranged our SF

ambush. I think we need to go to the Council ourselves," he replied.

"Agreed. But we'll need to be careful. After that ambush, they'll be on high alert. Every government building will be locked down tight."

Samuel closed the surveillance terminal, his expression thoughtful. "I might be able to help with that," he said, a hint of excitement creeping into his voice. "I know a few back channels, ways to get you into the Council building without attracting too much attention. It won't be easy, but it's doable."

Soren turned to him, hope kindling in his chest. "How soon can we move?"

Samuel glanced at Jane, clearly assessing her condition. The Admiral held her injured arm stiffly at her side, but her eyes were clear and focused.

"Give me an hour to make some arrangements," he said finally.

"Do it," Jane said. "We don't have the luxury of more time."

CHAPTER 15

Soren stood looking out of Samuel's living room window, adjusting the collar of his faded blue jacket. He couldn't help but feel slightly uncomfortable in the rather shabby jacket, plain gray t-shirt, worn denim jeans and the sturdy boots Samuel had provided him. It was a far cry from his uniform and the upper end civvies Jane had given him to wear. At least the spy had provided him with a nice wide-brimmed hat that would help hide his face.

She sat on the edge of the couch, carefully adjusting a standard medical sling over her injured arm. Samuel had given her a muted beige and cream-colored outfit consisting of a loose-fitting checkered blouse, a cable knit sweater vest, comfortable slacks, and sneakers, the entire outfit designed to avoid drawing attention to her injury while still allowing for ease of movement. It would be out of place among the elite who could afford healing pods when needed, both sets of clothes helping to sell the idea that they were rank and file nobodies.

"How do the clothes fit?" Samuel asked, his eyes darting between the two of them as he came out of his spare bedroom carrying two earpieces.

"Perfectly," Jane replied with an appreciative smile.

Soren nodded in agreement, though his expression remained serious. "They'll certainly help us blend in. Thank you, Samuel."

"Good. Now, these earpieces are encrypted," he explained, handing one to each of them. "They'll allow me to communicate with you from here. The range isn't fantastic, but it should suffice for what we need."

Soren inserted his earpiece, impressed by how seamlessly it fit. "Clever," he remarked. "I assume these are untraceable?"

Samuel nodded, a hint of pride in his eyes. "Absolutely. I purchased these on the black market from a trusted source and modified the internals to improve the security."

"It's almost like you expected this to happen one day," Jane said, adjusting her own earpiece.

"The most valuable trait of being a proper intelligence agent is preparation for when things go wrong. I was never sure how I would use the earpieces, but I always suspected I would need them at some point in time."

"I like the way you think," Soren said. "Now, what's our next move?"

"The Council building is about a kilometer north of our position. I need you to make your way there on foot. Try to look casual, hold hands like you're just out for a stroll. The best path is probably through the Central Gardens. It's hard to miss—lots of greenery and a big fountain in the middle. You can see the Council building from there. It's the tallest structure in the area, with a domed roof."

"I've been to the Council building before," Jane said. "Though I never stopped to enjoy the scenery."

"That's it?" Soren asked. "Just walk to the Council building?"

Samuel chuckled. "Of course not, but the less you know

ahead of time, the better it is for everybody in the event things go sideways."

"And if things do go sideways?" Soren asked.

"Let me know immediately," Samuel replied. "I'll be monitoring the local security channels. I'll do my best to create a diversion so you can get out of there and come back here. We'll figure something else out if we run into the worst case scenario. Other than that, be careful out there. And good luck."

Soren clasped Samuel's hand. "Thank you, Samuel. For everything."

"You're welcome," he replied. "But I'm the one who should be thanking you. If everything you told me is true... well, you're a much braver man than me, Captain."

Soren and Jane exited the apartment, making their way back down to the street. The artificial daylight was beginning to dim, simulating the approach of evening. Street lamps designed to mimic candles had flickered to life, casting a warm, almost romantic glow over the sidewalks. For a moment, Glaston felt like the most peaceful place in the universe, though Soren had a sense that peace wasn't destined to last.

They set off at a leisurely pace, Soren holding Jane's hand as Samuel had suggested. To any casual observer, they would appear to be nothing more than a couple enjoying an evening stroll. But beneath the facade of normalcy, both were hyper-aware of their surroundings, eyes constantly scanning for potential threats.

"Two o'clock," Jane murmured, her lips barely moving. "Man in the dark blue jacket. He's been glancing our way a bit too often."

Soren resisted the urge to look directly at the individual Jane had spotted. Instead, he used a nearby shop window as a mirror, catching a glimpse of the man in question. "I see him. Let's duck into this cafe up ahead. We can lose him in the crowd."

They veered into a bustling coffee shop, standing at the back of the line until the man in the blue jacket continued past the cafe, his gait unhurried.

"False alarm, I think," Soren said softly. "But good catch. We can't be too careful."

They continued their journey, passing through the Central Gardens as Samuel had described. The space was a marvel of engineering, a vast expanse of greenery and flowing water that Soren was certain had used New York's Central Park for inspiration, though its scale was smaller. Life went on as usual, with families out for an evening walk and joggers circling the shallow lake. He even spotted a few dogs. Knowing what he knew—and considering what had happened to them only two hours earlier—the whole scene felt surreal.

As they neared the Council building, the crowd began to thin. The massive structure loomed before them, its domed roof practically scraping the holographic sky. A fence surrounded the building, with numerous guards posted outside and along the entire perimeter. Armored vehicles also squatted nearby, at high alert after the earlier attack.

"How are we going to get around them?" Jane asked.

"Samuel must have a plan," Soren replied. He tapped his earpiece, activating the comm link. "We've reached the Council building," he said, his voice barely above a whisper.

There was a moment of static before Samuel's voice came back. "Good work. There are a lot of guards posted outside, so take a wide path around it to the back. You'll see a bank across the street. Let me know when you spot it."

Following Samuel's instructions, they went west two

blocks before continuing north, retracing their steps east until they reached the bank. "We see it," Jane confirmed.

"Excellent," Samuel replied. "There's an alley alongside it. Enter it and proceed about halfway down. You'll find a door marked as an emergency exit. Tell me when you're in front of it."

They crossed the street, trying to appear nonchalant as they slipped into the narrow alleyway. The space was dimly lit, the walls on either side blocking out most of the artificial light. They found the door exactly where Samuel had said it would be. "We're here," Soren reported.

"Good," Samuel's voice crackled in their ears. "I just unlocked the door. Go inside, quickly."

They stepped inside and closed the door—which Samuel immediately locked again—finding themselves in a narrow stairwell.

"There's another locked door at the bottom," Samuel informed them. "I will open for you as well. Beyond that, you'll find a tunnel that goes beneath the street and across to the Council building. Move fast. The access through this area will be logged, and with what happened earlier it's very possible someone will notice you."

"Alright, here we go." Heart pounding, Soren led the way down the stairs. The promised door at the bottom yielded to his touch, revealing a long, dimly lit passageway stretching into the distance. Without hesitation, they plunged forward at a run.

The tunnel was eerily quiet, their footsteps echoing off the bare walls. If someone had noticed the doors being opened and sent guards down to check, it would have been so easy to cut them off from either direction, box them in and capture them. Then again, maybe that wouldn't be so bad. They needed to get the Council's attention. That might be one way to do it.

Soon enough, and without interference, they reached

another door. Just as Soren reached out to open it, it swung open, revealing a man in a dark suit. For a heart-stopping moment, Soren thought they were caught. His hands began to raise in surrender.

But the man simply nodded, ushering them inside. "Quickly," he said, his voice barely above a whisper. "We don't have much time."

As the door closed behind them, Soren allowed himself a moment to catch his breath. The interior of the building was cool and quiet, a stark contrast to the chaos outside.

"I'm Garrett," he said, leading them briskly down a narrow corridor. "Samuel told me you were coming."

"Where are you taking us?" Jane asked.

Garrett glanced over his shoulder. "To see Council-woman Bao."

The name didn't mean anything to Soren, but Jane seemed impressed. There was no time for her to explain before they reached a nondescript door at the end of the passageway. Garrett placed his palm on a hidden scanner, and the door slid open with a soft hiss, revealing another stairwell going up.

"This part of the building exists for one purpose—to get the Council out quickly and quietly in case of emergency," Garrett said as they went through the door. "It's not meant to sneak FUP rebels in, and I'm guaranteed to lose my job over this, but, well...desperate times and all that."

They climbed the stairs in silence, the only sound their footsteps echoing in the enclosed space.

After ascending nearly twenty flights that left Soren breathing more heavily and Jane red-faced and sweating, Garrett finally brought them to a halt. He slowly opened the door, peering out into the hallway before waving them through. The corridor up here was ornately decorated with rich carpeting and attractive wallpaper. Portraits of past council members clung to both walls.

Garret still didn't speak, motioning them to follow. They walked briskly down the hallway to the door at the end. Garrett pressed his palm to the panel, and the door slid open with a soft whoosh. They stepped into a spacious office, its walls lined with bookshelves and holographic displays showing various data streams and news feeds. At the far end of the room, behind an imposing desk of polished wood, sat a woman Soren assumed must be Councilwoman Bao.

She looked up as they entered, her eyes widening in shock as she took in Soren's appearance. For a moment, the only sound in the room was the soft hum of the environmental systems and the muted chatter from the news feeds.

Then, with a calm that belied the tension in the air, Councilwoman Bao spoke, her voice steady and controlled. "Well," she said, her dark eyes locked on Soren's face, "I must say, this is certainly not how I expected my workday to end."

CHAPTER 16

Councilwoman Bao's eyes darted between Soren, Jane, and Garrett, her expression a mixture of shock and wariness. The tension in the room was palpable, the silence broken only by the soft hum of the holographic displays and the muted chatter of news feeds. Bao's office, with its polished wood furnishings and state-of-the-art technology, seemed to shrink around them, the pressure of the moment crushing in from all sides.

"Garrett," Bao said, her voice calm but edged with steel, "would you care to explain what's going on here? And why you've brought these...unexpected guests into my office without warning?"

Before Garrett could respond, Jane stepped forward, her good arm raised in a placating gesture. The sling holding her injured arm was a stark reminder of the dangers they had already faced. "Councilwoman Bao, I'm Admiral Jane Yarborough of the—"

"I know who you are, Admiral," Bao interrupted, her gaze still fixed on Soren. Her eyes narrowed, studying every detail of his face. "What I don't understand is why you've brought Grand Admiral Strickland into my office." Her hand moved slowly toward a panel on her desk, no doubt to summon security. "Is this some kind of joke? Have you finally lost your mind, Admiral?"

Soren took a step forward, his hands raised to show he meant no harm. He could feel the weight of Bao's scrutiny, the suspicion radiating from her in waves. "Councilwoman, I know this must be confusing and alarming, but rest assured, I'm not Grand Admiral Strickland. If you can spare us ten minutes of your time, we can explain everything. I promise you, it's of the utmost importance. What we have to say could save your planet, and this entire galaxy from the Strickland Federation, not to mention an even more dire situation."

Bao's hand hovered over the panel, her eyes narrowing as she studied Soren's face. The tension in the room was thick enough to choke on. After an interminable few seconds, she leaned back in her chair, expelled a breath, and folded her hands on the desk. The polished surface reflected the pulsing lights of the holographic displays, casting a soft glow on her features.

"Very well," she said. "I assume if you were here to kill me, you would have done so already." She tipped her head, her eyes narrowing as she obviously considered the situation. "You have ten minutes to convince me not to call security and have you both thrown into the deepest, darkest pit I can find. Sit."

Soren and Jane exchanged a glance before taking the seats in front of Bao's desk. The chairs were comfortable, at odds with the uncomfortable situation. Ready to move at a moment's notice, Garrett remained standing by the door, his hands folded in front of him, his posture tense and alert.

"Thank you, Councilwoman," Soren began, leaning slightly forward. "We've just come from a meeting with

Wilf Delaney. I shared some critical information with him, as well as a proposal. What I told him—what I'd like to tell you now—could change the course of the war against the SF and potentially save billions of lives across multiple dimensions."

Bao's eyebrows rose at the mention of multiple dimensions, her skepticism evident in the slight curl of her lip. "Multiple dimensions? I hope you realize how fantastical that sounds."

"I do, Councilwoman," Soren replied, his voice steady. "But I assure you, every word I'm about to tell you is true. And the stakes couldn't be higher."

Bao gestured for him to continue, her expression one of disbelief and curiosity. "Go on then. Enlighten me about these multiple dimensions."

Soren took a deep breath, gathering his thoughts. "Mr. Delaney promised to relay this information to the Council, but we have reason to believe he hasn't—and probably won't—do so. In fact, circumstantial evidence suggests he may be working for the Strickland Federation."

Bao's expression darkened. "That's a serious accusation, Mister… I'm sorry, I don't know what to call you. You look like Strickland, but clearly, you're not him."

"Technically, I am him," Soren replied. "My name is Captain Soren Strickland, of the Federation of United Planets. Only not the FUP of this dimension. And I understand the gravity of the accusation, believe me. I wouldn't make it lightly."

"Not of this dimension," Bao mused. "Tell me, Captain. How many dimensions are there?"

"Total?" Soren replied. "I have no idea. But there are three affected by the situation I'm eager to describe."

Bao drummed her fingernails in a thoughtful rhythm on the desk. The sound echoed in the tense silence of the office.

"If what you're saying is true, it would be a shame. Wilf has been a trusted member of our intelligence community for some time. His work has been invaluable. His mother would be so disappointed."

"Unless she's in the Strickland Federation's pocket too," Jane suggested, her voice grim.

Bao's eyes widened for a moment before her expression settled into one of resigned acceptance. She let out a heavy sigh, her shoulders sagging slightly. "I suppose it's possible. The writing's been on the wall for some time, hasn't it? We've all been too afraid to see it, too comfortable in our belief that we could maintain our neutrality indefinitely."

Soren leaned forward, his voice urgent. "Councilwoman, I might be able to help."

"So you've said. Go on. I'm listening. You have eight minutes left."

"Thank you, ma'am," Soren said. "All I ask is that you keep an open mind. What I'm about to tell you will challenge everything you think you know about the universe."

"At this stage, I'm ready to believe anything that might offer the CIP, Glaive in particular, a glimmer of hope."

Soren explained the Convergence, the role of the vortex cannons, and his idea for an alliance with the FUPs of the other dimensions. As he spoke, Bao's expression shifted from skepticism to shock and finally to a somber understanding. Her eyes widened as Soren described the potential consequences of the Convergence, her face paling at the thought of entire realities collapsing.

"The attack on us earlier today," Soren concluded, gesturing to Jane's injured arm, "is proof that Strickland fears what we have to say. He wouldn't have risked such a brazen assault on CIP territory unless he felt truly threatened. He likely knows that if we can unite the forces of multiple dimensions against him, his days are numbered."

"And how would Strickland have learned about this Convergence and the situation in the other dimensions?" Bao asked.

"We don't have any hard evidence that he has," Soren admitted. "But he captured my son during an operation three weeks ago. If he's forced him…" Soren's voice broke at the thought of whatever tortures his counterpart might have subjected Alex to.

"I see," Bao said. "I'm sorry your son was captured. I'm a parent, too. And I know what it is to fear for my children's safety. Please, give me a moment. This is a lot to take in."

"Take your time, Councilwoman," Jane said. "As long as you aren't counting it against our ten minutes."

Bao chuckled. "Of course not."

She rose from her chair and walked to the window, gazing out at the artificial sky of the subterranean city. The simulated sunset had given way to a star-filled night, and the holographic projections were so realistic that, for a moment, Soren could almost believe they were above ground.

"You're asking for a lot, Captain Strickland," Bao said finally, her voice soft but clear. She turned to face them, her silhouette framed by the false starlight. "You're asking us to take an enormous risk based on cosmic events I can barely believe, let alone understand. You're asking us to believe in alternate realities, in a threat we can't see or touch, and to potentially sacrifice everything we've built to fight the SF over it."

"I'm asking you to stand against your oppressor," Soren said. "Before your oppressor takes away all of your options. At the root of things, it really is that simple."

"May I point out, Councilwoman, that I wouldn't be here," Jane added, "wouldn't be wasting my time to come here, if I didn't believe in this man's fantastical story as you put it. He is telling the truth. You have my word on that."

Bao paused, her gaze sweeping over Soren and Jane. "Your word is worth quite a lot to me, Admiral. But nothing is ever that simple. At the same time, I find myself tending to believe you. Perhaps it's because the alternative is too ugly to contemplate. Or perhaps it's because, deep down, I've always known that this fragile peace wouldn't last forever."

Bao returned to her desk, settling into her chair with a heavy sigh. "We'd all like to live in ignorance; it is bliss, after all. But I suppose the time for action has come. I always thought we wouldn't stand a chance against the Strickland Federation. But here we have an opportunity. A crazy, unexpected, and potentially miraculous opportunity."

She leaned forward, her eyes intense as she looked at Soren and Jane. "This council only represents one planet, but as its head, I can ensure our support and get it put to vote across the entire coalition. It won't be easy, and there will be those who oppose it, but it's the best I can offer."

"Anything you can do is better than nothing at all," Soren replied.

"Thank you, Councilwoman," Jane added. "Your support means more than you know. How long do you think it will take to arrange the vote?"

In response, Bao reached for a device on her desk that Soren hadn't noticed before. It looked different from a standard comm unit. A special, more secure tranSat device. She pressed a button on its face and began speaking.

"President Tyre," Bao said, her voice crisp and authoritative, "it's Bao. I am hereby executing my emergency powers under Article Three of the Interplanetary Agreement. I'm requesting an emergency vote held in one hour.

The fate of not just our coalition, but potentially all of reality, hangs in the balance. Details to follow."

She tapped to end the recording and tapped a few more times to send the message. She turned back to Soren and Jane. "I always expected to receive that request, not to send it," she said, a hint of irony in her voice. "Funny how life works out, isn't it?"

Bao's gaze shifted to Garrett, who had remained silent throughout the exchange, a silent sentinel by the door. "Garrett, tell Major Husk to send a team to the field office to collect Mr. Delaney. We need to get to the bottom of his involvement in all this. And make sure they're discreet. If he is working for the SF, we don't want to tip our hand."

Garrett nodded sharply and left the room, the door sliding shut with a soft hiss behind him.

"What now?" Soren asked.

"I've recorded this conversation and sent it to the rest of the Interplanetary Council. In one hour, they'll listen to what we've discussed and enter their decision. Then, we'll have our answer. One hour to decide the fate of...well, everything, it seems."

"That fast?" Jane asked, surprise evident in her voice. "I wouldn't expect anything in government to move that rapidly."

Bao grinned, a hint of dark humor in her eyes. "It is an emergency, is it not? Multiple realities hanging in the balance, the threat of total annihilation by the Strickland Federation looming over us? If that doesn't qualify for rushing things along, I don't know what does."

Bao's expression grew serious once more.

"But for now, we wait. And hope that the rest of the Coalition can see past their fear and recognize the opportunity you're offering us. Let us hope that they can put aside their petty squabbles and self-interests, along with their weak knees, to see the danger of these circumstances and the potential of your ideas. If you'll excuse me…"

"Of course." Soren rose as Bao did, taking his seat again as Bao left the room. Soren and Jane settled in to wait, hope and anxiety churning in their guts. They had come so far, risked everything to get to this point. Now, so much rested on the decision of a group of politicians scattered across the stars.

He glanced at Jane, seeing his own tension mirrored in her eyes. The set of her jaw, the way her good hand clenched and unclenched on the arm of her chair, all spoke of the same nervous energy that thrummed through his body. At least he had no doubts that they had done all they could.

Then, his attention settled on the artificial night sky, twinkling with holographic stars outside Bao's window. As the minutes ticked by, Soren studied them, wondering what the real ones looked like from the planets where the other Coalition leaders were even now considering their proposal.

Would they see the urgency? Would they understand the magnitude of what was at stake? Or would fear and skepticism win out, dooming them all to a future under Strickland's iron fist—or worse, to the chaotic collapse of reality itself?

Even after Bao returned, the silence in the room was oppressive. Bao busied herself with work on her terminal, but Soren could see the tension in her shoulders and how her eyes flicked to the corner where the time was displayed.

Finally, a soft chime from her desk rang out like a gunshot. The Councilwoman leaned forward, switching the view on her terminal. "The votes are starting to come in," she announced, her voice taut.

Soren and Jane exchanged a glance. This was it–the

moment that could change everything. Soren's heart pounded, his mouth suddenly dry with anticipation.

Bao's eyes darted back and forth, reading the incoming data. Her expression remained carefully neutral, giving no hint as to the nature of the votes. After a long few minutes, Bao looked up, her eyes meeting Soren's.

"Well, Captain Strickland," she said, her voice carefully controlled, "it seems you've managed to accomplish the impossible."

"You mean...?"

Bao nodded, a small smile finally breaking through her professional demeanor. "The vote is in favor of your proposal. Just barely, but that doesn't matter. A simple majority rules. The Coalition of Independent Planets is prepared to join your fight against the Strickland Federation."

The relief that washed over Soren was so intense it was almost physical. He sagged in his chair, feeling as though a great weight had been lifted from his shoulders. Beside him, Jane let out a shaky breath, her good hand reaching out to grip his in a moment of shared triumph.

"Thank you, Councilwoman," Soren said, his voice thick with emotion as he squeezed Jane's hand back. "You have no idea what this means. You've given us a fighting chance, not just for this dimension, but for all of them."

"Oh, I think I know the implications," Bao replied, her expression growing serious once more. The smile faded from her lips, replaced by a look of somber resolve. "We've just committed ourselves to war against an enemy we likely can't defeat, merely on the hope that we can negotiate alliances with leaders we've never met, in dimensions I didn't even know existed two hours ago. The road ahead will be difficult, to say the least.

"But it's a road we'll walk together," Jane added, her voice firm. "And it's our best, and possibly only chance, at a future free from Strickland's tyranny. A chance to save not just ourselves, but countless others across the multiverse."

Boa nodded. "You've already won us over, Admiral. You don't need to continue selling the idea. What you need to do is tell me how the CIP can best assist you right now, and in the coming days and weeks ahead."

Soren leaned forward in his seat. "I've already planned that out, as well."

Bao laughed. "Somehow, I knew you were going to say that, Captain."

CHAPTER 17

Alex opened his eyes, gaze sweeping across the prison block. The other inmates were mostly quiet at this hour, some sleeping fitfully on their thin mattresses, others lost in their own thoughts, staring blankly at the ceiling or pacing in their confined spaces.

He had something completely different in mind. A week after folding away from Earth, the time had come to break free of their prison, or die trying.

"How's it coming, Three?" Alex whispered, his voice barely audible in the cell adjacent to his. He could hear the subtle friction of Jackson working on removing the wash basin's bolts.

"It's delicate work, Gunny," Jackson replied. "But I'll get it done in time."

Their plan had evolved over the past week, adapting to the harsh realities of their confinement. Initially, they had hoped to reverse the polarity of the force fields on their cells, a plan that had seemed elegant in its simplicity. But that idea had quickly proven impractical, dashed against the unyielding design of their prison.

As it had turned out once Jackson removed the sink for

the first time, there just wasn't enough space to manipulate the wiring. Even with the parts from the baton to help hook the proper lines and pull them closer, the bolt holes were smaller than they anticipated, as were the pipes feeding through the bulkhead for the sink.

Instead, they had settled on a riskier strategy: using the baton's battery cell to short-circuit the force fields entirely. It was far from ideal, a blunt instrument where they had hoped for a scalpel. The sudden deactivation of the fields would be impossible to hide, a beacon announcing their escape attempt to friend and foe alike.

Alex's gaze drifted to the other side of the prison block, where the SF civilians were held. Despite their affiliation, Alex couldn't help but feel a twinge of sympathy for them. Many had been swept up in raids, arrested on flimsy pretexts of sedition or conspiracy. He doubted all of them were truly loyal to Strickland's regime.

"What do you think, Gunny?" Jackson asked. "How many of them do you reckon will cause us trouble? I mean, some of them look like they've never thrown a punch in their lives, but desperation can make people do crazy things."

Alex considered the question carefully, his eyes scanning the faces of the SF prisoners. Some looked beaten down, hope long since drained from their eyes. Others maintained a defiant glare, their postures rigid even in sleep.

"Hard to say," he replied after a moment, his voice low and thoughtful. "Some might see it as a chance to prove their loyalty, thinking it'll earn them better treatment. Probably the younger ones, still buying into Strickland's propaganda. Others might be too scared to do anything, just trying to keep their heads down and survive. But I'll bet at least a few will help us, if only to spite their captors. Not everyone here is a true believer. Some of them are just ordinary people caught in the crossfire. They might see us as their best chance at freedom."

"Let's hope you're right," Zoe chimed in, her whisper barely carrying to Alex's ears. "We'll need all the help we can get."

"We can't control what the other prisoners do," Alex said. "We can only react." His gaze shifted to the guards at the station, looking over the cell block. He knew their positions and postures so well at this point that he could nearly pinpoint exactly where they were in the nightly routine. "But the time is right. Jackson, I want those fields offline in forty-eight minutes."

Jackson's acknowledgement was drowned out as a familiar voice rang out from further down the block. "Guards! Hey, guards!" The shout echoed off the metal walls, sharp and insistent.

Alex growled beneath his breath. It was Gray. Again. The asshole had been trying unsuccessfully for the last week to convince the guards to search them and their cells, and based on the last few nights, he had a sinking suspicion that eventually they would acquiesce, if only to shut him up.

"This is ridiculous," Cassandra commented beside him.

"Will you can it, Gray?" someone shouted from a nearby cell, their voice hoarse with exhaustion and irritation. "Some of us are trying to sleep! Don't you ever give it a rest?"

But Gray persisted, his voice growing louder and more insistent with each call. "Guards! I demand you check the cells of the Scarab imposters! They're up to something, I know it! You'll thank me later, I swear. Just think of the commendations and bonuses you'll get when you catch them in the act of planning an escape."

Alex's jaw clenched when he heard the sound of approaching footsteps, heavy boots on metal grating. The two roving guards appeared. The taller of the two, a man with a face like weathered leather, glared at Gray. "Do you ever give up, maggot?" he asked.

"Every day I try to warn you," Gray said. "Every day you ignore me. But I'm trying to help. Those three are planning something. I've heard them whispering. You need to search their cells!"

The guard sighed heavily, clearly irritated by the disruption to his routine. He turned to his partner, a younger man with a nervous twitch in his left eye and a hand that kept straying to his baton. "What do you think, Merv? Should we humor him?"

"What's the downside?" Gray pressed. "If I'm wrong, at least you had something different to do than stalk up and down the block for the next eight hours. And if I'm right... well, you might just earn yourselves a promotion."

Merv laughed at that. "They don't give promotions, asshole. But we might score a word from the Grand Admiral himself. I heard he has a special interest in those three."

"It'll shut him up, at least," the other guard agreed. "And who knows? Maybe the rat's onto something. Stranger things have happened, yeah?"

"Let's do it," Merv confirmed.

Alex's jaw clenched, hands balling into frustrated fists as the leather-faced guard turned to face the cells. "Alright, you three," he called out. "Surprise inspection. Any funny business, and you'll wish you'd never been born. Clear?"

"Crystal clear," Alex replied, his voice steady despite the tension coiling in his gut. He knew they had hidden their makeshift tools well, but a thorough search would still uncover them.

As the force field to his cell flickered off with a soft hum, he exchanged a quick glance with Jackson, silently urging him to stay calm.

The guards entered each of their cells in turn, methodically tearing apart the sparse furnishings. They flipped the thin mattresses, ran their hands along the edges of the sinks and toilets, and peered into every corner and crevice. The sound of their search seemed unnaturally loud in the quiet of the prison block, each rustle and thud sending Alex's heart racing. Thankfully, they didn't bother to examine the bolts on his sink, missing that vector of culpability.

"Take off your clothes," the older guard ordered gruffly, his eyes hard and suspicious. "All of you. Underwear, too. We need to make sure you're not hiding anything. And don't try anything cute. We've seen all the tricks before."

Alex gritted his teeth but complied, aware of the eyes of the other prisoners on them. He could feel their gazes like physical things, a mixture of curiosity, sympathy, and in some cases, a perverse enjoyment of their humiliation. Through the reflection from the guard's faceplate, he could see Gray's face split in a triumphant grin, clearly relishing their discomfort.

"Enjoying the show, Gray?" Alex called out as he removed his prison uniform, his voice laden with contempt. "I hope it's everything you dreamed it would be."

Gray's grin only widened. "Oh, it is," he replied, his voice dripping with satisfaction. "I gave you a chance, Gunny. You made the wrong choice."

The Scorpions stood naked in the corridor, their dignity stripped away along with their clothes, as the guards performed a thorough pat-down. Alex forced himself to remain still, fighting against every instinct that screamed at him to fight back, to resist this invasion of his privacy.

"Nothing here," Merv reported, his voice tinged with both relief and disappointment. "They're clean."

The older guard nodded, his expression unreadable. "Alright, back in your cells. And put your clothes back on. This isn't a strip club."

As they were roughly shoved back into their cells, Alex couldn't help but feel a small sense of satisfaction at the frustration etched on Gray's face. The traitor's plan had failed, at least for now, though even he couldn't guess how the guards had failed to find Jackson's stash.

"I'm sorry you had to go through that," Cassandra said beside him.

"I'm sorry you had to see me like that," Alex replied, pulling on his underwear.

He was putting his jumpsuit back on when he realized the guards weren't finished. To his surprise, they turned their attention to the man who had instigated the search.

"Your turn, Gray," the older guard growled, a hint of dark amusement in his voice.

"What do you mean?" Gray replied, a nervous quiver in his voice. "I'm not hiding anything."

"So you say," Merv said. "But maybe all of this hooting and hollering about those three that turned up clean is to distract us from whatever you're doing in there."

"Yeah," Leather-face agreed. "If you're so concerned about contraband, you won't mind us having a look in your cell, will you? After all, we wouldn't want to play favorites, and you have nothing to hide, right?"

Alex could see Gray's smug expression vanish, replaced by a mix of anger and embarrassment. "What? But I'm the one who—" he sputtered, his face reddening. "This is ridiculous! I'm trying to help you!"

"Shut it," Merv snapped, his hand tightening on his baton. "You wanted a search, you're getting one. Now step out of your cell and get out of your uniform."

Alex watched with pure satisfaction as Gray was subjected to the same humiliating process they had just endured. The traitor's face burned red as he stood exposed before the other prisoners, many of whom jeered and taunted him.

"Not so fun when it's you, is it, Gray?" someone called out, their voice thick with schadenfreude. "Karma's a bitch, ain't it?"

Alex paid attention to the prisoners who seemed the most joyful to see Gray's comeuppance. They would be potential allies, and there were more of them than he had expected. He almost laughed out loud, knowing Gray had inadvertently helped him gather one last bit of intel. All it had cost was a little dignity, which he would gladly trade for a better chance of success.

When the search of Gray's cell also turned up nothing, the guards stepped back, clearly annoyed at having wasted their time. "Satisfied now?" the older guard asked Gray, his voice dripping with sarcasm. "Got any more helpful tips for us, or can we all get back to our jobs?"

Gray said nothing, simply glowering as he was shoved back into his cell. His forcefield flickered back to life with a soft hum, and the guards departed, leaving the prison block in tense silence.

As soon as they were gone, Alex whispered to Jackson, his voice barely audible, "Where did you hide the components? I was sure they were going to find something."

Jackson's reply was equally hushed, tinged with pride and discomfort. "Trust me, Gunny, you really don't want to know. Let's just say we should be grateful they didn't decide to X-ray us. Because they don't know all the tricks."

Alex winced, deciding it was definitely better not to press for details. "Good work, Three. Let's make sure we don't have to go through that again."

"Copy that," Jackson replied with a soft chuckle. "At least we got to see Gray get a taste of his own medicine. That almost made it worth it. Almost."

"Let's sit tight for the next rotation," Alex decided. "We missed this one."

They settled in to wait, knowing they would need to

bide their time before attempting their escape. The hours crawled by, perceptually slowed by Alex's eagerness. He used the time to run through their plan in his mind.

Finally, as the current guards were cycled out and most of the other inmates had drifted off to sleep, Alex knew it was time. He whispered to his team and Cassandra.

"Are you ready? Once we start, there's no going back."

"Ready as I'll ever be, Gunny," Jackson replied, his whisper tinged with nervous excitement. "The sink is hanging by the plumbing, and the wire and battery is set."

"All set here," Zoe confirmed, her voice calm and focused even in its softness. "Just say the word."

"I'm ready," Cassandra added.

Alex took a calm breath, checking the position of the guards one last time. Everything they had endured, everything they had planned for, had led to this moment. Success meant a chance at freedom and hopefully a return to the Wraith. Failure...well, failure wasn't an option he was willing to contemplate.

"Okay, Scorpions," he said. "Let's show these SF bastards what we're made of."

In the never-ending harsh light of the prison block, a small spark flickered to life in Jackson's cell—the first step in a plan that would either lead them to freedom or doom them all. As smoke wafted from Jackson's cell and the forcefields began flickering out, Alex felt a surge of adrenaline course through him.

There was no turning back now.

CHAPTER 18

His muscles coiled and ready, Alex exploded into action.

Bursting from his cell at a dead run, he vaulted over the railing and plummeted toward the guard station below. Assessing his targets during the brief moment of freefall, Alex slammed into one of the four guards caught unaware by the sudden chaos erupting around them.

The man's body broke his fall, the impact driving the air from the guard's lungs with an audible whoosh. Before the others could react, Alex was already moving, his body flowing from one strike to the next with fluid precision, until a baton whistled through the air, catching him painfully on the shoulder. He gritted his teeth, the adrenaline coursing through his system dulling the pain.

The guard's face twisted in shock as Alex grabbed his arm "What the—" He swallowed the rest of his words, crying out instead as Alex twisted his arm and slammed his elbow into his temple, dropping him.

"You're not getting out of here, scum!" another guard snarled as he charged Alex his eyes wide with determined rage. Alex ducked under his wild haymaker, the guard's fist whistling past his ear. He drove his fist into the man's solar plexus, feeling the air rush out of the the man's lungs before he doubled over, gasping for breath. Alex brought up his knee, catching him squarely in the face. The growing cacophony of shouts and alarms swallowed the crunching sound of cartilage.

One last guard, a younger man with a thin mustache, fumbled with his baton, his hands shaking visibly. "S-stay back!" he stammered, his voice cracking with fear.

"Sorry, kid," Alex muttered as he closed the distance in two quick strides, "but I can't stay here any longer."

In two strides, Alex was on him, a quick series of strikes —elbow to the ribs, palm to the nose, throw to the floor— and the kid joined his companions on the floor, a bloody mess curled up in pain.

On the level above, Zoe had made a beeline for Gray's cell, her face a mask of cold fury. The traitor barely had time to register what was happening before she was all over him, her fists flying in a blur. Each impact with his face and gut drove him back into his cell.

"What...what are you doing?" Gray gasped, his voice thick with panic. He tried to block her punches, but his moves were too slow. She bloodied his upper lip and opened a cut over his left eye that was streaming blood down the side of his face."You're all going to die for this!"

"Maybe so. But you're going to die first," Zoe snarled, driving her knee into his stomach. The traitor doubled over, wheezing. "That was for Sarah. And this..." Her fist caught him on the jaw, snapping his head back. "...is for Malik." Gray stumbled back hitting his cell wall, his eyes wide with panic as Zoe pressed her advantage. She slipped behind him and wrapped her forearm across his throat. "And this," she hissed, her menacing voice barely audible over the din. Grabbing hold of her wrist with her other hand, she tightened her hold under his chin, drawing a gurgling gasp for air from him. "This is for every other Marine who died because of your treachery." She jerked her forearm tighter to his throat, completely cutting off his air supply.

Gray's eyes bulged as he clawed at Zoe's arm, his face turning a vibrant shade of purple. "Please," he wheezed, the word barely audible. "I...I was just..." He coughed, struggling for air. "...following...orders..."

"So are we," Zoe replied coldly, tightening her grip even more. She felt his hyoid bone collapse beneath her wrist. His struggles grew weaker, his legs kicking feebly, until finally, he went limp, and she dropped his dead weight on the floor, leaping over his body to join the fight outside his cell.

Meanwhile, Jackson and Cassandra raced down the steps, their eyes darting back and forth as they assessed the rapidly evolving situation. The other prisoners, realizing what was happening, began pouring out of their cells behind them. A few hung back, uncertain, while others immediately chose sides.

"Weapons!" Alex shouted from the guard station, grabbing the fallen guards' batons and rifles. He tossed them down to Jackson and Cassandra.

"Now this is more like it," Jackson grinned, checking the magazine on the rifle he kept.

Zoe appeared at the top of the stairs. She descended quickly, her eyes scanning for potential threats before she snatched an offered rifle from Cassandra.

At the far end of the cell block, Merv and the older guard—Leather-face, as Alex had come to think of him—had shaken off their shock and moved to sound the alarm.

"Oh no, you don't," Alex muttered, one of the fallen guard's rifles in hand. He aimed and fired twice in rapid succession. The guards convulsed as the stunner rounds hit them, then collapsed to the deck. Unfortunately, Merv managed to trigger his emergency beacon, setting alarms blaring in the cell block, no doubt bringing more guards running their way.

Alex growled under his breath, but there was nothing he could do about it now. They'd have to deal with it. After all, their plan had accounted for the alarm being triggered.

He turned his attention to Zoe, his elevated position allowing him to provide her cover fire as she hurried to join them near the guard station. With the advantage of high ground, his rounds found anyone who even remotely looked like they might try to stop her, leaving a string of frozen prisoners among the growing crowds.

Jackson and Cassandra formed a defensive line at the base of the guard station, keeping the surging crowd of inmates at bay. "We need to move!" Cassandra shouted.

Alex gave up his position, stowing the rifle and clambering down the ladder at the center of the position. It brought him to a control room at the base of the block, where he quickly scanned the controls. The array of buttons and switches was daunting, but he quickly found what he was looking for.

"Bingo," he growled, activating the door controls. The heavy blast doors at the end of the cell block began to slide open with a grinding metallic screech. Satisfied, he took a few steps to the blast door leading out onto the block, opened it and stepped into the midst of his team.

Almost immediately, a group of prisoners approached. A wiry man with haunted eyes stepped forward, his hands raised in surrender. "We want to help," he said, his voice hoarse. "Name's Decker."

"Strickland," Alex replied.

The group behind Decker wasn't sure how to react. Decker chuckled awkwardly. "Yeah, sure. You can be the tooth fairy for all I care, as long as you can keep us out of the Teegarden mines."

Alex didn't even have time to try to explain. "Door's that way," he said, pointing to the opening blast doors.

"Copy that," Decker replied.

With that, the ragtag group of escapees surged forward, hope and fear driving them on in equal measure. As they reached the threshold, four prisoners surged past Alex and burst through the doors, only to be cut down in a hail of gunfire.

"Get down!" Alex shouted, jumping behind the door frame as more bodies jerked and fell, splattering the deck with blood. Cassandra and the rest of the Scorpions reacted instantly, their training kicking in. They took up defensive positions behind the door frame, Zoe and Cassandra kneeling to give the men the higher firing position.

The prisoners who had rushed ahead lay motionless on the deck, their bodies riddled with bullet holes. "Shit," Jackson hissed, his face pale. "They're not messing around with stun guns."

Alex peered around the corner, quickly assessing the situation. A squad of guards had taken up position in the corridor, their weapons trained on the doorway. Behind him, he could hear the sounds of fighting as SF loyalists among the prisoners, despite being jailed by their own, tried to take advantage of the chaos.

"So much for an easy escape," Zoe muttered, her grip tightening on her weapon.

"When has anything ever been easy for us?" Alex replied grimly. He turned to his team, his voice low and steady. "Three, Five, on my mark. We take them down fast and hard. Three, two, one—mark!"

They moved as one, stepping out just far enough to acquire targets. Their shots were precise, dropping guards with ruthless efficiency.

"Clear!" Jackson called out as the last guard fell.

"Three, pass your stunner to Decker. Five, hand yours

off, too. Swap out for the percussion rifles with standard rounds. Those guards won't be needing them anymore."

"Copy that," Zoe replied, she and Jackson already moving to exchange their weapons, checking the magazines and safeties with practiced ease.

"Feels good to have some real heat again," Jackson commented, a hint of his old swagger returning.

"Which way to the bridge?" Alex asked, turning to Cassandra.

She pointed down the corridor to their left, her voice low and urgent. "That way. But it won't be easy. The entire ship will be on alert by now."

"That's never stopped us before," Jackson quipped.

"What about the last two times we did this?" Zoe muttered darkly.

"So, we're due," Jackson retorted.

"Stay focused," Alex ordered.

They moved out, Alex taking point with Zoe and Jackson flanking him. Cassandra and the allied prisoners brought up the rear, watching for any threats from behind. As they navigated the ship's corridors, the sounds of alarms and shouting grew louder.

They pulled to a stop at one of the ship's elevator banks. Alex smacked the call button as the others took defensive positions. Within seconds, they fired at guards approaching from the rear, forcing them back around the corner. Alex spun back toward the elevators as the arrival tone sounded. The doors in front of him opened, and before he could react, Briggs exploded from the cab. His meaty fist connected with Alex's jaw, sending him staggering back. The rifle clattered from his grip, skidding across the deck. At the same time, additional guards moved out from behind Briggs, managing to down two of the escaped prisoners before Jackson and Zoe could intervene.

Alex recovered from Brigg's surprise punch. Blood

trickled from the corner of his mouth, but his eyes burned with determination. He barely registered the fighting around him, all his focus on the big sergeant.

Briggs grinned, a predatory gleam in his eyes. "Come on, maggot. Let's see what you've got."

Alex charged, feinting left to draw Briggs off-balance before striking right, his fist driving into Briggs' kidney.

The big man grunted but didn't go down. He retaliated with a wild swing that Alex barely managed to duck. Briggs' own momentum worked against him as Alex stepped in close, driving his elbow up into the sergeant's chin. Briggs' head snapped back, but he recovered quickly. With a roar of rage, he grabbed Alex in a bear hug, squeezing the air from his lungs.

"I'm going to crush you like the maggot you are," he snarled, his breath hot in Alex's face.

Alex struggled, ribs compressing under the pressure. Black spots danced at the edges of his vision as he fought for air. With a burst of desperate strength, he slammed his head into Briggs' nose.

The sergeant's grip loosened as blood gushed from his shattered nose. "You little bastard!" he howled, more in anger than pain.

Alex broke free, gasping for air as Briggs backed up and swiped his arm across his nose, wiping away a swathe of blood. Pressing his advantage, Alex unleashed a flurry of strikes to Briggs' face and body. A grunt of exertion punctuated each impact, Alex pouring all of his pent-up rage and frustration into every blow. A fist into Briggs' solar plexus. A kick to the sergeant's thigh, buckling his leg. The blow took him to a knee, and then a spinning kick to the jaw glazed his eyes over. The big man swayed for a moment.

"How…?" he mumbled, blood bubbling from his lips. Then he toppled backward, hitting the deck with a resounding thud.

Alex stood over him, hands braced on his knees and his chest heaving as he caught his breath. "Stay down," he gasped when Briggs opened his unfocused eyes and managed to center them on Alex's face. "It's over." Briggs' eyes finally rolled back in his head, and he passed out cold.

With Briggs subdued, the remaining guards quickly surrendered, throwing down their weapons and raising their hands. The Scorpions and their growing band of allies disarmed them and rounded them up.

"Damn, Gunny," Jackson whistled, looking at the fallen Briggs. "That was as good as the ass-whooping you gave... well, back on Jungle."

"Not quite," Alex replied, still fuming. "He's still alive."

"We need to keep moving," Cassandra urged, her eyes darting nervously down the corridor.

Alex retrieved his fallen rifle. He turned to the group of ex-prisoners, his voice carrying clearly despite the continuing alarms. "This is it, people. The home stretch. Stay alert, watch each other's backs, and remember—we're fighting for our freedom." A chorus of muttered affirmations and determined nods met his words.

They pressed on, their numbers now swelled to nearly a hundred as more prisoners joined their cause. The ship's corridors echoed with the sound of running feet and shouted orders as they neared their objective.

The bridge.

The heavy blast doors were sealed shut, a last line of defense against the advancing escapees. Alex could almost feel the tension radiating from the other side, imagining the frantic activity as the bridge crew prepared for their arrival.

"Five, can you crack the security on—" Alex started.

"I've got this," Cassandra said, cutting him off. She approached the control panel on the bulkhead beside the doors and quickly entered the code.

To Alex's surprised delight, the doors slid open. "Go, go, go!" he yelled.

The bridge erupted into chaos as the escapees poured in through the breach. More alarms blared, mixing with the crew's shouts of surprise and fear. Most surrendered immediately, throwing up their hands in the face of the overwhelming numbers. A few tried to resist, but they were quickly subdued.

"Weapons down!" Alex shouted, his voice carrying over the din as he and the Scorpions walked in behind them. "It's over! Don't make this any worse than it has to be!"

And that was it. The bridge and the ship were theirs.

CHAPTER 19

Alex surveyed the bridge, adrenaline still coursing through his veins. The alarms continued their incessant wailing. Sparks occasionally burst from a damaged console, casting eerie shadows across the faces of the subdued crew members.

"Five," Alex called out, his voice cutting through the chaos. "Take Decker and some of the others. I want every guard and loyalist prisoner rounded up and locked in the cells. And fix that short while you're down there. We don't need any surprises."

He turned to look at Zoe. A thin trickle of blood ran down her temple from a cut she'd sustained during the fight, but her eyes were clear and focused. "On it, Gunny. Come on, Decker. Let's show these SF bastards how it feels to be on the other side of those force fields."

"And show those other civvies that got caught up in the sweeps that they picked the wrong side," Decker agreed. Zoe and the former prisoners left the bridge.

Alex turned to another sizable group of prisoners who had helped them. "You. Split into two teams and search the rest of the ship. I want the rest of this vessel's crew accounted for and under our control, asap."

"Who died and made you king?" one of them, a younger man inked with tattoos, asked.

"Uh-oh," Jackson moaned softly.

Alex stepped up to the man. "There's only room for one person to give orders on a ship like this. Do you want to challenge me for the right?"

The man locked eyes with Alex. "Well, yea—"

He hadn't even finished speaking before Alex had clocked him hard enough on the jaw to knock him on his butt. He planted his boot on the man's throat. "Are you sure about that?" Alex asked.

The man tapped his palm on the deck, and Alex not only removed his boot, he helped him back to his feet.

"If you want to stay a free man, I suggest you follow the Gunny," Jackson said to him.

"Yeah, okay," the man replied. "I just don't want to go back to that cell."

"None of us do," Alex agreed. "But if we give this ship's crew time to sabotage something, we might end up somewhere worse."

"We're on our way," the man replied, the group quickly breaking into two teams like Alex had asked, and heading off the bridge.

Alex turned his attention to the ship's commander, a stocky man with a haphazardly trimmed salt-and-pepper beard. The man's eyes darted nervously between Alex and the other escapees, his hands raised in a gesture of surrender. His uniform was wrinkled and stained with sweat, but Alex couldn't tell if that was due to their takeover, or if he was already that disheveled beforehand.

"You," Alex said, pointing at the commander. "What's your name?"

The man swallowed hard before answering, his voice

hoarse but steady. "Commander Omar Hayes, Strickland Federation Navy."

Alex studied the man's face. There was fear there, certainly, but also a hint of defiance. "You can disable the alarm now, Commander."

Hayes hesitated, his eyes darting to his crew. The bridge fell silent, save for the continued blaring of the alarms. Even the captured crew members seemed to hold their breath, waiting to see how their commander would respond.

"Ensign Doe, kill the alarm," he said at last.

"Aye, Commander," the ensign at the comms station replied. A moment later, the bridge finally fell silent.

"I appreciate your cooperation, Commander," Alex said. "Let's keep it going. I want an emergency stop. Right now."

"What?" Hayes cried. "I...I can't do that. We're in the middle of a fold. If we come out inside a star or black hole or something, we could all die."

Alex stepped closer, his voice low and dangerous. "And what do you think is waiting for us on Teegarden, Commander? To quote Master Sergeant Briggs, there ain't no tea, and there sure ain't no garden. Your people planned to work us to death on that planet, or worse. And we both know the risks of what you suggested happening are minimal at best."

Hayes' jaw clenched, a muscle twitching in his cheek. "You don't understand. The fold drive isn't meant to be stopped mid-jump. The consequences could be—"

"Could be what?" Alex interrupted, his patience wearing thin. "Could tear us apart? Leave us stranded in the middle of nowhere? Again, whatever happens will be a hell of a lot better than what's waiting for us on Teegarden. Now, are you going to stop this ship, or do I need to find someone who will?"

Hayes glanced around the bridge, taking in the hard

faces of the escapees. His shoulders slumped slightly as he realized the futility of his position. "Alright," he said finally. "But I want it on record that I'm doing this under duress. The consequences—"

"Will be on my head," Alex finished for him. "Now do it."

With a resigned nod, Hayes called out to his helmsman. "Lieutenant Johns, kill the fold. Emergency stop."

"Aye, Commander," Johns replied.

Seconds later, the endless black vanished in a flash of light, depositing the prison ship somewhere in the expanse of space.

"Where are we?" Alex asked.

"Nowhere," Hayes replied. "Deep space, between Earth and Teegarden. Though we might as well be a thousand light years away if you're hoping anyone will find you out here."

"Actually, I'm hoping for the opposite," Alex replied. "What we need right now is time, without confrontation." He turned to Jackson and Cassandra, who had been working with the other escapees to secure the rest of the bridge crew at their stations. "We need to figure out our next move. Any ideas on how we might catch up with the Wraith and the FUP?"

"I might have a solution," Cassandra replied. "I have coordinates to a secure area where we can transmit a message to the fleet. The problem is, we have no way of knowing when they might pick it up. If they're not in tranSat range, they won't receive it until they are."

"It's better than nothing, but we didn't escape just to rot on this ship while we wait around for a response that could take weeks to come. What we really need is a safe destination."

"That's the problem," Cassandra said. "There aren't any. The FUP's primary location is the best-kept secret in the galaxy. And the CIP will capture us if we go to one of their planets. When they do, they'll return us to the SF because they don't want any trouble with the Federation. We're basically screwed no matter where we go."

Alex's jaw clenched in frustration. "Doesn't the CIP realize the SF won't pause their conquest? That they're next in line. They have to know that."

Cassandra nodded, her expression somber. She placed a calming hand on Alex's arm. "They do, deep down. But they don't want to face the truth. It's easier to pretend they can maintain their neutrality indefinitely. Fear makes people do strange things, makes them ignore what's right in front of their faces."

Alex sighed. "I need to think about this." He turned to Commander Hayes. "I want a tour. I need to see what we have to work with on this boat."

Hayes hesitated, clearly torn between his duty and the reality of his situation. "I'm not sure that's a good idea," he began.

Alex cut him off with a sharp gesture. "It wasn't a request, Commander. Move."

With a resigned sigh, Hayes nodded. "Follow me," he said, moving toward the bridge exit.

"Three, keep the rest of the bridge crew in line," he ordered before following after the commander.

As they walked through the ship's corridors, Alex studied the man. His posture was rigid, his eyes constantly darting around as if looking for an escape route. Of course, there was nowhere for him to run. The prisoners who had rightly given up on the SF were in control now.

"Tell me something, Commander," Alex said, breaking the silence. "Why are you so loyal to Grand Admiral Strickland? What has he done to earn your unwavering devotion?"

Hayes stiffened at the question, his pace faltering

momentarily before he recovered. "Grand Admiral Strickland keeps us safe," he replied, his voice clipped. "He's brought order to the galaxy, stability—"

"Safe from what?" Alex pressed, cutting him off. "Stability for whom? Because from where I'm standing, all I see is oppression and fear."

The commander opened his mouth to respond, then closed it again. "From... from..." He stuttered as if he couldn't remember his lines.

"You don't even know, do you?" Alex said. "You've bought into the propaganda so completely that you don't even question it anymore. Has it ever occurred to you that maybe, just maybe, Strickland is the one you need protection from?"

"The only propaganda comes from the FUP," Hayes insisted.

"Did you know one of Alexander Strickland's squad has cancer?" Alex asked. "And he can't get it treated because Strickland won't let him that far out of his sight? That's how much he trusts his people. That's how much he cares about them."

"You...you're lying."

"The sad thing is, I'm not."

Hayes glanced at him, remaining silent, but Alex could see the doubt creeping into his eyes. It was a small crack in the man's armor, but it was there.

As they moved through the ship, Alex immediately noticed a heavily reinforced door that stood out from the others. "Is that what I think it is?" he asked.

The commander's hesitation confirmed Alex's suspicions. Hayes' eyes shifted between Alex and the door, clearly weighing his options. Finally, he sighed. "It's...it's the armory," he admitted reluctantly.

A slow grin spread across Alex's face. "Open it," he ordered.

Hayes shook his head, taking a step back. "I can't," he protested, his voice rising slightly. "I don't have the clearance. Only the head of security has access to the armory. It's a safeguard against...well, against situations like this."

Alex's expression hardened, all traces of humor vanishing. He stepped closer to Hayes, his voice low and dangerous. "I have Briggs in custody, Commander. I can send for him if I need to. But if I find out you're lying…"

For a long moment, they stood there, locked in a silent battle of wills. Alex could see the conflict playing out across Hayes' face—duty warring with self-preservation. Finally, the commander's shoulders slumped in defeat.

"Fine. I'll open it," he muttered. With shaking hands, Hayes approached the control panel. He let it scan his palm and entered a passcode, his fingers trembling slightly. A series of lights on the panel flashed from red to green, and the door slowly groaned open.

Alex stepped inside, his eyes widening as he took in the arsenal before him. Racks upon racks of weapons lined the walls—rifles, pistols, and more. Crates of ammunition were stacked neatly in one corner. Body armor hung on hooks, enough to outfit a small army.

"This is a lot of ordnance for a prison ship," Alex commented.

"Do you think you're the first group to try to escape?" Hayes replied. "You're just the first one that succeeded, and that's only because we're running a reduced crew, thanks to the lower prisoner haul. And…" He trailed off.

"And what?" Alex asked.

"Usually they try to break free during rec time. Makes it easy to gun them down either during the attempt or after the fact. You're the first to overcome the cell shields. And the first to have so many prisoners come to your aid. I don't know if it's because you look like Alexander, or if it's just your bearing, but most times we can count on seventy, eighty percent of the prisoners to help us out."

"That doesn't answer why you need so many guns, then," Alex said.

"For when this boat is full, and we need to clean house."

"By clean house, you mean—"

"Just what it sounds like. No survivors. Word spreads to Teegarden of attempted escape, and the next thing you know, the prisoners there are cooking up their own crazy ideas. They need to know there's no way out."

Alex stared at Hayes, an idea beginning to form in his mind. It was risky, but it just might work.

"Thank you, Commander," Alex said. "You've been very helpful. Let's head back to the bridge."

"I didn't help you," Hayes replied.

"You sure did. More than you even know."

Alex hurried back to the bridge, startling Jackson and Cassandra with his quick return. They had been huddled over a console, discussing something in low voices. Both looked up as Alex entered.

"What is it?" Jackson asked, instinctively shifting his grip on his rifle. "What's wrong?"

"Nothing's wrong," Alex said. "In fact, I decided where we're going."

Jackson raised an eyebrow, a hint of his old humor creeping into his voice. "Oh yeah? Where's that, Gunny? Please tell me it's somewhere with beaches, lots of pretty girls, and drinks with little umbrellas in them."

Alex's grin widened. "Teegarden."

The silence that followed was deafening. Jackson's face wrinkled in confusion, and Cassandra's eyes widened in shock. Even the captured crew members exchanged uncertain glances.

"Teegarden?" Jackson finally managed to sputter. "No

offense, Gunny, but are you feeling okay? We decided to break out of prison and overthrow the crew so we can avoid going there, and now you want to go there on purpose? What happened to finding a safe destination?"

"Like Cassandra said, there is no safe destination," Alex answered. "In which case, what are the alternatives? To tranSat the FUP fleet from the middle of nowhere and hope for an answer? We're Marines, Three. Men and women of action. Twiddling our thumbs isn't the right move. There's enough gear in this ship's armory to equip an army. So let's equip one. We have a week, so let's train one. And when we get to Teegarden, the last thing they'll expect to come off this ship is a fighting force ready to seize the entire damn place."

The bridge was silent, save for the soft beeping of consoles. Alex could almost see the gears turning in his companions' heads as they processed his plan.

Jackson was the first to speak. "You want to free the prisoners on Teegarden? That's...that's insane. It's suicide. We'd be going up against the entire SF garrison. We'd be outnumbered, outgunned..."

"Maybe," Alex admitted, holding up a hand to forestall further objections. "But it's also our best chance. Cassandra, what do you think?"

Cassandra nodded slowly, a spark of hope igniting in her eyes. "It's risky, but...it could work. If we can pull it off, it would be a huge win. The SF would never expect an attack on Teegarden launched from one of their own prisoner transport ships."

"Question," Jackson said. "Let's say we take Teegarden. What's to stop Strickland from sending Alexander there to deal with us again? He could blast the hell out of us from space."

"That's quite likely, but it will take him time. And in

that time, we can gather up the former prisoners and get the hell out of there."

"And go where, though, Gunny? I'm not trying to go against you, man, but sometimes your eagerness gets ahead of your reason."

Alex exhaled, trying to slow himself down. "Yeah, you're right. Maybe we end up back at that tranSat position to wait. But even if so, at least we'll have a lot more resources to offer when Yarborough or my father arrive. Besides, tell me it wouldn't be fun."

Jackson grinned. "I don't know. I'm starting to worry a little about your perception of fun."

"We can access tranSat on Teegarden," Cassandra said. "We'll need to modify the encryption to get a message to the FUP, but of course, I can do that. We can coordinate a rendezvous point from there."

Alex pointed to her, grinning broadly. "See, Three? We've got our ace in the hole." He turned to Hayes, who had been listening to their discussion attempting to keep a stone face, but it frayed at the edges, his cheeks red with frustration and anger. "Open a ship wide comm," Alex told him.

This time, Hayes didn't bother trying to resist. He turned to the comms station. "Ensign…"

"Comms open," the ensign replied before he finished the order.

"Attention all hands," Alex said. "This is FUP Marine Gunnery Sergeant Alex Strickland, from the bridge. Yes, that really is my name. It's a long story, but one I'm sure I'll have time to tell you in the coming days. This ship is under my control, and will remain that way while we reach our destination. The question then is what destination. And that answer is Teegarden."

He paused to give the freed prisoners he couldn't see

time to react. Those still on the bridge looked shocked and confused. He wasn't surprised.

"But we're not going as prisoners," he continued. "With your help, we're going there as liberators. We can free everyone caught up in the Grand Admiral's nets, FUP and SF alike. We can stand against the lies he's told. His promises of safety and security when all he offers is war and persecution. I know this probably isn't what any of you were thinking of doing when you decided to join our escape. But we have a chance here—a chance to do something that matters—to strike a blow against the tyranny that's oppressed us all."

He paused, his gaze sweeping over the faces before him. Some looked scared, others skeptical, but he could see a growing light of hope in many eyes. "We can run and hide, always looking over our shoulders, always wondering when they'll catch up to us. Or we can stand and fight. Whether you're an FUP loyalist or an innocent Federation citizen brought here to fill some bullshit quota—or whatever reason they're rounding you up in droves—you don't have to take it anymore."

The bridge was silent for a long moment as his words sank in. Alex could feel the weight of the moment, the pivotal decision that lay before them all. Then, from the back of the room, a voice called out. "I'm in."

The former prisoner stepped forward, his voice gaining strength as he spoke. "Better to die fighting than live as a slave. If we're going to go down, let's go down swinging. Let's show Strickland and his goons what we can do."

His words seemed to break a dam. One by one, others began to voice their agreement. The energy in the room shifted palpably, fear and uncertainty giving way to resolve and purpose. Even some of the captured crew members were nodding, a grudging respect in their eyes as they watched their former prisoners rally around Alex.

Alex grinned, certain a similar scene was playing out across the different groups of freed prisoners helping him secure the ship. "The easy part's over. Now, let's get to work."

CHAPTER 20

Alex stood on the bridge of the commandeered prison ship, his eyes fixed on the holographic display that Cassandra had ordered Hayes to pull up. The sensor-constructed composite of Teegarden rotated slowly, a desolate world of harsh terrain and unforgiving climate. Craggy mountain ranges jutted up from vast plains, while deep canyons carved through the landscape like open wounds. The planet's single, sprawling ocean was a dark mass that covered nearly a third of the surface.

Alex leaned in, studying the layout of the penal colony with intense focus. The colony itself was hidden within one of the valleys, its entrance bored into a sheer cliff that had no doubt been dug out via water erosion millions of years earlier, before the planet had gone completely dry. There were no other settlements on the planet. No way to escape except via starship. The place was as desolate as they came.

"Look here," Cassandra said. She zoomed in on a large, flat plateau nestled in the valley. "This is the main landing area."

It was little more than a massive concrete slab, scarred and pitted from countless landings. Squat, brutal stone structures separated each landing zone, while a relatively narrow metal bridge with no guardrails crossed from the slab to the prison's entrance.

"That's our starting point," he said. "Do we need authorization codes to land?"

"On a typical SF military ship, no," Cassandra replied. "But a ship like this one? I don't know."

Alex turned to Commander Hayes. "Well?" he asked.

"There are no special codes," Hayes replied. "Everything you need is already programmed into the transponder."

"Want to take bets that he's lying?" Jackson asked.

"He can lie if he wants," Alex replied. "Five can check the transponder as soon as she's done with the force fields in the prison block." He glanced at Hayes again. "Of course, I've already tried to warn the commander what will happen to him if we catch him in any lies."

Hayes' face darkened. He exhaled in a low growl. "Fine. There are codes. I can give them to you."

"I see," Alex said. "Lieutenant," he turned to the ship's navigator. "How many of the crew have access to these codes?"

"Only me," Hayes replied.

"I wasn't asking you, Commander," Alex replied. He approached the navigator, who swallowed hard as he neared, clearly fearful. "Do I need to ask you again?"

"Sir...I...uh...Lieutenant Chalms on the helm knows the codes."

"Traitor!" Chalms barked. "I'm not giving you anything. You're nothing but a group of maggots. The Grand Admiral will stomp you out as soon as—"

"Three, stun him," Alex ordered.

"Gladly," Jackson replied, approaching the pilot and hitting him with the stun baton. He slouched in his seat and fell silent.

"We'll get the codes from you and him separately," Alex said to Hayes. "They'd better match up." He turned back to Cassandra. "What else can you tell me about Teegarden?"

She zoomed the view out slightly from the colony, pointing to another plateau on both sides of the valley, where thick towers rose out of the rock. "Anti-aircraft batteries," she said. "Intended to take out any incoming dropships. These plateaus are the only other place beside the landing zones to touch down. If we succeed in claiming the colony, this is where the main attack will come from should we need to defend it."

Alex studied the topography. It looked like a cakewalk for power-armored Marines. More challenging if not armored, but not impossible.

"Is the bridge the only way in or out?" he asked.

"I don't know. I would suspect there's a bolt hole somewhere on the prison side of the terrain. And you can see there's evidence of thruster scarring on the plateau there."

"Yes, I see it," Alex said. "They have to send the ore out from somewhere. I doubt they're carting it all the way across the bridge."

"You're right. There must be another way in on that side."

"It doesn't matter for our purposes. Our only way in is across the bridge. But like you said, if we do need to defend the place…"

"We'll have to locate the second entrance," she finished for him.

"Exactly. What else can you tell me about the facility?"

Cassandra shook her head. "This is about all we can get without digging deeper into the ship's data stores and logs. And even then, any information we pull may be outdated or too high-level to be of much use. My work focused on tracking logistics through Earth-based private sector manufacturing. Of course, while the companies were private they pretty much had to produce whatever Strickland demanded."

"But there might be some nuggets of value hidden inside the ship's network?" he asked.

"We might be able to find something actionable, Gunny."

Alex nodded, shifting once more to Commander Hayes. "You heard her, Commander. I need those data banks unlocked."

Hayes didn't put up a fight. With a resigned sigh, he moved to the command station. "You don't understand what you're doing," he muttered as he tapped the control surface. "The Grand Admiral will—"

"The Grand Admiral should have killed us when he had the chance," Alex finished. "He didn't, and now he's going to regret it. Stop whining, and do what I've asked."

Hayes finished inputting the commands. "There," he said, his voice bitter. "It's done."

Cassandra immediately occupied the command station. She used the control surface to delve into the data stores. Alex waited patiently for her to speak up. "Like I expected," she said after a few minutes, "there's nothing specific about the planet's defenses. I'd guess they're pretty light, since I doubt Strickland considers people high-value assets. They likely rely mostly on the guards to control the prisoners and the lack of importance to keep it secure."

"I don't see it that way," Alex countered. "Not after FOB Alpha. Strickland knows there are only so many targets the FUP still has a shot against. If he's considered Teegarden one of them, then he's likely bolstered defenses there already. And, since he sunk his teeth into my mind, he has to know my father will go to great efforts not to leave me behind." He turned to Hayes. "What do you know about Teegarden's defenses, Commander?"

"I...I don't know much," he admitted. "I'm just a transport commander. I never really paid attention. I can tell you there are more than just guards on the station. A company of Marines is usually deployed there for training."

"What kind of training?"

"Live fire exercises. They transport them and some prisoners out to the ranges. The Marines have set time periods to locate and eliminate all of the targets."

"Damn," Jackson growled. "They use prisoners like animals to be hunted? Do they at least give them something to shoot back with?"

"Freezer rounds," Hayes replied.

"That's disgusting. They don't stand a chance."

"That's the idea."

"How the hell can you support that?" Alex asked, his voice raising angrily. "Any of you? Have you traded every sense of morality you have for this unquantifiable concept of security?"

None of the other bridge crew spoke up.

After a moment, Alex's attention went back to the projection. "Whatever we think might be there, we have to plan for more. A lot more. Keep digging through those records, Cassandra. Look for anything that might give us a more detailed picture of the situation on the ground there. Everything helps."

As Cassandra continued her data mining, Alex turned to Jackson. "I'm heading down to the prison block to check on Five's progress. You've got the bridge. Keep an eye on our friends here, and let me know immediately if anything changes."

"You got it, Gunny," he replied with a nod.

Alex left the bridge on his own this time. He knew the way back to the prison block. He was glad to see all of the downed SF guards and loyalist prisoners had been removed from the corridors, collected and brought back to the cells to get a taste of what it was like.

The blast doors remained open as he neared the block. Already, he could hear Briggs' voice echoing off the metal walls, a stream of curses and threats that seemed to have no end.

"You think this changes anything?" Briggs' voice boomed. "You're all dead! You hear me? Dead! When the Grand Admiral finds out about this, he'll turn this entire sector into a smoking ruin just to get you! I don't even care if he slags me, as long as you get turned into piles of ashen shit!"

Alex allowed himself a grim smile as he entered the area. How the tables had turned. The once-powerful sergeant now raged impotently behind a renewed force field, his swollen face red with exertion and anger.

He found Zoe up in Jackson's cell, tightening the bolts on the sink to ensure whoever was in the cell next wouldn't be able to remove them. She had already deactivated the force field for the specific cell from the control panel on the outside. She picked up a tablet she had gathered from somewhere—likely the guard tower—and looked over as he approached, a satisfied grin on her face.

"All done, Gunny," she reported before checking something on the tablet.

"Good work, Five," Alex said, his eyes sweeping over the rest of the cells. About thirty guards, including Briggs, were now locked behind the shimmering barriers, along with a number of crew.

The sound of multiple approaching feet turned his attention to the block's entrance. A group of captured crew members were being marched in, led by the tattooed man Alex had thrown to the deck earlier. His face was flushed with excitement, and his eyes had a wild gleam.

"Got another batch incoming," he called out, shoving a captured crewman toward an empty cell. The prisoner stumbled forward. "I hope you got those fields online."

"They're online," Zoe shouted back. "Put them anywhere you like."

"Copy that, ma'am," he replied. He and his group herded the prisoners to cells on the bottom level while Alex and Zoe descended back to the deck.

The tattooed man finished tossing the crew in their cells before leading his group over to Alex.

"Boss," he said, nodding to Alex. "That should be the last of them, but we should send out teams to make sure nobody's hiding anywhere, and to keep watch over the sensitive areas of the ship, like the reactors."

Alex nodded. "Are you military?" Despite his rough appearance, there was an intelligence in his eyes that Alex found intriguing.

"Nope. But I was a lead foreman at a factory back on Earth, so I know a thing or two about giving orders and making sure things get done."

"What's your name?"

The man straightened, puffing out his chest slightly. "Drake," he replied. "Hunter Drake."

"What do you think about our plan to hit Teegarden, Drake?"

Drake's face split into a feral grin, his teeth startlingly white against his tanned skin. "I think it's about damn time someone took the fight to those SF bastards," he said, his voice filled with barely contained excitement. "I got swept up in one of their raids while I was sleeping in my apartment. According to the people I talked to who were brought in with me, they didn't pick up a single FUP sympathizer or spy. Just innocent citizens trying to make a living." He spat on the deck, his face twisting with disgust. "They took everything from me, even my dog. Can you believe that? My dog! I bet they put him down already."

Alex studied the man for a moment, gauging his sincerity. There was no doubting the hatred in Drake's eyes when he spoke of the SF. It was a hatred born of personal loss, the kind that burned hot and didn't easily fade.

"You're clearly good at organizing people," Alex said. "I need someone to help group the freed prisoners into fighting units. Six man squads with a squad leader. Think you're up for it?"

Drake's eyes widened, a mix of surprise and eagerness crossing his face. "Hell yes, I'm up for it," he said. "Tell me what you need, and I can get it done, boss."

"For now, pick out a few prisoners to guard the reactors, engines, and life support."

"On it, Boss." Drake turned to the other freed prisoners to make his selections.

"Hey! Strickland!" a voice called out. Alex turned to see one of the SF citizens who had chosen not to help them waving to him from his cell. The man's orange jumpsuit was disheveled, and his eyes were wide with fear. "I changed my mind. I want to help you fight back!"

Several other voices joined in, a chorus of pleas and promises echoing through the prison block. "We can be useful!" one shouted. "I can shoot!" added another one.

Alex approached the first man's cell, his expression hard. The prisoners fell silent as he neared, their eyes fixed on him, reflecting hope and dread.

"You had your chance," he said, his voice cold and unyielding. "You chose your side. You chose to stand with the Federation even after what they did to you by ripping you from your homes and sending you away. The way I see it, you're too deeply loyal to the SF to be trusted. I don't want to spend the rest of this trip looking over my shoulder."

He turned away from the cells, ignoring the continued pleas and curses that erupted behind him.

"Drake," he said, "the prison block is yours. Get these people organized."

Drake had just finished sending out nearly a dozen volunteers to guard the critical areas of the ship. Now, he snapped to attention. "You got it, Boss."

Alex nodded, then turned to Zoe. "Come on, Five."

As they left the prison block, Alex could hear Drake begin organizing the freed prisoners. His voice echoed down the corridor, full of enthusiasm and purpose.

"Alright, listen up, you sorry lot!" Drake bellowed. "Playtime's over. If we want to stay free, we have to earn it. I want to know every skill you've got—if you can shoot, if you can fight, hell, if you can tie your own shoelaces."

Alex allowed himself a small smile as Drake's voice faded behind them. The man's energy was infectious, and they would need that in the coming days. It was a start, at least—turning a disparate group of prisoners into a cohesive fighting force.

"Where are we headed, Gunny?" Zoe asked as they walked.

"Armory," he replied. "I want to get an inventory of everything. Once Drake has the units separated, we'll be prepared to outfit them properly. Then we can start with their boot camp."

"Not all of them are fit to fight."

"Mentally or physically?"

"That depends. Drake is a gem, but most of the Federation group are terrified. It's one thing to fight for your immediate freedom, another to go up against what they see as an intractable opponent."

"They jumped into action when they saw us succeed. If we lead the charge, and we succeed, it'll give them the confidence they need. So will spending the next week training."

"You seem pretty sure of that."

Alex shrugged. "What else can we do? The element of surprise here will be a massive advantage."

"As long as Strickland hasn't sent the Scarabs to Teegarden ahead of us. We can't eliminate the possibility."

"No, we can't. But you saw Theo. He's having doubts. Maybe that kind of virus can spread to the others."

"Don't get your hopes up."

They reached the armory, the heavy doors still hanging open from his earlier visit.

"Let's see what we've got to work with," Alex said.

Zoe whistled as she took in the rows of weapons and equipment. "Looks like Christmas came early, Gunny," she said, running her hand along the barrel of a nearby rifle. "With this kind of firepower, we might actually have a chance."

"It's too bad Harry isn't here. He would love the challenge of inventorying and distributing this gear."

They set to work, meticulously cataloging every weapon, every piece of body armor, every crate of ammunition. As they worked, Alex contemplated their situation. They had a week to turn a ragtag group of prisoners into a fighting force capable of taking on the SF garrison on Teegarden.

It was a daunting task, but looking at the arsenal before him, he felt pretty good about their odds.

CHAPTER 21

Soren leaned back in his seat, feeling the subtle vibrations of the armored vehicle as it wound its way through Glaston's streets. The tinted windows offered only glimpses of the subterranean metropolis outside, its artificial daylight now dimmed to a minimal glow. Jane sat beside him, holding her arm against her chest and watching Councilwoman Bao intently.

Across from them, the Councilwoman's fingers danced across the surface of her datapad, no doubt coordinating the myriad details that came with organizing Soren and Jane's return to their fleet while also helping the rest of the coalition prepare for war. Garrett stood nearby, his expression one of confusion. The man had risked everything to help them, but neither he nor Soren could figure out why Bao had asked him to come along for the ride.

And then there was Samuel. Soren had contacted him on their way down from Bao's office to the waiting car, letting him know that things had gone well.

"So," Bao said, looking up from her device, her eyes locking onto Soren's. "You mentioned that your next move involves an attack on Teegarden. I'd like to hear more about that."

Soren nodded, leaning forward slightly. "The idea is to draw out Alexander Strickland's ship, the Fist of Justice," he explained. "If we can destroy it, or at least disable its vortex cannon, we might buy ourselves some time."

"And you think attacking a prison planet will accomplish this?" Bao's tone was skeptical, but not dismissive.

"We're not sure," Jane said. "But success will help us replenish our crews, while at the same time giving the Federation an embarrassing black eye. My ex-husband doesn't like to be embarrassed. He'll respond to the action with inequivalent force, and to me that means the Fist of Justice."

"It's his largest, most powerful warship," Soren added. "Designed to crush dissent. He'll want to use it to finish off the FUP, once and for all."

"And if the ship isn't already near Teegarden, we'll make sure our next target is obvious enough to bring Alexander running," Jane picked up.

"And destroy the Fist," Bao said. "You aren't concerned about potentially killing your son?"

Jane sighed mournfully. "It's the last thing I want to do. It won't be me who orders the fatal blow. But if he dies fighting for the SF, that's beyond my control."

"I see." Bao leaned back in her seat as she considered their words. "And what exactly are you expecting from the CIP in this operation? You must understand, we're walking a very fine line here."

Soren met her gaze, his voice firm but not demanding. "If the CIP could commit even half a dozen ships, and more importantly, ground troops for the assault, it would significantly improve our odds. We're not asking you to bear the brunt of the attack, but your support could make all the difference."

The Councilwoman's lips pressed into a thin line, her fingers drumming a nervous rhythm on her datapad. "You're asking for a lot, Captain Strickland," she said after a moment. "The moment the CIP participates in an overt attack against the SF, it's a declaration of war. Strickland will begin maneuvering his fleets to strike our planets. If we're not perfectly positioned ahead of time, the consequences could be catastrophic. Especially if they have more vessels than the Fist equipped with these vortex cannons."

Garrett, who had been silent until now, cleared his throat. "If I may, Councilwoman," he said, his voice hesitant but clear, "technically, these military decisions aren't up to us. They fall under the purview of the Military Council on Trappist-e."

Bao nodded, a hint of frustration creeping into her expression. "You're right, of course. But there's also the simple fact that most of our fleet is over two weeks away. Even if the Council wanted to green-light the request, we can't provide the level of support you're hoping for, Captain."

Soren absorbed this information. There was nothing that any of them could do about the time frame involved. Time wasn't on their side. "Can we speak to the Military Council directly?"

"I'll handle them," Bao interjected, her tone leaving no room for argument. "That's why I'm in this vehicle with you. They'll need to hear all of this from someone they know and trust."

Soren nodded, accepting her decision. "And what about Garrett? Why is he in the vehicle with us?"

Bao offered a humorless smile. "Because he let you into my office without permission. Armed, no less. He may have had a good reason, but he's still fired. I thought he might want to come with you."

Garrett didn't seem surprised by this revelation. He

shrugged, a wry grin spreading across his face. "She's right. And yes, I do want to join you. If what you've told us is true, this is bigger than any one job or career. I want to help."

"Glad to have you aboard," Soren said.

The vehicle began to slow, and Soren realized they had reached their destination. Through the tinted windows, he could make out the imposing gate of what had to be the Glaston barracks. The vehicle reached the guard station and came to a stop. Bao rolled down her window enough for the guards to see her face, and they silently waved them through.

They continued through the gate and down a ramp into an underground garage filled mostly with armored military vehicles. The driver brought their ride to a stop and got out to open the door for them.

"The loop station is this way," Bao said, leading them out of the vehicle. "It'll take us directly to the naval space-port in Dome Seventeen."

As they approached the entrance, Soren noticed a figure waiting for them. The man stood ramrod straight, his uniform crisp and immaculate. As they drew closer, Soren could make out the insignia of a full colonel.

"Welcome to Glaston Barracks," the man said, his voice carrying the practiced tone of someone used to command. "I'm Colonel Vatar." He paused, sizing Soren up. "I must say, the resemblance is uncanny." His eyes lingered on Soren's face, a mix of fascination and wariness in his gaze.

"Thank you for meeting us, Colonel," Soren replied, extending his hand. "Captain Soren Strickland." Vatar hesitated for just a moment before shaking it firmly.

"Captain Strickland." He smiled. "Councilwoman Bao messaged me to expect the unexpected, but I wouldn't have guessed this. I'm sure there's a bigger story you don't have time to tell me." He gestured toward the nearby door. "If you'll follow me, I'll escort you to the loop station. A tram is waiting to take you to Dome Seventeen." As they walked, Vatar continued speaking. "Once you reach the dome, you'll meet with Captain Haji. She'll fly you up to the Athena."

Soren's eyebrows rose at this. "The Athena?"

Vatar nodded, a hint of pride in his voice. "One of our… special assets. She comes with a crew I think you'll very quickly come to appreciate."

"Stop being so obtuse, Colonel," Bao said. "The Lammergeiers are the best-trained SpecOps squad in the CIP."

"And you're loaning them to us?" Jane asked, surprised.

Bao didn't respond. Vatar reacted with confusion. "I'm not sure what either of you mean. The CIP isn't providing any aid. The Athena is an independently tagged private vessel with a very ordinary crew."

Soren caught on quickly, offering the colonel a knowing nod. "Of course. My mistake. I thought you meant something else."

They reached the loop station, where a tram waited. Its doors stood open, inviting them inside. Soren turned to Bao and Vatar, knowing this was where they would part ways.

"Councilwoman, Colonel," he said solemnly, "thank you for everything. We won't let you down."

Bao's expression softened for just a moment. "See that you don't, Captain." She turned to Jane, her voice softening further. "Admiral Yarborough, it was an honor to meet you. I hope we'll have the chance to speak again under less dire circumstances."

"Likewise, Councilwoman," Jane replied, her good hand clasping Bao's briefly.

With final nods of farewell, Soren, Jane, and Garrett boarded the tram.

CHAPTER 22

The journey to Dome Seventeen passed in a blur of dimly lit tunnels and occasional flashes of subterranean infrastructure. Soren used the time to brief Garrett more fully on their situation, filling in the gaps of what the young man had overheard in Bao's office. To his credit, Garrett absorbed the information quickly, asking pointed questions that revealed a sharp, analytical mind.

When they finally emerged into Dome Seventeen, Soren was struck by the contrast. Where Glaston had been all artificial light and climate-controlled comfort, the dome was a marvel of engineering that allowed a slice of the harsh Glaive environment to coexist with human habitation. Through the transparent panels, Soren could see the planet's icy surface stretching to the horizon, bathed in the pale light of its distant sun.

The naval spaceport occupied most of the dome's interior. As they disembarked from the tram, a woman in a flight suit approached them, her stride purposeful and her expression neutral. "Captain Strickland, Admiral Yarborough," she said by way of greeting. "I'm Captain Risha

Haji. If you'll follow me, we have a shuttle prepped and ready for immediate departure."

As they walked, Risha's eyes kept darting to Soren, a mix of curiosity and unease in her gaze. "Colonel Vatar warned me something was up, but I have to say, sir," she said finally, her voice low, "the resemblance is remarkable. If I didn't know better..."

"It's a long story, Captain," Soren replied with a small smile. "One I'll be happy to share once we're underway."

Haji nodded, seemingly satisfied for the moment. She led them to a small, nondescript orbital shuttle, its engines already humming softly. They boarded quickly, with Haji vanishing to the flight deck while they gained their seats in the back.

"Here we go," Jane muttered as the shuttle lifted from the tarmac and started climbing toward the aperture at the top of the dome.

"All in all, I'd say our mission here was a success," Soren replied. The craft didn't have any viewscreens to see outside, leaving him to imagine their progress based on the intensity of the engines. "I'm sorry you lost your job over us, Garrett."

"I'm not, Captain," Garrett replied. "Or I wouldn't have helped you in the first place."

"I think it was more than a success," Jane said. "Outside of being shot, of course. We've been fighting a losing battle against the Federation for years now. To convince the CIP to help us is one thing. Your plan to enlist the navies from the other two dimensions...I have hope for the first time in I can't remember how long."

They fell into silence for the remainder of the short trip. Soren sensed the final approach in the change in inertia and the short burst of intense burn from the thrusters, slowing them to enter a larger ship's hangar. Soon after, the shuttle rocked slightly on its landers and the engines shut down, signaling that they had arrived.

"Welcome aboard the Athena," Risha said, returning to the main cabin from the flight deck. She reached up and tapped the door control, opening the hatch. "Shall we?"

They stood and the four of them stepped out of the shuttle into the hangar bay. A tall, broad-shouldered man with close-cropped salt-and-pepper hair and the unmistakable bearing of a career soldier waited there for them. His uniform was impeccable, every crease sharp enough to cut paper, and his piercing blue eyes seemed to take in everything at once.

"Welcome aboard the Athena," he repeated, his voice a deep rumble that seemed to resonate in Soren's chest. "I'm Major Frank Kosta, commander of the Lammergeiers. We've been expecting you for, what? Thirty minutes now?" He laughed, his stern demeanor crumbling a little. "Colonel Vatar said we were in for a surprise. He wasn't wrong."

Soren nodded, extending his hand. "Major. I appreciate your discretion and your willingness to help. I'm sure you have questions."

Kosta's grip was firm but not overpowering as he shook Soren's hand. "More than a few, Captan. But I've learned in this line of work that sometimes it's better not to ask too many. We go where we're needed, and right now, it seems we're needed here."

The major turned slightly, gesturing to a group of six individuals standing at parade rest behind him. Their attire was nondescript, but everything else about them, from posture to physique, screamed 'military.'

"Captain Strickland, Admiral Yarborough, allow me to introduce you to the Lammergeiers," Kosta said, a note of pride in his voice. "Some of the finest operatives the CIP has to offer."

A lean woman with sharp features and dark hair stepped forward.

"Master Sergeant Elena Volkov," she said, introducing herself before quickly offering the names and ranks of the rest of her squad. "Whatever situation you need our assistance with, we're ready to resolve it for you."

"Thank you, Sergeant," Jane replied. "You came highly recommended, and I'm sure you won't disappoint."

"No, ma'am," Volkov snapped.

Kosta cleared his throat. "We'll have time for a full briefing once we're underway. For now, let's get you settled in." He turned, leading them out of the docking bay and into the Athena's corridors.

As they walked, Soren took the opportunity to study their new allies more closely. The Lammergeiers moved with the fluid grace of predators, alert even on their ship. Three men and three women, plus Volkov, Haji, and Kosta. A small force to be sure. But bigger wasn't always better.

"I understand you had to leave Glaive in a bit of a rush," Kosta said as they made their way from the hangar bay to berthing. "We have basics that should fit for you to wear during our trip. It's nothing fancy, but—"

"We're in no position to be picky, Major," Jane said. "We appreciate whatever hospitality you can provide."

"That's good, because I'm afraid we only have two spare bunks for the three of you," he said. "Someone will need to double up."

Soren glanced at Jane, seeing the same mix of resignation and amusement in her eyes that he felt. There was a moment of unspoken communication between them, and despite being born in separate dimensions, they reached a consensus without words.

"Admiral Yarborough and I can share," Soren said.

Jane nodded in agreement. "It's not ideal, but under the

circumstances, I think we can make it work. We appreciate you making room for us at all, given the short notice."

Kosta's shoulders relaxed slightly, relief evident in his expression. "I appreciate your understanding." He paused at the hatch into berthing, tapping the control to open it. They stepped through, revealing a similar setup to the shuttle they'd arrived in, only with a bit more overall space within and between the racks. All of them were immaculately kept, with individual lockers at the end of each to store the Lammergeiers' personal effects.

"Bottom port corner is yours," Kosta said to Soren and Jane. "Top starboard is yours, mister…"

"You can just call me Garrett."

"Top starboard is yours, Garrett."

"Thank you, sir," Garrett replied.

"I'll have Private Dorn deliver those basics, in case you want to get cleaned up. The head is straight back from here. The galley is back out the way we came, down the passageway and to your left. This isn't a big ship, and we only have three decks, so you should be able to learn your way around in no time. Now, if you could provide us with the coordinates for our destination, we can get underway."

Jane gave him the rendezvous point where they were to meet up with the Wraith and the remnants of the FUP fleet. As Kosta relayed the information to Captain Haji via his comm unit, Soren felt the subtle shift in the ship's vibrations that signaled they were preparing to depart.

"We'll be folding shortly," Kosta informed them, his voice taking on a more formal tone. "I'm sure you know, it's a ten day trip. I suggest you all get some rest. We can hold a full briefing in the morning."

"Of course, Major," Jane said. "Thank you again."

"Just doing my job, Admiral," Kosta replied with a grin. With that, he left them to settle in.

As the door slid shut behind him, Soren turned to Jane

and Garrett, seeing his own exhaustion mirrored in their faces.

"Are you okay, Garrett?" he asked. "This is a big change from a few hours ago."

"It is," Garrett agreed. "It's a lot to take in. But I'm happy to be here, sir. I'm just a low-level intelligence analyst, but I'll do anything I can to help."

"A shuttle mechanic and a revoked, drug-addicted freighter deckhand have become two of my most valuable crew members," Soren said. "Don't limit yourself by your position. I certainly won't limit you that way."

Garret smiled. "Yes, sir."

"I think Major Kosta has the right idea," Jane said. "I don't know about you two gentlemen, but I could really use some rest."

"Agreed," Soren said. "We've earned it." He looked at Jane. "Are you sure you're okay with sharing your bunk?"

"Jane Yarborough has slept beside Soren Strickland a thousand times before," Jane replied. "In your dimension and mine. And if I'm being totally honest, I've missed sleeping beside a Soren Strickland I don't want to strangle."

"And I've missed sleeping beside my Jane Yarborough," Soren agreed. "More than I can say."

"While I'm not her, I hope I'm a nice reminder of her," Jane said.

"You are," Soren agreed, though his heart ached with longing for his Jane. With the mission a success and the CIP joining the fight, maybe he would see her sooner than he'd dared to hope.

As long as he saw Alex again, first.

CHAPTER 23

Soren awoke to the gentle hum of the Athena's mechanical operations. For a moment, disorientation clouded his mind as he tried to reconcile the unfamiliar surroundings with his last conscious memories. Everything felt slightly off and surreal at first.

Especially when he glanced to his side, where Jane still slept peacefully. It was strange, seeing her face so close, yet knowing she wasn't his Jane. The same curve of her cheek, the same slight furrow between her brows even in sleep. But the differences served as a constant reminder of the bizarre situation they found themselves in. A small scar near her left ear, a feature his Jane didn't have. The way her shorter-cut hair fell across the pillow. The hardness of years of war had chiseled her much leaner face. That was the greatest difference of all, stark and sad, though a benefit to him because it set this Jane apart from his Jane. Still, he had come to care for her too, just in a different way.

Careful not to disturb her, Soren slipped out of the bunk. The cool metal of the deck against his bare feet sent a small shiver through him, fully waking him up. He gathered the basic clothing that Private Dorn had delivered earlier—a neatly folded stack of gray and black fabrics—and made the short trip to the head.

Once there, Soren took a moment to study his reflection in the mirror. The face that looked back at him was more haggard than he was accustomed to, with dark circles under his eyes and stubble on his face.

"You've looked better, old man," he muttered to himself, running a hand through his disheveled hair, more light gray now than blonde. But unlike Jack, at least he had hair. He was glad someone, probably Dorn, had left them each a new hairbrush, razor, and toothbrush and paste sometime during the night. "But first a shower..."

The shower was a welcome respite, the hot water washing away the grime and tension of his visit to Glaive. He wished he could stand there and enjoy it longer than it took to get clean, but his stomach was starting to gnaw at his backbone. After quickly drying off, he shaved before taking care of his hair and teeth and dressing in the provided basics—a simple gray t-shirt and black cargo pants.

Feeling refreshed, Soren retraced his steps back through berthing, where Jane remained fast asleep. That wasn't surprising. The loss of blood and the need for her body to heal had no doubt left her more fatigued. He had also gotten the sense that having him nearby provided some measure of additional comfort to her. He couldn't help wondering if, despite all Grand Admiral Strickland had done, she still loved the man. If he were in her place, would he?

Considering how much his Jane still loved him after all their years together and all that she'd gone through as his wife, he decided that he would.

Leaving berthing, he made his way to the galley. As he approached, he could hear the low murmur of conversation punctuated by occasional laughter. The smell of coffee and eggs wafted through the air, his stomach growling in response.

He stepped through the hatch to find Garrett seated at a table with Sergeant Volkov and two other Lammergeier members. They were in the middle of what appeared to be an animated discussion, with Garrett leaning forward, his eyes wide with interest.

"...and then," one of the Marines, a barrel-chested man with a closely cropped beard, was saying, his hands gesticulating wildly, "the captain realized we've not only disabled his ship but reprogrammed his computer to broadcast 'I'm a pretty pretty princess' on all frequencies!"

The table erupted in laughter, Garrett's eyes wide with a mixture of amusement and disbelief. "You're kidding!" he exclaimed. "How did you even manage that?"

The bearded Marine grinned, clearly enjoying his rapt audience. "Well, you see, Rivera here—she's got a wicked sense of humor and fingers quicker than..." He put a hand on the shoulder of the lean, red-headed Marine beside him, opening his mouth to continue speaking. He clamped it closed as he noticed Soren's presence.

"Captain on deck!" Volkov called out, her voice sharp and crisp. The Marines snapped to attention, chairs scraping against the deck as they stood at attention.

Soren waved them back to their seats. "As you were. Please, don't let me interrupt what sounds like a fascinating story."

The Marines relaxed slightly, but remained respectfully upright as Soren made his way to the serving line. He helped himself to a tray of reconstituted eggs, some kind of starch mash and dried meat with gravy, and a cup of strong black coffee that promised to jolt him fully awake.

Turning back to the room, he hesitated momentarily before approaching the table where Garrett and the Marines sat. "Mind if I join you?" he asked, carefully balancing his tray.

Sergeant Volkov quickly nodded, gesturing to the empty seat beside her. "Of course not, sir. We'd be honored." She paused, a hint of mischief in her eyes. "We were just regaling Garrett here with some of our more...colorful encounters."

Soren sat down, sipping his coffee—strong and bitter, just the way he liked it—before digging into his breakfast. The eggs were predictably bland but filling. The rest was surprisingly tasty. "Space pirates, was it?" he said between bites. "Sounds like you've had some interesting missions."

The bearded Marine—his nameplate identified him as Corporal Swix—nodded enthusiastically, his earlier discomfort at Soren's arrival melting away in the face of a new audience. "Oh, we've seen our fair share, sir. Nothing you'll ever find in mission reports or on the news, of course. Some of our schtick, well, let's just say we overindulge at times to look less like professionals."

"Misdirection," Garrett said.

"Exactly. Nobody expects elite Marines to prank their targets. We look like thugs taking on thugs. It would be different if we ever had more, for lack of a better word... serious missions. But more often than not, speaking for myself at least, I feel like a wolf in a henhouse on these runs."

"I think you might find your next mission a bit more to your liking then," Soren said.

Swix suddenly looked uncomfortable, the jovial atmosphere dimming as his bright eyes darkened.

"Something wrong, Corporal?" Soren prompted.

Swix shifted in his seat, clearly wrestling with how to phrase his thoughts. "Well, sir, it's just... your comment, in combination with...well...your....resemblance to Grand Admiral Strickland. I mean, if I didn't know better, I'd swear you were him. It's...well, it's a bit unsettling, if I'm being completely honest."

The other Marines nodded in agreement, their eyes studying Soren with curiosity and wariness. Even Garrett, who knew part of the story, looked intrigued to hear Soren's response.

Soren set down his fork, meeting Swix's gaze. He could feel the pressure of the collective stares, the unasked questions hanging in the air. "There's a good reason for my appearance, Corporal," he said carefully. "But I think it's best we save all of the details for the full briefing. It's...complicated, to say the least, and I'd rather only go over it once." He paused, considering how much to reveal. "Let's just say that the universe is far stranger and more complex than any of us ever imagined, leave it at that, and enjoy our breakfast."

The Marines exchanged glances, a mix of confusion and intrigue on their faces. To their credit, they seemed to accept this cryptic answer, their training to respect the chain of command and the need-to-know nature of their work kicking in.

"Understood, sir," Swix replied. "We'll look forward to the briefing, then."

A moment of silence fell over the table, each person lost in their own thoughts about what Soren's words might mean. It was Rivera who broke the quiet. She leaned forward, her voice dropping to a near whisper as if afraid of being overheard.

"Speaking of complications," she said, "is it true? Has the CIP finally decided to join the fight against the Federation?"

Soren hesitated, fork halfway to his mouth. How much should he reveal before the official briefing? The Marines watched him intently, eager for any scrap of information.

He was saved from having to answer by the arrival of

Admiral Yarborough, who had entered the galley just in time to catch the question.

"It's true," Jane confirmed as she approached the chow line. The Marines once again stood at attention, which Jane acknowledged with a nod before waving them back to their seats. She grabbed her food tray before continuing, her voice carrying easily across the room. "The details are still being worked out, but yes, the CIP has agreed to join our efforts against the Strickland Federation."

A palpable wave of excitement passed through the group. Swix let out a low whistle, shaking his head in disbelief. "Well, I'll be damned," he muttered. "It's about time they got off the fence. No offense to present company," he added quickly, glancing at Garrett.

"None taken," Garrett replied with a small smile. "I think a lot of us have been hoping for this for a long time."

Jane joined them at the table, her tray laden with the same fare as Soren's. She took a bite of the eggs, grimacing slightly at the taste. "We'll go over everything in detail during the briefing," she said, washing down the bite with a swig of coffee. "But I can tell you this much, your team is going to play a crucial role. The tip of the spear, as the saying goes."

The Marines straightened at this, a mix of anticipation and professional pride evident in their postures. It was clear they were eager to be part of whatever was coming.

"Any hints you can give us, ma'am?" Rivera asked, leaning forward eagerly.

Jane shook her head, an enigmatic smile playing at her lips. "Patience, Private. All will be revealed soon enough."

As they continued eating and engaging in small talk, the galley hatch opened again, admitting Major Kosta. The Marines stood again, a reflexive action that spoke to their disciplined training.

Kosta waved them down, his eyes scanning the room

before settling on Soren and Jane. "Good morning," he said, his voice carrying easily across the space. "I trust you slept well?"

At their nods, he continued, "Excellent. We'll be holding the briefing in fifteen minutes. I suggest you finish up and make your way to the briefing room."

With that, he grabbed his food tray and sat at a separate table, maintaining a professional distance from the group. The atmosphere in the room shifted slightly, becoming more formal in the presence of the commanding officer.

The Marines quickly finished their meals and stood to leave. Soren and Garrett joined them while Jane remained behind, moving to sit with Kosta. As they filed out of the galley, Soren couldn't help but notice the way the Major had kept himself apart. It was a stark contrast to his own leadership style.

As they made their way through the corridors, Soren turned to Volkov, keeping his voice low. "The Major seems to keep his distance," he observed.

Volkov nodded, a hint of respect in her voice as she replied. "Major Kosta is an excellent commander, sir. But he believes it's important to maintain a certain...professional separation between officers and enlisted personnel. He thinks it's better for squad unity and chain of command."

Her tone was neutral, but Soren sensed there might be more to it. "And what do you think, Sergeant?" he prodded gently.

Volkov glanced at him, a small smile playing at the corners of her mouth. "With all due respect, sir, it's pretty clear you don't share that philosophy. Your approach seems more hands-on."

"True enough," Soren admitted, chuckling softly. "But I can see both sides of the argument. And I can't judge the differences between running a naval ship crew and a SpecOps unit. Different tools for different jobs."

The Sergeant nodded thoughtfully. "Agreed, sir. We all have a ton of respect for Kosta. Despite Swix's bravado, the Major's leadership has gotten us out of a few pretty tight situations."

They reached the briefing room, a compact space dominated by a large holographic display at the front. The Marines filed in, taking their seats with practiced efficiency. Soren remained near the front, watching the rest of the squad gathered. The air was thick with anticipation, each person eager to learn what lay ahead.

Jane and Major Kosta were the last to arrive. Their faces were serious as Jane motioned Soren over to sit beside her and Kosta at the table in the front of the room. Kosta cleared his throat, and the low conversations immediately died away.

"Alright, people," he said, his voice firm and authoritative. "We've got a lot to cover." He paused, his eyes sweeping across the assembled unit. "I'm going to turn things over to Captain Strickland, who has some...unusual information to share with us. Listen carefully, and save your questions for the end. Understood?"

A chorus of "Yes, sir" filled the room.

Kosta nodded to Soren. "Captain, you have the floor."

Soren stood and stepped around the table, every eye in the room on him, eager to hear what he had to say. He took a deep breath, then launched into his familiar explanation —the Convergence, the multiple dimensions, his journey through the Eye, and the danger of the Fist of Justice and its vortex cannon. He watched as expressions of disbelief gave way to shock, then a grim understanding of the stakes they were facing.

He went on to outline their plan to attack Teegarden, explaining the loss of his Marines on FOB Alpha and his gratitude to Councilwoman Bao for providing the FUP with a skilled insertion team.

"That's where you come in," he said, his eyes sweeping across the assembled Lammergeiers. "We need you to be death from above, living up to your namesake."

Corporal Swix grinned, his eyes wide with a mixture of excitement and curiosity. "You know what a Lammergeier is, sir?" he asked, clearly impressed.

Soren allowed himself a small smile, glad for the chance to lighten the mood slightly after the heavy revelations. "I do, Corporal. The bearded vulture, known for dropping bones from great heights to crack them open and get at the marrow inside. An apropos description of what I'll need you to do. Now," Soren continued, his voice taking on a more serious tone, "let me outline your specific objectives. We'll go over these in more detail as we get closer to execution, but I want you to have as much time as possible to prepare.

"Your primary task will be to secure the landing zone for our shuttle. We'll be bringing in a full complement of FUP Marines, along with additional ordnance to distribute to the prisoners. It's crucial that we establish a foothold quickly and efficiently. Once the LZ is secure, you'll take point, clearing a path for us to reach the prisoner population. Some of our Marines will stay behind to hold the LZ, while the rest will bring up the weapons. Once we start arming the prisoners, it should significantly ease your burden. Until then, the success or failure of the ground assault is in your capable hands." Soren paused, looking around the room. "Questions?"

PFC Rivera raised her hand. "What about air support, sir?"

Soren nodded approvingly at the question. "Good thinking, Private. You'll have air support from what's left of my ship's fighter squadron, the Hooligans. They're some of the best pilots I've ever seen."

Jane spoke up, adding, "We'll also have a squadron of

CIP fighters on standby, ready to deploy depending on the resources needed in orbit."

Another hand went up, this time from a tall, lanky Marine with a scar running along his jawline. "Sir, are there any particular prisoners we're looking to extract? High-value targets, maybe?"

Soren hesitated, caught off guard by the question. He felt a lump forming in his throat, the emotions he'd been holding back threatening to overwhelm him. "Why do you ask, Marine?" he managed, his voice slightly strained.

The Sergeant answered for him, her voice gentle but firm. "With all due respect, sir, it's clear from the strain in your voice that this mission is more personal than most. We just want to know if there's someone specific we should be looking for."

Soren felt a wave of emotions wash over him—surprise at being read so easily, gratitude for their perceptiveness, and a renewed surge of worry for Alex.

"You're right, Sergeant," he admitted, his voice thick with emotion. "There is someone. My son, Alex, and the two surviving members of his Force Recon Squad, the Scorpions. I believe they were captured during the assault on FOB Alpha. If they're there...I need them found."

A hushed silence fell over the room as the implications of this revelation sank in. The Marines exchanged glances, a mix of sympathy and resolve in their eyes.

Volkov's expression softened. "If he's there, sir, we'll find him. You have my word."

"Oorah," Swix added quietly, the other Marines nodding in agreement.

Soren felt a lump in his throat, touched by their immediate support. "Thank you. But I need you to understand— the mission comes first. We can't jeopardize our primary objectives."

"Understood, sir," Volkov replied, her tone professional

but with an undercurrent of compassion. "We'll complete both the primary and secondary objectives, sir. You can count on that."

"Now, let's talk about how we're going to prep for this mission," Major Kosta said, retaking the lead on the briefing.

As they delved into the specific skills and equipment they would need to sharpen up on, Soren was impressed by the Lammergeiers' professionalism and adaptability. As the briefing wound down, Soren couldn't help but feel a surge of hope. This was a skilled and dedicated team, and with their help, the chances of success had improved.

As long as they could get the Marines' boots on the ground. That challenge was his and Jane's to overcome. He didn't know yet what kind of defenses would be in place orbiting the planet, but he was determined to get through them.

"Alright, people," Kosta said. "You know what you need to do. Dismissed."

CHAPTER 24

Alex leaned against the railing of the prison block's upper catwalk, scanning the scene below. The deck bustled with activity, filled with the prisoners who had once been destined for a life of hard labor on Teegarden. Now—outfitted in body armor, rifles held at the ready—they moved in practiced formations under the harsh overhead lights.

It had been four days since their daring escape, and in that time, Alex and his fellow Scorpions had worked tirelessly to transform this ragtag group into something that would at least resemble an organized fighting force.

"Squad Three, tighten up that column!" Jackson's voice echoed from below, cutting through the din. "I've seen drunken rhinos with better coordination! Mendoza, if you bump into Soto one more time, I'm going to tie you two together and make you run laps around the perimeter!"

Alex couldn't help but smile at his teammate's colorful command style. Jackson had taken to his role as drill instructor with surprising enthusiasm, his usual wisecracks now peppered with sharp critiques and begrudging praise.

The squad in question scrambled to comply, their movements becoming more precise with each repetition.

Zoe's voice joined the chorus, her tone cool and professional as she guided another group through weapons drills. "Remember, smooth is fast. Don't rush the reload. Get it right, then worry about speed. Torres, that magazine isn't going to leap into the well on its own. Seat it firmly, then rack the slide. Again!"

The freed prisoners, now organized into squads and platoons forming a makeshift company, drilled with growing confidence. Their movements, while still far from perfect, showed marked improvement from the clumsy fumbling of just a few days ago. The rhythmic sound of their various efforts filled the air, punctuated by Zoe's precise instructions.

Alex's gaze drifted to the far end of the block, where the blast doors stood scorched and pitted. They had repurposed the heavy barriers as makeshift targets, allowing the newly minted fighters to experience live fire without the risk of damaging anything. The crack of rifle fire had become a familiar part of their days, each report a reminder of the deadly business for which they were preparing. They were fortunate for the overabundance of ammunition the prison ship had stockpiled, allowing them to burn dozens of rounds for each of the nearly two hundred freed prisoners that had joined their makeshift militia.

"You call that shooting?" a familiar voice sneered from one of the cells, cutting through the noise of training. "You're the most sorry pissant lot of maggots I've ever laid eyes on! I've seen better aim from a blind man!"

Alex's jaw clenched as he turned to face the source of the taunt. Sergeant Major Briggs stood at the forcefield of his cell, his face twisted in a mocking grin. The other SF loyalists and guards around him laughed heartily at his outbursts, often joining in. Their jeers and catcalls added another layer to the already chaotic soundscape of the prison block.

"Shut it, Briggs," Alex called down, his voice carrying easily to the big man.

"Or what?" Briggs shot back. "Are you gonna put me in prison?" He chortled with laughter. "Hey, little girl!" he cried, trying to get Zoe's attention. "Hey blondie! The way you teach firearms, I think you missed your calling as a secretary!"

Zoe didn't give him the time of day. While Alex could deal with Briggs' general heckling, he didn't take well to a direct verbal attack on his team.

"Briggs, that's two," he growled.

"What do I have to do to get three?" Briggs asked. "Oh, I think I know. You're supposed to be clones of the Scarabs, right? So where are your other three members? Not tough enough to make it out here?"

Alex's knuckles whitened around the railing. He let go, charging down four flights of steps.

"Uh-oh," Briggs mocked. "I think I did it this time, boys!"

The other SF prisoners laughed.

Alex stopped in front of Briggs, locking eyes with the bigger man. He could pull his sidearm, shoot him in the head, and none of the people out of the cells with him would care at all. But no matter how much he was taunted, he wouldn't stoop that low.

"I suggest you keep your mouth shut now, Sergeant," he hissed.

"Are you gonna make me?" Briggs asked.

"If you want another beat down, I'd be happy to give it to you. I'm sure the deck plating would love another intimate encounter with your face."

Briggs' grin widened. "Oh, I'm always up for a rematch, pretty boy. Question is, are you? Or are you too busy playing with these sorry excuses for soldiers to remember how real men fight?"

Alex felt a fresh surge of anger. Briggs had been a constant thorn in their side, his running commentary eroding morale and sowing doubts among the less confident trainees. The big man's voice carried an almost supernatural ability to find and exploit every insecurity in the fledgling soldiers. Something had to be done.

"I'll tell you what, Briggs," Alex said, his voice low and controlled. "Let's make a deal. One that might finally put that overactive mouth of yours to good use."

Briggs raised an eyebrow, curiosity replacing his usual sneer. He took a step closer to the forcefield. "I'm listening. What do you propose, maggot?"

"We go another round. Right here, right now. If I win, you stop your constant bitching and start helping us whip these people into fighting shape. Your experience would be valuable, and you know it. Unless, of course, you're all talk and no action."

"And if I win?" Briggs asked, a sinister gleam in his eye. The prisoners on both sides of the cells had started noticing the exchange and slowly begun to fall silent.

"If you win, I'll move you to an officer's berth for the rest of the trip. Better accommodations, better food, more space. Hell, maybe I'll even give you a massage."

A murmur ran through the assembled crowd. Even the other SF prisoners looked intrigued by the proposition, exchanging glances and whispered comments.

Briggs laughed. "Deal. But don't think I'll go easy on you this time. And I want the blonde to be the one to deliver the massage."

Alex reached for the forcefield controls, tapping them to release Briggs from his cell. He half-expected the man to bullrush him and try to toss him from the catwalk, but Briggs simply stepped out, still grinning.

"I'm going to destroy you, maggot," he growled.

"This way," Alex said, leading Briggs to the deck.

"Last chance to back out," he growled. "Spare yourself a world of hurt."

"Save your breath, Briggs," Alex replied, sliding into a fighting stance. "You're going to need it."

The other freed prisoners quickly formed a circle around them, eager for the spectacle. The air was thick with tension, the crowd holding its breath as the two fighters sized each other up.

"Five credits on Gunny," Alex heard someone whisper from the circle's edge.

"You're on," came the reply. "Briggs looks hungry for payback. I bet he takes him down in the first minute."

"Are you kidding?" Jackson scoffed. "Gunny's going to wipe the floor with that gorilla."

Alex tuned out the chatter, focusing entirely on his opponent. Briggs was a formidable fighter, his bulk belying surprising speed and agility. However, Alex had extensive training and experience on his side.

They began to circle each other, each looking for an opening. The crowd's murmurs faded into background noise as Alex studied Briggs' movements, looking for any tell that might give away his initial attack.

Briggs feinted left, his massive fist whistling through the air. Alex started to react but quickly realized it was a trick. The real attack came from the right—a powerful hook aimed at Alex's jaw.

He reacted instinctively, ducking under the blow at the last second. The wind of its passage ruffled his hair. Not wasting the opportunity, he countered with a quick jab to Briggs' solar plexus.

The big man grunted, more annoyed than hurt. "Lucky shot, maggot," he growled. "But luck runs out. Skill is forever."

He pressed forward, using his superior size to try to corner Alex against the circle's edge. Alex allowed himself to be pushed back, his feet sliding across the metal deck plates. He could feel the heat of the crowd at his back.

"Come on, Gunny!" someone shouted. "Don't let that SF bastard push you around!"

Alex ignored the encouragement, staying focused on Briggs. He waited for the right moment, letting the bigger man think he had the advantage.

It came when Briggs overextended on another haymaker. The punch went wide, leaving him off-balance for a crucial second. Alex seized the opportunity, slipping inside Briggs' guard to land a solid combination of two quick jabs to the ribs and a sharp uppercut to the jaw. Each impact sent a jolt up Alex's arm, a testament to Briggs' solid build. The sergeant staggered back, spitting blood.

"That all you got?" Briggs taunted, though Alex could hear the strain in his voice. A thin trickle of blood ran from the corner of his mouth. "I've had love taps harder than that."

They exchanged a flurry of blows, neither giving ground. The sound of flesh striking flesh echoed through the cell block, punctuated by grunts of effort and the occasional gasp from the crowd. Alex's speed and martial arts experience allowed him to land more hits, but Briggs' raw power meant each of his connected strikes took a heavier toll.

"Come on, Sarge!" one of the SF loyalists shouted. "Show this FUP punk what real power looks like!"

The encouragement energized Briggs. He pressed forward with renewed vigor, his massive fists becoming a blur of motion. Alex found himself on the defensive, ducking and weaving to avoid the onslaught.

Suddenly, Briggs caught Alex with a vicious uppercut. The world spun, stars exploding across Alex's vision. The taste of copper filled his mouth as he stumbled backward, barely staying on his feet.

"Not so cocky now, are you, pup?" Briggs sneered, moving in for the finish. "Time to put you down for good."

But Alex had been trained to fight through worse. He shook his head, clearing the cobwebs, and met Briggs' charge head-on. "I'm just getting started, old man," he spat, blood staining his teeth red.

A brutal exchange followed, both men landing and absorbing punishing blows. The crowd around them roared, caught up in the intensity of the fight. "Come on, Gunny!" Jackson yelled. "Remember Jungle!"

"Focus, Gunny!" Zoe added. "Find his weakness and exploit it!"

Alex could hear them shouting encouragement, their voices cutting through the fog of pain and adrenaline, reminding him of what was at stake. This wasn't just about beating Briggs. It was about proving to everyone—the freed prisoners, the SF loyalists, and even himself—that they had a chance against the odds they faced.

With renewed determination, Alex pressed his attack. He ignored the ache in his ribs, the throbbing in his jaw. Every lesson, every hard-won bit of experience, came into play as he searched for an opening.

Finally, he saw it. As Briggs cocked his arm, Alex noticed a slight hesitation, a barely perceptible wince. The big man's earlier beating had left his muscles tight.

Alex ducked low, driving his shoulder into Briggs' midsection. He heard the sergeant's breath leave him in a rush. Grappling, he used Briggs' size against him, pushing him off-balance and sending him crashing to the deck.

The impact was thunderous, Briggs' massive frame hitting the metal floor with enough force to rattle the nearby railings. Before he could recover, Alex was shifting his grip, scissoring the big man's head in a tight chokehold.

Briggs struggled, his face turning red as he tried to break free. His massive hands clawed at Alex's legs, but Alex's technique was flawless, cutting off the blood flow to Briggs' brain.

"Give it up, Briggs," Alex grunted, tightening his hold. "It's over."

For a moment, it seemed like Briggs would keep fighting. His eyes blazed with defiance, his muscles straining against Alex's grip. After what felt like an eternity, Briggs tapped the deck twice. The sound seemed to echo in the sudden silence that had fallen over the cell block.

Alex immediately released him, rolling away and climbing to his feet. He stood there for a moment, chest heaving, as he surveyed the scene. The crowd was silent, watching with bated breath to see what would happen next.

Finally, Alex offered a hand to Briggs. The big man lay there for a moment, staring at the outstretched hand as if it might bite him. Then, with a groan, he accepted it.

As Alex helped Briggs to his feet, a wave of cheers and applause broke out. The freed prisoners celebrated, while the SF prisoners looked on in stunned silence.

"Not bad, Gunny," Briggs wheezed as he found his footing. He rubbed his neck, wincing slightly. "Not bad at all. You didn't learn to fight like that in the FUP Marines. I would know."

"Actually, I did," Alex replied. "But not your FUP Marines. And Force Recon does things a little differently."

Briggs spat a wad of blood onto the deck. "You should have told me up front you were special forces. Maybe I wouldn't have given you so much shit. You hustled me like a champ."

The assembled crowd erupted in a new round of cheers and groans as bets were settled. Alex raised a hand, calling for quiet. It took a moment, but eventually the noise died down, all eyes turning to him expectantly.

"A deal's a deal," he said, still slightly out of breath. "Are you ready to start pulling your weight? These people need all the help they can get if we're going to have any chance on Teegarden."

Briggs looked around at the faces watching him—SF loyalists and freed prisoners eager to learn—all wondering what he would do. For a moment, indecision flickered across his features. Then, with a heavy sigh, he nodded. "Yeah, yeah. A deal's a deal. I'll help you whip these sorry excuses for soldiers into shape. But don't expect me to go easy on them."

Alex grinned, ignoring the twinge of pain from his split lip. "I wouldn't have it any other way."

Briggs turned to face the freed prisoners, his voice booming across the cell block with renewed authority. "Alright, maggots! Get in line! Playtime's over. You want to be real soldiers? I'll show you what that means! By the time I'm done with you, you'll either be the deadliest force on this side of the galaxy, or you'll be begging to go back to your cells!"

As the prisoners scrambled to comply, Alex made his way over to Jackson and Zoe. He could feel the beginnings of what promised to be some impressive bruises, but the sense of accomplishment outweighed the discomfort.

"Not bad, Gunny," Jackson said, clapping him on the shoulder. "Though I think you might have a shiner coming on that left eye. Guess Briggs isn't all talk after all."

Alex winced as he probed the tender area around his eye. "Yeah, he packs quite a punch. It was worth it, though. No offense to either of you, but Briggs has a way of motivating people that you two don't."

"It's called fear of punishment, Gunny," Jackson said.

"Probably not the best approach under normal circumstances, but nothing about this is normal."

"I'm sure they'll forgive me after we liberate Teegarden," Alex said. "We don't have much time left to turn these people into warriors."

"Do you really think we can pull this off?"

Alex nodded grimly. "We have to."

CHAPTER 25

Soren winced as the expected bright flash of light filled the viewscreen, signaling the end of the ten day trip back to the FUP fleet. Outside of the discussions from the first few days, the remainder of the journey had been relatively uneventful. The accommodations were much more enjoyable than the shuttle ride to Glaive, if only for the added space for him to stretch his legs. Although, as much as he didn't want to admit it, a part of him would miss sharing a bunk with this dimension's Jane at night.

Soren waited tensely for confirmation that the fleet was still there. In the back of his mind, he'd worried the SF had discovered their location through another spy. As the light faded and the sensors came fully online, a cluster of ships materialized both on the grid and against the backdrop of stars, their familiar silhouettes a welcome sight.

Relief washed over Soren. He immediately sought out the Wraith, its unique form standing out among the other vessels. Beside him, Jane let out a soft exhale, her gaze locked on her own flagship, the Spirit of War.

"There they are," she murmured, a hint of emotion

coloring her voice. "I wasn't sure if, after everything that's happened..."

Soren nodded, understanding the unspoken fear. He placed a reassuring hand on her shoulder. "I know," he said softly. "I was a little worried too. But here they are."

Their moment of relief was interrupted by Private Rivera's voice, sharp and alert from her station. "Incoming fighters, sir!" she called out. "Three squadrons breaking formation and heading our way. They're moving fast!"

"The Hooligans," Soren guessed, noting the number of marks on the tactical display, leading a pair of full squadrons in a wide formation. "And it looks like they've brought some friends."

"They're taking up escort positions," Haji reported, her tone professional but with an undercurrent of admiration. "Impressive response time. Whoever's in command over there doesn't mess around."

"Speaking of which, we're being hailed," Rivera said.

"Put it through," Kostas ordered from the command station.

"Unidentified vessel, this is Commander Jack Harper of the Wraith. You have entered restricted space. Identify yourself and state your intentions immediately. Any hostile action will be met with lethal force."

Major Kosta raised an eyebrow, looking at Soren. "Care to answer, Captain?" he asked with a grin. "I'd suggest we don't keep them waiting too long. Those fighters look like they mean business."

Soren nodded to Rivera to open the comms. He couldn't help the smile that expanded across his face as he responded. "Jack, it's Soren. You can tell Minh to stand down before he gets trigger-happy. It's just us, and some new friends."

There was a moment of stunned silence before Jack's relieved voice returned. "Captain? You couldn't have given us a heads up? We were about to go to battle stations. I've got pilots out there with itchy trigger fingers and a crew that's been on edge since you left."

"Sorry about that," Soren replied. "It's been an interesting whirlwind of a trip. We didn't exactly have time to send a postcard."

Jack's sigh was audible through the comm system. "I bet," he said, a hint of curiosity creeping into his voice. "How did it go? Were you able to convince the CIP to stop sitting on their asses?"

Soren glanced at Jane, who nodded slightly, her expression cautious. "We had some success," he said carefully, choosing his words with deliberation. "But it's probably best if we go over everything in person. There's a lot to discuss, Jack."

"Well, we'd better make it soon," Jack replied. "We're scheduled to depart for Teegarden in less than twenty-four hours. With everything that happened at FOB Alpha and Gray still MIA, the whole fleet's been on edge. Whatever you've brought back with you, I hope it's good news. We could use some of that right about now."

"It is," Soren assured him, his voice firm and confident. "We'll be docking shortly. Have the senior staff ready for briefing. Trust me, Jack, you're going to want to hear this firsthand."

As the comm channel closed, Soren turned to Captain Haji. The Athena's commander sat ramrod straight in her seat, her hands poised over the controls. "Bring us in nice and easy, Captain," Soren instructed.

Haji looked to Major Kosta, who nodded his approval of the order. "Aye, sir," she replied, deftly managing the flight controls as she guided the Athena toward the larger vessel. As they drew closer, Haji's eyes widened in appreciation, a soft whistle escaping her lips. "That's quite a ship," she murmured, her voice filled with admiration. "I've never seen anything quite like it. The design is sort of familiar, like a modified Komodo, but the color…what's the hull made from, if you don't mind me asking, Captain?"

"The hull is standard alloy," Soren replied. "But it's coated with a specialized material that when provided an electric current can bend both light and sensor signals around it."

"Like an invisibility cloak?" Kosta asked.

"Precisely," Soren replied.

"We sure could use something like that on the Athena, sir," Swix commented from the tactical station. "You don't have any more of that paint, do you, Captain?"

Soren chuckled. "I wish we did. One good hit on our hull and our stealth technology is done for."

The Athena approached the Wraith, maneuvering into position along the port side. Haji eased the ship in with practiced precision, aligning the two airlocks before giving Athena a soft push sideways with vectoring thrusters. The two ships came together with barely a whisper, the connection smooth and seamless.

"Docking complete," Haji reported.

"Put the reactor on standby," Kosta ordered.

"Yes, sir," she replied, tapping her console before rising from her seat. Soren felt the slight change in the vibrations through the hull as the reactor powered down. Major Kosta reached his control surface, opening a ship-wide comm. "Sergeant Volkov, meet me at the starboard airlock." He disconnected before the sergeant could respond and nodded to Jane and Soren. "Shall we?"

When they arrived, Volkov was already waiting at the airlock, coming to attention at their approach. Major Kosta set her at ease before opening the Athena's hatch himself. The Wraith's hatch opened simultaneously, and the difference in air pressure caused Soren's ears to pop.

Soren found himself face-to-face with Jack and, unexpectedly, Dana. He maintained a professional demeanor for a moment, but the sight of his daughter broke through his composure. Without hesitation, he stepped through the open hatches and pulled her into a tight embrace.

"Dad," Dana whispered, her voice thick with emotion. Her arms wrapped around him, holding on as if afraid he might disappear again. "I'm glad you're back."

After a moment, he released her, turning to Jack. The two men clasped hands firmly, years of friendship and shared experiences passing between them in that simple gesture.

"Welcome back, Captain," Jack said. "The Wraith is yours again. She's missed you. We all have."

"Thank you," Soren replied. "Jack and Dana, I'd like you to meet Major Frank Kosta and Sergeant Elena Volkov."

To Soren's surprise, a flicker of recognition passed across Jack's face. His eyes narrowed slightly, a thoughtful expression settling over his features. "The Lammergeiers?" he asked.

The shock on the CIP operatives' faces was evident. "How do you know that?" Kosta asked suspiciously. "Our unit is need-to-know within the CIP, never mind outside of it."

Jack held up his hands placatingly, a wry smile playing at the corners of his mouth. "I thought I recognized your ship on the way in. You just confirmed it for me. But there's no need for alarm. The CIP in our dimension was rolled into the FUP years ago. The Lammergeiers where we're from are part of our military."

"I see," Kosta said, clearly relieved. "Well, it looks like we're on the same side, again."

Jack turned to Jane, who had been observing the exchange with quiet amusement. "Does this mean the CIP has agreed to join our fight?"

"It does," she replied. "It wasn't easy, but we managed to convince them of the urgency of our situation."

Jack's eyes narrowed as he took in Jane's appearance, noticing how she held her arm close to her body. Although she had stopped wearing the sling after a few days on board the Athena, she still needed to regain her range of motion.

"Are you okay, Admiral?" he asked, concern evident. "What happened out there?"

Jane waved off his concern. "Nothing a bit of physical therapy won't fix," she assured him. "The Strickland Federation wasn't too eager to see us meeting with the Coalition, and did their best to stop us." She glanced at Soren. "Your Captain is proficient in more than just commanding starships."

Jack grinned. "After spending time in the so-called hospitality of the CIP, he decided he would never be an easy target again. I'm willing to bet you could run with the Lammergeiers if you wanted, Soren."

"I wouldn't go that far," Soren replied. "But it does mean a lot to me to be able to protect myself and those I care about."

Jane's face flushed slightly at his response. She recovered quickly. "The important thing is that our mission was a success. I'll head back to my ship after we brief your crew."

"Speaking of which, Jack, I'll need you to gather our staff," Soren said, his voice taking on the authoritative tone of a captain addressing his XO. "We have a lot to go over, and not much time in which to do it. The clock's ticking on Teegarden, and we need to be ready."

"Aye, sir," Jack replied, tapping his comm unit to relay the order to Samira. "They'll be assembled in the conference room in ten minutes."

As they made their way through the familiar corridors

of the Wraith, Soren couldn't help but feel a sense of home-coming. The ship hummed with life around him, each face they passed lighting up with recognition and relief at his return. Crew members smiled and offered warm words of welcome. The energy in the air was palpable, a mixture of excitement and nervous anticipation.

When they reached the conference room, Soren found the senior staff—Ethan, Keira, Liam, Tashi, Wilf, Dana, and Minh—already assembled. They sat around the large table, their expressions a mix of curiosity and relief. As Soren entered, they rose to their feet, a gesture of respect that touched him deeply.

He took his place at the head of the table while Kosta and Volkov found seats next to Jack. The room fell silent, all eyes fixed on him, waiting for him to speak.

"Welcome back, Captain!" Tashi blurted before he could.

"Yeah, welcome back, sir. We missed you," Wilf added, his fingers waving hello. "Ship's not the same without you."

Given the opportunity, the others offered similar words of welcome before Soren raised his hands to quiet them.

"Thank you all," he said. "It's good to be back. You certainly know how to make a man feel needed. Now, I expect this to be a brief meeting, but there are some developments I wanted to share with you right away. None of what I'm going to say is classified, and can be disseminated to your teams at your convenience." He paused to gather his thoughts before speaking again. "Most importantly, my mission with Admiral Yarborough to Glaive was a success. The Coalition of Independent Planets has agreed to join our fight against the Strickland Federation."

A wave of murmurs swept through the room, echoing shock, excitement, and disbelief.

Soren held up a hand, again calling for silence. The room quieted immediately. "I know this is a lot to take in," he continued, his voice steady and reassuring. "It changes the entire scope of our mission and this war. That's why I've asked Major Kosta and Sergeant Volkov to join us. They represent an elite CIP unit known as the Lammergeiers, and they're going to be instrumental in our assault on Teegarden."

Soren quickly laid out the plan, and Kosta and Volkov filled in the details of their roles in the ground assault. There were few questions, and the meeting ended within twenty minutes.

As the others filed out of the conference room, Soren caught Liam's eye. The lieutenant had been quiet throughout most of the briefing, his expression one of concentration as he absorbed the details of the plan. "Lieutenant, a word," Soren said, gesturing for him to stay behind.

Once the room had cleared, Soren made introductions. "Major Kosta, Sergeant Volkov, this is Lieutenant Liam Moffit. Liam is in command of the Marines on board."

"What's left of them, anyway," Liam said, his eyes expressing his displeasure over the possible fate of the rest of his men. "I'm happy to meet you. After what happened at the SF space station, especially after losing the Scorpions, we're seriously lacking in the kind of experience your squad can provide."

"Thank you, Lieutenant," Kosta said. "Captain Strickland told us about the mission, and the reasons things went poorly. I'm sorry for your losses. I'm sure it weighs heavily on you."

"That it does," Liam agreed.

"Liam," Soren said, "I want you to work closely with Major Kosta and his squad. Your units will be operating in tandem during the ground assault, and I need you to be in perfect sync."

"Of course, Captain." Liam glanced hopefully at Kosta. "I don't suppose your Lammergeiers are power-armored?"

"When the need arises," Kosta replied with a grin.

"Our Phalanx armor is superior to the SF's Kurota model," Volkov said. "With a higher density at a lower weight and a more powerful jet pack."

"Of course, the armor's always only as good as the Marine wearing it," Kosta said. "And we're the best."

"I wouldn't mind seeing your best go toe-to-toe with the Captain's son," Liam said. "For sport, of course."

"I hope we have that chance," Volkov said. "It's my personal objective to find Gunnery Sergeant Strickland and what's left of his squad among the prisoners."

"This mission is going to push all of us to our limits," Soren interjected, uncomfortable with the discussion turning to Alex. "We need every advantage we can get. Make it work. Train together, learn from each other. When we hit the ground on Teegarden, I want your teams coordinating like parts of the same body."

Liam straightened, a look of fierce determination crossing his face. "You can count on us, sir. We won't let you down."

"Good," Soren replied. "The Athena will remain docked with us for the fold, so you'll have every opportunity to train together for this."

"Yes, sir."

"Major Kosta, Liam can show you to the Marine barracks we've set up in the lower decks. If you'll excuse me, I have other matters to attend to."

"Of course, Captain," Kosta said.

With that settled, Soren made his way to the bridge, his mind already cycling through the details that needed attention before their departure. As he stepped through the hatch, a hush fell over the room, followed quickly by a burst of applause. The crew rose to their feet, faces beaming with relief and joy at his return.

"Welcome back, Captain," Mark called out.

Samira stepped forward, a warm smile on her face. "It's good to have you back, sir," she said. "Things just haven't been the same without you."

Like in the conference room, Soren was touched by the display. He looked around the bridge, taking in the familiar faces of his crew. Each one of them had sacrificed their lives back on Earth for him. Their loyalty and determination never ceased to amaze.

"It's good to be back," he said, his voice carrying across the bridge. He moved to the command station. "We've got one hell of a fight ahead of us, but looking around this room, I know we're ready for it. Each and every one of you has proven your mettle time and again. Now, we're going to show the Strickland Federation exactly what we're made of."

As he settled into the captain's chair, Soren felt a sense of rightness wash over him. The familiar contours of the seat, the hum of the ship's systems around him, and the quiet efficiency of his crew all came together to form a feeling of home. They had a long way to go, and the odds were stacked against them. But he knew he had the right people to go to war with him.

They were as ready as they would ever be.

CHAPTER 26

Alex kept his gaze fixed on the viewscreen as the dazzling flash of exiting fold space signaled their arrival. Jackson and Zoe stood nearby, while a unit of former prisoners outfitted in the arms and armor intended for the ship's guards stood close to each of the ship's bridge crew, ready to deal with them if they made any attempts to sabotage the planned attack.

"Remember, Hayes," Alex said, his voice low and menacing as he addressed the ship's commander. "Don't try anything stupid. You'll be dead before you can finish uttering any kind of warning. We have the clearance codes, which means we don't really need you anymore."

Hayes' jaw clenched, a muscle twitching in his cheek as he fought to maintain his composure. His eyes darted between Alex and the armed ex-prisoners, and then he nodded jerkily at Alex, "I'll comply," he said, his voice tight with barely contained anxiety backed by anger. "Just so you know, it won't be long before I'm standing over your corpse, laughing at you for thinking you could fight back against the Federation." The commander's eyes hardened, his voice taking on a tone of grim satisfaction as he continued. "You think you're clever, hijacking this ship, planning your little revolution. But you have no idea what you're walking into. You'll be slaughtered the moment you leave this ship."

Alex met Hayes' scowl with a cool stare of his own, unimpressed by the man's weak attempt at bravado. "Doubtful," he replied, his voice steady and confident. "You just do your job and get us to the surface without any trouble, and you'll keep breathing." His lips thinned, and he looked away.

As the brightness faded, the reddish brown orb of Teegarden filled the viewscreen. Alex's eyes narrowed, his attention immediately drawn to the dozens of silhouettes surrounding the planet.

"What the hell?" Jackson breathed beside him.

Orbiting the world were nearly two dozen warships, a combination of Rhinos, Komodos, and Valkyries that put the FUP's ragtag fleet to shame.

"This can't be right," Zoe added.

"I don't understand," Hayes muttered. Even he was surprised by the sight. "Why are there so many ships here? This doesn't make any sense. We've never had more than a token defensive force in orbit."

A flicker of unease disturbed Alex's gut. He scanned the assembled warships, searching for the Fist of Justice. To his relief, the massive dreadnought was nowhere to be seen among the orbiting vessels.

"They're not here for us," Alex said. "They're here for my father."

"Your father?" Hayes asked.

"Captain Soren Strickland."

Hayes tilted his head like a confused dog. Alex had explained the situation to the freed prisoners, but he'd never bothered to do the same for Hayes or his bridge crew.

"Do you think your father knows you're on your way here?" Jackson asked.

"I don't know. Maybe Strickland thinks he might come for us but isn't quite sure. That would explain why these ships are here, but the Fist isn't."

"Yeah," Zoe said. "It's not like he would go out of his way to rescue his kid if the shoe was on the other foot. He treats Alexander like shit."

"And Alexander takes it," Jackson said. "I'd feel bad for the guy if he hadn't been such an asshole to us." His tone darkened considerably. "If he hadn't killed Malik in cold blood."

"I don't have any sympathy for Alexander," Alex said. "He could have followed his mother and tried to do the right thing. He made his choice."

"Never mind Alexander," Jackson said, his voice low as he leaned in close to Alex. His eyes were fixed on the orbiting warships, a hint of worry creeping into his usually confident demeanor. "I don't like this, Gunny. That's a lot of firepower out there. Maybe we should reconsider our approach. It would take about five seconds for them to turn us into space dust."

"What choice do we have?" Zoe asked, her voice tight. "We can't exactly turn back now. What are we going to do, free all the guards and go back to our cells? 'Sorry for the inconvenience, we've changed our minds about this whole escape thing.' Yeah, I'm sure that'll go over well."

Alex took a deep breath, pushing aside his unease. When he spoke, his voice was steady and confident, carrying across the bridge. "Everything continues according to plan," he said firmly. "As long as we make it to the surface, we can free the prisoners. That's our primary objective, and it hasn't changed. We knew this wouldn't be easy, but we've come too far to back down now."

"And what happens when they start bombarding our

asses?" Jackson pressed, gesturing toward the viewscreen and the looming threat beyond. "Once we reach the surface, we'll be sitting ducks in a barrel."

"Don't combine idioms," Zoe said. "It's annoying."

"That doesn't change the point I'm making."

"The mines are too deep underground," Alex countered, his tone reassuring. "Bombardment wouldn't be an effective tactic. They'll have to deal with us on the ground. A counter attack. But I'm willing to bet those ships aren't carrying a lot of Marines. They were sent here to take out the FUP fleet, not launch a ground assault. By the time they're ready to hit back at us, we'll have the former prisoners armed and the entire place fortified."

"So let's say we take the colony," Jackson said. "Then what? Even if we can hold the SF ground forces back, we'll be trapped down there with no way off this rock. It's not like we can just hop on a shuttle and fly away with that fleet up there."

"Then we wait for our people to arrive," Alex said. "My father is coming, Jackson. I'm sure of it, and that fleet out there is proof. We just need to hold out until he gets here. Then our odds will be as good as they were ever going to get."

Before Jackson could hypothesize further, the comm station lit up.

"Commander, we're being hailed," the Ensign at the station said, looking over his shoulder at Hayes.

"Put it through," he replied.

A crisp, professional voice filled the bridge, cutting through the tension. "PTV-194, this is Teegarden Orbital Control. Welcome home. Transmit authorization codes for verification."

Alex pressed his sidearm against Hayes' temple, his meaning clear. The cool metal against his skin made the commander flinch slightly. Hayes swallowed hard, a bead of sweat trickling down his forehead, then began reciting the codes in a steady voice that belied the fear in his eyes.

There was a moment of tense silence as they waited for a response. Finally, the controller's voice returned, sounding bored and unaware of the drama unfolding on the incoming ship. "Codes verified. You are cleared for landing at dock two. Proceed on your current vector." A collective sigh of relief passed through the bridge.

Alex jogged Hayes with his sidearm. "Take us down," the commander ordered. "Nice and easy. Let's not give them any reason to suspect anything is wrong. I like my brain inside my skull."

The prison ship began its descent toward the surface of Teegarden b. Their ride down was smooth as they dropped through the thin layer of gasses surrounding the world. The barren landscape grew larger in the viewscreen, a sea of reddish-brown rock and dust stretching to the horizon. Jagged mountains rose in the distance, their peaks sharp and unweathered in the thin atmosphere.

As they neared the surface, the penal colony came into view. It already felt familiar to Alex after spending so much time staring at it with Cassandra and the Scorpions. Unlike the stored orbital imagery, a pair of ships were already docked at the thin terminals on the landing slab.

"Not getting off to a good start," Jackson commented. "More ships means more guards."

"Look on the bright side," Zoe countered. "It also means more ordinance to outfit the freed prisoners with once we're done kicking ass."

"True," Jackson admitted.

The helmsman guided the ship toward dock two, his hands steady on the controls despite the pressure of the moment. As they touched down, Alex noticed umbilicals stretching out to connect with their ship's exterior hatch to allow them to disembark. The facade of normalcy masked the tension thrumming across the bridge and, no doubt, across the ship.

"This is it," Alex said, his voice carrying across the bridge. He turned to Zoe and Jackson. "Three, Five, you're with me. We need to coordinate the initial push." Then, addressing the rest of the freed prisoners on the bridge, he continued, "The rest of you, escort the bridge crew to the cell block. Make sure they're secure. We can't afford any surprises."

As the freed prisoners moved to comply, Alex led his fellow Scorpions off the bridge. They made their way through the ship's corridors, their anticipation mounting with each step.

When they reached the main hatch, they found Cassandra, Decker, and the assault force waiting for them. The group was a mix of FUP spies and sympathizers, along with ordinary citizens caught up in Strickland's oppressive regime, now united in purpose. Each face was set with resolve, though Alex could also see the trepidation and fear dancing across the eyes of the least experienced among them.

Decker stepped forward, his tattooed arms crossed over his chest. "We're ready," he said, his voice low and intense. "Just say the word."

Alex looked around at the faces of the men and women who had followed him this far. They weren't professional soldiers, but they had something just as powerful driving them—the burning desire for freedom.

"This is it," Alex said. "Everything we've trained for comes down to this moment. We're not just fighting for ourselves. We're fighting for every prisoner in that colony, for everyone who's suffered under Strickland's rule." He paused, making eye contact with as many of his people as he could. "Remember your training. Watch each other's backs. Move fast, hit hard, and don't give them time to regroup. And no matter what happens, don't give up. We're in this together, and we're going to see it through to the end."

The faces around him hardened, hands tightening on weapons. Alex could feel the energy in the air, a palpable sense of anticipation and courage.

"One last thing," Alex added, a fierce grin spreading across his face. "Let's show these SF bastards what happens when mess with us."

With that, he turned to the hatch controls. Everything that followed would depend on what happened in the next few minutes. A single wave of hesitation crashed through him, but he rode it out, refusing to give in to his doubts. He took a deep breath, steeling himself for what was to come. He could hear the steady breathing of his team behind him and feel their eyes on his back. This was it. The point of no return.

"Ready?" he asked, glancing over his shoulder at Zoe and Jackson.

They nodded, their expressions mirroring his own.

"Born ready, Gunny," Jackson said. "Let's go create some mayhem."

CHAPTER 27

Alex's hand hovered over the hatch controls, his heart pounding. The moment of truth had arrived. With a deep breath, he pressed the button, and the hatch hissed open.

The docking terminal beyond was a stark, utilitarian space. Harsh lights illuminated the gray synthcrete floor and walls, creating shadows in every corner. A handful of SF personnel stood near a bank of computer terminals, their faces transitioning from boredom to shock as they registered the armed group emerging from the ship.

"Now!" Alex shouted, his voice echoing off the bare walls.

The freed prisoners surged forward, their weapons already raised. The air filled with the sharp crack of gunfire as they opened up on the stunned SF crew. Spouts of crimson erupted from their bodies as they crumpled to the floor, puddles pooling on the pristine gray surfaces.

One of the SF technicians managed to dive behind a console, fumbling for his sidearm. Alex tracked his movement, squeezing off two quick shots. The bullets punched through the thin metal of the console, eliciting a cry of pain from behind it.

"Move, move!" Alex urged, leading the charge across the terminal. "Decker, leave a team here to secure the area."

Decker nodded, motioning to one of his six-person squads. "You heard the man! Lock this place down!"

Alex led the main force toward a set of heavy doors at the far end of the terminal. A sign above them read "PRIMARY INTAKE."

"This way," Alex cried, leading them toward the doors, pushing through to the bridge leading from the landing slab to the rest of the facility inside the cliff face. With the element of surprise still intact, the prison workers at the far end had yet to notice them, but that wouldn't last for long.

They charged across the bridge, their footsteps thundering on the metal grating. The sound drew the attention of the workers, freezing most of them in shock. Three of them had already fallen by the time they recovered, the majority turning tail and trying to get away. At the end of the main corridor, a guard fumbled with the controls to seal the doors leading into the main intake area.

"Five!" Alex shouted.

Zoe had already raised her rifle. She took a split-second to aim, and fired. The guard's head snapped back, a spray of red misting the control panel. His body slumped forward into the doorway, holding the door open.

"Nice shot," Alex said as they reached the threshold. "Keep going!"

They poured into the primary intake area, a cavernous space with rows of processing stations ahead of three doors that branched off in three directions. Alex knew from Briggs that one led to the mines and prison, one to the guard barracks, mess hall and kitchens, and the other to administration and the prison control room. A handful of guards had managed to take up defensive positions behind overturned metal desks and steel barriers.

"Take cover!" Alex yelled as bullets began to whistle past them.

The freed prisoners scattered, diving behind whatever shelter they could find. Alex found himself crouched behind a heavy metal desk, Jackson and Zoe on either side of him.

"Suppressing fire!" Alex ordered. "We need to push through!"

The air filled with the deafening roar of gunfire as both sides exchanged volleys. A burst of fire from an SF guard shredded the desk next to Alex, sending splinters of metal flying. He felt a sharp sting as a fragment grazed his cheek, drawing blood.

"We can't get bogged down here," Zoe shouted over the din. "We need to keep moving!"

Alex nodded. "Three, flank left. Five, right. I'll draw their fire. On my mark!"

He waited for a lull in the shooting. "Now!" he shouted when he saw it, bursting from cover.

He sprinted across the open space, zigzagging to make himself a harder target. Bullets whizzed past him, so close he could feel their passage disturbing the air. One hit him in the chest, failing to penetrate his armor but knocking the breath out of him before he ducked behind a divider. Hoping that out of sight meant out of mind, he knew the divider wasn't thick enough to stop a bullet. He was getting his air back, but his chest throbbed where the first round had impacted. He didn't need another one.

With the guards zeroing in on him, Jackson and Zoe maneuvered to better positions. They opened fire from Alex's flanks, catching the defenders by surprise and giving him cover.

Their success motivated the freed prisoners, who broke cover to charge the guards, rifles spewing slugs that chewed through the flimsy desks some of the enemy had chosen for cover. Return fire chattered back at them from behind a sturdy steel, open-frame staircase leading up to the second floor, where there were more offices. Those rounds found many of their marks, picking off the freed prisoners in the lead. Even so, their superior numbers quickly overwhelmed the stairwell defenders.

They'd gained a foothold, but at a high cost. Bodies lay scattered across the floor, a mix of SF guards and too many of their own people.

Alex motioned to the door on the right. "They've got us pinned down here. We need to reach the control room, now!"

"I can take care of that for you," Decker said, dropping down at his elbow after catching up to him. "Just give me platoons four and five and consider it done."

Alex reached into his pants pocket, withdrawing a pair of comms units. They had found a limited number in the armory, too few to pass out to everyone. He handed one to Decker. "Do it," he told Decker, hanging the other around his right ear like an old-fashioned hearing aid.

Decker grinned and turned to the fighters. "Platoons Four and Five, you're with me!" he cried, eliciting a round of shouts from the members of the two groups. They following him to the right, quickly regrouping into practiced formations before disappearing through the doorway. Moments later, gunfire echoed from the direction, fading quickly as the teams swept through whatever defenses they encountered.

"Rojas!" Alex called out, getting the attention of the FUP Marine-turned-spy. He held a comms unit out to him. "Take platoons six and seven through the door on the left. Hit the guard barracks and cut them off before they can reinforce the deeper positions, then clear the mess hall and kitchen. We can't afford to get boxed in."

Rojas, a short, muscular man with a handsome face,

accepted the comm with an overly bright smile. "Consider your ass covered, Gunny," he said before turning to his group and shouting for them to follow.

"The rest of you are with me! We're going to take the cell blocks!" Alex shouted before pressing his hand to the comms unit. "Decker, Rojas, comms check."

"Copy, Gunny," Decker said.

"Copy," Rojas replied.

The remaining group of over a hundred fighters followed Alex as he pressed on, moving deeper into the compound. The utilitarian architecture—bare concrete walls, harsh lighting—continued, with an oppressive sense of confinement at every turn. They encountered sporadic pockets of resistance, but as expected, the entire colony was unprepared for an attack that originated from one of their ships. Then, alarms began to blare throughout the facility.

"Looks like someone finally managed to sound the alert," Jackson said.

"Then we'd better pick up the pace," Alex replied. "We need to get into the prison blocks before the guards can lock them down."

They pushed forward with renewed urgency, the fighting growing more intense as they encountered larger groups of defenders. Both sides took losses, the corridors echoing with screams of pain and the relentless chatter of gunfire.

After what felt like an eternity, they finally reached a massive set of blast doors that, according to Briggs, led to the cell blocks and mines. Unfortunately, the doors were sealed tight in response to the blaring alarms, leaving the area beyond them unreachable.

"Damn it," Alex growled, slamming his fist against the unyielding metal. "We're moving too slow." He put his hand to his comms unit. "Decker, what's your status?"

"Almost at the control room, Gunny," he replied. "There are more of these bastards here than I expected."

"We need the blast doors leading to the prisoners open asap," Alex snapped.

"On it."

Alex turned to Zoe. "Decker's getting hung up trying to reach the control room. Can you crack that thing?" He motioned to the door's control panel.

"I think *I* can," Cassandra said, stepping forward. She examined the control panel, her eyes narrowing. "Zoe, can you get the cover off this thing?"

Zoe joined her, pulling the limited tools she had collected from the prison ship from her pocket. "Just give me a minute."

Zoe quickly removed the panel's cover, and while she and Cassandra spoke in hushed tones about the wiring, the others took a knee behind them. Watching anxiously, they were acutely aware that every passing second gave the defenders more time to prepare for their attack.

"Cassandra?" Alex asked impatiently after a few tense minutes.

"Almost there," she answered.

"Everyone, get ready," Alex ordered, all of them taking cover behind the door frame. "They've had time to set up a defense."

"Got it!" With a spark and then a whiff of ozone, the blast doors began to groan open. Cassandra and Zoe immediately ducked out of the line of fire as a hail of gunfire blasted through the opening.

The SF guards had fortified their positions in the hollowed-out cavern, which appeared to be storage for the processed minerals and an overflow area for mining equipment. The guards had hastily moved the massive pieces of mining equipment and large wheeled crates filled with ore into a barricade stretching across the breadth of the cavern's stone floor. At least two dozen defenders peeked out from the spaces between them or rested their rifles across the tops, only the top of their heads visible.

Behind them was the wide-open tunnel entrance leading to the prison cells, and the mine tunnels blasted down through a hundred or more feet of rock. Additional guards had taken positions around the cavernous area.

"Three, Five, we have the flanks," Alex called out. "Push forward!"

He rushed through the open doors into the massive room, cutting to the right while Jackson and Zoe went left. Almost immediately, a pair of rounds impacted his body armor, one to his shoulder, another to his left hip, the force nearly knocking him off his feet. The pain was excruciating, but he ignored it and pressed on, his weapon blazing.

The freed prisoners followed his lead, letting out a collective roar as they surged forward, spreading throughout the cavern. The scene was pure chaos. The deafening rattle of gunfire, the screams of the wounded, the stench of discharged weapons.

Alex picked off two guards trying to fire at him from behind the first stack of crates, their heads snapping back as his rounds found their targets. He took off again, dropping into a slide around the corner of another crate. The guards hiding there, expecting him to come around at a run at his full height, had aimed too high, their bullets whipping well over his head as he shot from the hip. His rounds sprayed the four enemy guards, chewing into their body armor before finding flesh and killing all four.

Alex dropped down behind the crates, exchanging his spent rifle with one of the enemy's and then rifling through the man's zippered pockets, pulling out several fresh magazines for his new gun.

"Gunny, we have the control room," Decker reported in his ear. "What do you need us to do?"

"Stand by," Alex snapped back, shoving the spare cartridges into an empty compartment in his armor. "Rojas, sitrep."

"Guard barracks is quiet as a graveyard, Gunny. Because we turned it into one. The kitchen and mess are secure."

"Copy. Both of you, leave a squad to hold each space. I need the rest of you over here at the mine entrance, asap." Both of them confirmed they were on their way.

Alex sprinted toward the following stack of crates, rifle spitting rounds into the guards, who hadn't realized he was even there. Swapping magazines without slowing, the enemy went down one after another, reacting too slowly to save themselves.

Ahead of him, he could hear the cries of the freed prisoners, who had rushed the forward barricades and were now struggling to break through the defenses. He quickly scaled the crates, hopping from one to the next like a video game character. From that high ground, he unleashed hell on the defenders below, wiping out half a dozen before his rifle clicked empty. He drew his sidearm, but as bullets blazed his way, he jumped back behind cover.

Answering gunfire exploded from the opposite flank until the fire targeting him went silent. He peeked from cover, and there, coming out from behind the barricades, were Zoe and a grinning Jackson.

"Don't say we never saved your bacon, Gunny," Jackson said, circling the crates and vaulting the barricade just ahead of the rest of their forces.

"I know better than you that I couldn't do this without you and Zoe, but let's keep moving, We're not done yet," he said as he took stock of the situation. They had suffered more losses, but they had broken through. The path to the mines lay open before them.

They pressed deeper into the complex, the air growing

cooler and damper, carrying the musty scent of earth and rock. The walls were rough-hewn stone, supported by thick metal beams. Overhead, a complex network of pipes and conduits snaked along the ceiling. The steady hum of machinery grew louder as they progressed, punctuated by the occasional hiss or clang of distant equipment.

As they reached the door leading to the prison cells, the sounds of gunfire erupted once more. But this time, it wasn't directed at them. "They're shooting the prisoners!" someone shouted, just as Alex realized the same thing, his blood running cold.

A wave of fury swept through the group. Without waiting for orders, the freed prisoners charged through the doors.

"Wait!" Alex called out, but it was too late. The group surged ahead, heedless of the danger.

Bursting through an abandoned security checkpoint and continuing deeper, they followed the source of the gunfire, instantly stymied by a sealed blast door.

"Decker," Alex said through his comms.

"Yeah, boss?" Decker replied. They had gone so deep, his voice crackled in Alex's ear, along with almost too much static to understand him.

"We need the cell block doors unlocked."

"Which ones?"

"All of them."

"Your wish is my command."

The light over the door went from red to green. The others, seeing this, roared as they yanked it open and charged through.

The scene that greeted them was one of horror. SF guards were methodically moving from cell to cell, executing the prisoners inside. Bodies lay slumped on the floor, exterminated like rats in a cage.

The freed prisoners fell upon the guards with unbridled

ferocity. It was less a battle than a slaughter, the guards overwhelmed by the sheer numbers and rage of their attackers. Those who tried to surrender were shown no mercy, cut down where they stood.

Alex pushed his way to the front of the group, his stomach churning at the carnage around him. "Enough!" he shouted. "We need to save those we can!"

His words seemed to break through the red haze of vengeance. The freed prisoners began to focus on opening cells, helping the shocked and terrified inmates to safety.

Alex moved from cell to cell, his heart heavy. So many lives lost, so needlessly. But as he continued, he found more survivors—miners huddled in the backs of their cells, eyes wide with fear and disbelief.

"It's okay," he said softly, helping a trembling woman to her feet. "We're here to get you out. You're safe now."

As the reality of their rescue began to sink in, the freed miners began to rally. Those who were able-bodied volunteered to guide them to other areas of the complex.

"There are more cell blocks deeper in," one grizzled miner told Alex. His face was lined from years of hard labor, his hands calloused and scarred. "And the main shaft access is past them. That's where the bulk of us are, out working the mines. There are some in sorting and processing too. I just hope they haven't killed them all by now."

"Do you know how to shoot?" Alex asked.

The man grinned. "Lance Corporal Leon Brown, FUP Marines." His eyes narrowed. "You know, you look a lot like—"

"Alexander Strickland," Alex finished for him. "I get that a lot. But I'm with the FUP." He handed Leon a rifle from one of the downed guards. "Lead the way. As we go, we'll free as many as we can."

The militia split up, with multiple groups entering the

different tunnels leading deeper into the bowels of the mining complex. The deeper they went, the temperature rose noticeably, fed by the heat deeper within the planet. The twisting rock passages and steep inclines began to glisten with moisture. The hotter it became, the thicker the air grew. It was laden with dust and the tang of industrial chemicals. Harsh work lights cast shadows through the gloom, creating an eerie, otherworldly atmosphere.

They encountered more guards as they went, but they were disorganized and demoralized. Many surrendered without a fight, while others were quickly overwhelmed. As Alex and his group moved through a narrow passageway lined with massive drills and rock crushers, a group of guards ambushed them from behind a large excavator.

The initial volley caught two of the freed prisoners in the back, dropping them before they could react. Alex found cover behind the treads of a hauler, bullets ringing out against its metal frame. "Five, left flank!" he shouted. "Three, suppressing fire!"

The Scorpions moved with practiced efficiency, their coordinated assault quickly turning the tables on the ambushers. Within minutes, the last of the guards had fallen or surrendered.

Finally, they reached the main mining shaft. It was a vast cavern easily a few hundred meters across and descending into inky blackness. The smell of raw ore and machinery oil hung heavy in the air. It was so thick with dust now that breathing was nearly impossible.

Here, they found the last organized group of defenders, but as Alex and his forces poured into the cavern, weapons at the ready, he saw the fight go out of the guards' eyes. They laid down their weapons one by one, raising their hands in surrender.

As the last guards were secured, Alex allowed himself a

moment to catch his breath. They had done it. Against all odds, they had taken the compound.

"Gunny," Jackson said, approaching with a grin. "I gotta say, that was easier than I thought it would be."

Alex's face remained bereft of a matching smile. "Don't get too comfortable, Three. Taking the compound was the easy part. Now comes the hard part...keeping it."

CHAPTER 28

Alex stood at the edge of the main mining shaft, his eyes scanning the vast cavern before him.

A complex network of catwalks and scaffolding criss-crossed the open space, connecting to countless tunnels that honeycombed the walls. Elevators and conveyor systems hummed ceaselessly, despite the sudden absence of workers to monitor them. The constant drone of machinery echoed through the cavern, punctuated by the occasional clang of metal on rock or the hiss of pneumatic equipment.

"Impressive, isn't it?" Leon's gravelly voice came from beside him. The former Marine's weathered face was a map of harsh years spent in this subterranean world. Deep lines etched his forehead and the corners of his eyes, attributed to both age and a hard life. His hands, resting on the railing beside Alex, were gnarled and callused, the knuckles swollen from years of hard labor. "I bet Hell's pretty impressive, too. But I wouldn't want to live there. Just like I don't want to live here."

Alex nodded, his expression grim. "Unfortunately, it's still home. At least for the moment." He turned to face the older man, taking in the details of his appearance. Despite the years of hardship evident in every line of his face, there was a spark of hope in Leon's eyes. "We need to secure this place fast. Can you gather the other prisoners? We need to know who we can trust, who has useful skills."

Leon grinned, revealing a set of stained teeth. "Sure can. Most of the folks down here are ex-military or FUP sympathizers. And even if they did support the SF when they got here, they sure as hell don't now. They'll be glad to help." He paused, his eyes narrowing slightly as he studied Alex's face. "You know, I never did get your name."

"Gunnery Sergeant Alex Strickland," he replied, putting up a hand to cut off Leon before he could question the name. "It's a long story. I'll tell it to you once we have this place fortified."

Leon nodded, seemingly satisfied for the moment. "Fair enough. I'll round up as many folks as I can and meet you in admin. Any particular skills you're looking for?"

Alex thought for a moment. "Anyone with combat experience, obviously. But we also need engineers, medics, cooks. To be honest, I'm not sure how long we'll need to be here."

"You got it, Gunny," Leon replied with a mock salute. "We've been waiting for this day for a long time. Thought the FUP had forgotten about us, to be honest. But here you are, like avenging angels. At first, I thought that meant the FUP had found a way to turn the tide. That maybe we were winning this war. I have to admit, it hurts a little that you were prisoners like us, and that we're still waiting on a real rescue. But damn, I'm proud you broke the chains and at least are giving us all a fighting chance. You're sure the FUP will come for us?"

"Grand Admiral Strickland seems to think so," Alex replied. "He's got a whole fleet of warships waiting…" He pointed up. "…up there for them to arrive. They'll be here."

Leon laughed. "I can't wait for the fireworks. Catch up

with you later, Gunny." With that, he disappeared into one of the many tunnels branching off from the main shaft.

As Leon moved off to gather the miners, Alex headed back through the main tunnel, trying to get into comms range. "Decker, what's our status?" he repeated until he finally got a reply.

Decker's voice came back, slightly distorted by static. "We've secured the upper levels. Rounding up the last of the guards now. Cassie's monitoring things in the control room. No sign of incoming reinforcements so far."

"Copy that. Get those guards locked down. Use the cells in the upper levels."

"You got it. Anything else?"

Alex considered for a moment. "Yeah. Once the guards are secure, I want you to start checking our supplies. Food, water, medical equipment—anything we might need for a prolonged siege. We don't know how long we'll need to hold out."

"I'll get teams on it right away."

Alex continued back through the winding tunnels. As he walked, he passed groups of newly freed prisoners. Some looked shell-shocked, as if they couldn't quite believe their situation had changed. A young woman, sat huddled against a wall, her eyes wide and unfocused. Alex paused, crouching down beside her.

"Hey," he said softly. "You okay?"

She blinked, seeming to notice him for the first time. "Is it...is it really over?" Her voice was barely a whisper.

Alex nodded. "You're free now. What's your name?"

"Gina," she replied. "Gina Chow. I...I was arrested for attending a protest. They said I was a traitor."

Alex felt a surge of anger, but kept his voice calm. "Well, Gina, you're not a traitor. And you're not a prisoner anymore. Can you stand?"

She nodded, allowing Alex to help her to her feet. "What happens now?" she asked.

"I wish I could say we're going to hop into the prison ships and ride them back out of here, but Grand Admiral Strickland has a huge fleet waiting for our reinforcements. So we need to stick it out here until they arrive. Can you help with that?"

A spark of determination lit in Gina's eyes. "Yes. Yes, I can help."

Alex smiled. "Good. Wait here for Leon. Do you know him?"

"I...I think so. Older man. Dark skin, deep voice?"

"That's him. Tell him Gunny sent you. He'll find a place for you."

"Okay," she replied, her posture shifting from a frightened huddle to an eager watch.

Alex continued on his way. Others were already mobilizing, following the lead of Alex's fighters to secure different areas of the compound. The air was charged with excitement and apprehension. They had won their freedom, but now they had to hold onto it.

He exited the mines and through the door on the left side of the intake room, where some of the newly freed miners and his teams were working to remove the dead guards and collect their gear. A similar scene played out in the corridors leading to the control room, which Alex entered to find a hive of activity.

Cassandra sat at the main console, eyes narrow, hands hovering over the controls as she worked to gain access to the tranSat network. Zoe sat at a nearby terminal, coordinating with the teams spread throughout the complex.

"How's it coming?" Alex asked, moving to stand beside Cassandra.

She didn't look up from her work, her voice tense with frustration. "I'm pretty familiar with the Federation's systems, but it looks like this one was recently upgraded. Every time I think I'm close, I hit another layer of security. But I know I can crack it. I just need more time."

"Do what you can. We need to get a message out to the FUP as soon as possible."

"I know, I know," Cassandra muttered. "Believe me, I want to contact them as much as you do. But if I rush this, I might do more harm than good."

"You're right," Alex conceded. "Just... keep at it. Let me know the moment you break through."

Jackson entered the room, his rifle slung over his shoulder. "Gunny, we've got the last of the guards rounded up. They're secure in the upper-level cells."

"Good work. Any trouble?"

Jackson shook his head. "Nah, they're pretty demoralized. Most of them gave up without a fight. A few tried to resist, but..." He shrugged. "Let's just say they won't be causing any more problems."

Alex raised an eyebrow. "You didn't—"

"Relax, Gunny," Jackson interrupted. "They took a few extra hits with stun batons, but they're alive. We're not them."

Alex nodded, relieved. "How are our people holding up?"

Jackson's expression softened slightly. "They're scared, excited, angry—you name it. But they're holding it together. I think having a purpose, something to do, is helping. They're in control of their own destiny now, you know?"

"Yeah, I know," Alex replied. He turned to address the room at large. "Alright, listen up. We've taken the compound, but that was the easy part. Now we need to hold it. We have a good defensive position, but we need to be smart about fortifications. We have to expect that SF reinforcements will include power-armored Marines, and maybe even our old friends, the Scarabs."

"I'll check the galley," Zoe said. "Maybe we can bake them some cookies."

"Laced with arsenic," Jackson joked.

"My point is, we need to get creative," Alex said. "Let's take stock of everything we have, mining equipment, vehicles, anything that we might be able to use to build barriers, create cover, and offer our people better defensive firing positions. Or anything we can use as a weapon that may not have been designed as one."

"I hear those rock splitting lasers they use are pretty bad-ass," Jackson said.

"Perfect example. Let's see if we can weaponize them. Five, I want you leading that angle."

Zoe nodded, her eyes gleaming with the challenge. "Copy that, Gunny. I've got some ideas already."

"Three, work with Decker and Leon on organizing both our current regiment and the newly freed prisoners. The good news is that most of the miners here are former FUP fighters, so they already know how to shoot, but let's make sure we use everyone as effectively as possible."

"Consider it done," Jackson replied.

"Cassandra, keep working on that tranSat. The moment you break through, I want a message sent to the FUP fleet. Let them know the situation down here, and in orbit."

"Will do," Cassandra replied, her focus never wavering from her task.

"Gunny," Zoe said. "We're receiving an incoming video transmission."

"Oh, this should be good," Jackson quipped.

Alex moved to her station, which displayed the incoming signal. "Looks like it's coming from one of the orbiting ships." He straightened and turned to the primary viewscreen at the front of the control room. "Five, put it through."

The viewscreen flickered to life. A stern-faced SF officer appeared, his uniform immaculate. He did his best to appear straight-faced and unimpressed, but Alex could see absolute fury in his eyes.

"This is Admiral Nikolai Vance of the Strickland Federation Navy," the man said, his voice clipped and authoritative. "To the.." He trailed off suddenly as he saw Alex staring back at him from the control room, dressed in a guard uniform and body armor scuffed and dented from the fighting. "Commandant Strickland?" he asked, confused. "I...what..."

"Don't get yourself too twisted up, Admiral," Alex said. "I'm not *that* Alexander Strickland. I'd love to tell you why I look just like him, though, if you'll give me the chance. Our universe is under a grave threat, and it's not the FUP, CIP, or the SF. And if we work together—"

The transmission cut out.

"Damn," Jackson said. "This feels like one of those romantic comedies where the entire plot happens because the two leads won't take half a minute to clear up whatever misunderstanding started the whole thing."

"Yeah," Alex agreed. "I tried." He shrugged. "The fact is, if they thought they had sufficient reserves to come at us right away, they'd be doing it already. They obviously know they need additional reinforcements to take back the prison, and that means we have time."

"Copy that," Zoe agreed. "But how much time?"

"We can't assume any amount, which means getting everything done asap is the only right answer. You already know what we need to do. Let's get to work."

CHAPTER 29

Alex's eyes burned with fatigue as he made his way through the winding corridors of the mining complex, the air still thick with a mixture of dust and the smell of sweat. It had been twenty-four hours since they had seized control of the facility, and he had yet to find a quiet moment to close his eyes for more than a few seconds at a time.

Emerging from one of the tunnels, Alex found himself in the main ore processing area, where the dug up rock was sorted and treated to extract the precious metals inside. Massive conveyor belts snaked their way across the ceiling, still laden with chunks of raw material. Towering vats of chemicals used in the extraction process loomed over the walkways, their contents gurgling ominously.

But now, instead of the usual flow of minerals, the conveyors were being repurposed. Freed prisoners swarmed over the machinery, welding metal plates to create makeshift barricades. Others were dismantling heavy sorting equipment, repurposing the sturdy frames to build up their defenses, the constant hum of the machinery providing a backdrop to the cacophony of voices and clanging metal echoing through the vast network of tunnels and chambers.

This was only a fallback position, deep inside the mines. A place Alex hoped they would never need to retreat to when the SF forces came. Similar activity played out throughout the complex.

"Watch out!" a voice called out, and Alex instinctively ducked as a length of metal piping swung overhead, carried by a group of burly miners. They nodded to him as they passed, their faces streaked with grime but eyes alight with purpose.

He made his way to a raised platform where Jackson stood, overseeing the controlled chaos. His friend's usual easy-going demeanor had been replaced by an intense focus as he barked out orders and coordinated the various teams.

"How's it coming, Three?" Alex asked, joining him at the railing.

Jackson turned, a grin breaking through his serious expression. "Like you wouldn't believe, Gunny. These folks are something else. Give 'em a wrench and a welder, and they'll build you a fortress out of scrap metal and spite."

Alex nodded, surveying the scene. "Good. We're going to need every advantage we can get."

"No kidding," Jackson agreed. "Check this out." He pointed to a group working on what looked like a mining vehicle. Its massive treads and reinforced frame were being augmented with additional armor plating and what appeared to be a hastily mounted gun turret. "They're calling it the 'Mole Tank.' Apparently, it can burrow through solid rock. Figure we can use it to create some nasty surprises for any SF ground forces who poke their noses down here."

"Impressive," Alex said, genuinely amazed at the inge-nuity on display. "How many of these do we have?"

"Three operational, with parts for maybe two more," Jackson replied. "But that's not all. Come on, I'll show you what else we've cooked up."

As they made their way across the chamber, Alex was struck by the transformation. What had once been a place of oppression and forced labor was now buzzing with energy and determination. The freed prisoners moved with purpose and dedication. They had tasted freedom, and they weren't about to let it slip away again without a fight.

Jackson led him to a side tunnel where a group was working on modifying what looked like mining drills. "We're reinforcing the motors on the drills, and working on the software so they'll rotate faster. We catch the SF in the shafts, we can push them back, or go through them, with these."

Alex nodded approvingly. "I like it."

Jackson's grin turned predatory. "Oh, we've got traps too. See those chemical vats? We're running lines from them, and rigging some of the tunnels with a nasty surprise. The acid is strong enough to eat through power armor in seconds."

"Damn," Alex muttered, impressed and slightly unnerved by the ruthlessness of it. "I didn't know you had it in you, Three."

"You know me, Gunny," Jackson replied with a shrug. "I like to be thorough. And I owe those bastards big time for Sarah and Malik. I'll never forgive. And never forget."

"That makes two of us," Alex said.

They continued their tour, with Jackson pointing out other improvisations—repurposed mining lasers turned into defensive turrets, and modified ore carts turned into mobile cover.

As they finished their circuit, Alex clapped Jackson on the shoulder. "Great work, Three. Keep it up. I'm heading to check on Five next."

Jackson nodded. "You got it, Gunny. And hey, try to get some rest soon. You look like you're about to fall over."

"You don't look much better yourself," Alex replied.

"I'm hitting the first soft landing spot I can find as soon as we're done down here. You should do the same."

Alex waved him off to direct a team hauling scrap metal, knowing he wouldn't be resting until he was satisfied they had done everything possible to secure their position. He made his way through more winding corridors, the rock walls giving way to more finished surfaces as he neared the upper levels of the complex.

He found Zoe in what had once been a maintenance bay, now transformed into a bustling workshop. The air was filled with the smell of burning metal and the constant whine of power tools. Sparks flew as Zoe bent over a workbench, her face protected by a welding helmet, making precise adjustments to what Alex recognized as one of the mining facility's laser cutters.

"Five," he called out, raising his voice to be heard over the din.

Zoe looked up, pushing her helmet back to reveal a face streaked with sweat. Her eyes were bright with the manic energy of sleep deprivation and intense focus. "Gunny!" she said, waving him over. "Perfect timing. I think we've got something here that'll make those SF bastards think twice about charging in."

Alex made his way over, careful not to trip over the various cables strewn across the floor. "What have you got?"

Zoe's grin was fierce as she patted the modified laser cutter. "We've managed to seriously boost the output of these babies. Had to jury rig a new cooling system and power supply, but it'll be worth it. These should be able to cut through power armor like a hot knife through butter."

"Impressive," Alex said, examining the device. It looked

far more lethal than its original industrial design, with additional focusing lenses and a more robust housing. "How many can we deploy?"

"We've got five fully modified, with components for maybe a dozen more," Zoe replied. "But that's not all. Check this out." She led him to another workbench. Alex immediately recognized Gina, who was hard at work on what looked like a smaller, handheld version of the laser cutter.

"Gina here had the idea to make portable versions," Zoe explained. "They won't have the same punch as the big ones, but they'll give our people a fighting chance in close quarters."

Gina looked up. "I hope they'll be useful, Gunny," she said. "I used to work as a mechanic before the protests. I figured I might as well put those skills to use."

Alex nodded approvingly. "Good work, both of you. How long until we can start deploying these?"

"The big ones are ready to go now," Zoe said. "We're still working out some kinks with the portable versions, but I'd say another twelve hours and we'll have a decent number operational."

"Excellent," Alex replied. "Keep at it. And Zoe? Try to get some rest soon. I need you sharp."

Zoe waved him off, already turning back to her work. "I'll sleep when you do, Gunny. Or I'm dead. Whichever comes first."

Alex shook his head, knowing it was pointless to argue with her. As he headed for the intake area, he made his way out of the workshop, the sounds of intense activity fading behind him.

The massive space that had once processed new arrivals to the prison had been transformed into an impromptu training ground. While the experienced FUP fighters were using their other skills, rows of freed civilian prisoners stood in formation, many of them holding a rifle for the first time in their lives.

Sergeant Major Briggs stood at the front of the group. His booming voice echoed off the walls as he barked instructions, his face set in a perpetual scowl.

"Listen up, maggots!" Briggs shouted, pacing back and forth in front of the group. "I don't care if you were a pencil-pusher, a professor, or a prostitute before you got here. If you ever want to taste freedom again, you'd damn well better be ready to fight for it. I can lead you horse's asses to water, but I can't make you drink. So pay attention!"

Alex watched as Briggs demonstrated proper firing stance, his movements crisp and precise despite his bulk. The freed non-military prisoners struggled to mimic him.

"No, no, no!" Briggs bellowed, striding over to correct a man who was holding his rifle awkwardly. "You hold it like that, and the only thing you'll kill is yourself. Like this!" He adjusted the man's grip, his touch surprisingly gentle despite his harsh tone.

Alex approached, and Briggs noticed him, barking out a quick "As you were!" to the trainees before turning to face him.

"Gunny," Briggs said, his voice gruff but respectful. He'd had an epiphany since Alex put him on the deck a second time. Maybe slamming his head down hard enough made him realize how much he hated life under Strickland. Or maybe it was forced sobriety. Whatever changed his outlook, he'd become one of their most staunch supporters, eager to teach everything he knew. "Come to check on our fresh meat?"

Alex nodded, his eyes scanning the rows of nervous faces. "How are they coming along?"

Briggs grunted, both frustration and admiration evident in his tone. "Better than I expected to be honest. Most of them have never held a weapon before, but they're eager to learn. Might make halfway decent fighters out of them yet."

"Good," Alex replied. "We're going to need every able body when the Federation comes knocking."

Briggs nodded, his face darkening. "Yeah, about that. You really think we can hold this place against an all-out assault?"

Alex met the older man's gaze steadily. "We have to. And we will."

Briggs was quiet for a moment, studying Alex's face. Finally, he nodded. "Alright then. I'll make sure these maggots are ready to give the SF one hell of a fight." He turned back to the group, his voice rising once more. "Alright, ladies! Break's over. Back in formation!"

As the trainees scrambled to comply, Alex made his way out of the intake area, the sound of Briggs' bellowed instructions fading behind him. His next stop was the armory, where he found Decker overseeing the distribution of weapons and equipment. He stood at a makeshift command post, a datapad in his hand as he directed the equipment flow to several pushcarts.

"Boss!" Decker called out as he spotted Alex. "Perfect timing. We've just about got everything inventoried and ready for distribution."

Alex made his way over, nodding to the busy workers as he passed. "What's our situation look like?"

Decker consulted his datapad. "We've got a decent stock of standard-issue rifles and sidearms from the guards' armory. Not enough for everyone, though."

"We can supplement with the gear Zoe and Gina are cooking up from the mining equipment," Alex said. "For some of the defenders, anyway. Maybe those who are any good with rifles."

"Great. Ammunition is going to be our biggest concern. We've got enough for a couple of attack waves, but if this turns into a siege, we'll need to start rationing pretty quickly."

Alex frowned. He'd expected as much, but the truth still hurt. "What about body armor?"

"Not great," Decker admitted. "We've got the guards' gear, of course, but that's only going to cover a fraction of our people. We're working on improvising some protection from the mining equipment by repurposing what meager protective gear they bothered to provide, but it's not going to stand up to heavy weapons."

"Have you met Leon yet?"

"Sure have, Boss. He introduced me to these fine gentlemen." He motioned to the freed miners helping him load up the carts.

"Work with him to get the best weapons and ammo to those with combat experience. We'll need the rest to be prepared to use whatever we can recover from dead SF soldiers and our own casualties."

"That's dark, but I follow," Decker replied, making notes on his datapad. "Oh, and one more thing. We found a cache of cigars in the Warden's office after we locked him up. I took a few for myself and each of my helpers, but there are still a good number left in the box." He reached under a blanket he had used to hide them and opened the lid, offering one to Alex.

"I'll pass, but make sure you save one for Jackson and Leon."

"What about Zoe?"

"She doesn't smoke, either." He paused before reaching into the box. "But I'll take one up to Cassandra. I don't know if she'll want it, but she's certainly earned one."

"Sure thing, boss."

As he left the barracks, Alex felt the gnawing emptiness in his stomach. Being so close to the mess hall, he couldn't ignore the smell of cooking food. He needed sleep, but he also needed to eat.

The large dining area was bustling with activity. Long tables that had once been reserved for the guards were now filled with former prisoners holding animated conversation and the clatter of utensils. The serving line was busy, with cooks ladling generous portions of what looked like a hearty stew. They would need to ration whatever stores they had in preparation for a potential siege, but unless he wanted a full-on mutiny, he wasn't about to try to stop them from indulging tonight.

He spotted Leon at a table near the back, surrounded by a group of freed prisoners. He made his way over, nodding to those who greeted him as he passed.

"Gunny!" Leon called out as he approached, pulling out a chair. "Go grab yourself some grub and come sit. You look like you could use a good meal."

"That I can," Alex answered. He grabbed a tray, waited in line to be served, and joined the table, his stomach growling audibly. "Looks damn good," he said, digging in.

"That it is." Grinning, Leon slapped him on his back. "The cooks are calling it Liberation Stew. Best not to ask too many questions about what's in it. I'll tell you this, though. It beats the hell out of the slop they served us down below. Now, I know we'll have to eat said slop again if we're stuck in here too long, but it's nice to live like a normal human for a day or two."

"I had the same thought when I walked in," Alex agreed, tasting the stew. Whatever was in there was hot, filling, and far more flavorful than he'd expected. As he ate, he listened to the conversations around him. The freed prisoners' mixed emotions—excitement at their newfound freedom, anxiety about the coming battle, and determination to see this through to the end—ran the gamut.

"So, Gunny," one of the miners, a wiry man with a bald

head and a thick white beard, asked. "What's the plan? How long do you think we can hold out here?"

Alex set down his spoon, carefully choosing his words as he swiped his tongue around his lips to mop soup dribbles up from his lengthening stubble. "As long as we need to," he said finally. "We've got a good defensive position, and every hour gives us more time to prepare. The SF is going to throw everything they have at us, but they can't match our motivation or our will to survive."

Leon raised his cup in a toast. "To freedom," he said, his voice gruff with emotion.

"To freedom," the others echoed, and Alex joined in, proud to share a meal with these people.

As he finished shoveling in the stew with manners he knew his mom would deplore, Alex knew he had one more stop to make before he could even think about getting some sleep. He made his way to the control room, where he found Cassandra still hunched over the main console, her fingers hovering over the keys.

"Any luck?" he asked, coming to stand beside her.

Cassandra looked up, her eyes red-rimmed from staring at screens for hours on end. But there was a triumphant gleam in them as she spoke. "I've done it," she said. "Just finished cracking the last layer of security. We've got full access to the tranSat system."

Alex grinned, reaching into his pocket to produce the cigar. "I had a feeling this would be a celebratory gift when I carried it up here."

Cassandra gently plucked it from his hand, giving it a sniff. "This is Cuban," she remarked.

"It is?" Alex asked, surprised.

"Do you have any idea how much this cost? Where did you get it? You weren't carrying it around in your orange jumpsuit."

Alex laughed. "Decker found them in the Warden's office. I grabbed one for you."

"Where's yours?"

"I don't smoke."

Cassandra started cracking up.

"That's funny?"

"No. But I just realized I don't have a light."

Alex laughed too. "Save it for later. There's lots of heat sources down in the mines." He motioned to the terminal. "You have access. That means you can get a message out to the FUP, right?"

"We can send it, but depending on their position, it could be weeks before it's received. This is a message in a bottle, not an emergency line."

"Understood. Let's do it anyway."

Cassandra nodded, already pulling up the necessary protocols. "Ready when you are, Gunny."

Alex took a deep breath, composing his thoughts. Then he leaned in toward the comm pickup as Cassandra hit the record button. "This is Gunnery Sergeant Alex Strickland of the Federation of United Planets Marines. We have successfully taken control of the Teegarden penal colony. I repeat, Teegarden Prison is under FUP control." He paused, letting the magnitude of that statement sink in before continuing. "Be advised, there is a significant Federation fleet in orbit. At least two dozen warships, a mix of Rhinos, Komodos, and Valkyries. We are fortifying our position and are prepared to hold out, but we will need support. To any FUP forces receiving this transmission–we are here, we are fighting, and we need your help. We have access to encrypted and active tranSat, and can receive any messages you send in reply."

He nodded to Cassandra to end the transmission, tense while he waited for confirmation of its passing.

"Message sent," Cassandra confirmed. "It's encrypted

and bouncing through several relays. With any luck, it'll reach the FUP fleet before it's too late."

Alex nodded, the adrenaline that had kept him going for the past day finally started to ebb. "Good work, Cassandra," he said, his voice heavy with fatigue. "Now get something to eat and get some rest."

Cassandra nodded, stifling a yawn. "You too, Gunny. You look dead on your feet."

Alex couldn't argue with that assessment. The weight of the past twenty-four hours finally caught up to him, his body screaming for sleep. He exited the control room, his feet feeling like lead as he trudged through the corridors.

He found an empty office near the control room, likely belonging to one of the mid-level prison administrators before their takeover. The room was spartan, with a desk, a few chairs, and a couch against one wall. It wasn't much, but at least it was long enough to accommodate his long legs. It would do.

Alex sank onto it, his body protesting every movement. As he lay back, staring at the featureless ceiling, his mind raced with everything they still needed to do: fortifications to reinforce, weapons to distribute, strategies to plan.

But even as his thoughts whirled, exhaustion finally claimed him. His eyes drifted shut, and within moments, he was asleep.

CHAPTER 30

A soft chime lifted Soren's attention from the daily status reports to the door of his ready room. With only three days remaining until their arrival at Teegarden, the unscheduled visit immediately set him on edge. Everything had been running so smoothly to this point—from engineering to operations, to the Marines training with the Lammergeiers —that he had started to wonder when something might go wrong.

He exhaled, silently chiding himself for his foolish superstition as he set the data pad down on his desk. It was probably just Dana, coming to check on him in person and make sure he was taking time out from his duties to eat and rest. Now that he thought about it, he hadn't seen or heard much from her since they'd executed the fold.

"Enter," he called out, straightening in his chair. He smiled and started to rise when Dana appeared behind the opening door, a large grin already plastered to her face.

"Captain, do you have a few minutes?" she asked, immediately setting the tone of the visit as formal.

He couldn't help feeling a little disappointed that it

wasn't a personal drop-in, but he didn't let it show. He settled back in his seat, waving her in.

He was surprised when Dana stepped into the ready room, not alone, but followed by Lukas, clutching a datapad to his chest like a treasure, and then Ethan and Tashi.

All four of them displayed a nervous excitement that immediately piqued his interest. "Please, sit," he said, gesturing to the two seats on the other side of his desk. Dana and Lukas claimed them, while Ethan and Tashi stood behind them. "I don't recall setting you four on a specific task," he said, his voice light. "What is this about?"

Lukas cleared his throat, his fingers drumming nervously on the datapad he still clutched. "You didn't give us a specific task together, Captain," he began, his voice carrying a slight tremor of excitement, "but we found ourselves working together after I started asking Tashi and Chief Engineer Kaine questions about the Wraith's vortex cannon."

Soren leaned forward, joining his hands on the desk, even more interested now. "I see. You have the look of a group that's stumbled onto something promising."

"We have," Lukas agreed, relaxing slightly in response to Soren's positive reception. "Quite by accident at first, but we've spent the last few weeks, since just after you left for Glaive, working together on better understanding the vortex cannon. Trying to unlock its secrets, so to speak." He paused, glancing at Ethan and Tashi as if seeking reassurance. "And as you suspected, I think we've made a breakthrough."

Soren smiled. "Don't keep me in suspense, Doctor."

Lukas took a deep breath, his words tumbling out in a rush. "I believe I've developed an algorithm that describes how the cannon, at the right resonance and frequency, created the instability in the fabric of spacetime that threatens to lead to the convergence."

Soren stared at him in silence. It was a simple statement, but it carried so much depth and meaning, and he needed a moment for his mind to wrap around the idea.

"That's…beyond my ability to truly appreciate," he said at last. "I can't even begin to guess how you managed something like that."

"With help, of course," Lukas said. "I don't want to sound cold, Captain, especially in light of what happened to Alex. But I don't know if there's another way to put it. With regard to understanding the Convergence, our encounter with the Fist of Justice and its use of the vortex cannon is the best thing that could have happened to us. Studying the effects in relation to the data we captured in the Eye has been crucial to the discoveries and conclusions we've made since then."

"I understand," Soren said. "I'm glad that something good came out of it, at least."

"Maybe more than we could have hoped for, sir. With the help of my new algorithm, Tashi and I have been running simulations of setting Wraith's cannon to different frequencies and resonances. The results are…well, they're better than we could have hoped for."

Ethan jumped in, unable to contain himself any longer. "It's incredible, sir," he said. "We can't replicate the Fist's exact use as an unstoppable EMP of sorts. The Wraith just doesn't have the power supply for that. Well, we could if we didn't want shields, but that's obviously a bad idea."

"But," Tashi interjected, his usual easy going demeanor replaced by an intensity Soren had rarely seen in the young engineer, "we think we've found another option. A new way to use the cannon that could be especially useful when we reach Teegarden."

"Elaborate," Soren said simply.

Dana took over, her voice steady and clear as she laid out the details. "While we can't recreate the full EMP effect, the simulations suggest that we could potentially disable their shields," she said. "They'd need to be reset to bring them back online, which as I'm sure you know can take anywhere from a few seconds to a minute, depending on how quickly the ship's crew realizes what's happened and how complex their shield systems are."

"With the help of the FUP fleet," Lukas added, his excitement building as he explained, "we'd essentially have a chance to target multiple ships while their shields are down. It could be a powerful one-two punch, Captain. Imagine being able to neutralize an entire enemy formation's defenses in a single strike."

Soren leaned back in his chair, trying to temper his excitement over the possibilities. The tactical applications were staggering. If it worked as they described, it could change a battle's entire nature. But years of command had taught him to look for the catch.

There was always a catch.

"What are the downsides?" he asked, his voice carefully neutral as he studied each face. "A weapon like this, there have to be tradeoffs involved."

The group exchanged glances. Finally, Lukas spoke up, his earlier enthusiasm tempered by the answers to Soren's question. "There are a few, sir," he admitted, his fingers tightening on the datapad. "First and foremost, we've only modeled this effect in simulation. It's untested in the real world. We're confident in our calculations, but..."

"But simulations aren't reality," Soren finished for him. "The outcome could be slightly different, not as effective, or a non-starter. What else?"

"To make this setting work efficiently," Ethan said, "we'd need to divert all power from the third reactor to the cannon, which would reduce the strength of our shields significantly. It would be temporary, but we can't switch the flow back in the middle of a fight. Once we're committed to the reduced shield strength, we have to live with it for the duration."

"There's more, Captain," Tashi said. "We believe this configuration could add more strain to the interdimensional instability. According to our calculations, it's not as severe as the Fist's use, but it's not negligible either. We'd be playing with fire, sir, potentially accelerating what we're trying to prevent."

"Plus," Dana spoke up, her earlier excitement now tinged with worry, "we'll only have limited time to inform Admiral Yarborough of the plan once we exit the fold. It may be too late to adjust tactics now, which means we'd be throwing a major unknown into an already fraught battle plan."

Soren inhaled deeply. Each potential benefit seemed balanced by an equally significant risk. It was a tactical minefield with consequences that could ripple far beyond a single battle.

"I see," he said, his voice measured as he exhaled. "It would be nice if it were an easy decision to make. I'm interested to hear your opinions on the matter. Should we convert the vortex cannon to operate as you've suggested?"

The group fell silent, each carefully considering their response. Soren hated to put such pressure on them—ultimately, he would decide for himself—but he trusted their expertise in the technological side of the equation. Their opinions would at least help him come to a more educated conclusion.

Lukas spoke first, his voice hesitant but gaining strength as he continued. "It's a risk, sir. A big one," he admitted. "But if Teegarden is heavily defended, it could give us a powerful first strike. It might be the edge we need to break through and reach Alex. In fact, it could potentially be the difference between life and death for him and us."

"I agree with Lukas," Ethan said, nodding thoughtfully. "The potential benefits are enormous. But the strain on the ship and the dimensional stability are impossible to ignore. We'd be pushing the Wraith to her limits, and possibly beyond. If something goes wrong with the power distribution, we could be dead in space at the worst possible moment."

Tashi frowned, his usual enthusiasm tempered by the gravity of the situation. "I'm torn, Captain," he confessed, his eyes meeting Soren's. "The engineer in me is excited by the possibilities. The benefits. But the risks are significant. If something goes wrong, if our calculations are off even slightly..."

"If something goes wrong, we could make the Convergence worse," Dana picked up, her voice soft but intense. "Or leave ourselves vulnerable at a critical moment. But if it works..." She trailed off, leaving the implications hanging in the air. After a moment, she continued, "We could save Alex. We could save everyone. It might be our best chance at ending this war before it's too late."

Soren stood, unable to remain seated under the weight of the decision before him. He pushed back from his desk and began to pace behind it, the eyes of his team following him. The possibilities of their discovery whirled in his mind, a dizzying array of potential outcomes branching out like the roots of some vast, cosmic tree.

On one hand, the ability to disable multiple ships' shields simultaneously could indeed be a game-changer. If Teegarden was heavily defended, it might be their only chance at a decisive first strike. Combined with this new tactic, the element of surprise could turn the tide of battle before it even began.

But the risks...Soren's jaw clenched as he considered

them. Untested technology was always a gamble, and there would be no room for error in the heat of battle. And if it failed, they would be left in an extremely vulnerable position, potentially dooming not just their mission but the entire resistance.

Then there was the matter of the Fist of Justice. If Alexander's ship was present, Soren wanted to be able to potentially destroy it with one hit. The vortex cannon used conventionally might be their best chance at that. But if the defense around Teegarden was as formidable as they feared, they might not even survive long enough to take that shot without this new approach.

Soren turned back to the group, his expression grave. "How long do I have to make this decision?" he asked. "The stakes are too high not to consider all the angles. All the possibilities."

"We'd need at least a day to make the proper adjustments to the power supply and vortex cannon," Ethan said. "Two would be preferable, in case anything goes wrong in the setup so we would have time to revert to our current state."

"So, twenty-four hours," Soren said.

"That's a safe estimate, sir," Lukas said.

Soren nodded, his expression calm despite the turmoil within. "Thank you for your diligence on this, and for bringing it to my attention," he said, his eyes meeting each of theirs. "I'll consider it carefully and let you know my decision."

"Of course, Captain," Dana said, standing. The others followed suit. "Thank you for hearing us out."

As the door closed behind them, Soren returned to his seat, leaning back and contemplating the conversation. The possibilities of their discovery whirled in his mind, a dizzying array of points and counterpoints. This could be the most important decision of the war. The fate of not just their mission but potentially of multiple dimensions could hinge on this choice.

As he sat there, weighing the options, a memory surfaced—a conversation with his Jane years ago, when he agonized over a different, but still difficult, command decision.

"You can't always know the right choice, Soren," she told him, her hand warm on his shoulder, her eyes filled with love and understanding. "Sometimes, you just have to trust your instincts and be prepared to live with the consequences. That's the burden of command. And it's why they chose you. Because you have a warrior's instincts, and a leader's heart. When the moment comes, you'll make the call that needs to be made. And no matter what happens, it will be the right call, because you made it to the best of your abilities and intentions."

Soren closed his eyes, drawing strength from the memory of her voice, the phantom warmth of her touch. When he opened them again, the doubt had given way to assurance.

Following his instincts, he had his answer.

CHAPTER 31

Alex stood in the intake area, his eyes sweeping over the rows of freed prisoners as they moved through their drills under Sergeant Major Briggs' watchful eye. Four days ago, the intake area had been a scene of bureaucratic darkness, laden with sterile desks, terminals, and other bland equipment used to move the incoming prisoners from ship to shore. Now, despite the open area where the newly christened freedom fighters trained, the cavernous room looked more like the dam it was designed to be. Of course, it wasn't intended to stop water from breaching through, but people.

Massive ore sorters, their conveyor belts stripped away formed the backbone of barricades that snaked across the room. Overturned desks mounted with thick plating along with reinforced mining carts provided additional cover, creating a deadly kill zone that any invading force would struggle to pass through.

The walls, once bare save for warning signs and security cameras, bristled with jury rigged weapon racks. Standard issue rifles liberated from the guards' armory stood alongside mining tools modified into brutal melee weapons.

Plasma cutters, repurposed from their original task of slicing through rock, waited to be unleashed against power armor. The air retained the sharp smell of ozone and hot metal from welding torches, a reminder of the frantic preparations finished in this area, but still taking place throughout the complex.

Near the rear door leading to the mines, a group of former miners worked on what appeared to be a repurposed ore processing laser, mounted on a swivel base cannibalized from a mining rig. Its focusing lenses had been adjusted, transforming it from an industrial tool into a weapon capable of punching through the toughest armor. Cables snaked across the floor, connecting the device to a makeshift power supply cobbled together from a dozen batteries that had been scavenged from the docked prison ships.

Briggs' voice boomed through the chamber, echoing off the metal walls and high ceiling. "Move it, you sorry excuses for soldiers! You think the Federation is going to wait for you to finish wiping? Every second counts!"

The big man stalked between the rows of trainees, his face set in a perpetual scowl. He paused to correct a young woman. "Like this," he growled, though there was an undercurrent of patience in his tone. "You want to be able to squeeze the trigger without disturbing your aim. Breathe in, hold it, then exhale as you fire. Got it?"

The woman nodded. "Yes, Sergeant Major."

Briggs grunted in approval before moving on to the next trainee. "You there! What do you think you're doing? That's not how you reload. Do it again, and this time pretend your life depends on it. Because guess what? It does!"

As he observed the training, his comm unit crackled to life. Cassandra's voice came through, tense and urgent. "Gunny, we've got movement in orbit. New SF ships just arrived."

Alex's stomach tightened, but he kept his voice steady as he responded. "How many? What class?"

"At least six capital ships, but I'm not familiar with their configurations.'

"Understood," Alex replied. "They may be assault transports, delivering ground troops. I'm on my way to you now." He turned to Briggs, catching the corner of the man's eye. He paused his instruction and cast Alex a questioning look. "Training's over. Get these people to their assigned positions. It looks like we're out of time."

Briggs nodded. Rather than a fear reaction, a predatory grin spread across his face. "About damn time. I was starting to think those bastards had forgotten about us." He turned to the assembled fighters, his voice rising to a bellow that seemed to shake the very walls. "Alright, you heard the man! Move out! This is not a drill, people. Get to your stations and prepare for combat!"

As the intake area erupted into controlled chaos, Alex sprinted toward the control room. The winding corridors of the mining complex flew by in a blur. He burst into the room, immediately moving to Cassandra's side at the main sensor display. The holographic projection showed a swarm of red dots descending from orbit, their trajectories unmistakable.

"Sensors just picked these up," Cassandra said. "I'm not sure what to make of them, though. I don't have a ton of experience reading sensor data."

"They're missiles," Alex replied. "You can tell by the size and volume."

"But they can't hurt us with missiles," she countered.

"No, but they can make sure we're out of interceptors before they start sending the dropships down. It's standard operating procedure for a raid like this." Alex moved from the terminal to the window, pointing skyward as the first missiles appeared high overhead, streaking toward the surface at terrifying speed. "There they are."

Cassandra joined him just in time to watch the automated defense systems spring to life. Streaks of light crisscrossed the sky as interceptor rockets raced to meet the incoming threat.

The first few barrages were mostly neutralized, exploding harmlessly in the thin atmosphere high above the complex. But the missiles kept coming, and finally the defenses were exhausted. Alex watched as multiple warheads slammed into each of the prison ships on the landing pad, the detonations ripping gaping holes in the vessels and rendering them useless. Flying debris tore through the terminals, ripping gashes in the walls and leaving the whole area a mangled wreck. Some smaller pieces reached the control room, pinging off the reinforced transparency.

"Well, there goes our escape plan," Cassandra joked. They both knew there was no escape plan.

"Now they'll send in the dropships," Alex said. "With an escort if they're smart."

He backed away from the window and reached for the facility-wide comm system, his voice ringing out through every corridor and chamber of the vast complex. "All hands to battle stations! I repeat, all hands to battle stations! This is it, people. The enemy is on their way down." He put down the microphone, picturing the sudden controlled chaos in his head. Everyone knew their responsibilities. Now was the time to turn practice into performance.

Cassandra's voice was tight from the sensor grid. "I think…you're right, Gunny. I think those are dropships and fighters breaking off from the capital ships. I count…eighteen dropships, plus a lot of starfighters."

Alex did some quick mental math and cursed under his

breath. "Eighteen dropships is five thousand power-armored troops, or nine thousand standard, give or take. They're not taking any chances." He activated his comm unit. "Rojas, are you ready with the outer defenses?"

The response came back almost immediately, punctuated by distant explosions. "We're as ready as we'll ever be, Gunny. Got the anti-air batteries primed and waiting for targets."

"What's your ammunition situation?" Alex asked.

"We've got enough for about ten minutes of continuous fire," Rojas replied.

Alex nodded to himself. It wasn't ideal, but it would have to do. "Understood. The incoming fighters are going to target the batteries. Do what you must to stay alive, but try to hold your fire until the dropships are within range. Take out as many as you can before they reach the surface."

"Copy that, Gunny," Rojas responded. "We'll make these SF bastards regret ever bringing us here in the first place."

"Here they come!" Cassandra called out, the SF starfighters shooting downward in formation, like birds of prey diving toward their next meal.

"Rojas, you've got company!" Alex shouted into his comm.

"We see 'em, Gunny!" Rojas replied, his voice nearly drowned out by the sound of the AA guns opening fire.

The sky lit up as the batteries unleashed everything they had. Several fighters were immediately caught in the barrage, their shields flaring bright before failing under the onslaught. One fighter took a direct hit to its engine, exploding in a brilliant fireball. The rest of the fighters split formation, spiraling away from the penetrating rounds while fighting back with missiles, sending them streaking to the surface where they detonated out of sight. Alex only knew Rojas still had guns left because the bullets kept coming, following the fighters when they peeled away to circle back for another run.

"These boys aren't as tough as they think they are," Rojas growled through the comms.

"I've got visual on the dropships," Alex said. "Focus your fire on them."

"Copy that."

The remaining AA batteries opened up, filling the air with a deadly barrage of fire. Several dropships took a heavy pounding, their shields absorbing the brunt while their escorts swept in low, strafing the gun emplacements. Alex could see the smoke rising from them, along with the dwindling number of rounds targeting the incoming dropships.

Finally, one of the troop carriers succumbed to the defenses, smoke pouring from its breached hull before its reactor exploded, creating a much larger fireball than the fighter. The concussive force rocked the dropship beside it, sending it off-course and slowing its descent.

"Rojas, you've done all you can," Alex said. "It's time to fall back." He waited but didn't receive a reply. "Rojas!" Still nothing.

As he turned to check the tactical grid, a group of SF fighters screamed past the control room, so close that the entire chamber seemed to shake. They couldn't target the facility directly—the control center was too well protected —burrowed as deep as it was into the cliff face. It was a message, Alex knew.

We're coming.

Alex switched channels. "Three, what's your status at the secondary entrance?"

"Locked down tight, Gunny," came the reply, Jackson's voice steady. "We've disabled the lift to the surface and rigged enough explosives to turn this area into one hell of a death trap. If they try to come up this way, they're in for a nasty surprise."

"Good work," Alex said. "Keep your people alert. If they can't break through here, they might try to force their way down through that shaft."

"Don't worry about us, Gunny," Jackson replied. "We've got enough firepower here to make them think twice about trying to breach."

Alex cycled through the other team leaders–Leon, Zoe, Decker, Drake, and Briggs–getting similar readiness reports. They were as prepared as possible, but the real test was yet to come.

He watched the first wave of dropships descend out of view, landing at the top of the valley to unload their troops, who would have to first descend to the prison before they could get inside. The sensors lost track of them as they disappeared behind the rocky terrain, leaving an agonizing gap in their intelligence. The ground forces would be out there soon enough, but Alex had no way of knowing exactly where they would attempt to breach their defenses or in what numbers.

An eerie calm settled over the control room and likely the entire compound as they waited for the enemy's arrival. Alex struggled to keep his mind calm and focused. This was no time to second-guess decisions or wonder if they had done enough. He turned to Cassandra, his voice low but firm. "There's nothing more we can do from here. We need to help the defense."

"Right behind you, Gunny," Cassandra replied.

They quickly made their way through administration. The closer they got to the entrance, the more fortified the passageways became.

They reached the intake area just as the first distant

explosions of the improvised explosives they had planted signaled the SF's approach. Briggs was there, his massive frame unmistakable as he hunkered down, waiting with the other defenders. Their side of the corridor was heavily fortified, with overlapping fields of fire from their positions and easy fallbacks should they need to beat a hasty retreat.

Alex made his way to Briggs' side, taking in the resolved faces of the men and women preparing to make their stand. He couldn't help but notice the way Briggs' hands tightened on his weapon, a flicker of... something...passing across the big man's face.

"Having second thoughts, Sergeant Major?" Alex asked quietly.

Briggs turned to him, his expression hardening. "About what?"

"About shooting at people you considered allies just a couple of weeks ago," Alex elaborated.

For a moment, Briggs was silent, his eyes distant as if looking at something only he could see. When he spoke, his voice was low and intense.

"You know, Gunny, I've had a big damn hole in my heart for the past five years. Didn't even realize it was there most of the time. Just felt...empty, you know? Going through the motions." He paused, his gaze sweeping over the assembled defenders before returning to Alex. "But you knocked some sense into me. And now I'm fighting for something that actually matters. It's like that hole's finally starting to close up. For the first time in years, I feel alive again. I feel like I'm on the right side of history. So no, I'm not having second thoughts. I'm more than ready to show these SF maggots what real courage looks like."

Before Alex could respond, a second series of detonations rocked the area across the bridge. Smoke billowed through the entrance, and for a moment, everything was silent and calm.

Too calm.

The first wave of SF troops emerged from the haze like demons from some hellish realm. Their power armor gleamed in the harsh light, weapons at the ready as they charged across the bridge.

CHAPTER 32

Soren drew a deep breath, in through the nose and out through the mouth, calming himself against the anticipation of what was soon to come. The familiar tension before a battle coursed through his veins, a mixture of eagerness and dread that he had come to know all too well over the years.

His eyes drifted to the countdown timer on his command surface, the bright blue numbers having reached fifteen seconds. No time at all. His thoughts wandered to the decision he had made two days earlier.

A choice that could either save multiple universes or lead to their ultimate destruction.

He had followed his Jane's advice to trust his instincts. So why was he doubting them now? It was only natural, only seconds away from the reckoning of that decision and those instincts. He remained committed to his choice, and not only because it was too late to change his mind. His gut still said he had done the right thing, for all the right reasons.

Let the chips fall where they may.

He could still see the hopeful faces of his team as they

presented their findings, the excitement in their eyes as they explained the potentially powerful modification. But in the end, the risks had been too great, the unknowns too numerous. He had to prioritize the bigger picture, even if it meant potentially sacrificing their best chance at rescuing Alex.

"Preparing to exit fold space," Bobby said, counting down from five.

Soren had already set all hands to battle stations. Everyone was ready for a fight, though they had no idea what kind of fight they would have on their hands. Did the SF know they were coming? Had the Grand Admiral bolstered the planet's defenses? Would the Fist of Justice be part of any additional assets deployed to the planet?

They were all about to find out.

The darkness of the viewscreen exploded in a dazzling burst of light, momentarily blinding the bridge crew. As their vision cleared, the red-orange orb of Teegarden b filled the screen, its barren, rust-colored surface standing out against the blackness of space. But it wasn't the planet that drew their attention; it was the swarm of SF warships surrounding it, their silhouettes breaking up the consistent color of the distant terrain.

The sight of the SF ships hanging in space like a cloud of metallic locusts sent a chill down Soren's spine. Their formation tight and disciplined, the enemy's strength was unfortunately at the high end of what they had anticipated. Maybe even higher. He knew immediately that they would be in for a hell of a fight. That the impressive skills of the captains and their crews would be the only thing that might help them win the day.

"Twenty-seven SF capital ships detected, sir," Mark reported. "A mix of Rhinos, Komodos, and Valkyries." Soren could easily make out the distinctive and differing silhouettes of the lumbering but powerful Rhinos alongside the more balanced Komodos and the nimble Valkyries.

"Sensors are also detecting multiple fighter squadrons inside the atmosphere." He paused, his eyes widening slightly before he continued more animatedly. "Captain, I'm picking up numerous dropships about to touch down on the planet's surface."

Soren's jaw clenched. Were they reinforcing the garrison at the penal colony? It seemed strange to him that such a procedure wasn't already completed.

Before he could consider it further, Samira called out, her tone urgent but controlled. "Captain, incoming transmission from the Admiral.."

"Put her through," Soren ordered.

"Captain," she said, her voice carrying a note of barely contained emotion. "We've received a tranSat message from the surface. It's from Alex! He's not only alive, he's seized control of the penal colony. He and the prisoners are holed up there, waiting for us to come and rescue them."

A wave of relief washed over Soren, momentarily overwhelming the tactical concerns that had been dominating his thoughts. His son was alive. The news hit him like a physical force, causing him to grip the edge of his station for support. But the relief was quickly tempered by the realization of what the former prisoners were facing on the surface.

The SF dropships were moments away from touching down, carrying thousands of troops ready to retake the colony. With those numbers, Alex and his people wouldn't have had a chance on their own. Now, with the Lammergeiers set to ram their small number of Marines through the fortified defenses—as daunting a task as it was —their chances were better than he could have hoped for. Now at least, they had a chance down there.

Just like they did up here.

"Copy that," Soren replied. He could feel the eyes of his crew on him, watching for his reaction. "Then we'd best be the rescuers they're hoping for, but not at all costs. We need to stick to the original plan. We can't help Alex or the prisoners if we can't help ourselves."

"I'm glad we agree."

As Jane put their comms channel on standby, Soren turned back to the sensor projection, his mind already shifting gears to focus on the battle ahead. The holographic representation of the system floated before him, showing the positions of both fleets in real-time. The SF ships were already changing vectors, their formation shifting to confront the newly arrived FUP fleet. It was like watching a deadly dance begin, each side maneuvering for the best position before the real fighting started.

"Keira, activate the cloak," Soren said.

"Aye, Captain. Cloak activated."

"Sang, peel us away from the FUP fleet and set a course for orbit. Get us in position to deploy the Marines."

"Aye, Captain," she replied.

"Mark, is there any sign of the Fist of Justice?"

"Negative, Captain," he replied, his voice tight with concern. "But we may have a different problem. I'm detecting something odd about one of the Komodos."

"Can you put it on the secondary?" Soren asked.

Mark moved to comply. A moment later, the ship in question appeared on the secondary display, the camera zooming in. "It looks like they've hollowed out the center section."

Soren's blood ran cold as he realized why. "That ship is carrying a vortex cannon." He quickly opened the channel to the Spirit of War, his voice urgent. "Admiral, be advised we've spotted a modified Komodo. It appears to be equipped with a vortex cannon. Marking and transmitting it now."

"Understood," Jane answered. "Marker received. Thank you for the heads up."

Soren opened another channel. "Major Kosta, this is Strickland. We're moving on Teegarden now. Prepare for immediate deployment on my mark. Be advised, the prison is under friendly control. Your team will need to hit the enemy hard from behind and catch them in the crossfire."

"Yes, sir," Kosta replied from the Athena, where he would provide overwatch and comms for the ground units. "The Lammergeiers are locked and loaded."

He switched channels again, his fingers moving swiftly over his command surface. "Phoebe, get the Pilums into launch position. Minh, standby for launch on my command."

"Yes, sir," Minh replied.

Soren's attention returned to the sensor projection. The SF ships were spreading out into a wide attack formation while Jane's fleet maneuvered in an attempt to outflank them. He could tell by their positioning that they were trying hard to stay clear of the Komodo toting a vortex cannon.

"Three minutes to orbit, Captain," Sang announced. Three minutes until they could do anything to help the FUP with the rest of the fight. The good news was that none of the SF ships seemed to have noticed them before they cloaked and didn't appear to be tracking them now.

"Keira, charge our cannon," Soren ordered.

"Aye, Captain."

The seconds ticked away, the two fleets approaching one another, each ship constantly updating its velocity and vector, doing its best to gain a firing solution on its chosen target while avoiding a target lock on itself. It was a silent dance that might have looked like pure chaos to an inexperienced observer.

Soren could tell that both sides knew exactly what they were doing. The main thing in question was who would execute better.

As the two fleets began reaching optimal firing distance, the space between them quickly filled with criss-crossing projectiles. Railguns opened fire, and missiles launched from both sides, creating a light show of flaring shield energy and explosive flashes. The Wraith slipped silently around the chaos, out of the fight…for now.

Soren watched the battle unfold with a mixture of pride and concern. The FUP ships fought valiantly, their tactics honed by years of guerrilla warfare against a superior force. But the SF fleet was formidable, their numbers and firepower making every exchange costly. Soren could see FUP ships taking hits, their shields flaring as they absorbed the punishment. But they gave as good as they got, their weapons finding weak points in the SF formation.

"Thirty seconds," Sang announced.

Soren peeled his eyes from a particularly nasty exchange between the Fearless—the Valkyrie the FUP had only recently captured—and a second SF Valkyrie. The two ships were hammering one another with missiles, each desperate to breach the other's shields, so far without success.

He didn't get to see how it ended. Instead, he opened the comm to Kosta and Liam, ready to give the order when Sang told him they'd arrived planetside.

"Five seconds," Sang said.

Soren finished the countdown in his head. "Frank, Liam, deploy."

"Yes, sir," Liam snapped back.

He changed comm channels. "Minh, deploy. Cover the assets."

"Yes, sir," Minh replied. "Consider them safely delivered."

Soren watched on the sensor projection as the Stinger—loaded with Marines and escorted by the nimble Pilum fighters—launched from the Wraith on the ship's port side.

Behind them, the Athena separated from the hull and the cover of the Wraith's cloak, its thrusters flaring to quickly catch up to the Marines. Facing the planet, the two groups were out of both sight and sensor range of the warring fleets.

With that done, the Wraith could refocus its efforts on the starship battle playing out before them.

CHAPTER 33

Cloaked, the Wraith glided silently through the battle, unseen and undetected. Debris from destroyed ships and fighters drifted past them, a somber reminder of the cost of this conflict. While the Wraith had been busy launching their ground forces, it appeared the FUP was losing two ships to the SF's one and in danger of losing even more.

Soren had barely finished the thought when the vortex cannon's whorl of distorted spacetime lanced out from the bow of the modified Komodo, cutting into an FUP Valkyrie. The ship's shields flared brilliantly for a split second before collapsing entirely and allowing the vortex beam to slice the Valkyrie in half as if it were made of paper. The two halves of the ship drifted apart, secondary explosions rippling along each length. The resulting devastation left no chance for the crew to evacuate.

"Damn it," Soren breathed, watching the sensor projection update as the ship's icon faded out, replaced by a spreading debris field. He immediately recognized how quickly the battle had shifted with the destruction of the Valkyrie. The SF ships were suddenly pressing their advantage, sensing increasing weakness in the FUP defenses.

Their formations tightened, concentrating their fire on key targets in an attempt to accelerate their losses.

Soren made a quick decision. "Sang, bring us around to the nearest SF capital ship. Keira, standby to drop our cloak and fire as soon as we're in range."

"Aye, sir," both officers responded in unison, their hands moving swiftly over their respective consoles.

As they closed in on their target—a Rhino-class battle-ship—Soren felt the familiar surge of adrenaline coursing through his veins. In an instant, the Wraith shimmered into view, her vortex cannon already charged and ready. "Fire," he barked, failing to keep the emotion of the moment out of his tone.

Before the SF ship could react, the spacetime vortex erupted from the Wraith's bow, tearing through the Rhino's shields and ripping a massive hole in its hull. The beam continued through, emerging from the other side of the ship in a spectacular display of destructive power and slicing into a second SF vessel.

"Two direct hits! One destroyed! The second disabled!" Keira called out, a note of fierce satisfaction in her voice as the second ship immediately began venting atmosphere and personnel.

Soren allowed himself a small smile of grim satisfaction as the Rhino began to break apart. The massive ship quickly morphed into nothing more than a rapidly expanding cloud of superheated gas and twisted metal. The second ship peeled away, unable to staunch their bleeding as their shields flickered and died.

There was no time to celebrate. As soon as they revealed themselves, a few of the SF ships pivoted to bring their weapons to bear on the Wraith.

"Evasive maneuvers," Soren ordered, his voice calm but urgent. "Sang, keep us out of their firing solutions. Keira, recharge the cannon."

As Sang expertly guided the Wraith through a series of complex maneuvers, the sensor projection drew Soren's immediate attention. The modified Komodo had broken off from the main group, angling toward their position with clear intent.

It was coming for them, and coming fast.

"Sir," Mark called out, his voice tense. "The Komodo's cannon is likely recharged by now."

Soren considered their options. They couldn't risk taking a direct hit from that cannon, but they also couldn't keep running forever, especially when there was nowhere to run except into the thick of the fighting. They needed to neutralize that threat, and quickly.

He thought back to years of experience, mentally searching for a viable answer. The idea struck him. Risky, borderline reckless, but he doubted the SF had ever seen anything like it before.

"Sang," he said. "Prepare for the Comet maneuver. We're going to give our friends a little surprise."

Sang's eyes widened slightly, but she nodded. "Aye, sir. I remember the Comet maneuver well."

Soren intently watched the sensor projection, waiting for the perfect moment. The Komodo was closing fast, working to put its bow in line with any part of the Wraith, while Sang made evasive maneuvers, keeping them from getting a solid bead. The tension on the bridge was suffocating as the crew waited for Soren's command.

"Just a few more seconds," he murmured to himself. "Now!" he barked, his voice cutting through the silence like a knife.

The Wraith's engines and starboard vectoring thrusters flared to life, pushing the ship into a hard turn under maximum thrust. Soren gripped his chair tightly, fighting to stay upright as the inertial dampeners struggled to compensate for the sudden change in vector. The Wraith slipped right through the crosshairs of the Komodo, offering the enemy ship a split second to fire.

The Komodo reacted too late, caught off guard by the unexpected move. The deadly beam passed harmlessly by the Wraith's stern as she completed her ninety-degree turn, leaving the Komodo facing the wrong direction and trying to slow behind them.

Sang had already cut the main thrusters and activated top bow and bottom stern vectoring jets at full blast, throwing the Wraith into a hard rotation on its axis. The bow swung up toward the starboard side of the Komodo with such force that Soren couldn't have risen from his seat if he wanted to.

"Keira, fire!" Soren cried, seizing the moment of opportunity.

The Wraith's vortex cannon erupted again, the beam catching the broadside of the Komodo. The SF ship's shields collapsed almost instantly, unable to withstand the beam as it sliced through the hull, leaving the ship severed in half amidships. Sang continued the Wraith's rotation until the ship fully flipped back around, leaving the SF warship dead in its wake.

Soren clenched his hand into a celebratory fist, the limit of his expression over the hard-won fight. Vortex cannon or not, it was still only one ship and the full battle was far from over. He glanced at the projection, picking out another target. "Keira, get a solution on that Valkyrie, conventional weapons. Sang, take us in."

"Aye, Captain," they replied.

In no time, they had the next target in their sights. With its enhanced shielding, the Wraith took the attacks it received in stride, the shields depleting slowly. Closing on the Valkyrie, Soren once more gave the order to fire. Railgun rounds and missiles tore into an already damaged Valkyrie, breaking through its shields. The missiles opened gaping holes in the hull while flechettes sought critical systems inside. Finally, the Valkyrie's guns went silent.

"Target disabled," Keira reported, the ship going completely dark, able to do nothing but drift.

Soren's gaze swept the projection. Against all odds, the FUP was gaining ground, and its remaining ships were now outnumbering the SF vessels. No doubt, their four kills had helped even the odds immensely.

As Soren began to sense a rising degree of hope, the sensor projection suddenly lit up with new contacts emerging from fold space. A dozen new ships materialized at the edge of contact, their energy signatures unmistakable. Soren's heart sank as he recognized the silhouette of the ship leading the new reinforcements.

"Sir," Mark's voice was tense as he confirmed Soren's quick observation. "The Fist of Justice has arrived."

CHAPTER 34

The Karuta-armored SF Marines charged across the bridge, metal boots clanging, rifles shouldered and ready to fire the moment they breached the intake room where Alex waited with the freed prisoners.

Briggs' massive form loomed beside Alex, the big man's fingers dancing over the detonator in his hand. His face was hard and angry, all traces of his former allegiance to the SF pounded away.

"Just say the word, Gunny," Briggs growled beside him, his voice low and eager. "I'll send those bastards straight to hell."

Alex nodded, his own anticipation building. "Not yet," he murmured. "Let them get nice and close. We want maximum effect."

The first of the SF Marines reached the halfway point. More followed, forming a solid wall of armored troops advancing steadily toward them.

"Steady," Alex called out, his voice carrying to the defenders. "Hold your fire. Wait for my signal."

The tension ratcheted up with each passing second. Alex could hear the nervous breathing of the fighters around him, could almost taste their fear and resolve. The SF Marines drew closer, their heavy footfalls sending vibrations through the bridge.

Just as the first row of power-armored troops neared the end of the bridge, Alex gave a sharp nod to Briggs. "Now!"

Briggs' thumb came down on the detonator without hesitation. For a heartbeat, nothing happened. Then, pure hell erupted.

The bridge exploded, the spectacular chain of detonations tearing through its structure and throwing the armored forms of the leading SF Marines into the air like rag dolls. Those behind them stumbled, trying to regain their footing on the disintegrating surface. Failing, some managed to activate their jump jets to make an escape. Others weren't quick enough, plummeting into the depths.

As the dust began to clear, Alex saw the true extent of the devastation. The bridge was gone, leaving a gaping chasm between them and the enemy. Several SF Marines hung precariously from the jagged edge, their jump jets sputtering and failing.

But the victory was short-lived. Even as Alex allowed himself a moment of satisfaction, he saw the remaining SF forces regrouping. "Here they come!" Alex shouted as they began leaping the gap with a series of coordinated bursts from their jump jets. "Light 'em up!"

The defenders didn't need to be told twice. The air filled with a deadly barrage of weapons fire. Standard rifles chattered alongside the distinctive whine of repurposed mining lasers. The first wave of SF Marines was caught mid-jump, their armor initially absorbing the assault before failing under the concentrated assault. Several Marines fell from the air, joining their squadmates at the bottom of the chasm.

But more kept coming. They landed hard on the near side of the chasm, immediately taking up defensive positions and returning fire. The exchange was brutal and intense, the confined space of the intake area amplifying the din of battle.

Feeling the heat of near-misses as enemy fire peppered his position, Alex ducked behind a twisted piece of metal that had once been part of an ore sorter. He popped up, squeezing off several quick shots at an advancing Marine. His rounds pinged off the Marine's armor, but a sustained plasma burst from Zoe's position finally breached the suit's defenses. The Marine went down hard, twitching as electricity arced across the damaged armor.

Almost simultaneously, Briggs backed up to the large laser they had set up. "Come on you piece of shit!" he cried, hastily smacking the side of it. "We've got maggots to toast." He smacked the malfunctioning laser one more time and it hummed to life, its beam lancing out with deadly precision. It caught an SF Marine squarely in the chest, slicing through armor and cutting the Marine's scream off short.

Adjusting the laser, Briggs took out three more Marines before the reclaimed power supply went dead. "Son of a bitch!" he growled, kicking it as hard as he could for good measure. The laser remained offline.

Switching to his rifle, he fell in rank with Alex and the rest of the freed prisoners, firing at the incoming SF Marines. Already, nearly a dozen of the armored fighters were on the floor bleeding out, their armor smoking. For Alex, it was an impressive display, equal to, if not better, than the rebellion on Jungle, but for the lives of those few Marines, the defenders paid a heavy price.

Alex watched the SF Marines breach the prisoner's front line, their heavy weapons tearing through the makeshift barricades and killing his people one after another, including a freed prisoner Alex knew only as Jerry, who rose to meet the threat, only to be cut down in a hail of gunfire.

"Fall back to the secondary doors!" Alex ordered, knowing they couldn't hold their position much longer. "Move!"

The defenders fought in retreat, laying down covering fire as they withdrew deeper into the complex. Alex ran beside Zoe, alternating bursts of suppressing fire to keep the advancing Marines at bay.

"Just like old times, eh Gunny?" she quipped, her face streaked with sweat and grime.

Alex managed a dark grin. "To think there was ever a time when I lamented all our experience being limited to drills and sims. I'd love to have those days back."

"No kidding," she replied.

They reached the blast doors leading to the entrance of the main mining complex. As the last of the defenders made it through, Alex hit the door controls, and the massive slabs of metal began to slide shut, the process agonizingly slow compared to the speed of the rapidly advancing SF troops. Just as the gap narrowed to a few feet, a Marine made a final, desperate lunge. His armored form wedged in the opening, servos whining as he fought against the closing mechanism.

"Oh no, you don't." Briggs charged forward, his massive shoulder slamming into the Marine's chest. The impact, combined with the force of the doors, sent the soldier tumbling backward. The doors slammed shut with a resounding clang, sealing them off from the immediate threat.

However, Alex knew it was only a temporary reprieve. "Everyone, take positions!" he ordered. "They'll be coming through any second."

The defenders scrambled for cover, weapons trained on the doors. The narrow corridor behind the doors was a calculated choke point, designed to funnel the attackers into a deadly, concentrated crossfire.

Seconds ticked by, each moment stretching into an eternity. Then, with a screech of protesting metal, the doors began to buckle. The smoking penetration of cutting torches appeared along the seams, slowly carving through the reinforced barricade.

"Steady," Alex called out, his voice calm despite the tension. "Wait for a clean shot."

The doors finally gave way, crumpling inward with a thunderous crash. SF Marines poured through the opening, only to be met with a wall of gunfire. The defenders' weapons found their marks, downing several armored figures in the initial rush.

But the Marines quickly recovered, and their return fire was deadly accurate. Alex watched as fighters fell around him, their improvised armor no match for the SF's advanced weaponry. A young woman to his left—he thought her name was Maria—took a direct hit to the chest, her body crumpling to the floor.

"Keep firing!" Alex shouted, trying to rally his people. "Aim for the joints, the helmet seals!"

He squeezed off a series of precise shots that caught a Marine in the knee joint. The soldier stumbled, his armor's leg servos sparking and failing. A few more rounds caught his neck seal, a bullet slicing through the Marine's throat and leaving him gurgling, drowning in his blood, on the floor. Following his lead, more fighters refocused their efforts, cutting down the armored Federation fighters with increasing efficiency.

It wasn't enough.

For every small victory, the tide of battle pushed relentlessly against them. The Marines' superior numbers and equipment began to tell, slowly but surely forcing the defenders back. Alex found himself retreating step by step, each foot of ground given up, feeling like a personal failure.

"Gunny!" Jackson's voice crackled over the comm, tight with urgency. "We've got incoming at the secondary shaft!"

Before Alex could respond, a massive explosion rocked the entire complex. The force of it sent him stumbling, ears ringing from the concussive blast.

"Shit," he muttered, realizing Jackson had blown the shaft and taken some of the incoming Marines with it. "Three, fall back to the rendezvous point! We'll meet you there!"

Alex turned to the remaining defenders, his voice rising above the chaos. "Everyone, to the mines! Now!"

CHAPTER 35

More a frantic rush than an organized retreat, the defenders laid down suppressing fire as they reached a massive set of blast doors—the final barrier before the mines and prison cells.

Alex positioned himself near the controls. "Go, go, go!" he shouted, waving his people through.

The sound of pursuing Marines grew louder, their armored footsteps echoing off the stone walls. Alex's heart raced, knowing they were cutting it close. Just as the last of his fighters made it through, he caught sight of the lead Marine rounding the corner.

"Five!" he called out. "A little going away present!"

Zoe grinned, hefting what looked like a modified mining charge. "With pleasure, Gunny." She armed the device and tossed it down the corridor, the impromptu grenade bouncing and skittering toward the advancing Marines.

Alex slammed his hand on the door controls, diving through the narrowing gap. The blast doors slid shut just as an explosion rocked the passage behind them, the sound muffled but still impressive.

"That ought to slow them down," Zoe said, her grin fierce despite the exhaustion evident on her face.

Alex nodded, allowing himself a brief moment of satisfaction. But the reprieve was short-lived. The sounds of battle—Jackson's group, no doubt, engaged with the Marines who had breached the secondary entrance, despite the explosion—echoed from deeper in the mines.

"Alright, people," Alex called out, his voice carrying across the assembled fighters. "We expected this. We've still got reinforcements positioned further down, waiting for us to lead these bastards in. Five, get that drill into position. Briggs, I want you on the big gun. Everyone else, find cover and make every shot count!"

The fighters moved with courageous resolve, taking up positions among the mining equipment and stone outcroppings. The cavern was vast, its ceiling lost in shadow high above. Massive excavators and ore processors loomed like silent sentinels, their bulk providing additional cover.

Zoe maneuvered the drill—a massive piece of machinery nearly the size of a small shuttle—into place. Its business end was a wicked array of diamond-tipped drills capable of chewing through solid rock. Now, those same drills were aimed at the blast doors, ready to give intruders a nasty surprise.

Briggs hefted the heavy gun they had taken from one of the anti-aircraft batteries, a weapon so weighty only the strongest of men could even lift it. "I don't give a shit if I live or die," he growled, his face set in a fierce grin as he sighted down the barrel, eager for the coming fight. "I just want to take as many of those bastards with me as I can."

They didn't have to wait long. The blast doors began to glow red-hot as cutting torches worked on the other side. Alex tensed, his finger tightening on the trigger of his rifle. "Steady," he called out. "Wait for my signal."

With a shriek of protesting metal, a section of the door

fell inward. SF Marines poured through the gap, their weapons already blazing. The defenders answered in kind, the cavern erupting in a storm of weapons fire.

"Now, Zoe!" Alex shouted.

Zoe hit the activation switch, and the drill roared to life. It surged forward, its massive drills spinning with deadly intent. The lead Marines, caught off guard by the unexpected attack, were bowled over. Those unlucky enough to be caught directly by the drills were torn apart, their armor offering little protection against the industrial-grade equipment.

"Briggs, light 'em up!" Alex ordered.

Briggs opened fire with the AA gun. The heavy rounds punched through armor like it was cloth, sending Marines flying backward in smoking ruin. He was spewing hot metal everywhere when a round caught him in the chest, sending him to the floor, the gun clanging heavily down beside him. He tried to get up, only to take another round to the head. Alex didn't have time to lament his loss.

With the AA gun out of action, the SF forces regrouped quickly, their training and discipline evident even in the face of such an unorthodox defense. They kept their calm, their return fire brutally effective. They cut down several defenders in the opening salvo.

Alex found himself in the thick of the exchange, alternating between shooting and shouting orders to coordinate their defense. He watched in horror as fighters fell around him, good people he had come to know over the past days cut down by the relentless SF advance.

A Marine charged his position, jump jets flaring as the armored figure leaped into the air. Alex dove aside, rolling and coming up firing. His first rounds sparked off the Marine's armor, but he corrected his aim, sending two shots through the Marine's faceplate. The panicked Marine lost control of his jets and crashed to the floor, where Alex seized the opportunity. He closed the distance, jamming the muzzle of his rifle against the man's cracked faceplate. A quick burst and the Marine fell back, dead.

Like before, the ferocious defense wasn't enough to carry the day. By Alex's count, they had killed at least a hundred of the power-armored Marines, and probably a lot more. Still, their numbers were dwindling rapidly, and they couldn't match the SF Marines' superior firepower and protection. They had no chance if the entire landing force was wearing high-tech gear. He hoped that only the vanguard had the best equipment, with the secondary troops more traditionally outfitted.

Alex's comm crackled to life, Jackson's voice tight with strain. "Gunny, we can't hold them! They're pushing us back toward your position!"

Alex's heart sank. Caught between two advancing forces, their situation was rapidly becoming untenable. He made a split-second decision, one he knew might be their last. "Everyone, fall back to the main shaft! We make our stand there!"

The defenders continued their fighting retreat, withdrawing deeper into the cavern. Alex found himself beside Zoe again, alternating covering fire as they fell back.

Soon enough, they reached the mines, centered by the yawning chasm that plunged deep into the planet's crust. Ready to defend the mines, Leon's fighters already occupied the catwalks and elevators crisscrossing the open space. With dozens of tunnels leading from the area, they could split into the deeper mines and harass the SF fighters for days if needed, but it was here that Alex had chosen to make their most crucial—and likely their final—stand.

Alex's comm crackled again. "Gunny, we're almost there!" Jackson's voice was breathless and urgent. "They're right on our six!"

"Understood," Alex replied. "We'll cover you. Every-one, watch that far tunnel! Friendlies coming in hot!"

Moments later, Jackson's group burst from one of the side passages, a ragged band of survivors with SF Marines in close pursuit. The defenders opened fire, their concen-trated barrage forcing the thankfully traditionally outfitted Marines to pull back.

"Three, are the mole tanks ready?"

"Ready when you are, Gunny."

"Move them in behind the attackers. Catch them from the rear."

"I like the way you think, man."

A few seconds later, the mines began to shudder with enough force to dislodge small rocks, sending them tumbling into the nearby depths, where they could be heard rattling off the stone floor. The SF Marines suddenly slowed their assault, uncertain what was causing the disturbance and wary of another trap.

A few seconds after that, shouts rose up from the back of their lines, followed by screams. The Marines abandoned their cover and moved into the shaft, where Leon and his fresh shooters began picking them off with the most ruth-less efficiency yet. The traditionally armored Marines fell by the handfuls, while the remaining power-armored fighters succumbed more slowly.

Alex could hear them shooting at the mole tanks to no avail. Their armor was too thick, their boring drills deadly. The tanks pushed the wave of fighters toward Alex and his fighters, where they were easily picked off.

Within minutes, the front ends of the tanks appeared, the Marines caught between the mines and the spinning drills all dead.

An eerie quiet fell over the masses as the drills fell silent. By Alex's quick estimate, they had already lost nearly a quarter of their four thousand fighters.

"Is that it?" Gina asked, having stuck close to Zoe during the fighting. "Is it over?"

Alex wished he could have told her it was. "No," he replied. "This is just the calm before the real storm. But we're going to weather it, together. Okay?"

Gina nodded nervously. "Okay."

Alex turned away, raising his voice to a shout. "Reset the tanks! Reload and take cover! This isn't over yet, and we're lucky for it. We get to kill a lot more of the bastards who locked us up here and worked many of us to death."

A collective shout rose across the mines, echoing in the huge open chasm.

Alex closed his eyes, thinking of the message he and Cassandra had sent to the FUP, and suddenly realized that he had lost track of Cassandra. His eyes snapped open, and he glanced around, failing to locate her. His hand clenched into a fist. She might have already moved away to find cover. He didn't want to consider the alternative.

His thoughts returned to the tranSat. He could only hope Admiral Yarborough had heard it. He could only hope the fleet and his father were on the way.

He had badly underestimated the force Grand Admiral Strickland would so quickly bring to bear against them. For all his positive talk, it would take a miracle for them to have a chance to survive.

CHAPTER 36

Alex crouched behind a piece of mining equipment so twisted he couldn't tell what it had once been. He scanned the cavernous space before him, a haze of smoke still lingering from the fierce battle they had just endured. Dust particles danced in the beams of the mines' lighting, casting eerie shadows across the cavern walls. His ears still rang from the now-faded cacophony of explosions and gunfire, but he forced himself to stay alert, listening for any sign of the enemy's approach.

Around him, the surviving defenders huddled in small groups, tending to the wounded and redistributing what little ammunition remained. Their faces were already etched with exhaustion and tension, a far cry from the hopeful expressions they had worn just days ago when they had seized control of the prison. The floor was littered with spent shell casings and the bloodied fallen, though there were thankfully only a few bodies this deep into the mines.

So far.

And there were so many more on the two paths leading to this fortification, where they hoped to hold out before spreading into the surrounding shafts.

"How're we looking on ammo, Three?" Alex asked, his voice low as he turned to Jackson.

Jackson's face was streaked with soot. A fresh cut above his left eye had crusted over, giving him a fierce, almost feral appearance. He grimaced at the question. "Not great, Gunny. Decker says we've got maybe two more good firefights left in us, tops. After that, we're down to rocks and foul language."

Alex nodded, unsurprised but disappointed nonetheless. "We'll have to make every shot count."

He surveyed the makeshift fortifications—overturned mining carts filled with rubble, improvised barricades made from twisted metal and chunks of rock—they had cobbled together earlier. It wasn't pretty, but it had served them well so far. "We've bloodied their nose pretty good. Maybe they'll think twice before charging—"

His words were cut off by a distant rumble, growing steadily louder. The defenders tensed, weapons raised and ready. Alex could see the fear in their eyes, but also the steely resolve that had kept them fighting against impossible odds.

"Alright. Here they come," Alex growled, tightening his grip on his rifle. "Everyone, to your positions! Remember, aim for weak points—joints, visors, anywhere the armor's thinner! Make your shots count."

The echoing rumble grew to a crescendo, and then the next wave of SF Marines burst into view. They poured through the tunnel entrance like a flood, their boots pounding the stone floor. "Well, I'll be damned," Jackson muttered beside him, a note of dark satisfaction in his voice. "Looks like they ran out of the good stuff." Instead of the hard, imposing forms of power armor, these troops wore standard combat gear. They were numerous, but vulnerable.

Alex allowed himself a ferocious smile. "Then let's make them regret coming down here at all. Open fire!"

The cavern erupted in a storm of gunfire. The crack of rifles created a deafening cacophony that shook fresh dust from overhead. Muzzle flashes lit up the darker corners like strobes, casting shadows that danced and flickered across the rock walls. The defenders, entrenched in their positions, unleashed a devastating barrage.

Caught off guard by the ferocity of the response, the SF Marines crumpled to the ground—some crying out in pain, others merely falling silent and still. Their standard armor was no match for the hail of bullets, their formations disintegrating under the overwhelming assault.

"Push forward!" Alex shouted, seizing the momentum. His voice carried over the din of battle, rallying his fighters. "Don't let them regroup!"

Alex led the charge, the defenders surging ahead, driven by a mix of adrenaline and furious determination. Vaulting over a fallen ore cart and sprinting toward the entrance, his boots slipped on the blood-slicked floor, but he pushed on. He could see the shock and fear in the eyes of the surviving SF Marines as they realized their advance had turned into a rout.

The SF retreated, finding little cover as they backtracked the way they had come. The Scorpions and freed prisoners harassed them all the way back through the main shaft, picking them off one after another. Soon enough, the doors leading back to the main above-ground complex loomed ahead, the defenders reclaiming part of the territory they had surrendered. The struggling SF Marines broke completely there, turning to sprint away, desperate to escape from the charging defenses.

The former prisoners fired into the mass of retreating Marines, cutting them down as they tried to race back to their lines. Some made it out of the line of fire, leaving a trail of bodies in their wake, a macabre line of breadcrumbs leading back up toward the surface.

"Hold position! Hold!" Alex had to scream at the top of his lungs to halt the near-berserker rush, preventing the freed prisoners from rushing too far, too fast. There would be more Marines still entering the compound, and he didn't want his people cut down in their reckless abandon. Leon joined the cry, his deep voice echoing in the chamber and finally stopping the rest of the defenders.

A fresh silence fell over the battlefield, eerie after the chaos of combat. Alex took a moment to catch his breath, his chest heaving as he surveyed the carnage around him— not only the routed SF Marines but also the defenders who had fallen earlier during their initial retreat.

It was then that he spotted a familiar face among the fallen SF troops. "No. Damn," he whispered, though he had already feared the worst. His heart clenched as he moved to kneel beside Cassandra, her body sprawled at an unnatural angle, eyes staring sightlessly up at the cavern ceiling. He laid his hand over her eyes and closed them with a gentle touch. "I'm sorry, Cassandra. We'll make your sacrifice count. I promise."

"Gunny!" Zoe's urgent call snapped him back to the moment. The note of panic in it echoing off the cavern walls sent a chill down Alex's spine. "We've got movement up ahead. Looks like they're regrouping."

"Defensive positions!" he called out, his order driving the defenders to cover behind their prior barricades. "Check your ammo!"

The sounds of empty magazines falling on the rock floor and the collide of full ones slammed into wells filled the air. From behind the thick steel plates of a former ore cart, Alex shifted his gaze to the end of the corridor, where the approaching assault force was coming back into view.

A new wave of SF Marines advanced, and this time,

they were clad in the formidable powered armor that had already caused them so much grief.

"Shit. I guess they had some good stuff left after all," Jackson muttered, the sight of that imposing armor like a punch to the gut.

"Fall back!" Alex ordered. "Back to the mines! Move!"

The defenders scrambled to obey, laying down covering fire as they retreated, but the power-armored SF Marines were relentless, their heavy weapons cutting down defenders with terrifying efficiency.

Alex found himself beside Jackson and Zoe as they fell back, the three of them working to cover the retreat. One of the Marines pinned down a group of defenders, the massive rounds chewing through their cover in a spray of pulverized stone and twisted metal. Alex could see the fear in the eyes of the trapped fighters, their ammunition running low as they huddled behind rapidly disintegrating shelter.

"Three, with me! On my mark!" Alex called out. "Five, cover us!"

At his signal, he and Jackson broke from cover, sprinting to flank the Marine, exposing themselves to enemy fire. Zoe's precise shots kept them covered, her rifle cracking out a steady rhythm that bought them precious seconds. As they closed in, Alex saw the Marine start to turn, alerted to their approach by his armor's sensors.

"Now!" he shouted, his voice raw with exertion and tension.

In perfect unison, they opened fire. The Marine staggered under the assault, his weapon faltering as he tried to bring it to bear on the new threat. Sparks flew as their rounds impacted his armor, searching for weak points. One of Jackson's bullets found a vulnerable spot in the neck seal, and the Marine went down hard, his massive form crashing to the ground with a resounding clang.

Even so, the retreat quickly became a desperate scramble, the defenders fighting to get back to the mines. The tunnel echoed with the sounds of combat—the staccato of gunfire, the whoosh of jump jets, the screams of the wounded and dying. The air grew thick with smoke and dust, reducing visibility. Alex lost count of the number of times he felt the searing heat of near-misses, and a few hard stings of bullets absorbed by his body armor.

By the time they reached the main mining shaft, their numbers had been cut nearly in half. Alex's heart raced as he assessed their dwindling forces, the faces of the fallen flashing through his mind in a grim slideshow. They were running out of options. Fast.

"Three, get the mole tanks in position," Alex ordered, formulating a last-ditch plan. "We'll use them to bottleneck the Marines in the tunnel. It's our best shot at evening the odds."

As Jackson moved to comply, Alex turned to address the remaining defenders. Their faces were a mix of exhaustion, fear, and flagging courage, but in each pair of eyes he saw a fierce resolve, a refusal to go down without a fight.

"Listen up!" he shouted, his voice carrying across the cavern. "We've got one chance left. When those tanks engage, I want everyone concentrating fire on any Marines that make it past them. Aim for the weak points. Understood?"

A ragged chorus of affirmatives answered him. The sound of approaching Marines grew louder, the rhythmic thud of their armored footsteps echoing through the cavern like the heartbeat of some monstrous beast. Alex tensed, his finger resting lightly on the trigger of his rifle. He could feel his pulse pounding in his ears, each beat a countdown to what might be his last minute of life.

"Steady," he called out, his voice low but carrying in the tense silence. "Wait for my signal."

The first power-armored Marines appeared at the mouth of the tunnel, their weapons already blazing. The rifle fire chewed at the ore carts and rock piles, quickly eating away at their defenses. At that moment, the mole tanks roared to life, surging forward to meet the enemy head-on.

These Marines, like the earlier group, were caught off guard by the massive mining vehicles as they emerged from what had moments earlier appeared to be solid stone. The tanks' reinforced drills tore into their ranks, the hardened tips designed to bore through solid rock proving equally effective against power-armor. The sound of grinding metal filled the air as armor buckled and tore under the surprise assault.

"Now!" Alex shouted, his voice rising above the din of battle. "Light 'em up!"

The defenders opened fire, their concentrated barrage catching the disoriented Marines in a deadly crossfire, and for a moment, it seemed like they might actually turn the tide.

But then, disaster struck.

With a sputtering groan, one of the mole tanks ground to a halt, its engine giving out under the strain. The other, pushing too far into the Marine ranks, found itself under heavy fire, its thick armor unable to absorb the massive attack. In no time, its deadly drill slowed to a stop, its power supply destroyed.

The SF Marines, seizing the opportunity, pushed forward with renewed vigor. Their jump jets flared to life with high-pitched whines. They soared into the cavern and over the defenders' positions, raining down fire from above and wreaking havoc.

"Spread out!" Alex yelled, dodging a burst of gunfire from an airborne Marine. The rounds whizzed past his head, close enough that he could feel the heat on his skin.

"Don't bunch up! Make them work for it!"

But it was a losing battle. The exhausted and outgunned defenders couldn't match the Marines' mobility and firepower. Alex watched in despair as more of his people fell, their bodies joining the growing number of casualties littering the cavern floor.

"Fall back to the tunnels!" Alex screamed. "Fall back!" He swung his rifle toward an approaching enemy, rolling to the side as bullets threaded the floor where he had just been standing. Coming up on one knee, he aimed and fired, hitting the Marine's jets. They sputtered out, and he dropped like a stone into the deep chasm of the mines.

Looking around, Alex watched the armored SF Marines swarm and surrounded his defenders, overwhelming them from every side. He gritted his teeth as a powered Marine landed on a catwalk and shot down from a higher catwalk at Leon below him. The man's body writhed under the assault before dropping over the railing and tumbling into the darkness below.

"Gunny!" Zoe cried, the fear evident in her voice, a tone he had never heard from her before.

"Fall back!" he shouted back at her, pushing her toward one of the mine entrances, where a few other defenders had already started disappearing.

An SF Marine landed at the entrance, rifle chattering as he cut down the prisoners trying to escape. "There's nowhere to go," Zoe cried, losing hope.

Alex struggled not to do the same when an SF Marine landed on the floor to his right, only a dozen feet away, rifle pointed straight at him. He didn't want to accept that his life would end like this, but there was no way in hell he could avoid the killing shot.

Resigned, he straightened. His heart pounded, and his eyes narrowed.

His life would end like this, whether he liked it or not.

CHAPTER 37

Accepting his fate, Alex closed his eyes. And waited.

But the killing shot never came.

Instead, a high-pitched whistling sound he had never heard before, followed by a sound like tearing paper, cut through the chaos.

When Alex opened his eyes, he found the Marine he'd expected to take his life face down on the floor, his back riddled with holes. Alex looked up in disbelief as a group of power-armored figures, their jets firing, flew across the cavern, their deep red armor unlike anything he had ever seen before.

The newcomers hit the ground running, immediately engaging the SF Marines with skill, speed. and coordination that left Alex in awe. Their reflexes seemed superhuman, all moving with a fluid grace that spoke of extensive training and advanced augmentation. They dodged incoming fire and retaliated with devastating effect, making the SF's power-armored troops seem to clunk along like iron snails.

Beyond that, their advanced weaponry cut through the enemy with terrifying ease. One of the new arrivals went toe-to-toe with three SF Marines, ducking and weaving through attacks with inhuman grace. One of the enemy Marines smashed into a stone pillar with bone-crushing force, the impact leaving a spider web of cracks in the solid rock. The faceplate of another's helmet cracked and then shattered, exposing the shocked face beneath for a split second before a gunshot finished the fight. The third, realizing he was outmatched, retreated, only to be brought down by a precisely aimed shot to his jets. This Marine vanished into the tunnel's depths.

"Push them back!" Alex shouted, his voice hoarse but still carrying over the din of battle as he rallied his remaining forces. "Don't let up!"

With renewed determination, they turned away from their failing retreat and rejoined the fight. Moving with renewed purpose, their earlier fatigue was forgotten in the rush of impending victory, they pressed their advantage. Caught off guard by this new threat, the SF Marines found themselves on the defensive, and in an instant, the tide of battle dramatically shifted with devastating effect.

Alex found himself fighting alongside one of the newcomers, their movements syncing with an almost preternatural ease. Together, they engaged a group of SF Marines who had taken cover behind a fallen mining cart. The newcomer's armor hummed with energy as they activated a shield, deflecting incoming fire with ease. This gave Alex the opening he needed to flank the Marines, catching them unaware.

As the battle raged on, it became clear that the momentum had shifted drastically. The SF Marines, once seemingly unstoppable, were now being systematically dismantled. Soon, only a handful remained. These last few fought with the desperate ferocity of those who expected no quarter if they failed. They had seen their comrades fall, had witnessed the tide of battle turn against them, and now they fought with the reckless abandon of those with nothing left to lose.

One Marine, his armor scarred and smoking from multiple hits, ignited his jump jets, propelling himself at Alex with terrifying speed. Before Alex could react, one of the newcomers launched into the enemy like a human rocket. Their fight was brief but brutal, a whirlwind of strikes and counterstrikes that left Alex struggling to follow the action. In the end, the two fighters slammed together in an echoing crunch, the SF Marine crashing into the wall and toppling to the floor, where he remained motionless, his neck obviously broken.

"Surrender!" one of the newcomers called out, his helmet speakers distorting a voice that still carried an unmistakable note of authority.

For a tense moment, Alex thought the Marines would refuse. He could see the conflict in their body language, the way they shifted uneasily, weapons still raised, a few still firing. Then, as the last echoes of gunfire faded, quiet fell over the cavern. The air was thick with tension, the silence almost deafening after the chaos of battle, broken only now by the occasional groan of a wounded fighter. Everyone was acutely aware that the slightest provocation could reignite the battle.

Then, slowly, almost reluctantly, one, then two more dropped their weapons, others soon following suit. The fight gone out of them, they sank to their knees, arms raised in surrender. The gesture was one of defeat, but also one of profound relief. Even through their armored suits, Alex could see the fatigue in their slumped shoulders. Around him, the acrid smell of spent ammunition and burned flesh hung heavy in the air, an ugly reminder of the cost of war.

Alex stepped forward, his mind still reeling from the sudden turn of events. His body ached, a tapestry of cuts, bruises, and burns making themselves known now that the adrenaline was wearing off. He pushed the pain aside, focusing instead on the mysterious armored figures who had turned the tide of battle.

He approached the group of newcomers. "Who are you?" he asked, his voice nearly gone from shouting orders. "Where did you come from?"

One of the figures stepped forward, their movements liquid smooth despite the bulk of their armor. With a soft hiss of releasing pressure, the helmet retracted, revealing a woman's face. She was striking, with sharp features and intense eyes that seemed to look right through him. There was an almost regal quality to her bearing. To Alex, she was an avenging angel delivering the miracle for which he had only dared to hope.

"Sergeant Elena Volkov," she said, a small smile playing at the corners of her mouth. Her voice was husky, with a hint of an accent Alex couldn't quite place. She eyed him curiously. "You look familiar." Her small smile expanded, two perfect rows of white teeth belying her animalistic ferocity in a fight. "You must be Alex, no?"

"Gunnery Sergeant Alexander Strickland," he replied. "FUP Marine Force Recon, Scorpion Squad."

"Pleased to meet you," Elena replied. "I'm grateful to find you alive. I promised your father I would bring you back, or die trying."

Alex felt a rush of emotions—relief, excitement, and a sudden, unexpected flutter in his chest as he met Volkov's gaze. The mention of his father sent a jolt through him, a reminder of the larger conflict raging beyond the confines of their underground battlefield. "My father? He's here?"

Volkov nodded, her expression softening slightly at the hope in Alex's voice. "The Wraith and the rest of the FUP fleet are engaged in orbit as we speak. We were sent ahead to secure the ground and extract you and your people."

A second member of Volkov's team moved in beside her. "We ran into a few minor obstacles on the way," he said. "Nothing we couldn't handle."

The news hit Alex like a physical force. After everything they had endured, rescue was finally at hand. He suddenly felt lightheaded, the constant pressure that had been exerting down on him for days lifting ever so slightly.

"It doesn't look like there's anything you can't handle," he said, his eyes still on the sergeant.

Her next words tempered his elation, bringing him back to their situation's harsh reality.

"Don't get too excited just yet," she warned, her expression growing serious. The intensity in her gaze sharpened, reminding Alex of a predator assessing its surroundings. "The battle above is fierce, and there's no guarantee of victory. We need to be prepared for any outcome."

Alex nodded, forcing himself to focus on the immediate situation. The brief moment of relief faded, replaced by the familiar tension of the ongoing threat. "Understood. What's our next move?"

Volkov gestured to the captured SF Marines, her movements economical and precise. "You know how to use FUP power armor, correct?"

"A little," Alex replied with a sly grin. "I've never seen armor like yours before though."

"It's a special edition," another newcomer said. "That's why it's red."

"Swix thinks he's a comedian," Volkov said. "We're not FUP resources. We're on loan from the CIP. We call this Phalanx armor. Developed in hopes that it will help slow the Grand Admiral's conquest of our planets."

Jackson and Zoe closed in on them as she replied, having overheard everything.

"The CIP?" Jackson said. "Damn, I'm glad you aren't the bad guys in this dimension."

"What do you mean?" Swix asked.

"Ignore him," Alex said, drawing an indignant look from Jackson. "Three, Five…" He motioned to the captured SF Marines. "Let's get suited up. We're not out of this fight yet."

CHAPTER 38

Soren's gaze remained fixed on the sensor projection, watching as the Fist of Justice materialized out of fold space, flanked by a dozen more warships. The massive dreadnought dwarfed its escort vessels, its imposing silhouette a stark reminder of the destructive power it wielded. His jaw clenched, a mixture of dread and conviction coursing through him.

"Sir," Mark's voice cut through the tense silence on the bridge, "I'm detecting multiple launches from the new arrivals. Dropships and fighters, sir."

Soren nodded as he assessed the rapidly evolving situation. "Put it on the primary," he ordered.

The viewscreen shifted camera feeds, zooming in on the newly arrived warships and revealing a swarm of smaller vessels pouring from their hangars. The dropships, bulky and heavily armored, formed tight formations as they began their descent toward Teegarden's surface. Starfighters moved into an escort position around them, their thrusters leaving brief trails of blue-white exhaust in the void.

"They're not wasting any time," Soren muttered, more

to himself than to the crew. He straightened, his voice rising as he addressed the bridge. "Our primary target is the Fist of Justice. Everything else is secondary. Sang, get us clear of the main fighting so we can cloak and make our approach."

"Aye, sir," Sang replied. The Wraith veered away from the chaotic melee of ships and breaking into open space. The Valkyrie continued to harass them, sending volleys of missiles into their shields, which held strong against the effort.

"Minh," Soren called out, opening a channel to the Hooligan's leader, "what's the situation on the ground?"

Minh's voice came back over the comms. "Ground team is planetside, Captain. Volkov's squad is en route to the prison, moving in right up the enemy's tail. To be honest, I hope they have what it takes to break through that mess."

"That's their problem now. Another round of reinforcements are on their way down. I need you to intercept them. We can't let them add more fuel to the fire. But be careful; they have a formidable number of fighters escorting them."

"Copy that, sir," Minh replied. "We'll see how formidable they are."

As Soren closed the channel, another comm alert chimed. "It's Admiral Yarborough, sir," Samira announced.

"Put her through," Soren ordered, bracing himself for what he knew would be a difficult conversation.

"Captain, it looks like the Grand Admiral took the bait," she said.

"That he did," Soren replied. "We're moving into position to make a run at her now."

"Captain, I know that was the plan, but...we're taking a beating out here. We didn't anticipate this many ships, and if Alexander triggers the vortex cannon—"

"This is the reason we're here," Soren interrupted. "To rescue Alex and the FUP prisoners, and take our shot against the Fist. We can't abandon that mission now. We'll never get another chance like this."

"And what about getting ourselves killed in the process?" she snapped. "If we're destroyed here, the war is over, Soren."

"If we don't stop the Fist, the multiple universes will be over, Jane," Soren growled back. "Yours and mine. I know you're scared. We all are. But we can't give up now. Keep your ships tight to the enemy targets. It'll make the Fist think twice about using that cannon, knowing they'll destroy so many of their own assets in the process. We have to hope that'll be enough to deter them."

"And if it isn't?" Jane asked.

Soren didn't answer. They both knew what would happen if the Fist fired on its own again.

"Fine," she said agreed. "But you'd better destroy that damned ship."

The ferocity of the comment surprised Soren since it was Alexander's ship. Or was it? Her son and his squad had probably left the Fist to descend to Teegarden's surface. If they were going to destroy it, now was the time.

Alex had already killed one of his doppelgängers. If he was still alive, still fighting down there, Soren was confident he would deal with this one, too.

"Keira, prepare to activate the cloak," Soren said. "Sang, prepare to execute evasive maneuver Echo-4."

"Echo-4?" Jack asked from beside Soren while the two officers affirmed the orders.

"We need to lose that Valkyrie," Soren replied, watching the tactical projection. He didn't blink, preparing for the precise moment when the maneuver would be most effective.

"Sang, now!" Soren barked.

Her response was immediate and impressive. The

Wraith pivoted sharply, the inertial dampeners straining to compensate for the sudden change in vector. The Valkyrie couldn't hope to adjust to the sudden maneuver that made the Wraith seem more like a starfighter than a capital warship.

"Keira, activate the cloak."

"Already done, sir," Keira replied.

Soren grinned, comfortable with his tactical officer anticipating him. "Nice work, both of you," he said. "Now, get us a good angle of attack on the Fist. Make sure we stay clear of its vortex cone."

"Aye, Captain," Sang replied.

With immediate danger averted, Soren returned his attention to the larger battle. "Mark, find the Spirit of War and put a visual on the primary."

"Aye, Captain," Mark replied.

The Spirit of War appeared on the viewscreen, locked in a fierce engagement with a Komodo-class cruiser and a nimble Valkyrie simultaneously. The sight was both awe-inspiring and terrifying.

Jane's ship weaved expertly through a storm of enemy fire. Railgun rounds crisscrossed the void between the ships, peppering the Spirit's shields with glancing blows as she danced between the opponents. Jane followed his advice, keeping close to the enemy to negate the Fist's main gun.

Soren watched, his heart in his throat, as the Spirit unleashed a devastating broadside against the Komodo. The barrage struck home, a dazzling light show of destructive energy as the enemy's shields flared brilliantly, struggling to absorb the onslaught. It seemed the Komodo's defenses would hold for a moment, but then a critical failure cascaded through its shield grid. The protective energy vanished, leaving the ship vulnerable.

The Spirit's follow-up salvo was merciless. Armor-piercing flechettes punched through the Komodo's hull plating like tissue paper, leaving gaping wounds in the ship's flank. Atmosphere vented in violent bursts. As internal systems overloaded and ruptured, secondary explosions blossomed along the cruiser's length, quickly snuffed out by the vacuum of space.

As the Komodo reeled from the assault, the Valkyrie seized the opportunity to swoop in and unleash a swarm of missiles. Soren held his breath, watching them streak toward the Spirit of War's exposed flank. The Spirit's shields, still recovering from the exchange with the Komodo, flickered and strained under the barrage.

Most of the missiles detonated against the weakened shields, their energy dissipating harmlessly into space, but two managed to slip through just as the defenses failed. They slammed into the Spirit's hull, leaving angry, glowing scars in their wake.

Soren winced, almost feeling the impact himself. He knew Jane's ship had to have shuddered violently under the assault, but it didn't falter. Instead, it came about with surprising grace for a ship its size, bringing its railguns to bear on the Valkyrie. The ensuing exchange was brief but brutal, both ships trading salvos at near point-blank range. Shields on both ships flared and failed, armor plating melted and twisted under the onslaught.

Soren's knuckles whitened as he gripped the edge of his command seat, watching the Spirit take hit after hit but give as good as she got, her return fire precise and devastating. A mix of relief and satisfaction washed through him as a final shot from the Spirit found a weak point in the Valkyrie's armor, breaching its core. The smaller ship suddenly went dark and drifted through space on its current vector. The Spirit of War adjusted speed and heading to match, clinging tight to the damaged enemy ship as it moved away from the larger exchange between the FUP and the SF fleets.

Shifting his attention to the sensor projection, Soren found the Fist of Justice, surprised to see that it was only now beginning to accelerate to join the fray. The sight, even from a distance, sent a chill down his spine. He could almost feel the malevolent intent radiating from the vessel as if it were a living thing hungry for destruction.

He didn't like the formation of its escort vessels, either. They stayed behind the flagship, remaining clear of its vortex cannon. Would the ship fire on its own to disable the FUP fleet? It had at FOB Alpha, but how many starship losses could the SF endure? And if he were still onboard, would Alexander have the will to disable his mother's ship, which would surely falter once life support went fully offline? If someone else was in command, they might not be so hesitant. Soren knew he had to reach the Fist before it could get in range of the Spirit. It was the only way to ensure its cannon couldn't be used against the FUP flagship.

"Sir," Mark called out, his voice tense, "The Hooligans have engaged the dropships."

Soren turned his attention to the relevant quadrant of the projection as the black triangles representing the Hooligans merged with the fighters escorting the incoming dropships. The space around Teegarden lit up with weapons fire, the Hooligans getting off the first shots.

Zooming in on the frantic melee, Soren could almost feel the g-forces as Minh's Hooligan darted and wove through the frantic furball. The captain's extreme skills were on full display as he rolled and juked his bird to avoid targeting locks on it while brief flares marked the demise of the enemy ships in his reticle.

Two SF fighters fell to Minh's guns rapidly, their hulls rupturing in silent explosions that illuminated the battlefield. Debris scattered in all directions, adding another layer of danger to the already treacherous environment, but for every enemy Minh downed, another appeared to replace it. If nothing else, the overwhelming number of SF fighters threatened to swamp the Hooligans just through attrition.

Soren watched as one of the Hooligans suddenly found three SF fighters hot on his tail. He flew with amazing skill, twisting and turning in ways that seemed to defy the laws of physics, but in the end, it wasn't enough. A storm of enemy fire overwhelmed the fighter's shields in a brilliant flash, sending it into an uncontrolled spin before turning it into a fireball that quickly flared out.

His wingman climbed up past all three enemy fighters, yawed his fighter around and rolled, screaming in from above, guns blazing in a textbook ambush. For a moment, it looked like he would succeed, but in his fury, he had overlooked a descending dropship. A burst of rounds spat from one of the dropship's turrets, punching through the Hooligan's shields and catching the fighter squarely in the cockpit. Its pilot dead, the Pilum spun out of control, gravity pulling it down to crash into Teegarden's rocky surface.

Despite the losses, the Hooligans fought on. Soren monitored the action as Minh staged a daring attack run on the same dropship, weaving through its web of defensive stream of railgun fire to close on it with almost reckless abandon. At the last possible moment, he unleashed a full salvo of missiles before breaking off in a tight roll that had to strain the limits of his Pilum's structural integrity.

The dropship's shields flared brilliantly as it struggled to repel the assault. For a heartbeat, it seemed they might hold, but then Minh's missiles tore through them into the dropship's hull, triggering a cascade of internal explosions. This culminated in the entire transport breaking up, and the debris scattered to take out two unlucky SF fighters.

A second dropship fell to a coordinated strike from three Hooligans, their combined firepower overwhelming its formidable defenses in a dazzling display of precision flying and gunnery. The victory was short-lived, however, as the remaining dropships slipped past the embattled fighters, streaking toward Teegarden's surface with single-minded purpose.

"What are the odds one of those downed dropships had Jane's kid on board?" Jack asked, watching the more minor battle play out beside Soren.

"One in five," Soren replied, noting that eight dropships had reached the surface. "But with our current streak of luck, zero."

"That ought to mean our luck's about to change for the better."

"I hope so."

Minh's voice came over the comms, strained but determined. "We waxed two dropships, Captain. But these bastards are putting up one hell of a fight, and we're down two of our own."

"Nobody said this would be easy, Minh," Soren replied. "Those prisoners need every bit of help we can provide. Keep up the pressure."

"Copy that," Minh replied.

"Captain!" Liam's voice filled the bridge, breathless but excited. "Good news! Sergeant Volkov has made contact with Alex and his squad. They're alive, sir!"

"Well, there you go," Jack said. "Our luck is changing."

A wave of short-lived relief washed over Soren. Staying alive was hardly a given for anyone right now. "Good work, Liam. You need to warn them, more enemy forces are incoming, including from the Fist of Justice."

"Understood, sir," Liam replied. "We'll make sure they're warned."

As the communication ended, Soren took a deep breath, centering himself. Alex was alive. They had a chance. He just had to hold up his end.

It was time they ended this, once and for all.

CHAPTER 39

"Now this is more like it," Jackson said, throwing a couple of air punches with the SF Karuta power armor the Scorpions had taken from the captured Marines. "Not quite as good as our stuff, and it smells kind of funky." He turned to the enemy Marines, bound and sitting on the cavern floor. "What? The Grand Admiral doesn't let you use deodorant either? What an asshole."

Despite the continuing desperation of their situation, Alex couldn't help but crack a smile. Jackson's familiar humor was a welcome respite from the tension that had been their constant companion for days.

The moment was interrupted by the arrival of a platoon of Marines Alex immediately recognized as what was left of the force he'd trained on the Wraith. They pushed carts between them, loaded with weapon and ammo containers, the sight of which sent a surge of relief through him.

A Marine at the front of the group approached the Scorpions and Lammergeiers, trying to see through their faceplates, obviously looking for Alex.

"Here, Sergeant Mackie," Alex said, raising his hand to help him out.

"Gunny," Mackie said, turning to him with a broad smile. "It's good to see you. We've brought supplies and reinforcements. Lieutenant Moffit and Captain Strickland send their regards."

"Thank you, Sergeant," Alex replied. "Your timing couldn't be better. Let's get this fresh ordnance distributed."

As Mackie's team began handing out weapons and ammunition to the freed prisoners, Sergeant Volkov approached Alex. "I've received an update from orbit. Your father knows you're down here. They're doing everything they can to clear a path for evacuation."

Alex nodded, a complex mix of emotions swirling in his chest. Relief at his father's knowledge of his survival and a gnawing worry about the dangers he must be facing. "What's the situation up there?" he asked, dreading the answer but knowing he needed to hear it.

Volkov's expression tightened, the lines around her eyes deepening. She glanced up, as if she could see through the layers of rock to the battle raging in orbit. "It's not good," she said, her voice low and grave. "The Fist of Justice has arrived, along with significant reinforcements."

Alex exhaled, not all that surprised the Fist had finally joined the party. "That's not good."

"There's more," she said. "Dropships have deployed with ground reinforcements, including from the Fist. We've slowed the assault, but this is far from over."

"The Scarabs will be on one of those dropships," Alex said. "Watching you fight, I assume your squad is augmented?"

She nodded. "I don't know if our version is quite as advanced as the FUP's, but our armor should help balance that equation, if needed."

"Oh, it'll be needed. We don't have our augments anymore. The Grand Admiral saw to that."

"I'd give my left arm for them right about now," Jackson muttered, his voice a mix of frustration and longing.

"Seconded," Zoe said.

Alex looked to Volkov. "You're more familiar with the situation out there," he said. "What's our next move?"

"We push forward," she said. "Test their strength and resolve and retake as much ground as we can before those reinforcements arrive. The more territory we control, the better our chances will be of holding out until extraction."

"Agreed," Alex replied. "I like the way you think, Sergeant."

With a plan in place, they moved out, leaving the most entrenched defenders behind. The combined force of freed prisoners, FUP Marines, Scorpions, and Lammergeiers advanced through the winding tunnels of the mine complex. The immediate area remained clear, the SF forces clearly regrouping further up in the complex, waiting for the reinforcements to arrive before making another push.

They made it all the way back to the mine entrance without confrontation, but Alex could hear echoes of movement from further ahead. At once, his SF armor's comms flared in his helmet, the speaker demanding a report of their status, so Alex gave him one.

"This armor is now property of the Federation of United Planets," he growled as his eyes landed on Cassandra's corpse for the second time. "My status is motivated and pissed off, and I'm ready to kill any of you SF bastards who're unlucky enough to find themselves in my reticle." The comms cut off while Jackson and Zoe laughed at Alex's reply.

"Contact!" Volkov called out, interrupting their grim amusement. The Lammergeiers moved with inhuman speed, launching ahead of the rest of the force. Alex, Jackson, and Zoe quickly joined them, surging forward to join the fight.

A skirmish broke out in the tunnel as they met the first ranks of SF troops, perhaps nothing more than scouts. They turned out to be conventionally equipped, their armor lacking the imposing bulk and protection of the suits Alex and his team now wore. Still, they fought with desperation, their weapons chattering ceaselessly as they tried to hold back the larger advancing force.

The firefight was intense but brief. Outmatched by the power-armored assault, the SF troops, caught off guard by the ferocity of the attack, quickly crumbled, the survivors retreating.

As the last gunfire echoes faded, Alex took stock of their situation. They had suffered zero casualties, while the SF forces had been utterly routed. But it was hardly a decisive victory. It had been nothing more than the enemy's probe to see what they were facing.

"Good work, everyone," he called out, his voice carrying through the suit's external speakers. "But stay alert." He knew better than to let his guard down. In his experience, moments of triumph were often followed by the nastiest surprises.

They pressed on, moving up the main passageway toward the intake area, with the Lammergeiers leading the advance. They had almost reached the area when Volkov's voice echoed through the corridor. "Contact!" she shouted. "Multiple hostiles!"

"Charge!" Alex cried, leading the rest of their forces forward. He burst out of the corridor into the large, open space strewn with defeated fortifications, destroyed furniture, shell casings, and bodies from their earlier fighting. A mass of enemies occupied the space now, a mix of Marines in traditional and power armor.

The Lammergeiers went for the armored Marines as the intake area erupted into a fresh storm of gunfire. The freed prisoners and FUP Marines poured everything they had into the SF positions, trading heavy fire. As Alex rushed the powered opposition, rounds pinged off his armor, though he couldn't tell which side it was coming from. Alongside Volkov, he tore into the enemy position, making good on his threat over the comms.

The battle had barely started in earnest when Alex thought he heard someone crying out for Gunny. He turned to the rear, finding Decker desperately waving his arms. With a quick jump back from the fighting, laying down his suppressing fire as he went, he landed behind the still-intact barricade next to the man.

"What's wrong?" he asked.

Decker put his hand on the comms unit in his ear. "Contact behind us!" he shouted. "They found another way in! Our rear guard is getting decimated!"

Alex's blood ran cold. There were only supposed to be two entrances to the mines, and Jackson had collapsed one after the first SF units had breached it. It meant there had to be a third way in. An unmarked entry the prisoners didn't know about, and the guards they'd questioned hadn't divulged. Or maybe they didn't know about it either.

While pushing forward, a second force had slipped in, flanking them completely. But it couldn't be an ordinary force, or the rear guard wouldn't have quickly fallen into such dire straits.

"The Scarabs." It had to be.

They had fallen right into Alexander's trap and were now caught in its jaws.

CHAPTER 40

"Three, Five, fall back!" Alex shouted, already turning to race back the way they had come. "Volkov!" he shouted, his voice echoed off the cavern walls, filled with urgency, but she apparently didn't hear him. "Volkov!"

Giving up on calling for her, he doubled his efforts, racing for the mines. Jackson and Zoe were close behind, the Lammergeiers finally breaking contact to join them. The rest of the force remained at the intake area, defending that front.

They rocketed through the complex, Volkov and her team catching up to them in no time. Racing alongside them to confront the enemy ambush, their jump jets cut the time to reach the entrance to the mines in half.

Continuing from there without slowing, they descended as the metal flooring changed to carved rock and the air became cooler and damper. The disabled mole tanks came into view, the echo of gunfire on the other side of them, muzzle flashes visible at the end of the tunnel. A form blurred past the opening, the dark blue power armor of a Scarab impossible not to recognize.

"Son of a bitch!" Alex heard Jackson cry.

They picked up their pace, rushing forward with reckless abandon. Reaching the mole tanks, the world seemed to suddenly slow down, every detail etched with crystal clarity.

Flame blossomed as explosive charges went off, detonated by a tripline or other sensor. The sudden fireball radiated out, the frames of the tanks distorting and warping as they melted, bent, and shattered. The heat and flames of the explosion reached out for him, smoke billowing, debris flying everywhere.

Out of the corner of his eye, Alex caught sight of Rivera right behind him, her hand reaching out to shove him forward with incredible force. As he flew through the air, he turned just in time to see her take the brunt of the blast, flung back by it to disappear in the debris filling the air.

Blinded by the dust and choking on it, Alex could barely breathe. His ears rang, drowning out all other sounds and leaving him stunned and disoriented.

When the dust finally began to settle and his senses slowly returned, he found himself lying on the mine side of a newly formed wall of rubble. Volkov and Swix were there, along with Jackson and Zoe. But… "Rivera," he gasped, staring at the pile of rock and debris. His voice was hoarse, barely audible over the ringing in his ears. "She…"

"Saved your life," Volkov finished, her voice tight with emotion. She stood above him, her helmet retracted to show her face, her eyes burning with grief and anger. The rest of her Lammergeiers were also missing.

Alex turned over, pain wracking his body as he pushed himself up, dust and small rocks falling off him as he slowly stood. He suddenly realized that not only had he lost his rifle, the rest of the fighting had gone silent following the explosion. He turned toward the mines, eyes narrowing to glare through the haze. But there didn't seem to be anyone to shoot at, anyway.

"I don't understand," Volkov said. "What's going on?"

Alex wondered the same thing until a familiar voice echoed through the cavernous chamber. "Alex, are you still alive?" Alexander shouted.

Alex gritted his teeth. "Yeah, asshole!" he replied, wondering what his doppelgänger was up to. "I'm alive!"

"Tell your people to hold their fire. No one else needs to die here today," Alexander said. "I've ordered my forces to stand down."

"What is it you want, Alexander?"

There was a pause before the response came. When Alexander finally spoke, there was something different in his voice. "I want to fight you, Alex. One-on-one."

The request caught Alex off guard. He exchanged another glance with Volkov, who looked equally surprised. Her eyebrows were raised, her head tilted slightly in a silent question. This time, Alex was just as confused as she was. "Why should I agree to that?" he called back, his voice laced with skepticism. "It's hardly a fair fight with your augments."

"I won't use them," Alexander replied quickly, almost too quickly. There was an edge of desperation in his voice now "I swear it." Alexander's armored form appeared through the haze, He stopped no more than ten feet away from Alex. "Just you and me. No tricks, no backup. One-on-one."

"Why?" Alex asked, shaking his head in disbelief.

"It's…what I saw," Alexander said. "When my father used the neural link on you. Your memories. Your family. I…I never had that. I hate you for it, and envy you at the same time."

Alex glanced at Zoe, who shrugged, unsure what to make of his admission.

"We don't have to do this, Alexander," Alex said. "We don't have to fight at all. We don't even have to be on opposite sides. You might not have grown up with those experiences, but that doesn't mean you can't make your own. That doesn't mean you can't have what I've had."

"That's where you're wrong," Alexander answered. "I can't have those things. They were never meant for me. I was born to follow in the greatness of my father and inherit the galaxy. Without warmth. Without compassion. Without compromise. I need to know that it was the right path. Killing you, my counterpart, but also my inverse in so many ways, will prove it. Cheating would prove nothing. Please. I...I need this."

Alex hesitated, caught off guard by the unexpected vulnerability in Alexander's voice. The tactical part of his mind screamed that this was a trap, that trusting Alexander was foolish at best and suicidal at worst. But there was something in Alexander's tone that gave him pause, a note of genuine emotion and sincerity that he had never heard from him before.

Alex glanced at Volkov, searching her face for guidance. The Lammergeier sergeant's expression was guarded, her eyes narrowed in thought. She gave a slight shrug, leaving the decision to him.

"Alright," Alex said finally, his decision made. He could hardly believe the words coming out of Alexander's mouth, but something deep in his gut told him this was the right call. "You've got your fight. But if you try anything..."

"I won't," Alexander cut in quickly, relief evident in his voice. "You have my word."

"Are you sure about this, Gunny?" Jackson's voice came through his comm, tight with concern. "It smells like a trap to me."

"It may well be," Alex replied, his voice low. "But if we can end this here, maybe we can avoid more bloodshed."

"And if it goes sideways?" Zoe asked, ever the pragmatist.

"Then you two better be ready to pull my ass out of the fire. Again."

With a nod to Volkov and one to his team, Alex stepped forward, walking closer to Alexander.

"So," Alexander said, his voice strained. "Here we are."

"Here we are," Alex agreed, his voice steady despite the adrenaline coursing through his veins. "Let's get this over with."

Without warning, Alexander lunged forward, his fist whistling toward Alex's face. Alex jerked back, the blow missing him by millimeters. He countered with a quick jab to Alexander's midsection, the impact reverberating through his armor.

And so it began.

Alex had fought a copy of himself on Jungle. It was the hardest fight of his life, but it was nothing like this. That version of him had fought with the belief it would save his galaxy. This version fought believing it was the only way to save himself.

They exchanged blows, the clang of metal striking metal echoing through the chamber. Alex managed to land a solid hit on Alexander's faceplate, the impact sending cracks spider-webbing across the transparent material. Alexander retaliated with a vicious knee to Alex's midsection, driving him backward before landing a furious series of blows on the sides of his helmet, forcing him to jump back and fire his jump jets to clear the immediate area. He drew his sidearm and flew backward, firing at his eagerly pursuing opponent. One of his rounds hit Alexander's faceplate, creating more cracks in the protection.

Alexander answered with gunfire of his own, and the two of them ranged farther apart. Each of them used their armor to take their fight up to the catwalks high above the cavern floor. The metal grating rattled beneath their armored feet as they traded blows, each impact threatening to send one or the other plummeting into the depths below.

Alex was again on the defensive, driven back by Alexander's powerful kick. He would have gone over the railing into the depths if not for his jump jets, activating them just in time to crash land on a lower catwalk. As he struggled to his feet, Alexander leaped down, landing with a heavy thud that threatened to dislodge the entire catwalk structure.

They continued their brutal dance, neither willing to give ground. Alex could feel his strength waning, his reactions slowing. But he pushed on, knowing what was at stake. He landed a third blow to Alexander's faceplate, shattering the transparency, a good deal of it falling away to expose his forehead and one eye. His eyes were narrowed, lips twisted in an animalistic fury. He swung at Alex, but Alex blocked the blow and twisted his arm, drawing it back almost far enough to break it. Alexander grunted and threw his other fist at Alex's face. Alex ducked beneath it, cocking his fist back to land another decisive blow. Alexander grabbed the arm holding him and slammed his elbow on it, crushing the armor against Alex's limb. He cried out as pain lanced up his arm.

He knew immediately he had been betrayed.

Alexander had triggered his augments.

Before Alex could even finish the thought, Alexander had him pinned to the catwalk, his armored boot pressing down on Alex's faceplate. Cracks formed in the protection. The pressure increased, the initial breaks spider-webbing out as it began to fail.

"You cheated," Alex gasped, his voice strained.

"I can't lose," Alexander replied. "I just...can't."

If his face weren't about to be crushed, Alex would have felt sorry for the man. It was pathetic how desperately he needed to justify his existence and everything he had done and would continue to do in his father's name.

Alexander raised his foot to deliver the killing blow.

But it never came.

Instead, the explosive crack of a bullet split the air, followed by the thud of it striking flesh and bone as a bloody hole appeared in the center of Alexander's exposed forehead. He stumbled backward, held in place for just a moment by the railing before he toppled over it, disappearing into the depths below.

Alex turned to search for the gun the bullet had come from and the hand behind it. To his shock, he found one of the Scarabs on the trigger. The rest of the squad stood frozen, staring at the Scarab who'd killed Alexander as he stepped forward, his movements hesitant but purposeful. He reached up, removing his helmet to reveal a face etched with conflict, grief and resolve.

"I couldn't let him do it," Theo said, his voice carrying across the cavern. "This ends now."

The other Scarabs stared at Theo, mouths agape and uncertainty clear in their body language. But none of them raised their weapons against him.

"We all know this wasn't right," Theo continued, addressing his team. "Even Alexander knew. He just couldn't accept it. We have a chance to make a different decision right here, right now. I'm standing down. Who's with me?"

For a moment, no one moved. The silence stretched out, taut as a wire. Then, one by one, the Scarabs removed their helmets, their faces marked with relief and despair.

Alex stared at them, dumbstruck and grateful that in the end, his long game had played out exactly as he'd so desperately hoped. Perhaps they had a chance after all. The battle was far from over, but for the first time since this ordeal began, victory seemed possible.

The real fight, he realized, was just beginning.

CHAPTER 41

The Wraith glided silently through the chaotic battlefield, her cloaking device bending light and sensor signals around her sleek hull, rendering her invisible to both friend and foe. On the bridge, the air was thick with tension, the crew's breathing shallow and quick as they focused intently on their tasks.

Soren sat at the command station, eyes fixed on the sensors. The holographic projection showed a tight pack of ships circling the already destroyed and disabled ships as though they were trapped in their orbits. The Fist of Justice loomed in the tertiary viewscreen, its imposing silhouette to the Wraith's starboard as they worked to flank the behemoth and attain an unbreakable firing solution on it.

"The Fist is entering optimal weapons range now, sir," Mark reported, his voice taut, his face pale. A sheen of sweat beaded on his forehead as he monitored the sensor readings.

Soren nodded, his jaw clenched so tight his teeth were grinding, curious to see what the Fist's commander would do now that he had nearly reached the battlefield. To his surprise and momentary relief, the dreadnought began firing conventional weapons rather than its dreaded vortex cannon.

"Why are they holding their vortex cannon back?" Jack murmured beside him, voicing Soren's own thoughts. The XO's usually calm demeanor was strained, his eyes darting between the sensor projection and the main viewscreen.

Both erupted in a frenzy of activity, precluding Soren's answer. The Fist and its support ships had unleashed a devastating barrage against the FUP fleet. He watched in horror as two friendly icons blinked out, each representing a ship and crew lost to the assault.

"The Spectacle and Illusion are gone, sir," Mark reported, his voice cracking with emotion. "The Ever Valiant's taken heavy damage... she's breaking apart!"

"What's the status of the Spirit of War?" Soren asked.

"Still in the fight, sir," Mark replied, a note of awe in his voice. "Admiral Yarborough's giving as good as she's getting."

As if to punctuate Mark's words, the Spirit of War executed a daring maneuver, bringing its broadside to bear against one of the Valkyries. The FUP flagship's guns blazed, the display lighting up with the intensity of the relentless storm of metal tearing into the smaller ship's shields. Soren could almost feel the heat of the barrage through the viewscreen.

Soren opened up a channel to the Hooligan squadron leader. "Minh," he called out, his voice sharp, cutting through the chaos of the bridge. "I need you to join up with the other FUP squadrons. Focus your efforts on the Fist's support ships. Do what you can to harass and distract them from firing on the Spirit."

"Copy that, Captain," Minh's voice came back. "We're on our way."

Soren eyed the projection, watching as the seven remaining Hooligans formed up with the remnants of the

FUP fighter squadrons. The combined force streaked toward the enemy warships, launching their dwindling missile stocks once in range. The enemy responded with railgun fire, forcing the starfighters to take evasive action.

"Sir," Mark called out. "More tangoes from the Fist."

The space around the massive dreadnought exploded with activity as two squadrons of SF fighters poured from its hangar. They moved to engage the FUP squadrons, the two forces immediately filling the void with crisscrossing trails of weapons fire. Starfighters either disintegrated in the vacuum of space or escaped to come around for another pass.

"Sang, how close are we?" Soren asked, his eyes never leaving the projection. He could feel sweat trickling down his back, his uniform sticking uncomfortably to his skin. Their stealthy trip to stab the Fist in the heart seemed as though it was taking forever.

"Almost in optimal firing range, sir," Sang replied, her hands steady on the controls as she guided the Wraith through the chaos of battle. "Another thirty seconds and—"

Her words were cut off by a gasp from Mark. "Captain! The Fist... they're charging its vortex cannon!"

Soren's blood ran cold, an immediate chill spreading through his body. "No," he breathed, scarcely able to believe it. "They wouldn't dare...not with their own ships so close."

But the evidence was undeniable. The viewscreen showed an ominous energy buildup at the Fist's bow that seemed to grow with each passing second. Soren could almost feel the charge in the air, as if the very fabric of space was tensing in anticipation of the coming devastation.

"Sang, we need to close the distance now," Soren ordered, his voice sharp. "Get us into firing position before they can—"

"Captain!" Keira cried suddenly. "The Fist has target lock on us! They're firing their railguns!"

Sang was already desperately trying to escape the inexplicably aimed barrage when multiple thunderous impacts slammed into the hull. Alarms blared in a deafening cacophony as stressed meal groaned and rattled, reverberating throughout the ship.

"Multiple hull breaches!" Ethan's voice rang out from the engineering station.

"Shields up!" Soren commanded, gripping the arms of his station chair. "Evasive maneuvers!"

Another volley rocked the ship even as Sang twisted and rolled the Wraith to avoid the incoming fire. Sparks showered from overhead panels, and a fire erupted from one of the auxiliary consoles. Samira quickly grabbed a nearby extinguisher off the bulkhead and rushed to put it out before it could do any real damage. But now, with their cover blown, they were a prime target for the Fist's support ships.

More railgun rounds and missiles slammed into their hastily powered shields, the impacts rolling through the hull like thunder.

"Shields at sixty percent and dropping," Keira reported, her voice strained as she worked to redistribute power.

"Emergency bulkheads are sealed," Ethan added. "No injuries or casualties reported."

"Only because we're running a damned skeleton crew," Jack cursed. "How the hell did they see us? We removed the transmitter."

"They must be using some other method to detect us," Soren replied. "It doesn't matter now. We've lost the cloak. We need to stay focused."

Their surprise attack had been thwarted, but with the Fist's massive vortex cannon moments away from firing, his mind was working to devise an alternate plan.

"Captain, the Spirit of War..." Mark said, his voice trailing off, unable to describe what he saw.

Soren's eyes locked on the projection, where the Spirit and three other FUP ships had broken off from the main battle to power toward the Fist at full speed. The maneuver was bold, perhaps even suicidal, but it was born of the same desperation that Soren felt coursing through his veins.

"They're trying to take out the Fist before it can fire," Jack said, his voice filled with awe and dread.

"Then let's give them some cover. Keira, target the Fist with everything we've got. Sang, keep us moving. We need to keep drawing their fire."

The Wraith's weapons came to life, railguns chattering and missiles streaking toward the massive dreadnought. The barrage was little more than an irritant to the Fist's powerful shields, but it served its purpose, forcing the enemy to divide its attention. Soren could feel the vibrations of the weapons firing through the deck, a constant reminder of the deadly maelstrom they were drowning in.

As they maneuvered, Soren keenly noticed something on the sensor grid. A gap was opening in the defenses around the Fist—small but potentially large enough to land a killing blow.

"Sang," he called out, his voice steady. "Twelve degrees to starboard, mains at seventy percent. Fire port vectoring thrusters and pitch up thirty degrees, yaw right thirty. Bring us around one hundred twenty degrees, then full speed ahead. Keira, prepare to fire on my mark."

As Sang adjusted their course, Bobby's voice cut through the tension on the bridge. "Sir, that heading...we'll collide with the Fist!"

"Only if there's a Fist left to collide with," Soren replied.

The bridge fell silent. Every crew member understood the razor's edge between victory and annihilation. And they trusted Soren enough that nobody questioned the order or hesitated to follow it.

Sang carried out his heading change, bringing them into a sharp, rising vector that would swing them directly ahead of the escorts and turn them sharply head-on into the starboard side of the Fist. Soren could hear the ship groaning around them and feel the vibrations intensifying as they pushed the ship to the limits.

"Almost there," Soren murmured, more to himself than anyone else. His hands gripped his command station so tightly that his fingers ached, but he barely noticed. "Almost…" Soren repeated softly, every fiber of his being split between the projection and the viewscreen, watching as they completed the maneuver. With the Spirit of War rushing headlong into the fray, the Fist's commander had yet to notice their sudden course change.

The universe seemed to hold its breath. Time compressed to a near standstill before suddenly expanding again in a universe-rattling exhale.

With a silent flash of impossible light, the Fist of Justice unleashed its vortex cannon.

The cone of disruption rippled outward. Soren watched, stunned, as it passed through the Spirit of War and the other two ships racing alongside her. All three instantly went dark. But the disruption didn't stop there. It continued, carving through both the SF and FUP fleets, knocking the bulk of the remaining warships offline on both sides.

They were too late to stop the Fist from firing, but not too late to ensure that it never discharged the cannon again.

Now, it was their turn.

"Fire!" Soren roared, his voice raw with fury. In that moment, he poured every ounce of his will into the command as if he could guide the outcome through sheer mental force.

The Wraith's vortex cannon erupted, the fabric of space

twisting and warping around the beam as it lanced toward the Fist. For a moment that seemed to stretch into eternity, Soren feared it wouldn't be enough.

Then, the beam struck home.

The Fist's shields couldn't withstand the concentrated power of the Wraith's attack. The reality-warping lance sliced into the massive ship's hull with devastating effect. The viewscreen flared with the intensity of the impact as the dagger stabbed entirely through the Fist, slicing through multiple decks within seconds.

It was over in seconds. The vortex faded, leaving the Wraith on an inescapable collision course with the dreadnaught. Already, what remained of the ship began breaking apart, secondary explosions triggered as systems overloaded and ruptured.

"Brace for impact!" Soren shouted. He could hear the blood rushing in his ears, his heart hammering against his ribs as they plunged into a newly created gap between the two parts of the Fist.

The ship plowed into the opening, shields flaring brilliantly as they pushed through the split like a maul. Impacts with large pieces of debris reverberated through the ship, rattling teeth and threatening to shake the Wraith apart.

"Shields at twenty percent!" Keira called out, her voice barely audible over the cacophony of the proximity alarms. Sparks again rained from overhead, and the acrid smell of burning circuitry filled the air.

"Hang on!" Sang cried, her hands tight on the controls as she fought to guide them through the wreckage. With a final, bone-jarring shudder, the Wraith burst through the other side of the Fist.

"Hard to port!" he ordered, his voice cracking with the strain at the sight of one of the Fist's escorts sitting directly in front of them. The Komodo was nearly as mangled from the vortex cannon as the Fist.

Sang reacted instantly, throwing the Wraith into another sharp turn. The ship groaned in protest, inertial dampeners once again struggling to compensate for the sudden maneuver. Soren felt as if his insides were being pulled apart, the g-forces threatening to overwhelm him.

They swept over the Komodo by the skin of their teeth, immediately leveling off and cutting thrust, the forward thrusters shedding their velocity. Switching the viewscreen feed to the rear, Soren saw the two most prominent pieces of the Fist spinning away from their impact. The smaller aft section slammed into one of the escorts, punching through its damaged shields. The smaller vessel crumpled under the impact. The destruction was both beautiful and terrible, a reminder of the thin line they had just walked between victory and annihilation.

The larger bow piece careened away, barely clearing the path of the defunct Spirit of War as the powerless ship drifted through the area, mercifully still in one piece.

"Target destroyed," Keira announced, the edge in her voice carrying their collective anger, desperation, and ultimate satisfaction with it.

They had done it. They had destroyed the Fist of Justice.

CHAPTER 42

"Status report," Soren called out, his voice hoarse. He could taste blood in his mouth, feel the ache of bruises forming where he'd been thrown against his seat.

"Hull integrity at eighty-five percent," Ethan reported, his voice strained. "We've got multiple breaches, but emergency bulkheads are sealed."

"Weapons systems are operational," Keira added. "Our crews are reloading us now. The vortex cannon is recharging, estimated time to full power is one minute. Shields are down to fifteen percent, and the cloak is offline."

Soren's thoughts were already on their next move. The adrenaline still coursed through his system, keeping the fatigue and pain at bay. "Keira, as soon as the cannon is charged, I want you to target the nearest support ship. Sang, bring us about. We're not done yet."

As the Wraith maneuvered into position, Soren watched the remaining SF ships closely. With the loss of their flagship, they seemed momentarily directionless, their formations breaking apart as individual captains struggled to adapt to the sudden shift in momentum. He could almost feel their confusion and fear, sensing the opportunity it presented.

"Sir," Mark called out, a note of surprise in his voice. "The SF ships...they're changing vector. I think they're trying to disengage!"

Soren's eyes narrowed as he studied the sensor projection. Mark was right—the enemy vessels were pulling back—their fighters scrambling to return to their hangars. He could see the desperation in their movements, the realization that their seemingly invincible flagship had been destroyed.

"Should we pursue, sir?" Sang asked, her hands hovering over her controls, ready to give chase at a moment's notice.

Soren considered it for a moment, weighing the potential gains against the risks. The Wraith had taken a beating, and they had no way of knowing what other surprises the SF might have in store. The desire for total victory warred with the need to consolidate their gains and tend to their wounded.

"Negative," he said finally. "Let them go. We've accomplished our primary objective."

For a moment, silence reigned on the bridge. The crew sat frozen at their stations, as if unable to believe that the furious battle had truly ended. Then, slowly, a ragged cheer began to build. It started with a single whoop from Lina, her voice cracking with emotion. The sound was quickly joined by others until the entire bridge crew was celebrating their hard-won victory. Crew members embraced each other, tears of joy and relief streaming down faces that moments ago had been etched with desperation and purpose.

Soren allowed himself a small smile. He could feel the ache in his muscles, but the pain was a distant concern compared to the overwhelming relief that flooded through him.

But even as the celebration continued, Soren knew their work was far from over. The projection still showed the aftermath of the battle, where too many FUP ships had been knocked out by the Fist's cannon, the Wraith's killing strike seconds too late.

"Stations, everyone," he called out, his voice cutting through the jubilation. The crew quickly quieted and returned to their seats. "We defeated the Fist, we routed the enemy fleet, but this isn't over yet." He opened a comms channel. "Liam, what's the situation on the ground?"

"Sir," Liam's excited voice came back. "The fighting's over. The enemy ground forces have surrendered. Alex and the Lammergeiers...they've won!"

A wave of relief washed over Soren, so intense it was almost physical. He sagged against his command station, the full weight of the day's events finally hitting him. The fear and worry for his son that he had pushed aside during the heat of battle came rushing back, leaving him light-headed with relief.

"Thank you, Liam," he managed, his voice thick with emotion. He had to swallow hard before he could continue, fighting to maintain his composure in front of the crew. "Tell them...tell Alex we'll be there soon."

"Yes, sir. With pleasure."

Soren exhaled. The fighting might be done, but the cleanup was just beginning. "Bobby, I need you and Keira to grab Wilf. We' have rescue operations to coordinate."

As Bobby and Keira hurried off the bridge, Soren opened a channel to the Stinger. "Bastian, I need you to bring the Stinger back in to pick up Bobby, Keira, and Wilf. We have damaged FUP ships with no life support out there. We need to get those crews on board as quickly as possible."

"Copy that, Captain," Bastian replied. "I'm on my way."

Soren returned his gaze to the projection. The Spirit of War drifted lifelessly, her once-proud form scarred and battered. He could see the gaping wounds in her hull and hoped emergency bulkheads had shored them all up before the Fist's spacetime disruption passed through. Other FUP ships floated nearby, some still intact but disabled, others reduced to scattered debris fields. Each point of light on the projection represented lives hanging in the balance, waiting for rescue.

His thoughts turned to Alex, safe on the planet below. The image of his son, battered but alive, filled him with fierce pride and an overwhelming desire to see him, to embrace him and to know that he was indeed safe. For now, that was enough.

With a deep breath, Soren straightened, pushing aside his fatigue to focus on the tasks at hand. The real work was just beginning, but for the first time in what felt like an eternity, he had true hope for the future.

"Jack," he called out, his voice steady once more. "I want a full damage report and casualty list as soon as possible. Sang, plot a course to rendezvous with the Spirit of War. We need to rescue the Admiral and her crew."

"Aye, Captain," she replied.

Soren's gaze was drawn again to the viewscreen as the crew sprang into action around him. The stars shone steadily against the backdrop of space, indifferent to the battle that had just unfolded. Somewhere out there, he knew, the SF forces would quickly begin regrouping. They would lick their wounds and plan their next move.

The war was far from over.

But for now, in this moment, he and his allies had won. As Soren watched his crew work, he felt a surge of pride. Whatever came next, they would face it together.

And they would prevail.

CHAPTER 43

Soren waited impatiently at the starboard airlock, his eyes fixed on the small viewport as he watched the Athena maneuver into docking position. The past four hours had been a whirlwind of activity, a frantic rush to save as many lives as possible in the aftermath of their hard-won victory. The Wraith's sickbay was overflowing, every available space crammed with the wounded and shell-shocked survivors they had managed to rescue from the shattered remains of the FUP fleet.

He could still see the haunted looks in the eyes of the Spirit of War's crew as they were brought aboard. Some had faces smeared with soot and blood, the uniforms of others torn or singed. Many more had bruises and scrapes created when the ship lost power and gravity failed. They'd all been left huddling in the ship's core, the only area that had an air supply, though it would have only lasted them a few hours if not for their rescue.

Admiral Yarborough had been among the last to leave her ship, insisting on overseeing the evacuation of her crew before allowing herself to be rescued. When she finally stepped onto the Wraith's deck, her usual composure had cracked, revealing the weight of command and the toll of their losses.

He had held her tight while she sobbed over the deaths of so many good people, and doubly so for the death of her son.

They had defeated the Fist of Justice. But at what cost?

The question lingered in Soren's mind as they continued their rescue operations. Four other FUP ships survived the battle, but they were all in various states of disrepair. The Wraith, despite her own wounds, became the hub of their recovery efforts, her holds and corridors filling with survivors from across the fleet.

What surprised him most, however, was Alex's insistence that they extend their rescue efforts to the stranded Strickland Federation crews. At first, Soren had been hesitant, wary of potential security risks. But as they brought the first group of SF survivors aboard, he saw the gratitude in their eyes, the relief at being saved regardless of which side they fought for.

"Thank you," one young SF ensign had stammered, his eyes wide with disbelief as Soren helped him to his feet. The young man's uniform was filthy, his face streaked with tears and grime. "We... we thought you'd leave us to die out there."

Soren had looked at the young man, seeing not an enemy, but a scared kid caught up in something far bigger than himself. "Not today," Soren replied, his voice firm but kind. "This war has taken enough lives. It's time we started saving them instead."

The ensign nodded, his shoulders sagging with relief. "This isn't the peace and security we were promised," he murmured, more to himself than to Soren.

Now, as the Athena's airlock sealed against the Wraith's

with a soft hiss of equalizing pressure, Soren felt only excited anticipation. He glanced at Dana, who stood beside him, equally anxious to see Alex back safe. A vein of guilt threaded through Soren, that his son was alive when so many weren't. Why should he be so fortunate?

The airlock cycled, the indicator light flashing from red to green. As the inner door slid open with an equalizing hiss, Soren's heart pounded. The moment stretched.

And then, there he was.

Alex stepped through the airlock, his face was bruised and dirty, his fatigues stained with blood and sweat. But his eyes were bright and alive with a fire that made Soren's chest tighten with pride and relief.

For a moment, they simply stared at each other, father and son, the weight of all they had endured hanging between them. Then, as if a dam had broken, they surged forward, crashing together in a fierce embrace.

Soren clutched his son tightly, feeling the solid reality of him, alive and whole in his arms. He could feel Alex's body shaking, whether from exhaustion or emotion, he couldn't tell. Probably both.

"I thought I'd lost you," Soren whispered, his voice thick with emotion. "When we couldn't find you after FOB Alpha...I can only imagine what you've been through."

"I'm here, Dad," Alex replied, his voice cracking with emotion. "I'm okay. We made it. I never gave up. I never quit. I knew you'd come for me."

Dana joined the embrace, her arms encircling them as best she could. "I'm so glad you're safe, Alex. I'm so glad you're back with us where you belong."

They held the position for half a minute. As they separated, Soren took a moment to really look at his son. The physical toll of his ordeal was evident in the dark circles under his eyes and the dried sweat, grime, and exhaustion marking his face. But there was something else, a hardness in his gaze that spoke of the battles he had fought, both physical and mental. The experiences that hadn't killed him and would only make him stronger.

"I'm proud of you," Soren said, his hand resting on Alex's shoulder, gently squeezing it. "What you did down there...it was incredible. You didn't just survive, you led. You gave hope to people who had none."

Alex nodded, a ghost of a smile touching his lips. "I had help," he said, his voice humble and tinged with pride and grief. "Unfortunately, a lot of them died in the process." He turned back toward the airlock, where Jackson and Zoe had emerged, waiting patiently. Soren greeted them warmly, pulling each into a quick embrace.

"It's good to see you in one piece, sir," Jackson said, his usual grin in place despite the obvious fatigue in his eyes. "Though I gotta say, your welcoming committees could use some work. It just doesn't feel the same arriving somewhere without having my life threatened."

Soren chuckled, relief flooding through him at Jackson's familiar humor. "I'll be sure to hold you at gunpoint next time."

"Thank you, sir," Jackson joked.

"Captain," Zoe said, more formally. "It's good to be back."

Soren turned to her. "It's good to have you back. Both of you." He looked away from her as Sergeant Volkov and Corporal Swix stepped through the airlock, followed by Major Kosta and Captain Haji. Soren approached them, his expression somber.

"Sergeant, Corporal," he said, his voice heavy with gratitude and regret. "I can't thank you enough for what you've done. Your bravery, your skill...you and your team turned the tide down there. And I'm...I'm deeply sorry for your losses. Your people won't be forgotten."

Volkov nodded, her expression stoic, but Soren could

see the pain in her eyes. "Thank you, sir," she replied. "They died a warrior's death. We'll honor them by continuing the fight."

Soren was about to respond when movement at the airlock caught his attention. His eyes widened as the Scarabs stepped through, their postures nervous and uncertain. Alex had explained the situation beforehand, but it was still strange to come face-to-face with them.

One of them, a young man with haunted eyes, stepped forward. "Sir," he said, his voice hesitant, laced with fear and hope. "I'm Theo. These are...well, I guess you know who we are. We...we want to help. If you'll have us."

"Welcome aboard, Theo," Soren replied. "And the rest of you. I'm pretty sure I know your names. I've actually never met you before, though."

"Our Theo was discharged a few weeks before Jungle," Alex explained. "Cancer. He needed treatment. And this Theo...he may have cancer, too. The Grand Admiral never gave him leave to see a doctor."

Soren's eyes narrowed in anger at his alternate self. "Theo, we need to get you to sickbay right away," he said. "We'll do everything we can."

Theo looked surprised, then grateful. "Thank you, sir," he said, his voice barely above a whisper. "I...you don't owe me anything. Not after everything we've done."

Alex stepped forward and laid his hands on Theo's shoulders, looking him straight in the eye. "You saved my life, Theo. I hope we can save yours." Smiling, Theo nodded.

Soren placed a hand on Theo's shoulder beside Alex's, meeting his gaze steadily. "That goes double for me," he said firmly. "What matters is what we do now, moving forward. And right now, we're going to get you the help you need."

"Thank you."

As a waiting medic led Theo away, Soren greeted the other surviving Scarabs—Sarah, Zee, and Jackie. "I know this must be difficult for you," he said. "Confusing, maybe even frightening. But you're safe here. This is a chance for a new start, if you want it."

Sarah opened her mouth to respond, gratitude and relief evident in her expression. But before she could speak, a commotion behind them drew Soren's attention. Jackson suddenly stumbled, his face contorting in confusion and pain.

"Three?" Alex called out, concern etching his features. "What's wrong?"

Jackson tried to speak, but no words came out. His eyes rolled back in his head as he collapsed to the deck with a dull thud.

"Three!" Alex cried out, rushing to his friend's side, panic clear in his voice.

Before anyone could react, Jackie, Zoe, and Zee crumpled to the deck as if their strings had been cut. The impact echoed in the suddenly silent chamber, a chilling counterpoint to the joyous reunion moments before.

Chaos erupted in the confined space of the airlock chamber. Soren barked orders for medical assistance as he knelt beside the fallen soldiers, checking for pulses and breathing. They were still alive but unresponsive.

"What the hell is going on?" Dana demanded, her face pale with shock and fear. She knelt beside Zoe, gently cradling her head. "They were fine just a second ago!"

Before Soren could answer, his comms unit signaled an incoming connection. Lukas's panicked, urgent voice came through.

"Captain!" the scientist almost shouted. "I'm sorry to bother you but...I've been monitoring the sensor data since the Fist's final shot, and...sir, the patterns are changing. The energy signatures we've been tracking, they're...they're intensifying. I think... I think it's happening. The Convergence. It...it's started."

———

Thank you for reading! I hope you enjoyed the book! For more information on the next installment in the series, please visit mrforbes.com/convergencewar5.

OTHER BOOKS BY M.R FORBES

Want more M.R. Forbes? Of course you do!
View my complete catalog here
mrforbes.com/books
Or on Amazon:
mrforbes.com/amazon

Starship For Sale (Starship For Sale)
mrforbes.com/starshipforsale

When Ben Murdock receives a text message offering a fully operational starship for sale, he's certain it has to be a joke.

Already trapped in the worst day of his life and desperate for a way out, he decides to play along. Except there is no joke. The starship is real. And Ben's life is going to change in ways he never dreamed possible.

All he has to do is sign the contract.

Joined by his streetwise best friend and a bizarre tenant with an unseverable lease, he'll soon discover that the universe is more volatile, treacherous, and awesome than he ever imagined.

And the only thing harder than owning a starship is staying alive.

Forgotten (The Forgotten)
mrforbes.com/theforgotten
Complete series box set:
mrforbes.com/theforgottentrilogy

Some things are better off FORGOTTEN.

Sheriff Hayden Duke was born on the Pilgrim, and he expects to die on the Pilgrim, like his father, and his father before him.

That's the way things are on a generation starship centuries from home. He's never questioned it. Never thought about it. And why bother? Access points to the ship's controls are sealed, the systems that guide her automated and out of reach. It isn't perfect, but he has all he needs to be content.

Until a malfunction forces his wife to the edge of the habitable zone to inspect the damage.

Until she contacts him, breathless and terrified, to tell him she found a body, and it doesn't belong to anyone on board.

Until he arrives at the scene and discovers both his wife and the body are gone.

The only clue? A bloody handprint beneath a hatch that hasn't opened in hundreds of years.

Until now.

Deliverance (Forgotten Colony)
mrforbes.com/deliverance
Complete series box set:

The war is over. Earth is lost. Running is the only option.

It may already be too late.

Caleb is a former Marine Raider and commander of the Vultures, a search and rescue team that's spent the last two years pulling high-value targets out of alien-ravaged cities and shipping them off-world.

When his new orders call for him to join forty-thousand survivors aboard the last starship out, he thinks his days of fighting are over. The Deliverance represents a fresh start and a chance to leave the war behind for good.

Except the war won't be as easy to escape as he thought.

And the colony will need a man like Caleb more than he ever imagined...

Man of War (Rebellion)

mrforbes.com / manofwar
Complete series box set:
mrforbes.com / rebellion-web

In the year 2280, an alien fleet attacked the Earth.

Their weapons were unstoppable, their defenses unbreakable.

Our technology was inferior, our militaries overwhelmed.

Only one starship escaped before civilization fell.

Earth was lost.

It was never forgotten.

Fifty-two years have passed.

A message from home has been received.

The time to fight for what is ours has come.

Welcome to the rebellion.

Hell's Rejects (Chaos of the Covenant)

mrforbes.com / hellsrejects

The most powerful starships ever constructed are gone. Thousands are dead. A fleet is in ruins. The attackers are unknown. The orders are clear: *Recover the ships. Bury the bastards who stole them.*

Lieutenant Abigail Cage never expected to find herself in Hell. As a Highly Specialized Operational Combatant, she was one of the most respected Marines in the military. Now she's doing hard labor on the most miserable planet in the universe.

Not for long.

The Earth Republic is looking for the most dangerous individuals it can control. The best of the worst, and Abbey happens to be one of them. The deal is simple: *Bring back the starships, earn your freedom. Try to run, you die.* It's a suicide mission, but she has nothing to lose.

The only problem? There's a new threat in the galaxy. One with a power unlike anything anyone has ever seen. One that's been waiting for this moment for a very, very, long time. And they want Abbey, too.

Be careful what you wish for.

They say Hell hath no fury like a woman scorned. They have no idea.

ABOUT THE AUTHOR

M.R. Forbes is the mind behind a growing number of Amazon best-selling science fiction series. Having spent his childhood trying to read every sci-fi novel he could find (and write his own too), play every sci-fi video game he could get his hands on, and see every sci-fi movie that made it into the theater, he has a true love of the genre across every medium. He works hard to bring that same energy to his own stories, with a continuing goal to entertain, delight, fascinate, and surprise.

He maintains a true appreciation for his readers and is always happy to hear from them.

To learn more about me or just say hello:

Visit my website:
mrforbes.com

Send me an e-mail:
michael@mrforbes.com

Check out my Facebook page:
facebook.com/mrforbes.author

Join my Facebook fan group:
facebook.com/groups/mrforbes

Follow me on Instagram:

instagram.com / mrforbes_author

Find me on Goodreads:
goodreads.com / mrforbes

Follow me on Bookbub:
bookbub.com / authors / m-r-forbes

.

Made in United States
Orlando, FL
15 December 2024

55655727R00207